THE MILL WINDOW

JANELLE FREEMAN GARNER

For my mama
Who was wiser than I thought
And stronger than she knew

"One love had nothing to do with the other love. They were both good men; different men, I still love them both."

CHAPTER 1
IRIS

Standing in front of the newly placed headstone all I could see was the words forty-three; a lie carved inside the heart. The same lie that cast a shadow over the entirety of our marriage. He was gone; his body ravished from the disease that crippled our lives for so long.

Once again, I was forced to face the fallout of choices made long ago. It wasn't the first time I had suffered the death of a husband. Now I stood alone without either of them to face the collateral damage; the hurt it could cause the people I love the most. Looking back on the decisions we made, it all seemed so useless. The only thing I could think of was I needed to go home; my heart's home; LaGrange and the mill.

A feeling of peace came over me as I drove down the main street; the fountain still stood; the same as always. Pass Jefferson Street; down Jenkin Street; and onto Troup Street to the mill. I was standing in front of the place where it all started. Chills ran down the entirety of my body. I had mixed feelings as I noticed our bench had been replaced with a newer one. It looked the same but was missing the scars of time left by the heartbreak that happened there. Looking up at the mill where we all worked at

1

one time or another. I longed to sit in the mill window to let my mind rest; to listen to the whispers of God on the right thing to do, but the mill had long since closed making room for a new future. It's hard to explain how a simple window could be so important in one's life, but it had been my place since I was a young girl. Looking up at the window, my mind drifted back to a happier time and to the journey that led me to this day.

This is my LaGrange; the one where the mill still stands; empty now; the one I see when I think of the past; the one so important to the events that happened in this story.

The migration to a small southern town to work in the mills connected three families whose lives collided and change my life and the lives of the two men I would love forever. Yes, I said *two*.

CHAPTER 2
THE FAMILIES

My parents, the Reeds; along with the parents of Flynn Fisher and Elijah Foster were three of the families who came to the mill town of LaGrange for a better life. Elijah Foster and Flynn Fisher; are the names of the men I love; yes, I said love; present tense. Both men are gone now, but love doesn't die when the body dies, love lives in our souls forever. It's the only thing we carry with us when we leave this world to move on to the eternal one. I believe that.

That's why my story and their story needs to be told. So when the secrets of these families come to light, the people affected by decisions made long ago can have peace in their souls; for without peace, there is no rest. It is time.

CHAPTER 3
IRIS

All families have secrets, I'm sure of it. Secrets are kept for fear of being judged, most often by people who don't even know you. I grew up with silence surrounding my family. That silence prepared me for what was about to happen to me as a young girl of fifteen. Until Flynn, I had no secrets, because of society's taboo of who loved who during this time, keeping secrets became an unnatural part of my life.

My Daddy, Harley Reed, worked in the mills for years. That changed in 1930 when the mill workers went on strike across the South. With a family to feed, he crossed the picket line. The newly unionized mill workers promised he would never work in a mill in Troup County again, and he didn't. He was forced to work as a sharecropper on other people's property or work for the state to provide shelter and food for us.

Like most girls in our town, I stopped going to school after the seventh grade. The oldest of eight siblings, I was needed at home to take care of my younger brothers and sisters. We worked in the fields with my mother on a local cotton farm to make extra money for our family. For the next three years, I picked cotton, and dreamed of going to work in the local cotton mill. I especially wanted to work at Birch Mill. It was close to Troup Street and located on the river where my grandpa and I like to fish before it was built.

All parents during this time were strict, but mine were stricter than most. I learned early in my childhood "children were to be seen but not heard." My opinions were kept to myself, and my dreams were kept in my heart.

The world was a troubled place and war was all around us. Though our country was not yet involved in the war; we were fighting the war of survival during what would become known as the Great Depression, and I was fighting a war within myself to become a young woman. I took the first step when I was hired at the mill. The thought of a weekly paycheck was all I needed to start saving for my future.

I always loved the mills in LaGrange. Birch mill was especially beautiful and the place I was hired.

The entrance into the front offices resembled an old house made of rock and stone; big birch trees lined the walkways where workers entered each morning to begin their day. The front corner of the mill had one beautiful arched window outlined in big stones that framed it and emitted the music of the machines running inside.

As a young girl, I would walk to the mill to sit and look up at the window. It reminded me of the ones in the fairytales Nanny Wilson told me. I wasn't sure why but I was drawn to the window from a young age.

My first job at the textile mill was in the spinning room. I didn't know much about what that meant. I soon learned the spinning looms were filled with spools of thread that were woven into materials. My job was to make sure my portion of the line ran smoothly.

As I arrived the first day, I immediately noticed my work area was right in front of the mill window I had loved over the years. Each day my job became easier. I was taught early on in my life the pride of honest work for an honest wage. I was a loyal employee and always happy to have a job. The mill window became a mirror into the world outside; the place where I took my breaks and ate my lunch. It was my place to sit and dream about a new future.

It was sitting on the sill of the mill window I first noticed him; long before I met him or knew who he was. His reputation had proceeded him. He was handsome, no doubt. Though short in stature when compared to most guys, it was overshadowed by his dark black hair and his deep blue eyes. I didn't know much about him, except he ran with a group of wild boys, and always had a girl or girls with him or following close behind. I noticed the way he walked and how the other boys and girls surrounded him as he led them to school each day. He carried a confidence when he walked and had a laugh I heard clear up into the mill window. I felt jealous of the girls walking with him, and I was confused as to why I even cared.

Daydreaming during my break, I wondered who he was. I imagined he lived in a fine house with parents who insisted he finish school. My thoughts were interrupted by Naomi Fisher calling me for help on her line. As I turned, I could see the spools emptying. Naomi wasn't fast enough to replace them, and the line would soon shut down. That meant trouble for every-one. I hurried over, grabbing new spools as I passed the bin that held them, and helped Naomi Fisher get her line caught up again.

"Thanks Iris," Mrs. Fisher said. Shaking her head, "I just have the hardest time with changing those spools."

You couldn't help being drawn to Naomi Fisher, who I called by her request, "Mrs. Fisher." Her Italian heritage shown in her face. We became friends; even though she was fifteen years or more my senior, her childlike ways made her seem much younger.

Our house was in the mill village; just up the street, but Mrs. Fisher lived on Jefferson Street located in the part of the mill village directly in front of the owner's mansion. The houses there were bigger, decorated nicer, with a gated iron fence.

Most of the families who lived in that part of the mill village were men who were confidants of Mr. Clyborne, the mill owner. I knew most of their names and Fisher wasn't one of them. I wondered how she came to live there, though I dare not ask.

Leaving work one afternoon, Naomi Fisher invited me to come home with her for a glass of tea. After my work shift, I had a couple of hours of freedom each day before I was expected home. Out of curiosity about how the houses in that part of the mill village looked inside, I agreed.

Arriving at her house, I noticed an older woman sitting on the porch, tea prepared and ready on a beautiful tray with tea cakes beside it.

"Iris, this is my mother," Mrs. Fisher said with pride. "Mollie Burton." Shaking her hand, I could feel the warmth of her heart and knew instantly she was quite different from her daughter.

"Nice to meet you, Mrs. Burton," I said. Smiling, the small-framed woman insisted I call her Granny Burton.

"Not sure I would answer to anything else," she said.

Following Naomi's lead, I sat in a rocking chair and took a glass of tea. The front door opened and out ran two little boys and a little red-haired girl, right to their mother's lap. Naomi introduced me to Jack, Jacob, and Bobbie and explained her other son wasn't back from school yet; as those three ran to the yard playing tag.

Still wondering how Naomi lived on Jefferson Street. I noticed a man walking up the sidewalk. I know him, I thought, most everyone else knew him too. He works at the mill. As he opened the gate, I said, "Hello Mr. Burton," suddenly it made sense; Granny Burton was the wife of Mr. Burton; Mr. Burton was a friend of Mr. Clyborne, and worked at the mill. Naomi was a Burton. Chuckling to myself, I thought, so this is how she keeps her job and why she lives on Jefferson Street.

Mr. Burton leaned over to kiss his wife on the cheek. He smiled, "Hello Miss Iris, how are you today?" Before I could answer he looked at Mrs. Fisher, "Naomi, you heard from Harry today?"

She answered, "Yes PaPa, he is staying in Greenville for a while." Explaining to me that Harry Fisher was her husband and his father had recently passed away. He was helping his mother out. Half listening to her; I was trying to size up this family. Mr. Burton was a kind man; but people at the mill wondered what his job there was; officially he was the elevator operator; but he had an office and spent a lot of time with management and more importantly with Mr. Clyborne.

My thoughts were interrupted by Mr. Burton saying, "Mrs. Burton, don't you think it's time we have supper?"

She stood up, "I'm putting it on the table now."

Naomi was up and calling the three little ones inside to eat. "Iris, guess I better get these faces washed up for supper."

I smiled looking down at the three little Fishers, "I need to get home too. See you tomorrow." I waved as I went out the gate and down the street.

On my walk home, I thought about how different the Burton's house was from our house. I lived next door to Nanny and Paw Wilson with my parents, three brothers, three sisters, and my Grandpa Reed. As I walked inside that night, supper had already begun; the smell of Mama's cooking filled the air along with conversations of how each of their day had been.

"Hey Coot," Grandpa Reed said smiling up at me as I found a seat beside him in the crowded kitchen.

Leaning over toward him, I whispered, "Hey Grandpa" as I kissed him on the cheek. Grandpa was one of my favorite people, my daddy's daddy. He was a rebel, a wanderer. I found in him a kindred spirit.

He and Daddy lived from pillar to post after his wife died; he never had material possessions, but he was rich with the knowledge of how to live life. He understood the need in me to make mine different and that was something no one else could fathom.

After supper, the kitchen filled with me and my sisters; Tessa, Ester, and Loretta, cleaning up; washing and drying the dishes, wiping the table, sweeping the floor, and talking about boys and clothes. I made no comments, but my mind went to the mill window and the boy with no name. When the work was done, I slipped into the bathroom and got ready for bed. Lying under the covers, I listened to the radio as I drifted into the dreams of what I hoped the future held for me.

The next morning, I was up early to get ready for work at the mill. I cared how I looked and thought of every day as a new opportunity to show my bosses how happy I was to work there. I took pride in my job. It all had come very easily to me.

A lot of my time was spent helping my new friend, Mrs. Fisher. Her work was always a little behind, and most people thought she was incompetent or lazy. I thought she was shrewd. She managed to work without actually working. She had a way of making people enjoy helping her including me.

My afternoon visits to the Burton's house after work continued spring and summer and into the fall of 1939. Iced tea was prepared each day for Mrs. Fisher by her mother and sitting on the kitchen table with glasses ready to be poured and cookies ready to be eaten. We sat there around the table; gossip flowing about the people who worked in the mill.

Mrs. Fisher would stand each visit and announce it was time to get "those young'uns ready to eat" and off to the door she would walk; calling, "Jack, Jacob, and Bobbie supper time."

They ran inside for faces and hands to be cleaned for supper. That was my cue to head home to join my family, but not before lifting the three little ones to the counter to wash their face and hands. Off the counter, they would jump one by one as I finished wiping the day's dirt away. Jack, always hugging me and declaring his love.

Granny Burton often invited me to eat with them, but I knew I would be pushing my luck with Daddy. He was already unhappy about my new friendship with the Burtons and that included Harry and Naomi Fisher by proxy. The bad blood between the two families had spanned a few years by that time and stemmed from Mr. Burton's part in my Daddy losing his job after the mill strike.

Each night I made my way home in time to eat with my family; sliding into my seat beside Grandpa. I looked forward to the table conversations about each of their day, but I must admit the dynamics of the Fisher-Burton family on Jefferson Street fascinated me.

The arrival of Saturday was always my favorite time of the week; the day after payday. That morning, I cashed my check and gave my mother the weekly amount set by my father to help the family. I saved part of what was left by putting it in the bank, always leaving some to spend on shopping that day.

My sisters and I set out early to go downtown to look and buy. It was always fun; but this day, winter was setting in and we knew the cold weather months were around the corner. Loretta, Ester, Tessa and I walked briskly that morning. I was looking to buy much-needed warm work clothes; knowing the winter months still meant walking to work.

Approaching town, my eyes caught the boy, the same boy I watched from the mill window as I sat each morning to eat my biscuit. As always surrounded by a group of other guys and girls... there he was standing outside of Country Joe's Hot Dogs. I dare not ask my two little sisters if they knew him. As I walked by, he paid absolutely no attention to any of us. He was definitely handsome, but there was something different about this stranger that made my heart beat fast. I walked quickly by the group afraid to look in their direction.

Loretta, however, spoke to the group of four boys; "Hey y'all," she cooed.

"Loretta, for goodness' sake, have some pride" I whispered as the boy and I locked eyes for just a second. I pulled Loretta by the arm as we ran to catch up with our sisters.

Shopping finished, we decided to eat a quick sandwich at the food bar in Kessler's before we started for home. I was ready to escape the constant chatter of Loretta and how she was going to the movies next Friday night.

"Loretta, you know Daddy will never allow you to go to the movies," I sarcastically responded.

"I'm not going to tell him, Iris" She responded in an equally sarcastic voice.

Back into my own thoughts, I barely heard her mention the

word *him*, *school*, and the *movies* next Friday. I wondered who "him" could be. Loretta was only twelve but looked older and was boy-crazy beyond her years. I wasn't too worried about her plans for the next week, I knew Daddy would never let her leave the house alone.

The next week went by fast and Friday afternoon my sisters talked me into going to town to shop with them instead of waiting until Saturday. I should have realized Loretta was up to something and had other plans in mind but I was distracted by my thoughts of hopefully running into the mysterious boy.

As we walked toward town, we made our plans. Tessa and Ester headed off to hang out at McClellan's Five and Dime after they paid on their layaways. I was going to do my Saturday ritual that afternoon so I could sleep late the next day. Loretta said she was going to Country Joe's to meet her girlfriends. We all agreed to meet back at home by dark.

By the time I finished cashing my check and shopping for work shoes, the evening sun had begun to set. Looking at my watch, I thought I had time to grab a bite to eat at Country Joe's and meet back up with Loretta. In the back of my mind was the hope to run into the boy who had invaded my thoughts. Inside the small restaurant, my eyes scanned the place, no sisters, no boy. Thinking my sisters had headed home; I ordered a hotdog and drink. Knowing it was getting late, I decided to head that way myself.

Food in hand, I started the walk toward home. I turned quickly to see Grandpa calling my name, "Coot, Coot;" a nickname that only he called me.

Sensing something was wrong, I dropped my hot dog and ran toward him. Grabbing his arm, "Grandpa, what's wrong?"

"Your Daddy is on the warpath."

Cutting him short, I said, "I'm not late."

Shaking his head, "No, no, not you; Loretta isn't home yet, an hour late, and your daddy is worried and mad. I told him I would come to find her; do you know where she is?" he asked.

Realizing he could hardly catch a breath, I said, "Grandpa, sit down on this bench; I think I know where she is." I turned to head over to the theater, realizing we had fell for Loretta's plan. Looking back at the bench in front of the Big Store Grocery, I could see the old man I adored was worried, walking back a few steps to ensure he could hear me, "Grandpa, you go on back home after you rest a bit, tell Daddy, I'll bring Loretta home." He nodded.

The sun had set, and the city's lights were reflected in the fountain. I turned to start toward the Royal Theater. I was mad Loretta had tricked all of us. As I walked up to the ticket window, the boy inside chuckled and said, "She's here, you can go inside to get her." I smiled and said thanks wondering if I was supposed to know him.

I slipped inside the dark and waited while my eyes adjusted to the screen lit up with *Our Favorite Wives* playing. I quietly walked up the steps and scanned the rows as I made my way up to the balcony of the theater.

My eyes locked on the boy first, the one from the mill window, the light of the screen caught his blue eyes and a smile that melted a girl's heart. Thinking out loud, "Of course, he's with a girl."

Following his arm, he had encircled around someone…, I stopped dead in my tracks, "Loretta," grabbing his arm and pulling her from underneath it, "Daddy is on his way to town looking for you. You better hope we can get out of here before he finds us," I shouted; half angry from Loretta worrying everyone and half angry because she was with him.

Dragging her down the aisle and out of the theater into the street, I could feel the boy following us. Without thinking, I stopped, all the while holding Loretta by the arm like a mother hen, I shouted, "She is only 12 years old stupid." Stopping suddenly in front of us he looked frozen, unable to speak.

Loretta all the time screaming, "I'm going to be 13 soon." Slowly looking him up and down, He stood in front of me now, with no words, his annoying silence angered me. I jerked Loretta's arm and walked quickly, dragging her behind me.

Loretta tried to talk to me about the boy on our walk home,

but I stopped her at once, "Loretta, I don't want to hear anything about him."

She just smiled and said, "Ok, but you sound jealous…"

I stopped her, "Don't be ridiculous!"

I decided that night with a prideful heart, I would no longer entertain embellished thoughts of him.

Convinced he was an older boy who takes advantage of younger girls; I became consumed by the need to forget him; yet I didn't even know him.

I only sat in the mill window at lunchtime, knowing he wouldn't be passing by during that time of day. I was sure the familiar stranger wasn't going to be part of my life.

During this time my friendship with Naomi Fisher grew, and the Burton house became a haven for me. There was no way I would see him if I was there. I always knew Mrs. Fisher had a motive for our peculiar friendship. I was her safety at work and help for her at home, but she didn't realize my friendship with her provided me a sanctuary from facing the boy who consumed my heart.

I became attached to this family, spending afternoons playing with the three children, sitting, and talking with them, cooking with Mrs. Burton, I even developed a special friendship with Mrs. Fisher.

During the cold of the winter, the visits to the house on Jefferson Street were limited, but picked right back up in the early spring of 1940; work each day; home with Mrs. Fisher, tea on the porch or at the kitchen table depending on the weather.

It was on the porch one afternoon watching the Fisher children playing in the front yard I learned there was another Fisher child. His name was Johnny Flynn, and I could tell he was her favorite by the way she said his name. He was the oldest, still in school. She explained he was in Greenville visiting his other grandmother.

Mrs. Burton joined in the talk about Flynn, "He was moping around here like an old sick puppy; that boy I had to shoo him out from the house. I told him, "Go have some fun; do what young boys are supposed to do."

Mrs. Fisher interrupted, "Over some girl he doesn't even know; I sent him to visit his Granny; hopefully a change of scenery will do him some good." Listening to these older women talking about this boy I could sense he was missed.

I chuckled and without realizing I was speaking out loud, "At least he is old enough to wash his own face."

The visits to the Burtons had been good medicine for me in my quest to forget the elusive boy. I had begun to wash him away during the tea drinking, face washing, and helping with supper. Their daily invitation to stay and eat dinner with them was appreciated, but Daddy wouldn't allow it, "You're expected to be in your place by supper time." I didn't mind.

Each night just before I fell asleep, I thought for a moment about the boy who I had erased from my life. Little did I know things were about to change for this young girl in a noticeably big way.

CHAPTER 4
FLYNN

I need to preface my story by admitting I'm indeed a mama's boy. I recognized at an early age keeping secrets was a part of her life. I learned that art from her. Born so quickly after my parents were married, the story goes "I was premature." The truth is the honeymoon was premature; I was born right on time. As I grew older and I realized the math of my birth and the importance of keeping secrets to my mother.

She was a proud woman and cared about what people thought. It became natural to embellish a story or leave parts of a story out. I didn't think much about Mama's little white lies when I was young, but I was to find out how having secrets can destroy your life and change the journey you're meant to take.

I don't need to try to remember the first time I saw her. I remember it vividly. It was the Fall of 1939; I was thirteen years old. My mother, two brothers, and sister had just moved back to LaGrange from Greenville. Daddy had stayed behind; my grandfather had died, and Granny Fisher needed his help. It was a change I was used to by now; we had moved between Mama's and Daddy's families since I was born, never having a home of our own.

My daddy was working at Brighton Mill when the mills across

the south went on strike. He lost his job. With the need to stay with my grandmother, they decided my mother would go to LaGrange to work in one of the mills owned by the Clyborne family; who had managed to settle the strike long before other areas across the southeast. My mother was hired immediately because of my Grandpa Burton's relationship with the Clybornes.

We were living in my grandparent's house on Jefferson Street. It was a mill house, but the homes there were larger and nicer than most of the other houses in the mill village. My mother loved it there. She always fancied herself a little better than most, even though she wasn't.

It was easy to reacquaint myself with guys whose life I had come in and out of over the last 13 years. There was a group of us, Leon, Clyde, and Charlie, who always hung out together. We had decided that Friday night to see a movie, *Our Favorite Wives*. We immediately took notice of three girls in the balcony and sat right behind them. Before the movie was halfway over, I was sitting with my arm around a girl I had never met but had heard of, Loretta Reed.

Loretta was a beautiful girl, with crystal blue eyes, sandy long hair, and a reputation for being a little wild. Just what a 13-year-old boy was looking for on a Friday night.

About halfway through the movie, an angry hand pulled my arm from Loretta's shoulder, shouting at both of us, "Daddy is on the way to town to find you! Get up and let's get out of here." The girl was hurrying out of the side exit of the theater dragging Loretta behind her. I was following them shouting at the girl pulling Loretta alongside her, "Hey, what's the problem?"

The girl stopped suddenly and turned around to me just as I had almost caught up with them, "The problem is she's only 12 years old stupid. Why don't you run your game on someone your own age?"

I stared at her and could not speak, I wanted to scream, "So what, I'm only 13", but the minute I looked into her eyes, I was speechless. I was mesmerized by her beauty and the fire that radiated from her deep blue eyes.

The sound of my buddies running up behind us broke our stare as the girl and Loretta ran up the street and disappeared into the night. "Hey, you guys know that girl?"

Clyde spoke up, "Oh yeah, that's Iris Reed; she's way out of your league."

Charlie added chuckling, "Besides, her old man will kill you for coming near her or any of the Reed girls. Seriously, she is older than you, speaks her mind, and doesn't give any guy the time of day."

In a need to change the subject from the effect the elusive girl had on me, "Let's get something to eat." Unphased by their warning, I knew for sure Iris Reed's path and mind would cross again if I had anything to do with it, and it did in a very unexpected way.

The days of that fall ran into each other much the same; Mother was working at the mill, along with Grandpa Burton. That left Granny Burton to watch my two little brothers, Jacob and Jack, and my little sister Bobbie. Offering to help with them, Granny would shoo me away, "Go on now, have fun while you can. Life will catch up to you all too soon." Without a care and Iris Reed on my mind, off I would head to town and scan the places young people were hanging out, but no Iris.

I asked around about the Reeds and found out they lived down the street; two blocks over from me on Troup Street; the mill village. I can't remember how many times I walked by that house hoping to see her, but never did...what did she do all day?

When I asked Loretta about her sister, she would say, "I imagine you'll soon find out without me telling you," laughing the entire time.

I figured she had a boyfriend and decided to put any thought of her into the back of my mind. I told myself, "There are plenty of girls out there wanting my attention."

My days fell into the routine of playing with my brothers and sister after school and then heading to town until it was time for supper. Hoping I would run into Iris somewhere, but I hadn't seen her since that night. Her image was locked in my thoughts and haunted my heart. LaGrange was filled with girls I could spend time with, but none made me forget about the one girl who consumed me.

Thinking so much about Iris, had made me forget about my girl in Greenville, Joan. I'm sure she was wondering why I hadn't contacted her. My dad was still there, and mother decided, "I needed a change to get my mind back on "important things." I agreed. What better way to get Iris Reed out of my head? Joan was just the girl for it.

I was on a bus to Greenville the next day. I felt at home there as much as I did in LaGrange. It was much the same, a small mill town. I learned on my arrival that Daddy had gotten a job at a paint company. He had to travel out of town and needed me to be there with Granny Fisher.

Life had been difficult for her since my grandfather had died the previous year. I was glad to help her out and keep her company, especially during the winter months. A new school and Joan might help me to forget a girl I didn't even know. Yet I felt connected to her in some mystical way. Iris Reed, even her name haunted me.

Joan and I picked right up where we left off. I liked Joan. She and I had met at the Church of God in Greenville about two years earlier. We became fast friends mainly because she was the female version of me. She was a little wild; mature for her young age. She was pretty and smart; we thought alike. Over the next few months, we spent a lot of time together doing what young people like to do; another reason I liked her.

She began to talk about a future; I was only thirteen; about to turn fourteen in a few months, both good reasons to break it off with Joan. I couldn't lie about the real reason I ended it with her as I tried to explain, "I want the freedom to date other people." I had to try to meet the one person whose name I had mentally told myself I would never speak into words until I saw her face-to-face.

Joan took the break-up the way I expected; with a flip of her hair and a question, "Who is she?"

I poured my heart out to her, shaking my head in disbelief that I'd these kinds of feelings for a girl I didn't even know.

Joan's response wasn't expected "What are you doing here, get your butt on a bus to LaGrange! I've never known a Flynn who did not get the girl he wants, but... I'll be here if you change your mind." She leaned over; gave me a kiss on the cheek and walked away.

I left on a bus the next day for LaGrange with Granny's blessings and a promise from her she wouldn't call my mother to let her know I was on my way back. I told her I wanted it to be a surprise. If mother knew I was headed to LaGrange, she would demand I stay in Greenville.

On the bus ride back, I thought of Joan; hoping I had done the right thing; it's difficult when your head tells you one thing, and your heart wants the opposite. I knew one thing for sure, Joan and I would always be friends, and that proved to be right.

How was I going to see Iris Reed again? She hardly knew I existed and wasn't impressed with me during our first and only meeting. I decided when I got off of that bus, I was going straight to the Reed's house and walk right up to the front door to face her. I was convinced I had built her up to be something she wasn't. When I saw her, I would realize she was nothing special. Then I could discard her and any thoughts of her as I had other girls in my young life.

I was startled out of my thoughts as we pulled into the bus station and the doors opened. The cold air hit my face as I grabbed my bag. I ran two blocks out of town on Vernon Street, down by the mill, and up Troup Street to house number 3109. Not giving myself time to think about the chance of someone else answering the door, I pushed open the gate, walked up to the porch, and knocked expecting to ask Iris Reed who she thought she was. Trying not to show how nervous I felt, I had one arm on the door frame when the door opened; I jumped back.

An incredibly angry Harley Reed was in my face shouting, "Git out of here boy, and don't come back. We don't allow Fishers here."

Catching myself as I fell backward onto the walkway, I turned and ran three blocks up, and one street over to Jefferson Street. My mind was racing as I quietly opened the gate, then the screen door, and walked into the friendly fire of my home. "Anybody here?" I asked softly as I entered the house.

Mother grabbed hold of me like I was returning from war, and I was, but it was a war she knew nothing about. "You hungry son?" she asked me as we walked into the kitchen.

"You know I am, and something smells good!" I replied as I noticed Jacob and Jack sitting on the counter by the sink on the other side of the kitchen. Someone was washing their faces. I looked at Granny and half serious and half joking ask, "We have a maid now?"

CHAPTER 5
IRIS

The winter was behind us and 1940 began with a revelation that completely caught me off guard. The boy I was sure was gone from my life wasn't gone from my mind. This was partly due to my baby sister, who was tormenting me for the sheer fun of it. I had forbidden her to even utter a word about the mysterious boy, who she claimed to know personally.

She would find pleasure in saying to me, "Oh don't be sad; you'll see him again." Strangely enough, I found some solace in her taunting me with the hope that would come true.

Working at the mill filled my days. I took all the overtime I could. The afternoons I didn't work I would walk home with Mrs. Fisher, who was miffed by the fact I would rather work than spend afternoons helping her.

It was a Thursday, I remember, my daddy had finally agreed to let me stay for supper. He said, "You can eat with the Burtons, not the Fishers." Daddy, like everyone in LaGrange, liked Mrs. Burton. He would say, "She's a fine woman, but none of the others are worth one penny."

The walk out of the mill that day was silent except for the whistle that blew at quitting time. Mrs. Fisher hadn't been herself that day; her mind seemed to be elsewhere. She let her loom fall behind, nothing for me to do but help her as usual.

She had a troubled look on her face as we walked through the iron gate of the Jefferson Street house. She fell down on the rocking chair beside the prepared iced tea on the table beside it. Sensing something was wrong, I tried to weasel my way out of staying, "Mrs. Fisher tell Granny Burton I'll come for supper next week. I'm going on home."

Naomi's voice brought me back to the front porch, "Oh no… Mama has been looking forward to seeing you."

She rarely took no for an answer. I took a seat on the front step and Granny Burton came out the screen door. "Iris, it's so good to see you," handing me a glass of tea, "Supper is ready when Mr. Burton gets home." she said.

Bobbie was already running towards Mrs. Fisher, when she called Jack and Jacob to come, "Give your mother a hug." Her love for them showed in her eyes. We sat in silence for a moment, drank our tea, as Mrs. Fisher explained to her mother, "I've been worried all day about Johnny Flynn."

I whispered to Granny Burton, "Did something happen to him?" understanding Naomi's strange behavior that day.

She spoke up, "He's my baby son, he's having a tough time right now."

"I'm sorry to hear it," I said with a truthful heart. Before Naomi could explain why she was worried about her son, Mr. Burton came up the sidewalk.

"Hello ladies," he smiled. "Supper ready?" We all stood up and as I started to say I was going home, Mr. Burton took my elbow to guide me into the house saying, "Iris, I hear you're supping with us tonight, I'm so pleased," as he escorted me through the front door. I sat Jack and Jacob on the kitchen counter to begin washing their faces and hands.

With my back turned away from the door; I heard an unfamiliar voice, "I'm home." Mrs. Fisher's mood changed instantly.

"It's Johnny Flynn," as she ran from the kitchen towards the door. As I turned to sit Jack down from the counter, she walked into the kitchen with someone following close behind her. "Iris, this is my oldest, Johnny Flynn." I set Jack down quickly not to drop him from the shock of what I was seeing. Brushing the hair from my forehead, I was staring directly at the boy from the mill window, the movies, the street corners, and Country Joe's; the boy who I had worked so hard to avoid, the boy who haunted my dreams.

The look on his face matched my own as he uttered a pleasant "Nice to meet you," I responded as I turned to put the dirty washcloth down on the counter.

CHAPTER 6
FLYNN

By the look on her face, she was surprised as much as I was. Mother introduced me to the elusive Iris Reed. All the conversations with her I had practiced in my mind disappeared.

With a coolness in her voice, she asked, "So Mrs. Fisher, is this your other son? The little one you have been telling me about?" Looking directly at me she continued with sarcasm in her voice, "I think you're too old for me to wash your face; although I'm sure it needs it."

Jack and Jacob sat in their usual places at the table with Iris taking mine. Mother said, "Johnny Flynn, son sit here by me." As I sat down beside her, she continued, "Iris and I work together at the mill. We help each other keep the line running smooth."

I leaned back in my chair hiding my laughter at the thought of my mother working hard. I looked at Iris, who had undoubtedly found humor in Mother's comment; she winked at me. My heart jumped out of my chest as I thought, "Damn, what is it about this girl?"

Mother and Iris carried on idle gossip about the mill and the people there. I sat in silence wondering how Iris Reed had ended up at our kitchen table. I quietly concluded it was karma; another sign she was meant to be in my life. Just as the thought came to my mind, I was startled by my mother's voice, "Flynn, do you know where the Reed's house is? You need to walk Iris home."

Iris protested, "There's no need, I'll be ok."

Granny Burton spoke up, "Walk her home honey, it's getting dark."

I pushed my chair back from the table as Iris headed toward the front door. I looked at Mother, "Guess she's ready to leave," trying to act like it was no big deal to me.

Out the door; the walk to her house was quiet. There was so much I wanted to say, but was worried about seeing her father. I'm sure she was preoccupied about the same thing. Luckily, he wasn't out in the yard or sitting on the porch; seeing the coast was clear, she stopped me at the gate. She ran up the porch steps, and as I stood there just watching her; I could have sworn she turned and blew me a kiss.

CHAPTER 7
IRIS

Supper was served; Mrs. Fisher was telling her son all about what was going on at the mill. I was busy trying to ignore this cad that chases young girls. Yet, being near him made my heart beat so fast that I was sure someone was going to hear it. Finally, supper over, I took my plate to the sink and begin cleaning up.

Granny Burton said; "Honey, don't worry about those dishes." Taking her up on her offer, I said my goodnights, my thank you and headed toward the door into the sunset of the day.

Mrs. Fisher said, "Iris wait, Johnny Flynn, walk her home it's getting dark outside." I protested at once, as I kept walking toward the front door; thinking I would be out of sight before he caught up with me.

By the time I was on the sidewalk, he was right beside me. We walked silently down Jefferson Street; two blocks down; turn left onto Troup Street; counting the steps in my mind to prevent myself from saying something I might regret later. Things I thought I already knew the answers to.

Dusk was settling in as the sky was streaked with pink and blue; and with no words spoken between us; I quickly walked through the gate and up the stairs before my Daddy noticed I wasn't alone.

Without planning it; without thinking about it; I reached for the door handle, I turned to see if he was still there. Our eyes met for the second time and all sensibility left me as I blew him a kiss and ran inside.

CHAPTER 8
FLYNN

S leep didn't come easy that night. My mind was racing with the excitement of knowing Iris was sort of in my life. I finally fell asleep to the vision of her behind my closed eyes.

The next day I woke up filled with anticipation about seeing Iris again that afternoon. I hung around the house that day waiting to see them walk down the street after their shift at the mill. I was surprised to see Mother arrive alone. I was relieved. I wasn't ready for Iris to know the truth; I turned 14 years old that day.

That was a Monday, so Tuesday, Wednesday, and Thursday, came and went with no Iris. I was hanging around the house much more than usual and my mother and grandmother were beginning to wonder why.

By Friday I decided I was being stupid over this girl and I was through. As I stood up to go into the house to get ready to go to town, here they come walking up the street laughing and talking. Iris' hair was pulled back with a red bandana. I always noticed her face first and as usual I was mesmerized by her natural beauty. Even after work, wearing overalls, she was simply beautiful, and I suspected she knew it.

28

Calling the kids in from the yard, I stood up as Iris and Mother walked up the steps. Iris immediately let me know her feelings for me hadn't changed since the night at the movie theater, "Hello." The sarcasm in her voice said it all. The screen door slammed as she walked into the house, with Jack, Jacob, and Bobbie right behind her. I sat back down in the rocking chair on the porch trying to get my thoughts together.

Mother sat down in the chair beside me, "Johnny Flynn? You ok?"

"Yes, ma'am I am," I quickly responded.

She reached over, patted my knee, and brushing her hair away from her face, she said, "Good. Let's go eat supper." As she opened the front door she turned and said, "Your Daddy's coming home; he finished the job he was working on and has some time off."

I smiled, "It will be good to see him."

Alone on the porch, I decided to face her with everything I was feeling. I just needed to find an opportunity. Hearing Mother call my name, I went into the house to find them all seated at the table. Iris was sitting there with Jack on one side and Jacob on the other. Once again, the only chair left was beside my mother, which I'm sure Iris had planned.

I sat quietly, ate, got up, and thanked everyone, "Supper was good," as I kissed Granny on the cheek. I could feel my pride getting the best of me. I knew it. I felt it, but I couldn't stop it. Looking directly at Mother and Iris drinking their tea, I chuckled and confidently proclaimed, "I have things to do, see you ladies, later. Mother, I'll be back soon." Looking directly at Iris, "We're going to the movies." I knew this would spark a response from her and at this point, any response was better than nothing.

Iris sarcastically remarked, "You boys have a fun time now." I was sure the "boys" remark was related to my age.

In 1940, the social boundaries were different, and a lot of things weren't acceptable; people of different races, religions, and believe it or not age. It all felt so hopeless. I was tired of worrying about Iris, and decided the relationship between us was doomed before it got started; She was older than me. A relationship between a 14-year-old boy and an older girl would never be allowed. I didn't plan to see Iris for the rest of the weekend or ever for that matter. I convinced myself she was to be just a memory that would eventually fade.

CHAPTER 9
IRIS

I knew Flynn's comment about the movie was meant to get to me, and it did. I was ready at that point to leave the Burtons. Not offering to help with anything, I explained, "My head is killing me; just tired I guess." I fussed at myself all the way home for letting this boy bother me.

I was angry for giving this rogue any hope that I would let myself fall for him. Straight away, I said my good nights to my family and headed for my bedroom.

Loretta was waiting for me. She immediately jumped into my face and mockingly said, "I see you came home with Flynn in tow the other night. So, he is too old for me, but not too young for you?"

Confused by her nonsensical remarks I replied, "Loretta what are you talking about? I'm not interested in anyone who runs after little girls."

Her tone changed into mad as she got in my face, "What are you talking about?" She yelled with a quiet voice hoping Mama or Daddy wouldn't hear us talking about a boy, especially a boy with the last name of Fisher. She continued, her bright blue eyes sparkling with fire, as they often did when she had news she was happy to shock someone with, "I just turned 13 years old, right?"

"Yes, you are 13 now, right?" I mockingly replied.

She continued, her hands on her hips, her face nearly touching mine, "How old do you think Flynn is?"

In my best I don't care voice I replied, "I thought he was 16 or 17; now I'm not sure. Maybe he's older?"

Loretta, with delight, filled me in on the truth, "You're wrong, Miss Know It All, try thirteen, maybe fourteen by now. You're older than him."

Her words echoed in my head; I knew without a doubt that Loretta was telling the truth. Everything suddenly made perfect sense...why he was with kids walking to school, he wasn't driving, didn't work... but he sure looked older. Then suddenly, my heart dropped as I thought of what people would say; it was unacceptable for a soon-to-be 16-year-old girl to be with a 14-year-old boy. I knew I had to push my feelings aside. My face reflected my thoughts as I sat on the side of the bed.

Loretta sat beside me and placed her head over on my shoulder as I spoke softly, "You really like him, Loretta?"

She didn't speak for a moment and then she continued, "Not like that, he's a nice guy, but he's a big flirt.... lots of girls like him. He has a reputation."

"You like him, Iris?" Ester and Tessa sat on the other side of me on the bed.

All three of my sisters were waiting on my answer. "No, No, No," I said.

Ester interrupted my answer. "He's been asking about you all over town Iris. I heard he has it bad for you."

Looking at them all, trying to absorb what was happening, "I cannot like a 14-year-old ...No, I am definitely not interested."

During the next couple of weeks, I intentionally made excuses not to visit the Fisher's house after work. I couldn't chance running into Flynn. He was too young for me, yet when I was around him my heart was his. I was better off staying as far as I could from all the Fishers.

Sitting in the mill window that Friday, I was a million miles away when my thoughts were interrupted by the familiar voice of Mrs. Fisher. "Iris, Iris, no excuses, you must come home with me today. Mama said she is expecting you for tea, cake, and talk." I did miss spending time with Granny Burton.

I thought for a minute; thinking I had stayed away long enough, "Ok, sounds good," I said, as I stood looking out the mill window. I thought out loud, "Maybe he won't be there."

"Who?" Mrs. Fisher said.

I laughed and shook my head. "No, not at your house at my house, never mind, let's go," I said.

On the walk to the Burton's house, Mrs. Fisher talked incessantly, as I pretended to listen. Opening the gate, and walking up the sidewalk toward their house, my heart beating fast as I realized he was there.

What am I doing? I thought it was ridiculous to react this way to a kid. I smiled as I saw him playing football with his two younger brothers. He was shorter than most boys, even for a 14-year-old, but he was definitely handsome. I was staring at his every move.

"Iris, Iris..." Mrs. Fisher was poking my elbow... "Don't you agree?"

"Yes, I do" I stuttered, wondering what I had just agreed to. Mrs. Fisher was going up the steps to the porch. I followed along behind.

She turned and said, "Boys, time for supper."

Bobbie was already in the kitchen with Granny Burton washing her hands.

She handed me a washcloth, to clean up the boys as they ran into the house straight to me.

Mr. Burton remarked, "We've missed you, Iris. I'm so glad you decided to join us."

Flynn came in slowly behind his brothers. I couldn't help myself. "Hello kid," I said sarcastically in an attempt to embarrass him. I could tell he got the message. He stared at me as he sat down at the dinner table. With all hands clean, supper time started; Mrs. Fisher sitting right beside Flynn telling him his Daddy would be home in the next couple of days.

I quickly made an excuse not to stay for supper. I watched him as I gathered my things to leave for home; his eyes were unbelievably blue. I said my goodbyes and with no offering from him to even acknowledge I was leaving, the thought occurred to me that I had totally misread Flynn Fisher. He wasn't interested in any Reed girl. As I walked home, a feeling of sudden sadness filled my heart. I reminded myself that he was just a kid, too young for me. I was determined to forget the Fishers, the Burtons, and especially Johnny Flynn.

CHAPTER 10
FLYNN

It was Saturday morning and a group of us guys made our way downtown to the city fountain. We liked hanging out there because the main part of town encircled it and we could see everyone going and coming. I had hardly thought anything about Iris; so, for me, it had been a good month. I was sure I was over her.

The guys and I were pitching pennies in front of the fountain that faced the Hollywood Clothing Store. I was winning and it was my turn; I pitched my penny; it hit directly on the line. I won again. I bent down, picking up all my winnings; I glanced up just in time to see a pair of legs walking out of the store. My eyes followed the legs up to see what creature was attached to the short shorts and strapped heels...An auditable "Damn" came out of my mouth. It was Iris Reed. I just couldn't seem to get away from this girl.

Walking across the street, smiling at me with her famous smirk, "Like what you see?"

Before I could get words out of my mouth, I heard the voice of reality screaming down the street. "Iris, Iris." Good grief I thought it's the other woman I can't get away from, my mother.

As my brain settled on what was happening, I heard mother asking Iris to go home with her for a glass of tea.

Iris looked at me, "I would love to but…" As the two of them walked down Broad Street.

Mother yelled back at me, "Johnny Flynn, you be home by supper time." Hoping not to appear to be too anxious, I went back to my game.

The guys could see I was flustered by the whole scene. Trying to avoid any teasing from them, I shook my head in disbelief and said, "You believe those two? Whose turn is it?"

As the darkness of sunset began, I headed for home. I missed supper time and Mother wouldn't be happy. Hopefully, Iris' visit was over, and she had gone home. By the time I arrived, everyone was sitting on the front porch. Surprisingly, Mother was laughing and smiling. I realized why; Daddy was home. He said he was there for a while, and I was happy about that because he could handle mother better than anyone else. Especially right now, though she was smiling I could tell she wasn't happy with me. It was a moment before I realized Iris wasn't on the porch, assuming she was inside, I asked, "Where's your friend?"

Mother looked puzzled by my asking about Iris, "She went home, it's her 16th birthday."

My thoughts started going in all directions as I realized she wasn't one year older than me; She was two…

At that moment, Granny Burton opened the door holding one of her famous cakes, "Who will run this cake down to Iris' house? She's so good to us."

Daddy standing up said, "Flynn will" as he patted me on the shoulder and whispered, "Be careful son, those Reeds are dangerous," winking at me.

Taking the cake, I replied, "I will Daddy." Walking down Jefferson Street over to Troup Street, I was as nervous as a cat in a room full of rocking chairs; one because Iris was the only girl that made me doubt myself and two because the possibility of knocking on that front door again made me have flashbacks of Mr. Reed's threats.

36

Approaching their house, I saw right away, I wouldn't need to go to the door. I could see the whole Reed family and friends in the front yard. I opened the gate.

Loretta ran up to me; "Hey handsome, where you been? Oh wait, I know you've been mooning over my older sister," she said laughing.

Still holding the cake in my hands, "Girl, you are crazy." Just as those words left my mouth, Iris came out the front door.

"Well, hello Johnny Flynn." I ignored the fact that she was trying to irritate me, by calling me by both names. She knew I didn't like it.

I held my hands out and awkwardly replied, "Granny made you a cake."

Iris leaned forward to take it while saying, "She is the sweetest thing, tell her thank you." As she took it from my hands, she whispered, "We need to talk."

I could feel Harley Reed's eyes piercing me from under the old oak tree in their front yard.

I whispered back to Iris releasing the cake into her hands, "The fountain, Sunday afternoon, after church."

Her voice suddenly returned to normal, just as old man Reed was getting up from his chair, "Please tell Mrs. Burton thank you for me and tell your mother hello." With that, she twirled around quickly and met her father just as he was approaching us. I walked out the Wilson's fence gate shaking my head as I headed back home.

I wanted to feel excited about meeting her, but I had a bad feeling Iris Reed was about to read me the riot act. I was sure she planned to tell me what a stupid kid I was to ever think anything could be between us.

CHAPTER II
IRIS

I spent the month of August intentionally staying away from the Burton's house and I was feeling much better. I was sure I wasn't interested in Flynn. I woke up on my birthday morning to go to town.

Mama cooked me a special breakfast, "No cleaning up for you birthday girl. You go on to town and get back early," she said. I was happy to spend my day doing what I loved to do...shopping.

Wearing new short-shorts, sandals, blouse and knowing I looked good, I felt a renewed confidence... I was over Flynn Fisher. Laughing out loud, I silently asked myself "Flynn who?"

My last stop of the day was at Hollywood Clothing to pay on my layaway. As I finished paying my weekly $1.00 to the sales lady, I was ready to go home. I heard the bell ring as I opened the door to leave, but my eyes were focused on the group of boys who were pitching pennies by the city's fountain. I immediately recognized one as Flynn Fisher. Thinking I couldn't get away from this kid, I noticed he was focused on my legs. I whispered under my breath, "He doesn't even recognize me." At the same time, I was thinking how handsome he really was.

Just as I rounded the circular side of the fountain, Flynn was bent down picking up coins from the cement sidewalk.

Suddenly, a recognizable voice was in my head, "Iris, Iris." Lord, I thought, it is Naomi Fisher. When we all met, Flynn stood up on the sidewalk right in front of us. We all three just stood face to face for a moment. Mrs. Fisher spoke first; inviting me to supper at their house.

I stumbled to speak as I explained to her that my family expected me home, "but I'll walk a while with you."

I could feel Flynn's eyes fixated on me. Unnerving as the whole thing was; I realized one thing that shock me to the point I let out an audible gasp. I liked this boy, and I knew I shouldn't because he was only 14 years old.

The sound of Mrs. Fisher's voice brought me back to reality, "Iris you can stop long enough for tea." As she struggled with her packages she looked back at the group of boys, "Don't be late for supper Johnny Flynn."

We walked out of town to the Burton's house. I reminded her I had to go straight home, "It's my birthday."

She replied, "Well gracious, Iris, why didn't you say something, Happy Birthday," as we parted ways.

I walked toward home, still shocked by the attraction I felt toward Flynn. I kept telling myself that he was a child, but he didn't look like a child or act like a child. One thing I knew for sure, any relationship I had with Flynn Fisher would never be accepted by the people who mattered to me.

As I turned onto Troup Street, I could see my family gathered in the front yard. I was happy for the distraction; I was tired of thinking about Flynn. Walking through Nanny and Paw Wilson's gate; an audible "Happy Birthday" filled the air.

Knowing my Daddy didn't want us wearing short shorts, I couldn't help but notice his immediate disapproving smile. I made my way to the front door letting everyone know I would be right back.

Inside the house, the smell of my favorite dishes filled the air. Mama and Nanny Wilson were in the kitchen cooking my birthday supper. Both standing at the stovetop, I walked over and put my arms around the two women I admired the most in the world. Mama looked down at my clothes; I quickly replied, "I'm going to change into a dress."

Mama smiled, "Good idea. You know your daddy hates those short shorts all you girls are wearing." I squeezed them both and went off to my bedroom.

Changing quickly into a red-checked dress, I moved to the mirror to pull my hair back out of my face with my favorite red bandanna. Standing in front of the mirror, I could see Loretta talking to some boy.... wait a minute that some boy was Flynn Fisher. A wave of jealousy flowed through me as I hurried to go outside to see why he was there. Was it to see Loretta? Out the door, down the steps, I approached Flynn and Loretta. "Why Johnny Flynn Fisher, as I live and breathe," mimicking the name his mother called him.

He spoke quickly, his confidence shaken by all of the Reed eyes focused on him. Holding a beautiful coconut cake, his voice sounded awkward, "Granny Burton baked you a cake." I stepped closer to him to take it, I surprised myself as I whispered, "We need to talk?"

He whispered back, "The fountain on Sunday?"

I answered, "Two o'clock?" Not giving him time to respond, I twirled around just in time to see my Daddy rising from his chair. Looking back at Flynn, "You tell your Granny thank you, ok now?" I winked at him without even thinking.

My 16th birthday went on until late evening, eating, singing, and Daddy's storytelling. All the while, I was silently asking myself, "What in the world are you thinking Iris Reed? He is just a kid."

Finally, the party was over, and I escaped to my bedroom hoping sleep would come quickly, so I wouldn't think about him or what he might say to me the next day.

CHAPTER 12
FLYNN

Sundays had always been my favorite day. The entire town was closed. After church, everyone went home for a big dinner. The rest of the day was spent sitting on the front porch or window shopping downtown. This Sunday was to be no exception; I woke up by my mother's voice calling, "Johnny Flynn get your brothers up."

I walked across the room to Jacob and Jack's bed, shaking their shoulders and calling their names, "Get up. It's time to get ready for church." I dressed quickly, helping Jacob and Jack when they needed it. Tucking in my shirt, I yelled back to them, "Come on guys, breakfast is ready."

I walked into the kitchen where Granny was taking a hot pan of biscuits out of the oven; Paw was sitting sipping his coffee out of his two-handled cup. I grabbed one of the biscuits off the plate Granny was holding and headed out the front door. I always thought it was a strange thing, Granny Burton. She was the Godliest of all of us and yet she stayed behind on Sundays to cook dinner. Guess God knew Mother couldn't cook.

Smiling at Granny, with biscuits in both hands, I kissed her head and hollered. "Mother, I'm going ahead, Meet you there."

"Johnny Flynn," she said as the front door squeaked open, "You better be on time."

"Yes ma'am," I hollered back. As the door opened, I saw Daddy sitting on the front porch; coffee in one hand and a cigarette in the other. "See you Daddy," I said.

He smiled, "See you son." I opened the gate and started toward Troup Street. "Hey," Daddy hollered, "Church is the other way."

I pretended not to hear, waving bye without looking, and hurried toward the Reeds to hopefully catch Iris leaving for church too. I was going to ask her what she wanted to talk to me about that day. No luck, the only person visible was Ester Wilson, Iris's grandmother. She was sitting on the front porch of her house shelling peas. I couldn't help but chuckle out loud, "Another Godly woman making way for sinners to go to church," and in my mind, the Reeds could use all the God they could get.

"Good morning Flynn, you're going the wrong way, aren't you?" she asked. I shook my head and started toward the Church of God on Stonewall Street trying to beat my mother there. I didn't make it.

I slipped through the church doors as they were singing, "*Victories in Jesus*," the song that signaled church had officially started. My mother singing the loudest, looked over her shoulder in time to see my late arrival. I winked at her...Ok, that smile meant I wasn't in trouble. I settled back on the church pew. I tried to listen to the preacher, but all I could think of was Iris.

Church seemed long that day, finally, it was over; I hurried back to the house...12:30...one and one-half hours before I was to meet Iris Reed. The mere thought of her made my heart race and my forehead break out in a sweat. I hated that a girl I hardly knew had that effect on me. "What the hell," I thought. "She isn't that special."

Once again Granny Burton had outdone herself...fried chicken, mashed potatoes, green beans, cornbread. Normally, I would eat too much, but with thoughts of my meeting with Iris running through my mind; I pushed the food around on my plate, then announced, "I'm meeting the guys in town." I was up and out of the door before anyone could stop me.

Daddy pushed his chair back from the table and followed me to the front porch. "Son, be careful, protect yourself," patting my shoulder.

"I'll try, Daddy this girl has my head crazy."

He replied, "I think she may be worth it." Smiling, he turned and walked back inside.

I walked six blocks to town with a newly found confidence. At Broad Street, the fountain water was visible, it was blue this Sunday. "Hope that isn't a sign of what was to come," I whispered under my breath. My eyes traced the perimeter of the water fountain, but no Iris. I found a bench and sat down, thinking, "I'm not going to wait long." I was sure she was playing with my heart, as I got up to leave about an hour later.

I turned to start home and there she was out of nowhere. My anger vanished as I stood up from the bench. I watched her approach me. She looked nervous, constantly looking around to see if anyone was watching. Her beauty was undeniable, and that day was no exception; she wore a dress with flowers of blue and yellow, with her hair tied back with a yellow scarf, and heels that were blue. I didn't realize at the time how the memory of her that day would be etched into my brain and how many times I would lie in bed trying to erase it.

"Can we walk?" she asked.

CHAPTER 13

IRIS

Sunday morning came after a sleepless night... thinking I wasn't going to meet that "kid" ...to extreme excitement about the possibilities of what might be beginning with someone who had captured my heart...kid or not.

I attended a local church where my Paw Wilson was a deacon. It was located on the outskirts of LaGrange, and I was worried I couldn't make it there, home for dinner, and to town to meet Flynn. I decided to ride my horse, Moses, named after my favorite Bible character. Moses needed riding and I needed the time to think without my family's endless chatter. Plus, I could get home before them all; maybe I would have a decision on what I needed to do about all of these mixed feelings.

I dressed quickly, grabbed a biscuit and my Bible, and I was out the door while explaining to Nanny Wilson, "Moses needs riding; tell Mama I've already left." No time for her to respond. I was on Moses and on my way to church. The ride there went by quickly as Moses and I carried on a one-sided conversation about Flynn, who I referred to as "the kid."

I don't remember much about church that day, my mind was wandering. I answered my own question about meeting Flynn that afternoon about midway through the service. I began to worry if he would show up or not; deciding either way would answer my questions. I smiled as I realized how God gives us insight without us even realizing it.

After church, I untied Moses and headed for home. Jumping off, I fed and watered him. I started to the house then stopped and went back to Moses. I felt like he was my best friend that day, rubbing his nose, he nuzzled against my face. We understood each other.

Running into the house, I washed off quickly and changed into a blue floral dress, Flynn's favorite color. I heard him tell Granny Burton one night how nice she looked, "Nothing prettier than a girl in a blue flowered dress." I laughed at the time, but I found myself buying a lot of blues.

Back to reality, I checked myself in the mirror, declaring "I hope you know what you're doing." Heading out of the house, I grabbed a chicken leg from Nanny Wilson's well-dressed Sunday dinner table. "Tell Mama I'm meeting some friends downtown for a picnic, I'll be home before dark."

"Ok Iris," she said to me but under her breath, I heard an audible sigh "What in the world is happening to the young people today?" Shaking her head she continued, "Running here and there and on the Lord's Day."

Walking to town, eating my chicken leg carefully so not to get it on my dress, my mind was racing in a million different directions; One I didn't know this boy... two...he's just a kid. He's fourteen, a baby, yet he seemed much older to me. One part of me was hoping he wouldn't show up and the other was praying he would.

I turned onto Jefferson Street past his house, and no one was outside. Thank goodness, I thought. Turning onto Vernon Street, where Clyborne Mansion sat lined with magnolia trees; I thought what a beautiful day it was. At this point, I was sure about one thing; I really liked this boy, this kid, and I felt it was all wrong, but I couldn't stop myself.

Approaching the fountain my eyes searched its circumference, checking each bench to see if he was there. I saw him sitting on the other side, his back to me. He was nervously looking around, fidgeting with his shirt. As I neared where he was sitting, the fountain sprayed me with water, surprised I gasped; he heard and turned, and suddenly we were facing each other. Silent; neither of us knew what to say, finally I spoke first, "Can we walk?" He looked at me and for a moment I was unsure of what he would say next.

CHAPTER 14

FLYNN AND IRIS

I spoke up thinking I knew what she was about to say, "Look Iris," taking her arm and turning her towards me. "I know why you came here; Let's just get this over with." She looked at me with confused eyes; speechless like she wanted to say something but couldn't. I continued, "I know you think I'm a kid, 14 years old, and you're 16." I paused waiting for her to respond. Nothing. Frustrated and confused the words "I'll leave you alone," fell from my mouth as I turned and began to walk away.

I had taken a couple of steps when I heard, "Flynn Fisher, where are you going?" I turned and stayed where I was; just looking at her. "Loretta told me you're 14, I thought you were thirteen, which isn't much of a difference," as she walked toward me, "The problem is I can't get you out of my mind." She rambled on, "I tell myself, he's just a kid, but you don't look like a kid or act like a kid."

I interrupted, "Wait, wait, grabbing her hands in mine I started to say, "You like…" stopping myself realizing how juvenile it sounded. "Look, let's walk and see if we can figure this out," placing my hand on the small of her back, we headed down Hill Street and out of town.

We walked in silence. We were both searching for the right words; unsure where the other one stood. We ended up in front of Birch Mill, where she and my mother worked. We sat down on a bench facing the river that ran beside the mill. She glanced around, nervous I figured. I spoke slowly. "I tried to tell you the night I was with Loretta, that I was thirteen, but you wouldn't listen."

She interrupted, "I thought you were older and interested in my sister."

I stopped her there, "It's been you since that night. You're all I think of...dream of."

"No, no," she argued as she stood and walked a few steps away from me, "This is wrong, you're a kid. Still in school. Son of my friend. I shouldn't have these feelings for you."

I stepped toward her, took her hands, "I'm not a kid, my feelings are real." Our hands dropped. We stood there in silence.

After a few moments, she looked up at an arched window facing the bench where we had sat, "You see that window, the arched one."

"Yes, I see it," I said.

Iris explained, "I sit there every morning on my first break." I looked at her not understanding what that had to do with us. She continued, "I watch you each morning, I see you walking to school with your friends. You have a lot of girls around you."

I chuckled not sure how to respond. We walked on in silence again, both of us knowing we had to go home before we were missed from the normal routines of our Sundays. "Iris, let's just sleep on this and see how we feel about this in the morning?" I waited for a minute.

Her words came slowly... "I have work, you have school, let's give this a couple of days, ok?" she asked.

We walked on to the end of Troup Street, where we would go our separate ways home, "Look meet me Tuesday, five O'clock right here at Birch Mill; at the bench underneath your window. There will be so many people around they won't notice us."

She raised her head in my direction and smiled, "Ok five, Tuesday, underneath our window," she smiled.

I held her hand for a moment. We separated to go in opposite directions. I looked back at her and she at me; we smiled at each other. I had the loneliest feeling overcome me. I knew my life wouldn't be complete without her in it, and it scared me.

CHAPTER 15

FLYNN

Sleep escaped me each night as the two days that followed crept by. I spent the time reliving Sunday and going over every word Iris spoke that day. Thinking about the possibilities of our starting a relationship. I was sure about two things; what I felt for Iris was real, and I couldn't imagine my life without her in it.

Monday and Tuesday went the same as always. The only difference was Iris was not coming home with mother from work. She commented to Granny Burton with raised eyebrows when Jack asked where she was, "I think Iris has a boyfriend."

I pretended not to hear a word. After I finished my schoolwork, I headed out the door announcing, "I'll be back later." Not waiting for a response, I ran toward Birch Street Mill to the familiar bench. I stopped. Iris wasn't there.

CHAPTER 16
IRIS

Tuesday at 5 o'clock; it would all be decided. I told no one about my meeting with Flynn; I wanted the decision to be mine and not influenced by anyone else. I knew everyone would have their own opinion, probably not good ones. I stayed away from the Fishers and Burtons and the mill window for those two days.

I stood to the side of the window watching this boy as he walked passed below. He was alone and looking up all the time. I couldn't get past his age, but it didn't stop my feelings for him. I was confused…tormented on whether to let people determine who I loved or to risk the fallout we would face when and if our families found out.

Tuesday came; work went slowly by; on my way home, I was still unsure if I should meet Flynn or just let it be over with him. I knew in my mind I should end it, but my heart told me the opposite. I changed clothes; grabbed two sodas and started to the mill. At the end of Troup Street, I turned left, and in the distance, I saw him.

CHAPTER 17
FLYNN

I sat down on the bench, head in my hands. I raised it as a familiar voice asked, "You want a drink?" We sat silently.

Finally, I said, "Well...now what?" I felt unsure of myself; an uncommon feeling for me.

Iris broke her silence, "I thought a lot about you and all the things that seem wrong about us."

"Like?" I asked.

Half laughing, she continued, "Your age for one."

The uncertainty turned to anger that the subject of age had come up again. "Here's the thing; I'm done talking about age; mine or yours. We can't change it. Today we decide; we walk away or give this thing a shot." I learned that day Iris Reed isn't one who will be pushed into anything. She got up from the bench and began to walk away. I didn't move; I had run after this girl for what seemed like an eternity. The ball was in her court now. I told myself I could just move on. I sat watching her walk further away from me. I dropped my head.

"Flynn," I looked up. She was standing in front of the mill about fifty yards from me staring upward.

"What the hell," I whispered to myself as I got up and ran toward her. As I reached her, "What's wrong?"

Without looking at me, her voice shaky, "I start to work at six every morning just past that window." Thinking what that had to do with anything, she stopped me before I could speak. She continued, "You pass here every day going to school." Seeing the confusion in my eyes, she said, "I watch you...I didn't know who you were. Now I do, you look up and we will see each other at the beginning of our day." She chuckled, "Me at work; you at school."

"Does this mean..." I started.

She stopped me. "It means we'll try this to see how it works out, with one condition."

"Continue," I said.

"No one knows about us until we see what we feel for each other," she said.

Thinking silently that I couldn't believe I was allowing this girl to dictate to me, I said "Agreed." I stuck my hand out in a light-hearted gesture. Iris took it and pulled me briefly toward her... kissing me lightly on the cheek. I melted.

The daylight was beginning to turn into dusk. We headed up toward Troup Street; me turning off one block early to avoid any confrontation with her daddy. She looked back at me, "See you," as she disappeared.

The next morning, I told my school friends to go on ahead when they came by the house, partly because I was running late and partly, because I was afraid of my reaction when I saw Iris standing in the window or worse my reaction if she wasn't. Grabbing my books, I hurried out the front door and down the walkway; looking down the street to make sure my buddies were out of sight.

Iris' window was arched shaped and outlined in rock. It was the only one in the mill like it. You could hear the looms running. I always noticed someone sitting or standing in it peering out at the world with their work eyes. I learned it was Iris Reed.

That day was different, the window held the truth about my future; would Iris be there as she promised, or was she playing a cruel joke on me? That thought had weighed on my mind all night.

Now turning the corner to the riverside of the mill, I was about to find out. My heart was beating hard; I swear my shirt was moving up and down. Approaching the window, I turned to see if she was there; she wasn't. Dropping my head, I told myself not to look up again. Don't give her the satisfaction; she was probably hiding, laughing her head off. I was past the window now. I couldn't help myself; I stopped, turned around, looking straight at the window. There she stood. I backed up a few steps; I could see her clearly now. Iris always awed me with her beauty but framed by the arch of the mill window, I haven't seen a sight more beautiful to this day. She was smiling; I gave her the ok sign. She gave it right back to me; waved; slipped her hands back into her overalls and was gone. It was enough for me; I knew she felt the same way. Our feelings were real, and though most people thought of me as a boy; that day I made a promise to act like a man.

Early in my adolescence, I realized girls liked me, and I liked them. Not one had given me pause to think of my future at 14 years old. Until now, the image of Iris in that window changed everything. My mother was adamant that I would graduate. My future seemed out of my hands and in hers, but the one thing I knew for sure was my future was going to have Iris Reed in it.

After that morning, Iris came home with Mother from the mill, most days. We decided not to change our normal routines so not to cause suspicions. I found it hard to stay away from my house, but I knew I had to.

I came home from school, did my homework, and headed to town like I always did. Careful not to show excitement when I walked through the front door and saw her in the kitchen. I waited until mother would insist, "Flynn walk Iris home." Those walks became our favorite time of the day. We laughed, talked, and got to know each other. Our feelings became real as we begin to plan our future together.

At 14, I wasn't an innocent young boy; as I said girls liked me; and I like them; the answer is yes to the question you are wondering about as you read this. I had been with a girl. Iris Reed was different, it wasn't her age, it wasn't her beauty, it was her. She had it all in my eyes.

We couldn't keep our hands off of each other and many nights we would slip into the darkness of the evening to be closer, but never did I disrespect her. We hugged, kissed, and sat on the floor of an empty house and talked about our future.

We planned how we were going to see each other on the week-ends; ways to bump into each other on Saturdays and Sundays. Meeting by accident on the street, slipping into a movie. Each week we slowly became more comfortable with each other and more in love than ever.

As late summer and fall passed, our plans for a life together were made. Knowing at my age I couldn't marry right away, we decided the following summer after my 15th birthday, we would leave LaGrange and be married. Iris was sure she could win her parents over eventually.

Even though she was my mother's friend, my mother would never accept the age difference between us or the fact that Iris was a Reed. Mother's comments were unkind, "She is a nice girl. It's too bad she was born into a lower-class family."

I knew the decision to run away to be married was the only way Iris and I had a chance. We both began saving money for a life together. Little did we know the events to come would change our lives and the lives of our families yet to come.

CHAPTER 18
ELIJAH

My family was much like most others. Born to Sidney and Erma Foster, I was the baby of eight siblings: three brothers and five sisters. My parents were not strangers to the hardships and the hard work that was needed to support a large family. Married in 1899 at an early age; they suffered a tragedy experienced by many during that time.

They struggled to overcome the loss of three children during the influenza epidemic long before I was born. That tragedy changed them. I have always been told that they were never the same. I will say they had a sadness about them even in good times.

Working farms owned by others was a way of life for most people. It provided a good life for the landowners, but just a way to get by for families like mine.

By the age of seventeen, my older siblings were all married, and I was the only child of my parents living at home. I was a boy much the same as every other boy during the 1930s moving around from place to place trying to survive.

By 1940, my father was hired by a company that made electric fans and we moved to Thomas County. It was the first job he had working in a factory.

My older sister, Vivian, and I were close; she was fourteen when I was born and became somewhat of a surrogate mother to me. She had weathered a divorce and remarried. Wanting a fresh start, she and her new husband moved to LaGrange to work in the mill. It wasn't a coincidence my sister ended up working there; they took the advice of Alice Wilson, who was friends with my mother back in Tallapoosa.

I don't believe in coincidences, and it wasn't one that I ended up meeting Iris Reed in the fall of that year. The move to Thomas County was difficult for my parents; there was no way to make the move in one day. The perfect stopping place for us was at my sister's house.

Vivian and Allen, her new husband, lived in the mill village up the street from the Wilson's. I was always glad to see Vivian and she was equally glad to see me.

Vivian was short and round in stature but large in heart and personality. Arriving that September afternoon, she insisted after supper we visit the Wilsons. Mama decided they needed to rest for the continuing trip to Merrillville the next morning. I on the other hand was happy to visit the Wilsons. I loved Mrs. Alice and her cooking. It was during that fall visit; I caught my first glimpse of Iris Reed and lost my heart.

Sitting under the big oak in the freshly groomed front yard of the small mill house, Mrs. Alice and her daughter Anita Reed had set up a table with desserts.

As everyone was rising to help themselves, she handed me a large piece of coconut cake telling me, "I'm going to fatten you up."

I smiled, feeling a little out of place sitting under that tree with all of those older folks, Mr. Harley, Mr. O.H., my dad, and a few other neighbors who had joined us. I like being there, taking it all in.

Mrs. Anita was back and forth as her kids were running in and out of the house. I had met her son Robert and Loretta when they were visiting their grandmother back in Bowdon. They walked over to me, I said, "Hello y'all," as I stuck out my hand to shake

Robert's hand; I smiled at Loretta. I knew she liked me, but I wasn't interested in getting involved with anyone, especially a 13-year-old girl who seemed to like all boys.

Standing with my back to the house, I heard the front door slam and a voice saying, "Bye Mama, Bye Daddy."

In unison, Mr. Harley and Mrs. Anita said, "You be back by ten!" Under Mr. Harley's breath, I heard him say, "That girl is going to be the death of me." I turned to see who this girl was, just as he finished his sentence.

I'm a simple man, who happen to fall in love at first sight with a not-so-simple girl. The moment I saw her bounce down the Reed's porch steps, my heart jumped against my chest, "Robert, who's the little troublemaker?" I hoped he didn't see the sweat that broke out on my forehead.

Before he could answer, Tessa, another Reed daughter, said, "Oh that's Iris, our sister. She is having supper with the Burtons tonight, La-De-Da."

I could tell there was some jealousy in her voice, and I could see why. Iris Reed, simply put, was a knock-out. Wearing a blue dress with her hair hanging on her shoulders, she had an air of confidence that any 17-year-old boy would notice.

As she walked down the sidewalk, Robert called, "Iris, come here and meet Elijah."

She replied, "I can't, running late."

Quickly she looked my way, "Hi Elijah," as she swirled around, opened the gate, and disappeared up the street. Robert and I looked at each other and laughed, but Tessa sighed with disgust as she turned to walk away.

The rest of that night, I laughed, talked, and watched the side-walk hoping Iris would come walking back down it; all the time asking myself, "What are you doing? She is just a girl; you don't even know her." The night passed quickly and before Iris returned, we said our goodbyes and headed back up Troup Street to home.

The next morning, we were up early and on the road to our new life some 190 miles south of LaGrange. The trip down moved slowly; we spent one night taking a nap on the side of the road. I had a lot of time to think about what I wanted to do after I helped my parents get settled in their new house. Instead, my head was full of Iris Reed; a girl I had only seen for less than five minutes.

We arrived the next day at our new home in Merrillville. Settling into the house was a responsibility left up to my mother and me; my dad started his job the very next day. It was the first real job he had at something other than sharecropping. I saw a glimpse of hope for a better life from both of my parents that I had never seen.

Helping them the next few weeks kept me busy, but Iris Reed became a constant memory. I couldn't understand it. How could a girl I saw for such a short time have such an impact on me?

At my parent's suggestion, I decided to head back to LaGrange to visit Vivian. A trip we had planned when we were last there. I was excited to see her and hopefully run into Iris again.

As it turned out during that trip, Robert Reed and I became fast friends. He was an old soul at fourteen; a tall red-headed lanky fellow with a huge personality. A jokester by nature, he always bragged his only goal was to live life to its fullest and he did.

We had a fun time during that visit and the many that came after. We did what all teenage boys have done through the ages in the south; fished, swam in the backwaters, hung out downtown, and yes, we chased teenage girls.

I admit during all these trips, I was taking every chance to run into Iris, and occasionally I did. She became an elusive mystery to me, which enticed me even more. I could not understand it; girls liked me, but she wouldn't give me the time of day. At first, I took her coldness as a way to get my attention, but all too quickly she let me know that I was dead wrong. She was not interested in me or anyone else.

Robert watched my encounters with her and her lack of interest was comical to him. He shook his head and warned me, "Give it up man." His hand on my shoulder, he looked me directly in the eyes, "Iris isn't the kind of girl your efforts will impress."

I figured her brother knew her better than me and decided I needed to forget Iris Reed. I found out that was a hard thing to do.

The end of the summer seemed to come quickly, and my trips to LaGrange became slowed down by the cruel winter of the south. Iris Reed had convinced me that I was wasting my time.

Robert agreed, "It was time for me to move on, there are plenty of other girls."

Without thinking, I quickly responded, "They aren't Iris."

Two of my sisters and their families moved down to Merrillville near my parents. It was a perfect opportunity for me to head out to Laurel, Mississippi to pursue work opportunities. I heard the railroad company there was hiring.

By that winter, I had moved into a boarding house run by Miss Mattie Lloyd and began a job in the local mill, not with the railroad as I had hoped. People from all over lived in the rooming house; mill workers, oil drillers, factory workers, and rail workers.

I liked my job and was hoping I would come to love Laurel and make a life there.

Laurel was much different than LaGrange or Merrillville or maybe it was me that was different. I was a 19-year-old man trying to forget a girl I didn't know. I dated a lot during my time there, but no one could measure up to the perfect girl who eluded me on each trip I made to LaGrange.

While in Laurel, I took an oath that I wouldn't speak her name again. I hoped that it would help to erase her image from my brain. It was a long cold Mississippi winter and though I lived in a house full of people, I was terribly lonely.

CHAPTER 19
FLYNN

The easiness of Iris and I seeing each other ended when the Reeds decided to move to Mountville on the outskirts of town. Her visits to our house each day after work became impossible because getting home was more than just a short walk down the street.

The distance coupled with the record cold and snowfall during that winter made it difficult for us the see each other. We were living for the few moments we saw each other through the mill window and notes we left each other in a secret place under our bench. Those stolen moments in the mornings ended when schools were closed and our ways of seeing each other were over.

With each day's passing, I missed her more and my insecurities grew. Being separated pulled us apart. I convinced myself she still thought of me as a boy and had probably found someone else. Still, I couldn't look at another girl. All I could do was wait for the long winter to turn to spring.

Desperate to spend some one-on-one time with Iris, I hatched a plan. On the pretense to visit my mother at the mill, I carefully wrote a note for Iris and would find a way to pass it to her while I was there.

The early morning walk down the street to the mill was cold and treacherous, snow covered the mostly deserted streets and sidewalks. A moment of sadness filled me as I passed the empty mill houses where the Wilsons and Reeds had once live. The closer I got to the mill, the more nervous I became. Not being with her had made me doubt her feelings for me but had not changed mine.

Into the mill, through the weave room, into the loom area, my eyes caught sight of the window where Iris always sat. She was not there; no sign of her or my mother. I wasn't sure why I felt the need to sit in that window, but I did.

Staring out at the snow surrounding the mill, I felt someone standing near me. I turned to see Iris there. I stood up immediately. Looking behind Iris, I noticed my mother making her way over towards us. Holding the note tucked under my fingers, I stuck it out as if to shake Iris's hand. I slipped the note to her and winked; and she immediately responded,

"Why little Flynn Fisher, what are you doing here?" She strategically stuck the note in her overall pocket.

Surprised by her comment, I stammered, "Here to see my mother."

Iris responded, "Well here she comes." She moved around me to sit in the window. I met my mother as she approached and positioned myself to see Iris staring out what she called, "her" window. Suddenly, she stood, walked past us, and disappeared into the restroom. I wondered if she was reading my note.

CHAPTER 20

IRIS

Moving to Mountville and the unusual amount of snow we were getting that winter made it impossible to visit the Burtons. School had closed, so even the mornings of us seeing each other through the mill window as he passed by had ended. Talking to each other was impossible, neither of our families had a telephone.

Just getting to the mill each day on the snowy roads was a long ride on Moses. Sitting in the mill window mornings before work, I began to question my feelings for Flynn. Looking at the undisturbed snow, the sounds of the machines drowned out my audible self-questioning about a relationship with this 14-year-old boy.

The only communication we had were the notes Flynn would sometimes leave in our secret place under the bench at the mill. I don't know how he managed the simple declarations of love. They always melted my heart; not the words as much as the efforts it took for him to leave them there.

The whistle signaling starting time brought me back to reality. As I made my way to my machine to begin my day the feeling of despair covered me. I felt there was no hope of this relationship lasting. The morning went by slowly; the sound of Mrs. Fisher's voice began to make my skin crawl as she spoke of their perfect family to the other workers. I knew better, but I did listen carefully when she spoke of Flynn. It was my only connection to him.

Break time arrived and I quickly made my way to the bathroom then started over to sit in the mill window for what I hoped would be a few minutes of peace.

As I walked through the maze of the running mill machines, I noticed someone had beaten me there. "Hey" I shouted in my most irritated voice; I realized it was Flynn. Without thinking, I continued my sentence, "Why it's little Johnny Flynn Fisher." I knew I shouldn't have said it, but I was half irritated and half trying to disguise my sheer delight.

As Flynn and I chatted, he reached forward to take my hand as if to shake it, and I noticed a slip of paper, a note, and a wink. Out of fear of lingering eyes, I quickly jerked my hand back and slipped the note into the bib of my overalls. His smile, his eyes, that wink, my heart; I couldn't wait to read his note.

Standing there looking at each other wasn't something we should do. Mrs. Fisher had spotted us and was all but running over to Flynn. I quickly move to my window, pretending not to be interested in either of them. Realizing there was no chance of reading it without Mrs. Fisher seeing it, I quickly headed to the bathroom filled with anticipation of reading his note.

As I passed by Mrs. Fisher, I smiled and said, "Going to the bathroom to fix my lipstick."

Sarcastically she replied, "Your break is over."

"Oh no, I have eight minutes left," I replied just as sarcastically pointing at the clock above the mill window.

Flynn was chuckling as he said, "Mother, mind your business."

I slipped into the bathroom stall and pulled out the note, my hands were shaking as I unfolded it. It read:

"Meet me at the Royal Theater on Saturday. 2:30? Upper balcony? We'll be careful, we can't afford to mess up our plans for July, but I need to see you. Can't wait." A heart beside his name; *Flynn.*"

I hurried out of the stall to the mill floor, but he had already gone. I hurried to the mill window, now our window, on the pretense of leaving my red bandana. I noticed Flynn standing outside below it. I quickly gave him the ok sign; he smiled giving me the thumbs up.

The rest of the week went by quickly and Saturday finally arrived. The snow had stopped making it easier to make the three miles to LaGrange from Mountville. I would normally ride Moses, but I didn't want to leave him out in the cold all day. I left home early to walk to town, about a mile down the road a taxi pulled up; it was Charlie.

Smiling he said, "Flynn wanted me to pick you up. No charge. My contribution to love." He continued, "Not really, Flynn didn't want you walking in the cold."

I got in the front seat, "Thanks" I said. The ride to town was quick, and Charlie didn't talk anymore about Flynn; but as I was climbing out of the taxi he assured me, "I'll take you back home, ok?"

I nodded and smiled, "I need to be home by 4:00?"

He nodded.

I was to meet Flynn at noon, so I had a little time to do my shopping and to pay on my layaway. I arrived on time at the theater and made my way up to the upper balcony to the two seats where we usually sat. I stuck my bags under my seat; took out my mirror, brushed my hair, and put on fresh lipstick.

I remembered I hadn't eaten anything all day. I started making my way down the stairway of the balcony to get popcorn. The light on the steps shone just enough to light the faces of the people coming.

I noticed Flynn just in front of me with both hands full. As we passed each other, he said, "I got everything we need. Just slip back up here in a minute." I could tell he was as nervous as I was about people seeing us alone in the dark theater. The lights were down, the step lights dimmed, and I made my way back up to the balcony. Nervous, I turned and glanced at the clock above the exit door, 2:15. Walking back up the steps, I noticed the theater wasn't full.

"Thank goodness," I thought as I sat down beside Flynn. We

grabbed each other's hand with the sheer desperation of wanting to be together, he began telling me how much he loved and missed me as the cartoon before the movie began to play.

I whispered, "I feel the same way." We kissed as the movie began and to this day, I cannot tell you what the movie was; what happened next erased the memory out of my head.

As the kiss between Flynn and I ended, I felt a strong arm pulling me away from him. Looking up I saw my Daddy, my terribly angry daddy saying, "Iris Reed, you get yourself up and out of this place now," as he was dragging me down the steps. Screaming the entire time about how I had deserted our family for the Fishers and the Burtons. I glanced back at Flynn. Daddy dropped my arm as he turned around to face him.

With his finger pointed directly in his face I heard him say, "If you come around her again, you will pay. Stay away from her and my family."

My Daddy was a big man and could be intimidating; and I saw it on Flynn's face, which had changed from a young man to a scared 14-year-old boy.

That night and the next day were a blur. I was so upset and embarrassed; all I did was cry. I don't remember much, but I know my daddy visited the Burton's house to tell them, "To keep their no-good son away from his daughter."

I heard Mrs. Fisher and he had almost come to blows when she accused me "of chasing after a child." I stayed in my room that Sunday worried about Flynn. Everyone left me alone and I finally slept.

Relieved that it was Monday, I dressed to go to work; the house was quiet. As I started out the door; Daddy spoke to me for the first time since the theater; his words were sternly spoken: "Quit the mill or ask to be sent to a different one." As it turned out that wasn't necessary.

CHAPTER 21

FLYNN

I don't remember too much about that night. Old man Reed grabbing Iris' arm; pulling her down the theater steps. Her looking back at me with a look I had never seen. I can't imagine what she was going through.

I left the theater as quickly as I could behind Iris trying to follow her to make sure she was all right. She was gone before I could get out the theater door. I made it home and was faced with questions from my mother; Why was I home so early? What movie did you see? Who went with you?

Daddy spoke up and said, "Naomi leave him alone." I quickly escaped to my bedroom.

Laying in the quiet of the night, I planned to go to Iris' house the next day and speak with Mr. Reed. Practicing exactly what I would say to him; I drifted off into a restless night's sleep. I woke up the next morning to voices screaming at each other. Peeking out of my door, I saw Mr. Reed pointing his finger at my mother telling her to keep me away from his daughter.

Mother screamed, "It's Iris' fault. Coming here pretending to be my friend."

Mr. Reed screamed back, "It's your fault you old biddy; using her to do your work."

My Daddy stepped between them. "Wait a minute, both of you; it's nobody's fault. They are two young'uns who like each other,"

Mother looked at Daddy with only a look she could give, "Harry, Iris is too old for Flynn. She is a..."

"Watch what you say," Mr. Reed screamed at Mother, "You're the problem, using people, using Iris to do your work." He stopped short when I walked into the room. I stood there for a moment, unsure if it was real or a nightmare. Wiping the sleep from my eyes, I began to speak.

I spoke slowly; careful to be respectful of my relationship with Iris, "Look everyone, we love each other." Daddy walked over and put his arm on my shoulder. I continued, "Mr. Reed, I'm sorry we didn't come to you, ask your permission, but you weren't exactly friendly towards me sir."

He lunged toward me, "You..." he began.

Daddy stepped in, "Think it's time for you to leave Harley." As he pushed him toward the front door.

The man I was trying to win over was shouting, "You will never see Iris again," I was stunned and speechless; I didn't know what to say to anyone.

Granny and Paw Burton came from the kitchen, both looking a little shaken by what had just happened. Granny handed me a cup of coffee, "I like Iris," she spoke softly.

Paw Burton, always a thoughtful man spoke up, "We need to all calm down and think about this for a while."

Mother disappeared as the three little ones began to wake up. I escaped back to my bedroom with my coffee and laid down on the bed, what to do next? Mother appeared at my bedroom door on her way to church, "Johnny Flynn, don't leave this house, do you hear me?"

I just looked at her, "Yes mother. The whole house heard you!" I lay on the bed most of that day. Glaring at the ceiling, thinking;

planning; how I would get to Iris. I'm sure she was being watched by her Daddy. I passed the time sleeping until Sunday was gone.

Monday morning Mother had already left for work at the mill. Granny had my breakfast ready. I ate in silence; not knowing what to say, but I knew what I was going to do. Granny in her attempts to make things better, smiled at me, "Flynn, honey, you know I like Iris; sweetest thing; but she isn't right…"

I stopped her there by saying "I know Granny. I need to get to school." Out the front door, I hurried walking past Iris' old house and the mill. If I knew Iris like I thought I did, she would be watching out of the mill window.

Snow on the ground, my heart beating fast as I got closer to the mill, then the window. What I saw next filled my soul. Iris appeared; we waved. Knowing there was no way she could hear me, I picked up a stick, drew a heart, and wrote a message in it. I looked up; she was pointing to herself and holding up two fingers. Then she was gone. I knew exactly what her message meant, "me too." She still loves me too. I looked at my watch as I remember school was closed because of the weather. I turned and walked home. "The schools closed early," I told Granny as I escaped to my bedroom to thaw my frozen hands and feet.

I knew I wouldn't be able to see or talk to Iris until all of this calmed down some. I decided I would speak to her the only way I knew I could. I would get up before sunrise walk down to the mill and leave a message for her in the snow outside of the mill window. The next morning, I grabbed a hot biscuit off the stove and left the house sight unseen; making sure Mother had left before me.

CHAPTER 22

IRIS

The weaving room was a buzz with what had happened between the Fishers and Reeds, making the feud between the families worse. The whispering picked up as I started working. I knew Naomi Fisher started her handy work as people glared at me throughout the morning.

Break time arrived and I quickly made my way to my window. It snowed all morning and stopped just as the sun rose. As I sat down, I felt defeated and terribly alone; I was sure my relationship with Flynn was over. Looking out to the pathway between the mill and the river I noticed someone standing there.

It was Flynn writing in the snow with a stick. I smiled as I read his message inside a heart he had drawn; "Still the same; I love you!"

I motioned back to him, pointing to my heart and holding up two fingers, "Me too." He smiled and sat on the bench until I got up from the mill window to go back to work. Nothing else mattered; we were still together.

CHAPTER 23
FLYNN

The next morning, I wrote a new message inside a heart formed with rocks, "I love you with all of mine." Back at home, Granny Burton was upset, "You went to the mill?" The last thing your mother said was, "Tell Johnny Flynn to stay away from the mill." She followed me into my bedroom, "Flynn things aren't right at this house. Your daddy set off for Greenville."

As I closed my door, I tried to reassure her, "It's ok, Granny."

My mother came home that day raving about Iris, "She didn't help me keep my line running, I'll show her a thing or two." I closed my door and tried to sleep by letting my mind drift to the times' Iris and I had spent together.

Laying there listening to Mother call her things she didn't deserve; I made my mind up to leave a message every morning written in the heart I made from rocks below the mill window until all this died down. It was the only way I could think of to communicate with her. I couldn't send her a letter, call her, or go to her house for fear her daddy would find out.

What I didn't realize was I was a naïve 14-year-old boy who was about to get reality slapped in my face. By the time I woke up the next morning, all hell had broken loose. Mother had gone into work only to be told she was fired for lack of production.

Behind the door in my bedroom, I chuckled, knowing that Iris not helping her had caused it. Mother just couldn't work fast enough to keep up on her own. I opened my bedroom door, walked over poured myself a cup of coffee, and grabbed one of the fresh muffins Granny had just taken out of the oven. Without a word, I turned and walked back into my bedroom followed by Mother. I tried to close the door quickly, but she held the door-knob and shoved her way inside.

I had no idea what was about to come my way. "Johnny Flynn," she began, "I like Iris, but you see the kind of people she comes from." I remained silent and stared at her for a moment.

Trying to defend Iris, "Mother, I don't care about her family. I know what kind of people Iris is, that's all I care about. I love her, and we will be together." I could tell my words only made my mother madder.

She turned and going out the door she spoke, "We'll see." I felt victorious, everything was going to be ok. I had won the fight, but a real battle was about to come.

At that very moment of self-satisfaction, my mother marched back into my room with boxes and my suitcase, "Pack your things, we will be moving back to Greenville tomorrow."

Angered and defeated and with feelings against my mother I had never felt, I screamed, "I'm not going!" I pushed past her and went into the kitchen.

"Granny, I can stay here, right?" I knew I had put her in a bad spot.

She spoke softly, "Honey you know I can't go against your mother and daddy." Still, I refused to pack, thinking I could convince my Daddy when he got home.

The house was eerily quiet that night. Paw and Granny Burton ate and went immediately to their bedroom, I was sure they were tired of all the trouble our family brought them. Mother didn't speak to me again, a welcome change. I went to bed and closed my eyes and held my breath worried about what she would do next.

My brothers asleep, she slipped into the room and packed all of my things. I laid in bed that night trying to figure out what I was going to do. How would I ever get out of the house without Mother knowing it?

In desperation, before sunrise, I dressed quickly in the clothes left at the foot of my bed. Weaving through the packed boxes, careful not to wake anyone, I grabbed my coat and slipped out of the house.

I ran toward the mill. Knowing Iris would be getting there to start work, I hoped to catch her before she went inside. Out of breath, I got there just in time to see her clear the front door. As the sun rose over the river, I sat on the bench unsure of what to do next. How would I let her know what Mother had done? I sat for what seemed like forever, hoping she would see me; but she didn't. Sadness filled me, and it was at that moment that I knew it would be a long time before I would see, talk to, or touch Iris again.

I grabbed a stick and walked over to the heart I had built with rocks and wrote my message in the freshly fallen snow. Then, I took a piece of paper from my front pocket, scribbled a handwritten note, and stuck it under the bench; not sure she would ever find it.

Looking at the message in the heart I knew it would make her sad. I hated writing it as much as I hated being ripped from her life. I stood frozen partly from the cold and partly from the feeling of helplessness.

I felt a hand on my shoulder, it was Daddy. Sadness in his voice, he whispered, "Let's go son." The walk back home was filled with silence, except for one statement, "Your mother has made up her mind; You know how she is."

I looked over at him, "Do you agree with her about Iris?" He just shook his head to indicate no. I made a mental promise to never forgive my mother; and one day to marry Iris Reed.

We left that day, the car packed in a way, I knew we weren't coming back for a long time if ever. I didn't need to ask where we were going, we had bounced back and forth from Greenville to

LaGrange most of my life. I felt lonelier than I ever had, but knew there was nothing I could do.

CHAPTER 24

IRIS

For the next two days, as I arrived at work, I headed straight to the mill window hoping Flynn would be standing below; but there was no Flynn. Looking through that window with complete sadness my heart jumped as I realized there was a message written in the snow. He had outlined rocks in the shape of a heart and inside it read "Love you with all of mine." My heart was full as I thought of the trouble, he had gone through to leave the message. Sneaking out of the house under the watchful eye of his mother in the early morning. Using rocks, he found to form them in a perfectly shaped heart. The love I felt for Flynn at that moment was beyond words.

The day went by slowly as the mill floor was buzzing about what was going on with Naomi Fisher. She had come to work but then left suddenly. I wasn't too concerned about her. I was too busy trying to figure out how I was going to manage to see Flynn again.

After a sleepless night, I left for work earlier than usual. I arrived and went directly to the mill window with my coffee hoping to see Flynn as he arrived. He wasn't there, but a new message was written inside the heart. "She is taking me away...I'll always love you." I stood up and stared out the window; unsure of what to do next. I knew the "she" in the message was Naomi. I heard she was fired yesterday for lack of work. I felt a little responsible because I had stopped helping her after I heard what she said to Daddy.

What did Flynn mean she is taking me away? Suddenly, I panicked. I told my boss I was sick and left the mill. I ran the eight blocks to Jefferson Street. I slowed down as the Burton's house came into view. I walked through the gate unsure what I was facing. Granny Burton opened the front door as I walked up the steps. I was out of breath to the point where I couldn't speak.

She looked sad as she held my hand, "Honey, they are gone. I can't tell you where they went. I'm not sure, but I suppose Greenville." I turned as tears ran down my cheeks. I was going home, getting my money and buying a bus ticket to Greenville.

Before I made it to the gate, I felt a soft touch on my shoulder. "Iris don't go. Naomi has made up her mind about you and Flynn. She won't let you near him. Honey, he's only fourteen, give it some time."

I couldn't stop the tears as I collapsed into her gentle arms, I knew it was over for me and Flynn. He was gone forever. I'm not sure how I made it home that day. The next two days, I stayed home from work; I couldn't stand the thought of sitting in my mill window. I was heartbroken.

Saturday morning, mama made me get up and get dressed. I still wasn't speaking to Daddy; I blamed him for all of this. I left the house to walk and think, ending up at the mill. I sat on the same bench Flynn and I sat on the day we decided to give ourselves a chance. I stared up at the mill window and down at the heart with the words Flynn had written now covered in snow. Feeling lost and confused; I wondered what my life would be without the future Flynn and I had planned. My heart was broken. There was nothing else I could do but cry.

I heard someone calling my name, "Iris, Iris." I looked up. There stood a young man standing in front of me.

CHAPTER 25
ELIJAH

Laurel, Mississippi didn't turn out to be the place I thought it would be. I was looking for independence when I left home. I had a job there that paid well, but I was lonely and I missed my family. Going home to Merrillville was too far to travel over the weekend, but I could make it to LaGrange.

My trips to visit Vivian became more frequent and by February, I decided to leave Laurel for a job there. I was hired at Birch Mill. My training would start in nine days. I packed quickly and made it there five days before I was due to begin.

The winter weather in LaGrange was much like Laurel, cold and snowy. Vivian remarked, "Worst one we've had in a long time." I loved the cold weather.

She knew I liked Iris and made it a point to tell me the Reeds had moved to Mountville. I didn't say much as I wondered where Mountville was. I dare not ask. I didn't want anyone to know how much of my heart Iris Reed had taken.

As Vivian was mumbling something about the Fosters, I stopped the conversation with a lie, "Nothing to me where the Reeds moved."

Vivian glared back at me with her knowing smile, "Ok honey, we both know that's not true."

The Saturday before I was to start work, I took my usual morning walk and ended up on the riverside of the mill. I liked it there. I noticed benches along the walkway and decided to sit on one to drink my coffee and eat the breakfast Vivian had handed me as I walked out of the door. She knew I could get caught up in what I was doing and forget to eat. I chuckled at the thought of her knowing me so well.

At the mill, I looked around to find a bench to sit for a while, my eyes locked on a young woman crying; I didn't recognize her but felt I should find out if she needed help. I walked up to her slowly and was surprised to see Iris Reed sitting there. My heart was broken to see her like that. I felt her sadness and didn't understand the effect this girl had on me.

"Iris? Iris?" I spoke softly, "Are you alright?"

She looked up wiping her eyes, "Yes, No." She paused, "I really don't know."

I sat down on the bench beside her, "You want to tell me about it?"

She was silent. Then spoke in a confused voice, "I can't talk about it right now; It is too much," as she stared up at the mill. I wasn't sure what she was looking for... or at, but she seemed to be fixed on a certain window. I could tell she was hurting; I didn't know why or who caused it, but pain and sadness filled her. As we sat there, I realized how much I cared for this girl I hardly knew. I was feeling things for her I never felt before, and the realization of it caused me to gasp.

Suddenly, Iris stood up, "Enough of this," as she walked along the river's edge. No words were spoken. I walked with her, more behind her than beside her; not knowing exactly what to do or what to say, but I felt she needed someone with her. I opened my biscuit and handed her a piece. She took it and ate it slowly; still nothing but silence between us. I kept my eyes on her; hoping and praying whatever tormented her would leave her. She walked for what seemed like forever and I followed; not sure that she even knew I was still there.

Suddenly, she stopped and turned as if she just realized who I was, "Elijah... right?"

I grinned down at her and just nodded. She stepped back beside me as we started to walk. I glanced at my watch; we had been walking for an hour. "You hungry?" I asked as we approached Country Joe's Hotdogs. She nodded. I opened the door for her, she sat down at a small table in the back. I stepped to the counter and order two hot chocolates and two hot dogs. We sat together and ate in silence. The warmth of being out of the cold and drinking our hot chocolate seemed to change Iris' mood.

I spoke first, "I don't know what's happening to make you so sad... but..."

She stopped me there; one tear rolled down the length of her face. "You don't live here?" she asked. I knew she wasn't ready to talk about whatever was bothering her.

Letting her lead the conversation I replied, "I do, I just moved here to work in the mill. I'm staying with my sister, Vivian." I went on to tell her about my life in Laurel and how much I missed my family. She shook her head like she was listening to me tell her about the job I was to start on Monday.

I wasn't sure she had heard a word I was saying until she smiled, "I've met Vivian at the mill and now you're working there?" She stood up to collect the trash on the table; I followed her lead; took it from her hands and walked over to the trash can. Iris had put her coat on as we headed out the door. The rush of the freezing air outside took our breaths away. Her voice shivered from the cold, "I need to let you get home. It is getting late and the cold will set in after dark." Forgetting the Reeds had moved, I told her I would walk her home.

She explained, "I don't live in town. We moved. Moses, my horse is over by the theater." She smiled. It was one block from where we were.

As I walked her there, I asked, "Are you sure you are ok now?"

I helped her onto Moses, she smiled down at me, "I'm not ok, but I hope I will be." The sun began to set as Iris Reed disappeared down the road, what a picture. My perfect girl riding off into the sunset. The only problem was she was heartbroken over the love of someone else.

I walked quickly back to Vivian's house; my mind all over the place. My head was telling me I didn't have time to worry about Iris Reed, but my heart was telling me something completely different.

Over the next few weeks, I was busy training at the mill and making a trip back to Laurel to finish moving. I was sure I would run into Iris, but I didn't. I walked through the loom area every day but never saw her. The mill was a big place and Iris seemed to have disappeared in it.

Before it was time for my work schedule to begin, I decided to visit my parents in Merrillville. Hoping the trip would help me to forget the elusive Iris, but as hard as I tried I couldn't get her out of my head.

Returning to LaGrange, I was ready to start work, but found out the cold of the winter closed the mill and forced everyone to stay home. Time passed slowly as my need to work increased, not for money ...I needed to find Iris. My heart had completely been stolen by her.

The winter months slowly passed away to the arrival of March breathing a new life into LaGrange and the mill. The warmth of spring began to thaw out the city and Iris Reed.

CHAPTER 26
IRIS

After the day I had spent with Elijah, a boy I hardly knew, I was more confused than ever. I couldn't manage to do anything but survive. The rest of the winter was spent working when the mill wasn't shut down by the cold. It had always been a place of refuge for me, now it was just a job. I was drawn to the window, but now it only brought me sadness to sit there without Flynn sitting with me.

Looking at the bench below, where he and I planned our future, made my heart hurt. The promise we made, "to love each other no matter what" rang in my head. It was the place where I last heard from Flynn and where he left the messages to me.

No one knew about the brief note I found taped underneath the bench from Flynn the day Elijah found me sitting there. It had been a secret place planned by him in case we were ever separated. He knew his mother would try anything to get her way and break us apart. She had succeeded.

The note was short and broke my already shattered heart; how could I be happy when Flynn was so far away. I knew Naomi Fisher would never let him return.

"Iris, I will always love you; I will always be working my way back to you. Try to be happy while I am gone. Flynn".

The words hurt; I couldn't stop crying. I didn't want to do anything but stay at home and be by myself. The pain I felt was like the grief you feel when someone you love dies. I lost Flynn and the future I thought we would have. I tried to hang on to the memories of our times together, but they only brought me great sadness.

Slowly, I began to push them away, remembering the words of Granny Burton to "forget about Flynn." Facing Naomi Fisher had won, I realized I would never see him again. I had to do what Flynn said in his note and try to be happy; I had to let him go.

Elijah and I had become fast friends over the Saturday we had shared. He was adjusting to his new life in LaGrange, and I was adjusting to a life without Flynn.

Elijah told me "I fell for you the first time I saw you, but you were with Flynn. I know he moved away. Is that why you are upset?"

I responded, "We're not together." He was curious about what happened between us; but never asked me any questions. I explained to him, "It's still hard for me to talk about what happened."

The differences between Elijah and Flynn were obvious. Elijah was older and taller with a slender build. He was handsome but in a different way than Flynn. An old soul, quiet and shy when he met people, but always friendly to everyone.

Our lives had been similar; our family life much the same. The relationship between us was slow to come, but in time we became good friends. I was comfortable with him. I couldn't say that about many people since Flynn had left. Elijah always put me first and never pushed me.

He was close to his family, but they didn't rule him, unlike Flynn. He continued to live with his sister, Vivian, and her husband; saving money until he could afford his own house.

As time passed working together at the mill, we slowly became closer. The things we had in common pulled us together. Our lives just intertwined naturally. Still, I didn't allow myself to get too close to Elijah; my feelings for Flynn were as strong as ever. I told myself, "You can't love two men at the same time."

I thought about Flynn every day. He was becoming just a memory and the future we planned was slowly replaced by the days spent with Elijah. I eventually convinced myself it was time to move on; especially after I heard Flynn had come to town and didn't contact me. By winter, almost a year had passed since I had seen or heard from him, and Elijah was there.

At work, we shared the same break and lunch times, arranged by him, I'm sure. At first, we ate with the rest of the mill workers; then slowly we would find places we could sit alone. He knew not to ask me to sit in the mill window; I explained its importance in my relationship with Flynn. What I couldn't tell him was how afraid I was to sit in my window. Afraid if I sat there all of the feelings I had carefully convinced myself I no longer felt for Flynn would come flooding back.

CHAPTER 27
FLYNN

The first months in Greenville I was consumed by anger towards my mother. She was running my life and there wasn't much I could do about it. I tried to make the best of it there until I was old enough to live my own life.

Going to school and spending my free time with Joan was all I did. I made sure she knew about my feelings for Iris. I told her, "We could only be friends." She agreed, but I knew she secretly hoped it was different between us. I wished I could feel something for another girl, but my heart was no longer my own. It belonged to a girl 150 miles away; and in those days 150 miles might as well be a thousand.

LaGrange was off limits for me. My mother insisted the time away from there would allow me to "Get my mind straightened out; you will see Iris isn't right for you."

She encouraged me to see Joan, and she was thrilled when I told her I had gotten a part-time job at the mill and wanted to save my money. She thought I was planning a future in Greenville. I let her think what she wanted to think, but I knew I was working on a plan to go back to LaGrange for good.

Occasionally, I travelled to LaGrange with my parents to visit

Granny and Paw Burton. We didn't stay long; I was closely watched. My mother was happy to hear the Reeds had moved to the outskirts of town and no longer lived down the street.

My hopes of seeing Iris disappeared. It was hard to be that close to her and not see her. I decided I wouldn't return to LaGrange until I could stay. I had caused enough hurt; It was the best thing for Iris.

Charlie finished school and went to work in the mill and would tell me about Iris. He said, "She was sad and having a hard time." It broke my heart to think of her hurting. I did the only thing I could at the time, I wrote her a letter and mailed it while I was in LaGrange; to try to be happy and strong until I could come back to her; that I loved her. I hoped it made it to her hands.

Shortly after I mailed the letter, I heard from Mother that Iris was dating Elijah Foster. I didn't know what to believe. I was more determined to get back to Iris to see if it was true.

I hadn't been in LaGrange in over a year. The next six months, I worked harder at school and the mill. I was on the path to graduate from tenth grade and having enough money to move back to LaGrange by the first of the year.

Hearing Iris was seeing someone else haunted me; and convinced me I needed to forget her; A goal I didn't achieve. I had to face Iris to find out the truth so I could move on with my life. Without Joan, I don't think I would have survived.

Mother made it a point to tell me any news she heard about Iris, "I'm so glad Iris has come to her senses and moved on; the Fosters and the Reeds are better suited for each other."

She loved Joan; thought we were planning a future together. I told Joan what Mother had said, but instead of being happy, she was angered by my mother saying things to hurt me. Joan and I did grow closer, but I couldn't give her my heart. It wasn't mine to give; my heart belonged to someone who I was sure no longer knew I existed.

I made it to Thanksgiving and Christmas. I loved that time of year, and this year was more special. In January I would have the money for my bus ticket along with more than enough to start my life back in LaGrange.

It had been almost two years since I had seen Iris. With or without her, it was where I wanted to be. The hardest part of moving back was the hurt it would cause Joan, and I did have some guilt over the whole situation. Although I tried to be honest with her about my feelings, I selfishly held on to Joan "just in case."

The day after Christmas, I broke the news to my mother and father, "I'm moving back to LaGrange."

I spoke with Paw and Granny to make sure I could stay with them. They were happy to hear I was coming to live with them, "We could use your help around here."

Surprisingly, my parents agreed. Mother insisted, "It is your choice, but there are some conditions to your decision." I nodded. She continued, "You must finish school and go home every day to help Granny Burton, and not contact Iris." I nodded in agreement knowing I had plans of my own.

New Year's Day; Everything was ready for my trip back to LaGrange. My ticket was bought; clothes were packed; all that was left to do was tell Joan. Standing before her, the words spilled out. "I'm leaving tomorrow, moving back to LaGrange. It has nothing to do with you." I explained, "It's me."

She stopped me, "No it's Iris Reed. I'm not going to try to stop you. You need to figure it out. I'll wait, but not forever." She kissed my cheek. Suddenly an empty feeling filled my heart and I prayed I wasn't making the wrong choice.

After a sleepless night, I was on the bus back to LaGrange. I questioned why I felt such a need to return. The things I heard about Iris made me sure she had forgotten all about me and our plans.

CHAPTER 28

ELIJAH

My move to LaGrange and my job in the mill had proved to give me what I had hoped it would, a good-paying job and Iris Reed. Our relationship began slowly after that Saturday I ran into her outside of the mill. Iris' hurt was deep. I knew how she felt about Flynn.

At first, I was satisfied being her friend; hopeful that her feelings for me would replace her feelings for him. I learned when to approach the subject of Flynn, and when not to say anything. I sat silently with her at the city fountain and mill park bench; watching her as her heart began to heal. I allowed her that time; She cried often; it broke my heart, but I knew she had to get through the hurt to be able to love someone again. I was hopeful that someone would be me.

Working together in the mill, our friendship slowly began to grow. First, we just waved to each other, and spoke a short "hi." I would make sure I caught up with her on her walk home until our paths separated; she would get on her horse and wave bye as I turned on Troup Street. Those walks were often silent.

Looking at her, I wondered why I was so drawn to her. Yes, she was beautiful; but she had something most women didn't have during those days. She had an independent spirit; a confidence that most girls just didn't have, and it drew me to her. I saw her dismiss guys at the mill who were trying to get to know her without a second thought. It was that confidence that made her so desirable.

I knew Iris and I were friends. I let it be; thinking in time I could make her see we were made for each other. It happened slowly. Iris hadn't mentioned Flynn in a long while. When she did it was to tell me she hadn't heard from him.

She said, "He has moved on, and it's time for me to do the same." His absence from her daily life resulted in her opening her heart to me and our friendship slowly changed into a relationship.

Vivian worked at the mill when Flynn was there. She explained he came there daily, "They ate lunch in the window every day. I can't tell you how many times they sat there after work; talking and laughing together." She warned me, "Elijah, their bond was strong. I'm not sure if Flynn came back here, she wouldn't be with him again. I don't want you to get hurt."

I listened to her concern and explained, "My connection to Iris is strong, and there is no way I can or would stop seeing her. It's a chance I have to take."

I understood now why Iris insisted we eat in the mill's lunch-room. Why she would stand and stare at the window; never approach it or sit in it. Strangely enough, no one else would sit there either. It was if it was a sacred place meant only for Iris and Flynn. I decided if she would sit in the window with me; she was truly over him. I made a bold move the next day and told her to meet me in the loom area for lunch.

The next day at lunch time, I walked through the mill's loom area. I sat in her window with a pail holding the lunch I had made for us sitting beside me. If she sat there with me, I would know she was truly over Flynn. I was nervous, but soon found out the answer to that question.

I saw her as she came into the room; she walked around the last machine and saw me sitting in the window. My heart dropped as I saw the look on her face; as though she had seen a ghost. She immediately turned and walked away. I was half mad and fully hurt. Defiantly, I ate lunch alone. Sitting in Iris' window, I felt like an intruder into her heart. It was an uneasiness I had never felt.

I finished the day working silently and feeling deflated. I was convinced Iris wasn't over Flynn. After the shift ended, I walked quickly out the mill door and to the corner of my street. I saw her standing there. I was angry.

Iris began, "Elijah, I'm sorry. It's just the mill window has a lot of history for me; and my time with Flynn." She paused…I could see her struggling with what to say next. "Much of my relationship with him involved the window; not only us sitting there but in other ways that I cannot talk about right now. I'm afraid if I sit there all the memories I'm trying to forget will come rushing back. I don't want them to." She began to cry softly.

I couldn't stand to see her that way, "I'm sorry. I should have known that." I reached for her hand, "Let's just forget it."

For the first time, she took it, and we walked up to my house. From that day forward our relationship began to move from friends to something deeper. We promised each other to move slow and "have a good time," and we did.

It was still winter; the cold and lack of money limited what we did. We spent most of our time at my house, playing cards or games. However, the Reed's house was a different story. I wasn't sure why Harley Reed kept such a close eye on all of his daughters, but he did. No boys were allowed to visit them. He watched over them wherever they went. We didn't care.

Our time together was filled with riding horses, sitting on a bench talking at the fountain, or having something to eat at one of our favorite places. We went to the movies, fishing on the banks of the backwater, or listening to the radio on the front porch of my house. I was careful not to be disrespectful to Mr. Reed's rules. I wanted him to see he could trust me.

By the holiday season, I had become a member of the church in their little community. Iris and two of her sisters, Ester and Tessa sang there. What people didn't know about Iris was how incredibly shy she was; it took a lot for her to stand in front of people, but I loved watching her sing alto.

All and all, 1942 had been a good year for me. We celebrated Thanksgiving Day and Christmas together. Mr. Reed allowed me to come over and sit on the porch to exchange our gifts; she gave me a new pair of riding gloves; I gave her a little gold bracelet with hearts on it. She seemed happy and that made me happy.

New Year's Day, 1943, arrived with a new hope on the Reed's front porch, and our first real kiss. Yes, I waited that long; I wanted to be sure she was ready to move on. It was worth it. The minute the kiss happened; it was all over for me. I was head over heels in love with her. I was pretty sure Iris felt the same way.

After that moment, Loretta, appointed to watch over us, opened the front door, "Now, now, y'all keep your hands and lips off of each other or I'll have to call Daddy," she laughingly scolded us. The front door closed, and then opened again, "By the way, I heard some news in town today y'all might be interested in" ... she paused for a minute and walked out on the porch, "Flynn Fisher is moving back to town, in fact, he may already be here." Proud of herself, she twirled around on her heel and went back inside. Iris seemed surprised, but didn't let on that she felt anyway at all about the possibility of seeing Flynn.

Suddenly, all of my confidence in our relationship disappeared. Under my breath, I said, "I guess we'll find out if you're really over him." Iris pretended not to hear, but I knew she did. It unnerved me that she didn't assure me she felt nothing for him.

CHAPTER 29
IRIS

I 943 was to hold many changes for me. I never expected that my feelings for Elijah would grow into something more than friends. Our first kiss on New Year's Eve began to change how I looked at him. He was different in every way than Flynn. I told myself it was because he was older, but really it was just the differences in the people they were. Neither was better than the other. Flynn never had a chance to prove who he was because of the feud between our families. Elijah did, and he proved to me every day that I came first. What would happen the next day at the mill would change everything.

The mill had been closed for the holidays. The first day back was always exciting. Everyone was in a good mood sharing their Christmas memories, but that day there was an undercurrent of something happening I didn't know about. People whispering and looking at me; I tried to push it back as my imagination, but I could tell that it wasn't.

Right before lunchtime, Elijah came by my workstation; leaned over, and whispered, "Meet me at lunch; I'll be busy during my break, ok?" I nodded. I figured he was helping out someone whose line was behind.

After yesterday's news about Flynn coming back to town, I was worried he was upset. Elijah was normally a confident man, but he changed when anything to do with Flynn was mentioned.

The morning went by quickly; I knew something was happening, there was a strange silence among the mill's gossip pool. It was obvious it was something to do with me. I decided to work through my break. The looms' constant hum usually help me think. Not this day, I couldn't figure out what was going on with Elijah or anyone else and it unnerved me.

Lunchtime arrived. I grabbed my lunch pail and started toward the lunchroom. I took the long way around the work floor; I had made it a practice when Flynn seeped into my brain to avoid the area where our mill window was. The memories were too strong there. Walking through the dopher area I felt a touch on my shoulder. My supervisor, an old friend of Flynn's, was a strong supporter of me and Elijah. He had seen firsthand the pain Flynn had caused me at the hands of his mother.

Charlie made it clear he wasn't going to get in the middle of things, "I love Flynn like a brother, but he's got a lot of growing up to do," was his only comment. Now that he was my boss, we made a deal not to discuss Flynn, especially at work.

The touch on the shoulder startled me out of my thoughts, "Iris." Charlie was standing in front of me with a serious look on his face. "I need you to report to the loom area." It was more an order than a request. Thinking there was an emergency backup on the line there, I turned and walked quickly taking a deep breath as I entered the one area I didn't want to be near; especially after hearing the news Flynn was coming back home. It was the place where our relationship began and ended. I moved quietly and forced my thoughts back to my job; thinking the backup must be bad; my walk turned into a run.

As I entered the loom section of the mill the hum of the machines sounded familiar; like a normal run of cotton going through. Turning the corner, the mill window in full view I gasped; then held my breath for a moment, half angry at the trickery used to get me there, "What is going on?" I said as I surveyed my surroundings. Then I saw it, lunch was spread out on the ledge of the mill window; Elijah walked out from behind one of the looms and took a seat beside the food he had carefully arranged there.

The workers left the area for lunch, total silence as the looms were stopped. Elijah motioned for me to come over; I walked a few steps in his direction trying to keep my eyes on him and not the window.

He looked worried, "Let's try this again. Will you sit with me?"

I knew I couldn't sit in the mill window, Flynn's window, "You know I can't." Immediately the last time I sat there; the last day I saw Flynn rushed like a river back into my mind. I knew this was going to take me back to a place where I didn't want to be anymore. Elijah was angry. He got up from the window and walked away. I followed him, "Elijah, wait; Please listen to me."

His words were angry; a voice I had never heard; "No you listen, he's back, Flynn is back." My mind began racing, Loretta was telling the truth. Elijah took my silence as an affirmation I wasn't sure of myself, "You're still in love with that boy; I can see it in your face."

I couldn't answer him. I stood staring at the mill window wondering why Flynn hadn't found me; how could he be here and not come to see me? There was only one reason for that; he had really moved on; he was over me. I turned away from Elijah and went back to work. At that moment it was all I could physically or emotionally do.

CHAPTER 30

FLYNN

I returned home, LaGrange, the place I felt the most like myself, the day after New Year's Day, 1943. It was about seven months before my 17th birthday. I went to register for school the day it reopened. I was on the road to an early graduation from high school in March. It was a promise I made to my mother as part of the deal to return to my grandparents' house.

Paw Burton helped me get a job at the mill after school. I suspect he was trying to keep me busy; so, I would not get into any "trouble." I had one week before school and work started. I was torn over whether I should contact Iris or not. I heard about her relationship with this guy, Elijah. Charlie told me they spent all their time together. That concerned me most, Iris didn't give her time off work to just anyone. It did look like she had moved on to a new relationship. Frankly, I was hurt and mad.

Charlie got a job at the mill shortly after I was taken to Greenville. His tone of voice changed as he spoke honestly, "Flynn, it was hard for her after what your mother did to you; She lost the spark that you loved so much about her; cried all the time. Then Elijah appeared; he picked up the pieces. I thought they were just friends, but lately, it seems to be more."

He told me they were always together at the mill; how it seemed to be something serious between them. What he was saying was causing me a lot of different emotions; Seeing I was getting upset, he stopped; placed his hand on my shoulder, "Man, just leave it alone for a while; she is dealing with a lot, but she has begun to smile again." I pushed his hand from my shoulder and turned and walked away. "Hey Flynn," his voice changed to the joking Charlie I knew, "If it makes you feel better old man Reed doesn't let him come in their house either."

I kept walking holding up my hand for him to stop talking to me. I decided that day the best thing I could do for myself and Iris was to leave her alone. I wouldn't contact her. Everyone is saying she's doing good and was in a serious relationship with this fellow.

I knew eventually I would run into them, and the thought of seeing her with him made me sick. I had to do everything I could to avoid her; it was the only way I could survive here.

The week passed quickly; I hung around the house, helping with chores my grand-parents weren't able to do anymore. I enjoyed being back on Jefferson Street with them, especially my grandmother. She always had good advice, "Time takes care of most things Johnny Flynn." Her voice softly whispered in my ear, "If Iris and you were meant to be together, you don't have to do anything; God will take care of it."

I nodded, "Granny, I believe that, but for now, I need to try to avoid her. It is the best thing for her and me." Granny smiled in her "God will work it out" way. I prayed she was right.

Only a few people knew I was back in town, but LaGrange was a place where secrets were hard to keep. I started back to school the next week. I was anxious to get it done and start my new job at the mill. I walked through town to school. I couldn't stand the thought of seeing the mill window and no one sitting in it or worse see them sitting there. I was trying to live by "out of sight, out of mind," but Iris still filled my head and my heart.

School was different; most of my friends had left to work or had been drafted into the military. Charlie was at the mill and driving a taxi on his off days. Leon had been drafted and was married. Clyde had moved to Columbus to work. Having all my buddies out of school was a relief; I had no distractions. I was there for one reason; to make good on a promise I had made Mother.

After school, Grandpa Burton worked it out so I could begin my training at the mill to work in loom repair. I suspect he thought it would be better for me if I stayed busy. I knew the repair division of the mill was separated from the weaving section where Iris and Elijah worked. The thought of seeing them together didn't sit well with me.

My training at the mill was from 4:00 to 6:00 in the afternoons and Saturdays most weeks. It was a good schedule for me; I headed home after my last class at school, changed clothes; ate; rested; and then headed to the mill.

By the time I got to work; day shift workers were already gone, including Iris and her new guy. I avoided any place I thought I might run into her; I wasn't ready to face the truth about my relationship with Iris.

I learned the skill to repair looms quickly; I had a knack for it. Soon I was working as a loom apprentice, making 98 cents an hour, one of the highest-paying jobs at the mill. My time was filled, and I was happy about it.

Iris had to know I was back, but she didn't try to see me. I thought she had replaced me with Elijah and that hurt. I was sure I would never feel the same about anyone as I did for her. Granny Burton was right when she said, "Flynn, you will never replace the feeling you have for your first love."

I quietly walked over to her and gave her a hug, "I know."

I had one Saturday a month off; I had been working hard; saving almost everything I made. The only thing I spent some of my savings on was a telephone for Granny Burton. Now she didn't have to run next door to use the neighbor's. She was so excited and humbly scolded me about using my money for it. I knew secretly she was thankful.

A day off was a welcome relief. Leon was home on leave; me and Charlie were off from the mill, and Clyde was visiting his parents. The old gang was together again. We were meeting at Country Joe's for a dawg. I was nervous going into a local hang-out, but I couldn't hide forever.

I arrived to find everyone seated at a table in the back corner. I relaxed a little thinking maybe we wouldn't be noticed. I took the seat with my back facing the door.

We were happy to see each other and spent time catching up. I was most interested in Leon and what he thought about the military. I had considered joining. It would be a good way to start over.

Leon warned me, "Man, think long and hard about it. It is tough, being away from your family; not able to contact them. The war is heating up, so the chance of going overseas to fight is real, man."

Charlie always eager to lighten the mood placed an arm around my and Leon's shoulders; "What you guys need is a dawg." They called out our order just at that moment. Clyde stepped up to get them and proudly position the eight hot dogs and four milkshakes in the center of the table. He looked at me and winked, "Flynn, we're still Reed free in here, relax man." I grabbed my dawgs and shake and smiled at him, jokingly giving him a middle finger. At the very moment a familiar voice made me want to hide under the table. I knew Clyde had pulled a good one. He had seen a Reed.

Loretta Reed made her presence known, "Well, if it's not the four bad boys reunited, as I live and breathe." Looking directly at me, "Hello handsome, where have you been hiding since your big return?"

Trying to be cool I responded, "Waiting for you to grow up doll!" All of us, including Loretta, busted out laughing. We talked briefly; Loretta had grown up. She was as pretty as ever. Still, Iris was so much more.

Loretta turned to walk back to pick up her to-go order, leaned down, and said, "I won't tell anyone I saw you."

I winked at her, "Thanks, I appreciate it." She was gone.

Clyde, who knew me so well, could see the worried look on

my face, "Man, forget her; no dame is worth it, even Iris. Let's get out of here." At that point, I wasn't worried about Iris. I was too mad and hurt. Running into Iris Reed was the last thing I needed. I was afraid of what I would say or do if I did.

We decided to call it a day and to meet later in the week. I was relieved; my nerves were on edge, and I needed to think. I knew Elijah Foster was staying two blocks over from where I lived, so I took the long way home, down by the Piggly Wiggly, up Pine Street, to come out behind our house. It turned out to be the same route Loretta Reed took to the outskirts of town where they now lived. I saw her before she saw me and tried to duck between some cars parked on the street. It was too late.

She ran across the street to my side. I kept walking; She kept talking, "Flynn, look I knew you first. Besides Iris has a serious thing going with Elijah. I want my chance with you."

I stopped and spoke slowly so she would understand "Girl, are you crazy? We can be friends, that's all… if you promise to never say the name Iris in my presence again."

She put her arms around my neck, I removed them quickly. "You are crazy as ever girl." I turned and walked away.

"Flynn," she shouted, "a crack in the door, that's all I need."

I kept walking. Trying to shake a feeling I had never felt before; what was it? Then I realized for the first time I was jealous of another guy; Elijah Foster had something I didn't, he had Iris Reed.

CHAPTER 31
ELIJAH

I never met Flynn Fisher, but it was hard for me to imagine Iris with what I thought of as a boy two years younger than her. Maybe I could've understood it if they were both in their twenties, but he was only thirteen when they met. Maybes weren't important now; hopefully, neither was Flynn. Iris was with me. We were headed in the right direction, but Flynn was back in LaGrange; working in the mill. I knew and she knew, but we had not talked about it. She had kept her promise to me and stayed away from him.

She constantly reassured me that "We were just kids…he has been gone for a long time…I'm with you now."

I still worried she would always wonder 'what if' when it came to Flynn. She had become my world. I told her how much she meant to me, but stressed. "I won't be second best to anyone."

I had tried to forget about the mill window. Her refusal to sit in or even get too close to it still haunted me. How could a simple mill window be such a roadblock in our relationship?

Since the last incident at what had become *their window*, we were eating in the lunchroom with everyone else. Other times when we had something we needed to talk about in private, we would sit at a small table placed on one side of a wall just outside the doors that led to the mill offices. It was quiet and hardly anyone passed by it.

It was one of those days, while we sat and talked, Iris asked, "Your birthday is tomorrow, the big 21st. How do you want to celebrate?"

I winked at her and took her hand, "Well, I think you already know the answer to that…" Placing my hands on the outline of her face; I stole a quick kiss.

She playfully slapped my hands away, "No really…"

I finished her sentence; answering her questions, "I want you to have lunch with me; make me cupcakes and eat one with me sitting in *your* window." I figured if she said yes, it would show she was over Flynn. Her mood changed immediately. She was silent for what seemed an eternity.

Before she could answer the whistle signaling it was time to go back to work blew. "Let's go, time for work," as I stood up and offered her my hand.

She stopped for a moment and looked at me, "I'll try…ok?"

That was all I could ask of her. It was enough for now. I had some big news myself I hadn't told Iris. I planned to tell her tomorrow during our lunch break and hoped she would agree it was good news for us and our future. Silently laughing, I said under my breath. "Maybe we will be sitting in that damn mill window together."

I knew I was making a big deal out of a stupid window, but to her, it represented everything she had with Flynn Fisher. Everyone at the mill knew she hadn't sat in it or gone near it since he left. She avoided it; to the point that she asked to be transferred out of the area.

She explained, "It's a constant reminder of Flynn and what we had. His mother took him from me; he would have never left on his own." I knew she blamed his mother; but I wondered what she was thinking now that Flynn was back and hadn't attempted to see her.

On my birthday, I woke up with anticipation of getting to

work. I could tell right away that Iris had put a lot of time and effort into making the day special. My work area was decorated with crate paper and balloons. She was standing by my machine holding a sign; "Happy Birthday, Elijah."

She made her way to me, "Happy Birthday Baby," kissing my cheek. All my coworkers cheered and sang to me. I was happy and hoped lunch would be more of the same. The morning work whistled started the workday; Iris leaned and whispered in my ear, "See you at lunch; I have all your favorites."

My day was off to a great start, more than I expected. My excitement grew as the morning passed. I wondered about lunch; "Would she be able to sit with me in the mill window?" That would make it clear to me she was over Flynn. Under the hum of the looms running, I whispered, "She loves me; she loves me not." I shook my head and laughed at my silly behavior.

The whistle signaling lunchtime startled me back to reality. I made my way to the bathroom to wash up for lunch; then began the walk to the loom area where Iris would be waiting. She knew what I wanted and what it would mean to me. How could she not?

As I turned the corner where the mill window was…a table sat in front of it with the ledge as a seat and a chair on the other side. The table was set with the lunch she had made and cupcakes that formed the outline of a small heart. I knew which seat was meant for me and which was meant for her. I should've been angry, but I knew she did the best she could. I smiled and decided not to focus on the disappointment I felt. I sat on the window ledge.

Iris leaned over and whispered "Thank You" as she sat in the chair. We ate the beef stew and homemade sandwiches Iris had made "with my own little hands" she said. She lit three candles on seven of the cupcakes; the eyes watching us appeared and began to sing happy birthday. I blew the twenty-one candles out with one long blow: and instinctively hugged Iris.

Charlie told everyone to take their cupcakes and "let them celebrate alone." I knew he was a friend of Flynn's. I hoped he would tell him about this day and how happy Iris and I were together.

Charlie turned to leave, "Y'all enjoy it; Iris deserves it."

Alone as you can be in a mill starting back on a cotton run, I was ready to tell Iris my news; "It's going to change our lives," I said. I think she thought I was going to ask her to marry me; instead, I held my breath and said, "I joined the military."

She walked to where I was sitting on the ledge of the mill window and took my hands and softly asked me, "What?"

I stood up, "I leave in four weeks for basic training."

She dropped my hands, "But why? Because of Flynn coming back?"

Surprised she thought I would make a decision because of Flynn, I replied, "No...I was going to be drafted anyway. This way I get to make my own decisions...You know the war is getting worse. It has nothing to do with Flynn; it's for you and me. I'll make better money; we can have a better life when the war ends."

Iris was silent for a long while. My head dropped as I stared down at the mill floor; I was thinking how much I had begun to hate this damn window. Iris moved; I thought to walk away, "Iris," I started to speak, but noticed a shocked Iris staring out of the window, "Iris. Let me explain."

She stood frozen. I'd never seen her that way. I followed her stare to the sidewalk outside the window and realized Flynn Fisher was standing below it staring up at us...a cold chill went down my spine.

CHAPTER 32
IRIS

I got up from my chair and walked over to Elijah and took his hands, I wanted to comfort him; To tell him I understood his decision to join the service, but I glanced out the window and saw Flynn.

It was the first time I'd seen him in years. My eyes became fixated on him. I heard Elijah calling my name, but I couldn't speak. I was overcome by emotion; tears rolled down my face.

I heard Elijah say, "Well, I guess that answers my question; Happy birthday to me." I could feel the sarcasm in his voice. Out of the side of my eyes, I saw him walk away; still, I couldn't move.

Charlie showed up just in time to witness the entire thing, "Iris, you need to get back to work." He grabbed me by my shoulders and turned me away from the window, "Now Iris, go back to work.."

I finally got the words out, "Charlie, why is Flynn at the mill?"

As Charlie walked me back to my workstation, he explained to me Flynn was working to train as a loom repairman after school. "He comes in after you leave each day so he would not interfere with you and Elijah."

"Why didn't he come to see me when he got back to town?" tears streaming down my face.

Charlie tried to make me understand, "He thought it was best for you. He didn't want to hurt you." Charlie said Flynn had done the right thing, but I was angrier and more hurt than ever at Flynn.

"You should have told me Charlie!" as I made my way to my area to take over my job.

He responded, "It wasn't my place Iris; Don't put me in the middle of this."

Tying my hair back in a bandana; using my handkerchief to wipe my face, I hugged him, "I'm trying not to; thanks for everything." I turned and started to work.

My mind was all over the place. I realized Elijah was gone. Where was he? I didn't want to hurt him; I cared for him. I tried to concentrate on my job; all I needed was to get fired.

The rest of the afternoon passed slowly; I skipped my break; too afraid I would run into Flynn or Elijah. I didn't know what I would say to either of them. I was worried about Elijah and confused about Flynn. My brain was racing from thoughts of Elijah to Flynn… unsure where my heart was.

The whistle to end the workday blew. I grabbed my things. Charlie said he would clean up the mess from the party for me. I ran to find Elijah. I hated knowing he was hurt and was worried about all of this happening on his birthday. He was nowhere at the mill.

I hurried down the street looking for him all the way to his house.

Before I had time to knock on the door, it opened. "He's here Iris." Vivian answered my question before I had time to ask it. "No, he doesn't want to talk today; He told me what happened. Give him time, Iris. It's his birthday, leave it be… figure out what you want; all of this isn't fair to any of you."

I nodded, "Please, tell him I'm sorry, and I want to explain when he's willing to listen." I left and started home. I thought of going back to the mill to find Flynn. "Who does he think he is?" surprised at my anger at him.

My anger at Flynn made me feel worse about hurting Elijah; he didn't deserve it. He was kind, gentle, and I knew he loved me. I just didn't know if I loved him the same way. I cared about him; missed him when he wasn't around; but my feelings for him were nothing like the feelings I had for Flynn. Even now, when I thought of Flynn; angry as I was, my heart melted; memories of our times together were the sweetest. The walk home went by fast, and before I knew it, I was inside the kitchen with Mama.

She looked tired and worried. Things were in turmoil around our house. Tessa had been sick for weeks now; and had gone to the doctor today. "How's Tessa? What did the doctor say?" I asked with genuine concern. Mama shook her head; that was her signal she didn't want to talk about it.

I put my hands around her waist and gave her a big hug; she patted my hands. "Go on now Iris, take a bath and relax, I need to think. We'll talk later, ok?" I left the kitchen; worried Tessa must really be sick. I quietly entered our bedroom where I found her sleeping. I gathered a change of clothes and made my way to the bathroom. The warm water was calming as I lay in the tub trying to figure out what was going on in our house. I tried to think about Flynn and Elijah, but I was too worried about Tessa.

The noise from the kitchen told me supper was ready, and the smell of Mama's cooking made me hungry. I dressed quickly in my nightgown and joined the others at the table.

Robert always ready to cause a little trouble asked, "You and Elijah have a fight?"

Daddy was already on edge and Robert's comment set him off, "I don't want to hear anything about any boys coming around you girls; you hear me?" looking at me, Ester, and Loretta.

"Yes sir," we all answered in unison. Tessa was still in our room; I wasn't sure she was awake, but I knew something was wrong with her when Mama took a tray to the bedroom. I was worried about Tessa, and no one was willing to tell me what was wrong.

Supper was over quickly, no talking. It seemed like a big cloud was hanging over our house, but I couldn't figure out why. I finally told myself it was just my imagination colored by what had happened that day at the mill. Boy, was I wrong. Things around the Reed household were about to change in a big way.

It was Loretta and Ester's turn to do the dishes. I made my way to our bedroom to talk to Tessa. She was sleeping or pretending to; either way, I could tell she didn't want to be bothered. I turned my radio on softly and lay on my bed wondering where I should go first tomorrow; to talk to Elijah or to find Flynn. I decided I owed Elijah an apology and decided not to find Flynn at all; better left alone. Loretta came into the bedroom in her usual loud way, I motioned for her to be quiet, pointing to Tessa.

Loretta asked me, "What's wrong with her?" I shook my head I didn't know. She sat on my bed and turned attention on me, "You must have found out Flynn is back; that's the only thing that would put you in bed on a Friday night."

I answered her in a sarcastic voice, "How long have you known?"

She was silent; like she was considering whether she should tell me or not. I sat straight up in bed, "Tell me Loretta!"

She told me how she had ran into him at Country Joe's, "He was downtown with the guys. He made me promise not to tell you or anyone he was back."

It hurt me that he didn't want me to know, and it hurt me more that Loretta didn't tell me.

My hurt feelings turned to anger, "I don't care if he is back or not." I laid back down on my bed and turned over so she could not see the hurt in my face.

"Really Iris?" she asked, "You're over him?"

"Yes, really," I replied.

"Do you mind if I go out with him?" She stuttered, "I mean it's over two years since y'all were together."

She paused allowing me to answer. I turned back to face her; "Did he ask you out for a date?"

106

"No, No," she insisted, "but I wouldn't mind if he did, he is so darn handsome…. he's grown up; you can see it in his face."

I stopped her, "Loretta, do what you want to." Secretly, I was relieved he hadn't asked her out. As I turned back over to try to sleep, I told them all, "I'm with Elijah now." I wasn't sure they believed me, but I wasn't sure I believed myself.

That conversation made me decide to go see Elijah the next morning. His feelings was more important than looking for Flynn. He hadn't come to see me. I drifted off to sleep too worried about Tessa to worry about Flynn or Elijah.

Saturday morning, I felt better; a good night's sleep had helped me clear my mind. I dressed quietly in my light pink dress; one of Elijah's favorites. Tessa was up and hopefully feeling better. Loretta and Ester were both still sleeping. I made my way to the kitchen where Mama, Daddy, and Tessa were sitting.

I poured a cup of coffee and asked "Tessa you feel better?" I could tell Mama had been crying. Daddy looked half mad and half worried. "Somebody want to tell me what's going on here?" I asked.

Daddy said we would talk about it later; Mama assured me Tessa was fine; "Iris now you go on to town and pay your bills," she insisted. I pushed my chair back; walked over to the sink and placed my cup under the running water. Placing the cleaned cup in the dish drainer, I turned to grab my purse and walked over to the table.

I leaned over and kissed her on the cheek, "Mama, I'll bring you some candy from Kessler's." She patted my hand. "Tessa, you want something from town?" I asked. She shook her head. Daddy reminded me not to spend all my money; I nodded and walked out the front door a little irritated; I was unsure why.

I immediately began thinking about what I would say to Elijah. I was practicing speeches when Charlie drove by in the taxi he drives on the weekend and offered me a ride. I declined; thinking the walk to town would give me time to figure out the right thing to say when I got to Elijah's house.

The door was open. I could see them sitting at the table eating breakfast. I made my way up the front steps and knocked; my heart beating fast; my stomach turning. Vivian came and unlatched the screen door, "Hey Iris, come on in and have breakfast with us."

"Thanks, I'll just have coffee," I answered. Elijah nodded but didn't speak; his silence said everything. "Hey," I whispered as I sat in the empty chair beside him. He nodded, but no words. This was an Elijah I didn't recognize; he was still hurt. Vivian tried to fill the awkwardness with details of the supper she had cooked for his birthday as she cleaned the table.

Allen grabbed her coffee, "Viv let's finish this on the front porch." Vivian followed him out the front door looking relieved to be out of the room.

I took Elijah's plate to the sink and washed it along with the dishes left in the soapy water. Silence filled the room; I sat back down at the table. I knew I owed him an apology, "Elijah, I'm sorry your birthday was ruined."

He interrupted me before I could finish, "Iris I don't give a damn about my birthday." Clearly irritated he continued, "A year, Iris, a year, we've been together for a year; and never have you looked at me the way you looked at Flynn standing below that window yesterday." He got up and started to the back porch. "I just don't get it," he said looking back at me from the opened door. He was hurt. His eyes were filled with confusion. He walked outside and sat on the back porch steps. I followed him.

Choosing my words carefully in an attempt not to hurt him more, "I'm not sure how to explain it in a way that you'll understand; but Flynn and I were together almost every day for two years. Then he was ripped from my life without warning; not of his choosing. We had planned a future together; a life."

I stopped talking. Elijah was leaning forward with his hands folded; arms on his legs; I couldn't see his face. He turned his head toward me; I looked away. I continued what I was saying. It was hard; but it needed to be said, "I can't tell you I'll never speak to him. We'll probably run into each other eventually, but I can promise I'm not going to look for him." I leaned forward so he could see my face, "Right now, our relationship is more important to me than seeing Flynn. Ok?"

"Ok," he replied, as he traced the outline of my face with his hand. The coldness of February was in the air. We were both shivering, "Let's get back inside; it's freezing," he spoke for the first time that morning using the caring voice I'd become used to. We sat at the table, "Listen, Iris, I'm leaving for boot camp soon. I want to make sure where we stand before I leave." I started to speak. He silenced me with a finger over my lips and continued, "I need you to sort this out. My plans involve you; built around us. Figure out your feelings for Flynn; when you do let me know."

I reassured him again I wasn't going to chase Flynn around town; I explained to him what Loretta told me the night before; "Flynn hasn't even tried to speak to me. I'm with you. I'm not looking for him."

He explained, "I have about three weeks before I leave. I want to spend as much time as we can together." I agreed. He leaned over the table and gave me a light kiss on the lips, "I got to go, Allen is waiting for me."

I heard Allen's truck crank up in the backyard, "We're going to get some firewood. We'll drop you off at the bank." I smiled and nodded; thinking how well he knew me.

Vivian came back into the kitchen, "Well, I'm glad y'all made up!" I hugged her, and we were out the door. The ride to town was quiet; The truck stopped in front of the bank and I hopped out.

Elijah asked, "I'll pick you up tonight around seven? I'll be busy most of today."

I thought how glad I was I met him. I walked through the double doors of the bank not knowing I was about to run into the one person I didn't want to see.

CHAPTER 33

FLYNN

I'd been home about six weeks, and purposely not seen Iris. After running into Loretta, I was sure she knew I was back in LaGrange, but not tried to contact me. School and training at the mill, kept me busy, but at night my thoughts were of Iris.

I could date if I wanted, girls were available and always Loretta. She had continued to "run into me." Loretta was trouble and it just wasn't worth it. I did have hopes of getting back with Iris …dating anyone else would end that permanently.

After working at the mill on Friday, I arrived home to find a surprise visitor, Mother. She decided to check up on me, "To make sure I was keeping my end of the agreement." Granny Burton was happy to see her, but she wasn't happy to find out the reason for her visit.

Mother spent the day checking at school and the mill. The reports were good. I was happy she was only going to be there one day and night and leaving to go back on the bus early Saturday.

Saturday morning, I found out why she was really there. She was going by the bank to make sure I was saving my money. Her checking up on me angered me, but my bank account was out of the question, "Go ahead to the bank; I'll be happy to drop you off. You aren't on my account so; they won't let you see my balances or withdraw any money." I knew my mother well. I knew she would do more than check balances given the opportunity, and I had plans for that money.

Her bus back to Greenville left at 2:00; the bank closed at noon and she was determined to go there. It was fine with me; they were across the street from each other. I walked with her to the bus station to make sure she was set for her trip back to Greenville. She would have time to go across the street to the bank, and I would be able to go about my day. It was the only time I had to do errands and meet up with my buddies to hang out.

I told Charlie I didn't want to meet at Country Joe's, Loretta always showed up there, "I don't want to run into any of the Reeds; especially her."

Charlie chuckled, "She's a wild young thing; but I think she's harmless."

"Not for me; I don't need any grief from the Reeds," I answered back. I wasn't sure if Iris knew I was back in town or not. Charlie hadn't mentioned what had happened Friday at the mill.

We decided to meet at the Tasty Coffee Shop south of the town square. We had a quick lunch; catching up on each other's life. For old times' sake, the four of us decided to pitch some pennies on the sidewalk in front of the fountain across the street. I felt pretty safe in that area of town. It was where the older people gathered. I was sure I wouldn't run into Iris, plus I could see the bus station.

It was turning out to be a good day and a needed day of relaxation for all of us. Even better I was set to win a little extra change. Up at the line that divided the sidewalk; it was my time to pitch; I leaned over, eye on the target.

Things happen when you least expect them to, and I didn't plan to see a pair of legs walking toward me. Especially legs I still recognized after so much time had passed since I had seen them.

My face mirrored the shock I felt as I stood face-to-face with

Iris Reed. We both stood frozen, with no words; neither of us knowing what to do or say. The guys watching this were as stunned; no one said a word.

Iris finally said, "Well, some people never change; still a little boy playing games."

At that moment, I heard my mother's voice. It pierced my very being, "Johnny Flynn, my bus is leaving." She looked over and saw Iris, hands placed on her hips she declared, "Well, the nerve; you're still following Flynn all over town! I know what you are up to..."

I stopped her, "Mother, be quiet." Iris turned back towards town and hurried away from us.

The guys were shaking their heads, Mother turned and walked back to the bus station without speaking a word to anyone. I watched her step up onto the bus feeling glad she was on her way back to Greenville.

Behind me, Leon was talking to Charlie, "You need to tell him."

Surprised by the idea my buddies were keeping something from me made me angry. "What? What? Somebody tell me what the hell is going on," pushing Charlie's shoulder.

He replied, "Sit down; calm down." I sat down on the bench; Clyde sat beside me. Leon decided to bow out of "this mess" and headed home to spend time with his family before he had to leave to go back to the base. Charlie began to tell me what had happened at the mill on Friday. My head was reeling; I didn't know what to do with the things he was saying to me.

What kept ringing in my mind was that Iris knew I was back, and she hadn't tried to contact me. Nothing else was important. He kept talking about the window. I replied,

"So what, she wouldn't sit in the damn window; she hasn't tried to talk to me, and I'm here." Her actions said everything; Iris had moved on...

CHAPTER 34

IRIS

My conversation that morning with Elijah had gone well, and I was in a hopeful mood as I opened the door of the bank. As usual, it was busy; I stepped into the line to wait for my turn at the teller window; making a mental list of what I needed to do after cashing my check.

I heard a voice I hoped I would never hear again; chills traveled down my back as I turned my head to see Naomi Fisher. I stood in front of the man behind me so she couldn't see me. I reached the teller's window; finished what I had to do; and ducked through the double doors to the bank's bathroom to wait until she left. I didn't want her to make a scene in the bank; everyone there knew me and her. I didn't need any more whispers about my family. I waited; peeked out of the bathroom just in time to see her walk out of the front door. I left the bank determined not to let her change my day. I had a couple of hours to finish my errands before I needed to start home.

I smiled thinking of Elijah and our conversation that morning; I missed him. I slipped into the Tasty Café Coffee Shop, ordered a hot chocolate to go, and was on my way to The Five and Dime.

Outside the café sipping my hot chocolate, I felt renewed and calmed from the incident in the bank. I decided to walk down the south side of the fountain. It was lined with beautiful old craftsman houses; Flynn used to talk about us buying one after we got married. I shook my head scolding myself. I turned my thoughts to my date with Elijah that night, wondering what it was he wanted to tell me.

Suddenly, I felt something hit my shoe. Picking up the penny lying in front of me, I reached out to hand it to its owner and stood face-to-face with Flynn Fisher. We both stood there speechless. All the hurt he had caused me filled my heart; the lump in my throat stopped words from coming.

An eternity seemed to pass until the voice I escaped that morning was standing in front of me, "Iris Reed, have you no shame; following Flynn all over town…" Flynn spoke up; telling his mother to be quiet.

I interrupted him, "Some things never change. You're still a mama's boy." I turned and brushed by Naomi hurrying down the street to get as far as I could away from the Fishers.

I slowed down to a fast walk as I entered the busy section of town. I couldn't help but think of what had happened. Face with the sight of Flynn, a strange sensation flashed before me. I was seeing our relationship appear before my eyes like a movie.

"Iris, Iris, you ok?" I felt Elijah's arm around me, pulling his coat over me as much as he could. "You're freezing, get in the truck and warm up," as he walked me over and helped me inside.

CHAPTER 35
ELIJAH

Allen and I had worked all morning splitting firewood and loading it into the back of his pick-up. On our way back to the house, I was in deep thought going over the morning's conversation with Iris. Allen's voice interrupted, "Hey, you want a hotdog?" as he pulled up in front of Country Joe's.

I jumped out of the truck only to be met by a hurried Iris; "Hey girl, what's the hurry?" She looked visibly shaken; shivering from the cold.

"Just trying to get home," she hugged me so tight; like she had never done before in public. I hugged her back trying to warm her up. I didn't know the cold wasn't what was making her shiver.

Allen rolled down the truck window, "Iris get in, we'll take you home." I walked her over to the truck; opened the door and she climbed inside.

Still confused and worried, I walked over to Country Joe's window and order three hotdogs, two coffees, and a hot chocolate, Iris' favorite. Back in the truck, we ate, while Iris sipped on her drink. I leaned over and whispered; "You ok?"

She nodded, "Just cold. I'm glad I ran into y'all." She unwrapped her hotdog and took a bite.

The ride to her house was quiet; Allen was tired; I was confused, and Iris looked worried. Arriving at the Reed's house, I helped her down out of the truck, "You sure you're ok?"

She nodded, "Just a little tired."

"Too tired for tonight?" I asked, worried about her answer.

She shook her head to indicate no. I reminded her, "I'll pick you up around 7:00. We need to talk."

"I know," she responded as she ran up the steps and disappeared inside.

Looking in the truck window, I saw Allen had dozed off. I walked around to the driver's side, "Slide over brother-in-law." He slept all the way home. I was glad for the silence; I wasn't sure what to think or say about the events of the day but decided not to worry about every little thing Iris said or did.

Allen woke up as we pulled into the driveway. Deciding to unload the truck later, I pulled it to the backside of the yard. He made it inside the house to his chair and fell back to sleep instantly. I hit the bathroom to get cleaned up, so I could rest before getting dressed for the night out with Iris. Laying on my bed, I tried to sleep; but my brain was all over the place, from one thing to another.

CHAPTER 36
IRIS

Allen turned the heat in the truck up as I held my frozen hands up to the vents; I wasn't sure if I was cold or in shock. Elijah slid into the truck beside me with chili dogs and drinks. The smell of food made me realize I hadn't eaten all day.

I leaned over and whispered in his ear, "Thank you."

I could tell Elijah was worried about me; he kept rubbing my hands, "Maybe you should rest tonight?"

"No, I'm ok, I want to see you," I smiled at him. We pulled up to my house, and he helped me down from the truck. He walked me to the bottom porch step; he knew that was where he stopped, or my Daddy or Mama would be out the door.

Elijah made me feel safe. I was beginning to see the difference between the two men. I loved them both, but the love was different. I turned as I opened the front door and waved goodbye to the truck headed out of my driveway.

The house was empty. Everyone was at Nanny Wilson's Saturday supper. I smiled; glad I didn't have to go. I turned on my radio and ran a warm bath. While I was soaking I tried not to think about anything, not Tessa and especially not Flynn Fisher.

Seeing him was still a shock; he had changed. He looked older; more mature; more handsome. Any girl would want to be with him, and I'm sure he had dated a lot of them while he was in Greenville. I laid back into the tepid water and tried not to think about anything.

My thoughts went to Tessa and what she was facing; I'm not sure how or who, but she was going to have a baby. It had upset the whole family; Daddy the most and his strict rules had tightened even more. I was unsure what was going to happen with Tessa, but I was happy I wasn't in her shoes. I stood up from the tub, dried myself off. Looking at my unclothe body for a moment in the mirror, I realized it could have been me just as easily.

I dressed with extra care wanting to look pretty for Elijah, my blue dress, heels, and my hair down. I saw the headlights from his truck coming down the dirt driveway, grabbing my new white sweater; I went out the front door just as he started up the walkway. He looked handsome; his slender build looked good in dress clothes. He hugged me extra tight as he helped me into the truck. I could tell he had something on his mind; he had already told me earlier we had to talk about some things. I knew he was worried about the military, boot camp, and our relationship. All subjects I wanted to avoid because I didn't know the answers to the questions I was sure he was going to ask. On the ride to our favorite place to eat, The Fish Camp Restaurant, we were both quiet. He asked for a table in the corner; I was surprised, he usually liked being out in the open.

CHAPTER 37

ELIJAH

I was leaving for boot camp in four weeks; I wasn't sure what military life would be. The war in Germany had ramped up, and I was worried about where I would be sent. More important, Iris was on my mind. I was in love with her. I had never said it out loud, but I think she knew how I felt.

Knowing I was going to leave soon, made me realize it was time for me to put all my cards on the table. I didn't know how she felt about us. The last few days made me question if I had wasted my time on a girl who didn't care about me the same way I cared about her.

The ticking from the clock beside my bed told me it was time to get dressed to pick up Iris. I dressed in my best clothes; brown slacks and a new blue shirt. Looking into the mirror, I questioned everything about my appearance. I wasn't that tall and too skinny. I shrugged my shoulders at the face staring back at me from the mirror, "You are what you are." I told myself Iris could take me or leave me, but I didn't feel that way.

In the kitchen, I grabbed the truck keys from the hook hanging by the backdoor and thanked Allen for unloading the wood. I hugged Vivian, "I'll see you later Sis."

She hugged me back, "Yes you will brother."

I was nervous as I drove the short ride to the little community known as Mountville where the Reeds had moved. I was mindful walking up the sidewalk toward the house. Thankfully, I never got too close, Iris always came out before I reached it. Tonight was no different. As I stepped onto the sidewalk the door opened, and she was there. Each time I saw her was like the first; I was in awe of her, but tonight she looked especially beautiful. I wondered if it was for me and silently prayed it was. "Hey Baby," I spoke softly. We walked hand in hand to the truck. I asked her if she was feeling better.

"I am," she answered pushing her hair behind her ears.

"Ok, how about some catfish?" I smiled at her. I knew it was her favorite.

She replied with her standard, "Anything is ok with me."

At the local Fish Camp Restaurant, I picked a table in a corner hoping to have our conversation without interruption. We ordered our food; our sweet tea arrived, and I began the speech I had practiced in my head all day. "Iris," I began to speak slowly, "Will you wait for me while I'm away?" I startled myself with the boldness of my question, but I knew it was now or never; "You know how I feel. I want to marry you…be with you for the rest of my life." Iris looked surprised, no words, just confusion filled her eyes.

I kept talking unable to stop my feelings as they tumbled out, "I know you could do better, but no one," I took her hand, "No one could love you more, be better for you…" I stopped myself from speaking and waited for a response of any kind, but the only one I got was Iris staring into open air.

Slowly, she began to speak to me, "Elijah you know…" Before she could finish her sentence, the waitress was sitting two plates of hot fried catfish in front of us.

"Y'all need anything else?" She asked as she set a bottle of ketchup and tartar sauce on the table. The silence told her we didn't.

I looked at Iris hoping she would finish what she had begun to say. "Elijah, you're a special man; special to me; I know you're better for me..."

Sensing it wasn't going to be a short conversation, I stopped her from saying anything else. "Let's just eat, and enjoy our dinner; then we can talk, Ok?"

She nodded and slowly began to eat the food in front of her. I smiled as I watched her consume the fried fish. I wondered how someone so little could eat so much. Making small talk as we ate; I asked her what upset her that afternoon in town.

She thought for a minute, "Not upset; mad... I'll tell you about it one day, but tonight is about us." She took my hand in hers, "Elijah, I'll miss you when you leave; you're my best friend, and I have feelings for you, but..."

I stopped her by placing my finger softly on her lips, "Not here, you ready to go?" I was afraid of what the but was. I paid the waitress, and we were back in the truck with one hour left before Iris had to be home.

I thought a 9:30 curfew was strange for an 18-year-old girl. I wondered if I was the cause or had Mr. Reed heard Flynn was back in LaGrange.

At Iris' request not to be alone with me, we sat on a bench at the fountain. I took it as a good sign for her to be worried about being alone with me; at that point, we had only kissed a couple of times...nothing else.

The night air was cold. I wasn't sure if I was shaking from it or from fear of what Iris was going to say, "You were giving me a but..." I questioned her on the meaning.

"But, she started...I need some time; I think I love you. I want to be your girlfriend, but I need to make sure I'm over Flynn. I saw him today, by accident, and the only thing I felt was anger. We hardly spoke to each other."

We sat silent...each of us not knowing what to say..."When do you leave?" she asked.

Confused by what she had said to me, I responded, "About three weeks; I'll be gone for a while; 13 weeks or longer...."

She stopped me, "I want to spend my free time with you before you go; make memories for you to take to boot camp ..."

I stopped her there, "It's cold and getting late.... we better get you home." I didn't know how to feel about what she was saying. As I opened the door for her to get inside the truck I asked, "Are you going to see him too?" Her immediate response of "No" eased my mind as I rounded the truck and climbed inside.

She explained, "Maybe when you come home for leave after the 13 weeks then we both will know; we'll be sure if we belong together or..."

We drove in silence. Arriving home on time, "Ok", she asked?

I leaned over and kissed her, "Ok...I can never deny you anything, and you'll know for sure in thirteen weeks?"

She reached up, kissed me, and held my hand tighter as we walked up to the sidewalk, "Thank you Elijah."

I leaned in kissed her lightly and turned to walk back to my truck. I stood by the truck and called her name as she opened the front door, "Iris." She looked back at me. "I know. I already know." She smiled and disappeared inside the house.

CHAPTER 38
IRIS

He started to talk about boot camp; the war getting worse; he said he loved me. I stopped him there with a silent stare. I tried to find the words to explain to him how I felt. The waitress gave me a welcome chance to breathe as she placed the plate of hot catfish in front of us. I was thankful to have the time to think about how to answer the question I knew he was going to ask me. We ate in silence.

He leaned over the table, "You finished eating?" I nodded. "Let's get out of here," he said pulling my chair out from the table. He took my hand and led me out the door to the truck. He picked me up and sat me in the seat, I finally had the nerve to tell him how I really felt. Silence filled the truck as he looked into my eyes.

I nervously said, "Elijah, I think I love you; but I have to be sure I'm over Flynn." He said nothing; walked around to the driver's side; started it, drove to the town fountain. We parked in front of the place where we always had our most serious talks. I reminded him of my curfew. He was quiet. We sat silently looking at the pink flow of water spurting up from the fountain.

He explained he had three weeks before he left to report to

boot camp in Atlanta. He asked "Can you promise me you won't date Flynn until after I leave?"

I promised him I wouldn't. I wasn't planning to see Flynn at all. "I'll be here, missing you," I said as I kissed his cheek. He began to explain he would be gone for at least thirteen weeks; maybe I could figure out what I felt for each of them during that time.

I was too worried about being late getting home to think about him or Flynn. He questioned me about my Daddy being so strict, and more worried about his girls than ever before. I swore him to secrecy. I believed him when he told me he would never betray my trust. As we drove to my house, I told him about what I thought was going on with Tessa. "I'm not sure, but all the signs are there." I explained I didn't know who or how and I hoped I was wrong.

Always thoughtful with his words, he didn't speak for a while, and then in a reflective voice, "I hope she has found someone to love, and it will be ok for her" was his only reply, no insults, or ugly remarks.

We pulled in front of my house at 9:22; I was on time. I hopped out of the truck; he was right behind me. I took his hand, and for the first time, he walked me up to the sidewalk. He moved to kiss me. I pulled back, but his kiss reached my lips with a light touch. Worried Daddy was looking, I said, "Goodnight." He smiled as he turned and walked back to the truck.

My hand was on the doorknob when I heard him call, "Iris", he whispered, "Thirteen weeks, then we will know?"

I nodded, "Yes, we'll know." I watched him walk slowly down the sidewalk. Once again, I turned to go inside, I heard him call my name for the second time, I turned to look at him as he softly spoke, "I know. I already know." I smiled at him and closed the door.

CHAPTER 39
FLYNN

People automatically thought I didn't write, call, or try to see Iris while I was gone because I hadn't been serious about her. I was accused of never caring about Iris. My actions since I was ripped away from her were guided by my love for her.

The letter I sent to her wasn't easy to write. When she didn't answer it, I felt like she had moved on with her life without me.

The few times I was allowed to come to LaGrange were well planned by my mother to account for every minute of my visit. I never intended to allow her to run my life forever, at first, I had no choice. That changed as I got older; I decided to take my life back. Mother was a strong determined woman, so I had to be careful.

I started working in Greenville, saving my money, making my own decisions, and standing up to my mother. Joan had a big part in helping me change. I owed her more than people know, but she wanted something from me I couldn't give her. Although I did try. The simple truth was my heart wasn't mine to give. It belonged to a sassy girl in LaGrange who I thought had forgotten me.

My independence day began the first month of 1943; I

announced I was moving back to LaGrange. After all the arguments my mother threw at me, I made her one promise; I would finish school. With that, I began my return to Jefferson Street to see if there was anything or anyone left for me there.

I was back in LaGrange two weeks before anyone besides my grandparents knew I was there. My promise to my mother stood strong; I would soon finish high school and had begun to train for my job at the mill.

By the third week back, my days were full. I thought it best not to see or tell anyone I was there except Charlie. We kept in touch with each other, but we had agreed not to talk about Iris. He knew the whole story about us, and had his own opinions about me reuniting with her. I asked him not to tell anyone I was back. I wanted to let people know in my own time, but after running into Loretta at Country Joe's, I figured she told Iris. I was wrong. Iris didn't know until I went to work early that Friday.

Thinking everyone was back to work after lunch and no one would see me, I decided to go in early. I was feeling down that day; I decided to go to the other side of the mill to see our window. The place where our love story began and ended; it was our place. I had avoided that side of the mill afraid of all the hurt from the past coming back.

I didn't know about the whole birthday thing until the following Saturday. Charlie told me after Iris walked up outside Tasty's when we were pitching pennies. He also told me Elijah had joined the military.

I knew then he would be going to boot camp for a while. I told Charlie, "I'm giving him his chance out of respect. I won't contact Iris until he leaves. Then it's my turn to find out if Iris has any love left for me."

Charlie patted me on the back, "Man, love is love, you can't deny it; I do respect you for stepping back the next few weeks."

As bad as it was when we saw each other that day I knew my feelings were still there. Every moment we had spent together rolled in front of my eyes like a movie; I was so shocked I couldn't speak and stuttered as I tried to explain to the guys why I looked so stunned;

I headed home that day with a new resolve, glad to have seen Mother, glad she was gone; happy I got to see Iris regardless of the situation; and heartbroken she had found someone else.

CHAPTER 40

ELIJAH

I felt better about my relationship with Iris after our date that Saturday, but still worried about why she was so upset earlier that day. I was sure it was something to do with Flynn. She was visibly shaken by something or someone, but I had learned over the past year not to push Iris to tell me anything. She would tell me what she wanted me to know if or when she decided to. Whatever happened seemed to have made her move closer to me for that I was grateful.

Iris and I were both faithful churchgoers and during our talk on Saturday night, we decided to go to church together. I felt it was important to attend the church that her Paw Wilson had helped to establish in the neighborhood where they lived. She was a member there; maybe it would give me a chance to get to know her family.

My first Sunday went well; the singing and the preaching. Afterward, we went to my house to have dinner with Vivian and Allen. Iris volunteered us to do the dishes afterward and I didn't mind doing anything with her. Dishes done; we sat with a fresh cup of coffee and a slice of pie at the kitchen table. "Iris, I was thinking about going to talk to your Daddy. What do you think?"

She shifted in her chair, tracing the rim of her coffee cup with her finger while she thought about what I had said, "I think it's a good idea; I don't know what he'll say; even if he will talk to you, with all the stuff going on with Tessa, but he should give us a chance."

I was surprised she was ok with it, and took it as a sign she was thinking of the future with me. "Let's go right now" as I grabbed her hand, the keys, and headed out the back door.

The ride over was quiet; she questioned what we were doing, "You sure you want to try this? My daddy can be a hard man to deal with when it comes to" ...she thought for a minute, "Well with everything!" We both laughed as we pulled into the driveway.

I tried to reassure her, "I can handle it."

Their house was an old farmhouse with a huge front porch that I had never stepped foot on. I was nervous as we walked up the steps; Iris went in to talk to her daddy while I sat on the porch swing. I couldn't hear what was being said behind the closed front door, just a lot of whispering. I was unsure if Harley Reed would come out of the house; much less talk to me; unless he came out to tell me to get off his front porch. The minute I had the thought, the front door opened; then the screen door and he appeared.

He was a massive man, tall and sturdy, not heavy, just sturdy. Dressed in overalls, wearing a grey flannel hat that sat perfectly on his head, "Iris said you wanted to talk to me?" The screen door slammed behind him, and someone inside the house closed the door.

I have to admit I was a little scared and nervous but determined to make my point with him...politely, "Yes sir, should we sit?" I asked.

He walked over to the edge of the porch, hand placed inside the bib of his overalls, and spit out his tobacco, "Son, I have five daughters, lost one to the influenza seven years ago, bout killed me and Maw; he hesitated for a minute, "Got one sitting in the house there, fixing to have a baby, and we don't know who the father is, so if you have something to say about Iris, I hope for your sake it's good… otherwise this talk is over, and you need to get in that truck and head down that driveway."

I was surprised by his words; he was standing shaking his head at me. I wanted to let him know he didn't need to worry about me, "Sir, Iris is important to me. Her happiness is my main concern. She had a rough year or so…"

He interrupted me, "I warned her; the Fishers are trouble; she had to see for herself."

I continued, "Yes sir, don't know them, but I'll be leaving for boot camp, in three weeks. I want to be able to come here to spend time with Iris, get to know you and her family; want y'all to get to know me."

He sat silent for what seemed like forever, "Ok, we can give it a try; Anita says my mistake with Tessa was not letting…" He stopped there for a moment, "I have your word, no funny stuff, you have good intentions toward Iris?"

I stood up; "Yes sir, you have my word."

He walked over to the door and stepped inside, "Come on in son." I walked through the front door of the Reeds for the first time; Iris stood up from the sofa with a look of surprise. She walked over and took my hand as she introduced me to her family.

Our three weeks together were busy; I put in for leave at the mill with the hopes that my job would be waiting for me when I returned home. As I walked through the mill I thought about how much I was going to miss the place; it allowed me to make a paycheck and friends. I looked over at Iris. Our relationship had happened there; lunch, and walking home together. Slowly over time, we grew to love each other.

I spent my days getting things in order before I was to leave while Iris worked; evenings and weekends we spent every moment we could together.

She helped me pack the duffel bag they had given me. Getting everything ready to leave would have gotten me down, but Iris helped me feel better about it. We spent our time walking and talking, visiting with her family and my family.

Mr. Reed had been true to his word, letting me come to the door to pick up Iris for dates; a few times I was invited to supper. I liked the Reeds, but they were different from most families I had been around. I could sense the love between them, but it was through a seriousness that penetrated the house. I didn't see much laughter, joking, or hugging, yet you could tell they would do anything for each other. Being around them help me to understand Iris; I could tell she had softened; laughed more and showed affection. Still, she was a mysterious woman.

I was worried about what would happen while I was gone; would she see Flynn, and if she did would she feel the same for him? She would not answer the question directly; but with, "Aren't we planning to be together forever?" I had to be ok with that answer.

I was to report to the bus station on March 17th; there would be a bus waiting to take me and thirty other young men to a military base located in Atlanta to begin the induction process.

Vivian invited the family up to a going-away dinner. It was good to see them all, but I was secretly happy they needed to leave early to get home for work the next day. I said my goodbyes to my mama and promised to write to her as often as I could. Iris and I stood in the driveway and waved until they were out of sight.

I turned to Vivian, "Let's get the kitchen cleaned up."

Vivian shook her head, "No, you two need some alone time before you leave...go on now." She knew I was feeling nervous and insecure about leaving Iris.

I took Iris' hand "Let's walk awhile?"

She agreed with some hesitation, "It's cold."

I whispered in her ear, "I'll keep you warm." We walked down Troup Street. Approaching the house where her family had lived, I said, "This is where I first saw you."

"It's where I was born," she declared as she opened the gate to walk up the sidewalk, "Elijah, come on" motioning me to come with her. She knocked on the door and peered through the window. "It's empty," she whispered. As she spoke I noticed the moonlight reflecting a soft glow on her face. I was mesmerized by her. Not knowing why, I was staring so intently at her, she asked, "What's wrong?"

I took her hand and softly whispered, "You're beautiful; then and now." She sat on the step; I sat beside her as close as I could to keep us warm, "Look, I have to talk to you." I was pouring my heart out to her, "I need you to understand; I want to make sure when I leave here, we're on the same page about this thing. We are solid; anything else isn't fair to me or you."

Though she didn't speak, I knew she was listening; her head was bowed. She was thinking about what she was going to say. She spoke slowly, "I guess it depends on what you mean by solid; I told you I care for you. I'm worried about you going away, worried about the war. I'm not sure how I will get through one day without you here; seeing you; talking to you." She began to cry softly.

I felt sorry I brought the whole thing up; I put my arms around her, "Iris, I love you; everything I do, I do with you in mind."

She hugged me hard, "I love you too."

We both started to laugh, "Damn, I said, You are one..." I stopped there realizing it wasn't time for a joke. We sat for a while; silence surrounded us.

Realizing it was getting late we made our way back up to Troup Street; inside the truck on our way to her house, she surprised me with what she was saying, "I think this will be a test; What about you? You know there will be times when girls are around?"

I stopped the truck, took her hand, "Look, I tried to be with other girls to forget you even before I moved here, and I knew you were with Flynn. It didn't work."

She looked surprised as we drove. We agreed the time apart would tell if what we felt was real; "Look, thirteen weeks, right? We'll know for sure then how the other feels."

We were both silent the rest of the short trip to her house; I opened her door and walked her up the sidewalk to the front porch. I put my arm around her and pulled her close; she didn't pull away. Standing at her front door; we held each other tight, "I already know baby" I whispered, "In thirteen weeks maybe you'll know?" She kissed me softly and disappeared inside the house.

CHAPTER 41
IRIS

The three weeks before Elijah left for basic training changed a lot of feelings, not only mine but my family's. Nanny Wilson always influenced people, my Daddy, especially. His mother had left him and my Paw Reed when he was very young, so Nanny Wilson was like a mother to him. Nanny had known the Foster family when they all lived in Bowdon Junction and told Daddy they were good people; "Harley, you have to loosen the reins on Iris. She's a good girl; Elijah is a nice young man. Look at what happened to Tessa."

My sister had gotten pregnant and was waiting now for the baby to be born. The father was someone my daddy had trusted and allowed Tessa to babysit at their home. Daddy felt he had betrayed him and was extremely hurt by the whole thing. He had always been strict on us girls; "Boys are different" he would say. After Tessa got pregnant, he was determined "That it would not happen again." We tried to keep our business private; but I knew people were talking. My daddy allowing Elijah to come to our house was a sign. It showed he trusted him and me, and I didn't want to betray his trust.

Before Elijah left, he proved to me and my family his word was good. The few times Daddy did allow him to come inside the house, he was respectful and kind to everyone.

When he saw Tessa the first time he said, "Man, I feel bad for her. What guy would do that; leave a girl ….?" After that, he would bring her a candy bar; or flowers he picked from Vivian's to cheer her up; that tugged at my heart.

Family was important to Elijah; He was worried about his parents and thought it was important to see them one more time before he left. He asked my daddy for permission for me to spend two nights in Merrillville. I was surprised he agreed to it. I was never allowed to spend a night anywhere especially out of town.

I was nervous about the trip. I didn't know his parents or his sisters who live there very well. We were leaving Friday after I was finished at the mill; Elijah would pick me up there. I packed my bags the night before under the constant teasing by Loretta and Ester.

"You have to behave; Do you understand what I mean?" Mama said when she brought clean clothes into our room that night.

I felt bad for Tessa, laying on her bed, we all knew what Mama meant by behave. "You don't have to worry mama," wishing she would just be quiet. Tessa had been through enough pain.

I lay in bed that night thinking about how different my life turned out; so far from the plans I had only two years ago. I thought about Flynn, seeing him. I wondered if he ever thought of me or us and how we use to be.

I forbid Loretta to mention his name, and I had stayed away from places he hung out. I saw him from a distance once. I ducked into a store; so he wouldn't see me. I still felt love for him, but it was a different kind of love than I felt for Elijah. I wondered if we had met when we were older would it have worked out…I just didn't know.

The bedroom was lit up by the full moon shining through our window. Loretta was awake; I asked her, "Have you seen Flynn around town?"

She got out of her bed and walked to mine; sat down on the

side, "You mean have I seen him with a girl...don't you? Iris, are you sure about Elijah? You sure he's where your heart is?"

Ester sat up in her bed, "I haven't seen Flynn with any girls."

Tessa was next, "I saw him a few times at the Big Store Grocery. He carries sadness; I recognized it in his eyes." She turned over in her bed facing the wall.

I turned away from them all; I didn't answer any questions about Elijah or make comments about Flynn. My excitement about going to Merrillville had left me. I fell asleep unsure about anything or anyone. My last thought was, "In thirteen weeks maybe I will know." It made me smile just a little.

The next morning, I left for work with my suitcase in hand. Paw Wilson drove me. The thoughts of last night were still in my mind; I longed to sit in my mill window. It would give me time to think about things. It always had; the hum of the looms running seem to settle my mind, I saw things clearer; except my feelings for Flynn. I was taking a big step away from him by going on this trip with Elijah, and it scared me.

By lunchtime, I had told myself it had to be over with Flynn. I walked straight over to the mill window; it represented everything that had happened between us, and under my breath, I spoke the words out loud, "It has to be over." I stood directly in front of the place where it all began and ended it with him. I felt frozen, like it had a magical power over me. I took a deep breath; walked closer to the window and sat down inside of its arch. I crossed my legs and turned around to look out at the place where Flynn had left me those last messages; and I spoke to him, "Flynn it's over for now; it has to be for me to give Elijah a fair chance. He is so good to me." I said the words like Flynn was there and hearing me. I said it for me and for Elijah. I sat silent until the whistle blew telling us lunch was over, and it was time to work. I felt better as the mill floor filled with workers. I had a new start.

The workday ended, and I headed out of the mill to meet Elijah. I was happy to see him standing there holding my suitcase he had collected for me, "Hey beautiful" putting my bag in the back of the truck.

"Hey," I said as I hopped inside and closed the door. Elijah cranked the truck. I looked up at the mill window remembering my day. My heart dropped. Flynn was standing there framed by the rocks that formed the arch of the window...I had seen the image before in a dream. I looked away and looked again, it was real. It took my breath as the lump inside my throat stopped me from gasping out loud. He was staring down at me. The truck began to move; Flynn raised his hand to wave...I stuck my hand out of the truck and Elijah's view and waved back. Then Flynn was gone, along with my new start from that day; the thought of what he and I had together filled my thoughts...again. Would I ever be over this guy?

I tried to enjoy the ride to Merrillville, but between being tired and what had happened my mind was all over the place. The three-hour drive was nice and I tried not to think about anything else.

We arrived at his parents' house; his mother had cooked supper. His family was quiet. His mother treated him just the same as Vivian. It was obvious he was the baby of the family. Sidney, his father, was a no-nonsense man. It was a different atmosphere than the Burtons; the only other family I had gotten to know.

Elijah and his father took their coffee to the front porch; he later told me how against the war his father was; Jake his brother was drafted into the military right before he enlisted. He was at a base in military police school. His father was worried they both would end up overseas fighting.

Saturday morning, I helped Elijah's mother cook breakfast; I enjoyed it. She was quiet but had a good sense of humor and gave good advice. "Iris," she said, "Don't hurt my baby. He has never been in love."

Washing dishes at the sink, "I'm not trying to hurt him." Our talk was interrupted by two of Elijah's sisters, Ann and Betty, coming in the back door carrying food they had made for lunch. Throughout the day, family and friends dropped by to visit Elijah.

It was nice to see he was so loved. He always introduced me like I was someone special, but he was the special one.

Sunday morning came and we were on our way home, and only two days left before he was on a bus to Atlanta. I would be glad to get the thirteen weeks behind us; then in Elijah's words, "Maybe we will know." I smiled thinking of how he said it. Without warning my spirits dropped and a cloud formed over us as the image of Flynn standing in the mill window came to my mind. It was a quiet ride home.

CHAPTER 42
FLYNN

I had nothing against Elijah Foster; although he took advantage of Iris by weaseling his way into her life during a time when he knew she was vulnerable. He had been hovering around Iris a year before I was taken away by my mother.

With all of that, I still respected him for joining the military to fight in the war effort. It was because of that, I decided to give him the time with Iris before he left for boot camp without any interference from me. I was no fool; I had people keeping me filled in with what was going on between them. Some of it was hard to hear. I had intentionally avoided Iris because of Elijah, and I wasn't ready to answer the questions I knew she had. I had hoped the letter I managed to mail her right after I left answered them, but after her reaction when we ran into each other; apparently it hadn't. I only saw her that one time in the three months I had been back; it wasn't the happy reunion I hoped for.

It was hard to be in LaGrange and not see her. Charlie told me how difficult it was for her after I was forced to Greenville. He told me, "She's finally getting back to her old self." I could wait; Elijah would leave for boot camp in two days and would be gone for at least three months. I heard he had took a leave of absence from the mill and would be leaving soon. I decided to wait for my chance to win Iris back. The wait wasn't easy, and I fought the urge many times to go see her.

Loretta told me about Elijah being allowed to visit the Reed's house; something I never tried or even thought of trying. My encounters with Harley Reed had always told me it was out of the question. I knew Iris worried if we were together, she would be forced to choose between her family or me. I thought the same thing, and I'm not sure I would have won. I do know one thing for sure, Iris's love for me was deep, and it was real. Hopefully, something is still there; just a spark that I can ignite. I had thirteen weeks to try.

Friday before Elijah was to leave; Loretta told me they were going to visit his parents. I stood with arms on each side of the mill window, to keep me from falling in the floor as I watched her leave the mill and straight into his arms. She got into the truck and looked straight up at the mill window; I waved. She waved back. Charlie came up behind me, "Hey Flynn, boy what are you doing?"

I looked at him for a moment, then replied, "Waiting Charlie, just waiting."

CHAPTER 43

ELIJAH

March 7, 1943, a date I'll always remember, the notice in the mail from the armed forces read, "Report for Duty Notice." I was to be at the town's bus depot at 10:00 AM on that day. I woke that morning a little afraid of the unknowns I was facing in the days and weeks to come. I thought I was physically strong enough to handle boot camp, but being separated from my family and Iris worried me.

Iris and I had talked about how this day would go. We said our private good-byes the night before, supper at the Main Street Cafeteria, then a walk to our favorite bench in front of the city fountain. The nights had warmed a bit with the start of the spring season. The fountain water was flowing red, white, and blue in honor of all of us leaving the next day. We sat closer together than usual; it eased my worry as I spoke. "I'm not sure when I'll be able to write or call you."

She took my hand and locked her fingers in mine; "It's ok, I'll write to you," she whispered.

I remembered the stamps and envelopes I had for her in my jacket pocket. I handed her the bag.

She quietly opened it and smiled when she saw what was inside, "You're the most thoughtful…" as she leaned in to hug me.

Sitting on the same bench we sat on the day I happened upon a broken girl; I felt closer than ever to her as we clung to one another.

She finally said, "Come on soldier boy, you need to get some sleep."

Sleep was difficult to get that night as I lay in bed after I drove Iris home. Most of the night my mind was filled with wondering what I would be facing over the next few months and how I could get through one day without Iris.

The next morning Iris got to our house around eight o'clock. She had taken time off from the mill to be there with me when I left. It proved to me she really cared because the one thing everyone could agree on about Iris Reed, she was a loyal employee. She never missed work.

We sat around the breakfast table and made small talk as Iris held my hand. She kept looking up at the rooster clock hanging above the sink.

"Time to go," she announced as I squeezed her hand. The truck was loaded with a duffle bag carefully packed with the few things I was allowed to take with me. The ride to the bus station was short. As we parked, we noticed the bus to pick me and the others up was already in front of the bus station's front door. It was decorated with an American Flag draped on each side.

A soldier was standing beside the door of the bus ready to check us in as we arrived. I reported to him; he spoke first in a controlled stern voice, "Name?"

"Elijah Foster Sir," my voice was shaking.

"Number?" he never looked at me.

"02122192" I replied.

"You have 15 minutes to say your goodbyes." He took my duffle bag and handed it to the bus attendant to put it into the luggage compartment on the side of the bus. He saluted, and I returned the salute; he yelled, "Next." I turned and noticed Iris, Vivian, and Allen had been ushered into the waiting area.

Opening the doors, Vivian and Allen stepped forward, "Bye honey, you know we're right here if you need us." Allen shook my hand; Vivian hugged and they were gone.

Iris and I were alone with all the other couples saying their goodbyes. It was hard. "Baby, I'm going to miss you; I know you're strong; stay that way for us?"

She nodded, "I'll be ok Elijah; you be careful; call, write, whatever.... I'll write you." We hugged each other and noticed the bus station was filled with others just like us; men, husbands, and fathers, saying goodbye to women, girls, mothers.

Suddenly, the time was up and they called us to load the bus. I hugged Iris one more time; saluted the commander at the bus door; and I stepped into a new world; half scared to death, but excited to begin what I hoped would be a new chapter for me and Iris.

My seat was by a window; I tried to lower it. Iris had followed me outside down the side of the bus; she was standing below me. I couldn't speak to her for fear I would get up and run off that bus into her arms. I just pressed my left hand to the glass.

The bus started and began to pull away from the curb; Iris raised a small sign, "In thirteen weeks, we'll know" and waved with her other hand. I smiled and thought out loud, "How could any man leave her?" I couldn't understand how Flynn Fisher could have stayed away from her; I thought it strange that he was in my thoughts.

The bus turned and Iris was out of sight. It moved down Broad Street filled with people along the sidewalk to see us off. Searching the faces for any signs of people I knew; I only saw one; Flynn Fisher standing on the corner just watching as I left; just waiting for the time I would be gone.

CHAPTER 44

IRIS

The two days before Elijah was to leave was a blur. I asked for them off work; something I never did. They only let me off the day he was to leave. We went to dinner the night before; I knew he wanted to say something to me. I was ready to listen, "But not during dinner, Ok?"

He agreed. After supper, he reached for my coat and help me put it on. "Let's go," he smiled. I nodded and we headed out the door into the cool of the night. I didn't need to ask where we were going; we always ended up in the same place when we had something serious to talk about; the bench in front of the fountain. The same bench we sat on the day he rescued me from the one in front of the mill. Neither of us spoke for a while, I don't think we knew what to say that hadn't been said. Elijah reached into the pocket of his jacket and handed me a small brown paper sack. Inside it held envelopes with stamps already attached, and a bag of nut goodies, my favorite candy.

I smiled as I took it out of the bag, "Should we?"

He smiled back at me, "No, those are for you, to remember." He took my hand, "I'm not sure how long I'll be gone; at least thirteen weeks, maybe longer." He went on, "or when I'll be able to write."

I stopped him by handing him a card saying how much I would miss him, with a phone number at the bottom. Our family never had a telephone; few people did back in those days. I saved the money to have one put in our house. Elijah looked confused at first by the numbers. Suddenly, he realized what they were and just hugged me.

I spoke softly into his ear, "Call me collect when you can."

He squeezed me tighter, "I will." We held each other a little longer than we ever had. It scared me that I let another man get so close to my heart.

The next morning, I arrived early at Vivian's house. She had breakfast cooked, and they were eating. I poured myself a cup of coffee and joined them at the table. Sadness completely covered me as I thought of Elijah not being here anymore; he had become my security over the last year. He was there for me no matter what. It scared me to think of not seeing him. I felt the same emptiness I had felt when Flynn was taken away. I kept telling myself this was different; not to let Elijah see how sad I was. The kitchen was quiet as all the words left to say between us had been said.

The bus station was filled with people, yet there was a blanket of silence in the air as young men said goodbyes. Elijah went outside to report to the soldier checking them in. We were instructed to stay inside while Elijah reported to check in. I didn't know if he would come back inside or get on the bus. I was nervous. I saw him salute as another man in uniform that put his bag in the luggage compartment as he made his way back inside.

Vivian and Allen hugged Elijah and made their way back to their truck. I told them not to worry about me getting home. I was going to work later; it would fill the rest of the day.

Elijah whispered, "I only have fifteen minutes before I need to get on the bus." As he spoke, I tried to listen. I kept telling myself; I would be ok; he would be ok, and we would be ok. He whispered, "I'll be back soon."

The loudspeaker spoke over us, "Bus loading now; all soldiers report immediately." We walked outside; we hugged each other tight.

I whispered, "I'll be right here waiting for you." He kissed me quickly and was gone. I felt a cold chill go over my body as he stepped up onto the bus decorated with flags of red, white, and blue. I heard someone call my name; I looked down the row of seats until I found Elijah. He pressed his hand against the window; I held my hand up to meet his. The bus cranked, and I stepped back and held up a sign I made, "In thirteen weeks you'll know?" I saw a smile on his face; then he was gone.

CHAPTER 45
FLYNN

LaGrange is a small town. When a bus arrived to pick up young men to leave to serve in the military, everyone knew it. The city's street would be lined with people to see them off; to say goodbye; wish them luck.

The day Elijah was leaving, I stood hidden in the crowd about a block away from the bus station. I wanted to see them together; I would be able to tell if Iris loved him.

It was a shock to see her with him. The relationship between Elijah and Iris looked easy; like they had been a couple for a long time. The way she touched his arm; how she looked worried and sad. His look of anguish staring out of the bus window as he was leaving; all of these told me they cared about each other. I was struggling with what I should do...maybe I should just leave her alone; she looked happy, and she deserved to be happy. I made up my mind. I left town that day determined to move on, to stay out of her life. I could find someone else, but I knew I would never love anyone like I love her. She was a hard act for any girl to live up to.

I admit I was a bit traumatized seeing Iris with Elijah. To see her acting in the same way she did with me was hard. I was confused and unsure of myself, feelings I had never experienced.

Those feelings and seeing the two of them together made me determined to stay away from her, or any place I thought she might be. I was successful the first two weeks Elijah was gone. It had been hard to avoid Iris when I was at the mill, but I figured out a way. I would wait outside and watch her leave each day; then go to the other end of the mill where I was training. I had plenty to keep me busy; school, and the mill, and when I wasn't at either of those places I stayed home.

By the end of March, I finished school and my training as a loom repairman at the mill. I was ready to work full-time. I knew sooner or later I would run into Iris. Two weeks after Elijah left, I reported for my first full-time day at the mill. I arrived early to meet Charlie to go over my daily schedule. I was nervous being in the same place as Iris.

Charlie immediately picked up on it, "Flynn, you're acting like a cat in a room full of rocking chairs; what's up?"

I pushed by him and walked to the coffee pot in our office and poured a cup, "Where do I get my list of repairs I need to work on today?" I asked.

He handed me a roster with a list of machines, "I'll try to keep you out of her area, but sooner or later you will cross paths with her."

I responded, "No problem. Put me where you need me; Iris Reed and I are old news." I walked out onto the mill floor and began to do the work I had trained for the last three months.

The next two weeks went by quickly; I enjoyed my job, and I was good at it. It was strange not seeing Iris at the mill. I decided I was going to run into her sooner or later and just wanted to get it over with. I wasn't trying to avoid her, but most of my work had been at the far end of the mill away from the loom area.

It was Friday; the mill was silent as the daytime workers left; time to cleaned my tools and my desk. When I finished, I headed for the bathroom to wash up. I hadn't even stopped long enough to drink a soda that day and decided to relax for a minute before heading home. Drink in hand I made my way to the mill window; I hadn't seen it since the day I saw Iris leave with Elijah.

I stopped dead in my tracks as it came into view; Iris was sitting sideways, knees drawn up with her arms wrapped around them. She was perfectly framed by the outline of the arched window. It was quiet; my brain was all over the place as a flood of memories of our time together flashed through my head. I felt like I couldn't breathe. I stood still staring at her for a moment; her beauty still got to me.

I turned slowly, not to disturb her, and began to walk away. "Too late, I see you there." She spoke calmly, "You don't speak to me anymore?" as she turned to sit straight in the window.

I turned to face her and walked a few steps toward her, "I didn't want to bother you." She stared straight at me without speaking.

The shift change had started, and the evening crew was filling the mill floor. Iris got up from the window and walked over to where I was. We walked silently out of the mill into the warm air of the spring afternoon.

She broke the silence, "It was strange seeing you here that day; it had been a long time. I didn't think you would ever come back to LaGrange again."

I answered, "I knew I would make my way back here one day; I didn't always know how or when, and I didn't want you to sacrifice your life waiting for me. I felt like I had brought you nothing but pain. I didn't want that anymore." I stopped speaking for a moment waiting for her to react; but she didn't. I stuttered as I tried to explain my actions, "I know it had to be hard to read the letter I wrote you. It was just one, but…"

She looked confused, "What letter?"

I explained, "I wrote you. I wanted to call but couldn't…my mother…so I wrote you a letter; explaining my…."

She began to run away from me then turned, "Flynn, you're lying. I didn't get a letter."

Confused and angry to be called a liar, "Iris, I did; I promise."

She was angry, "Tomorrow, our bench? One?"

I was stunned by what had happened. I didn't know what was going on...I nodded; she was gone just that quick. I turned to head home, still confused. I had no idea what was going on with her; guess I would find out tomorrow. It seemed like I was always waiting for tomorrow when it came to Iris Reed.

I spent the next morning helping around the house with chores; Granny Burton and I rested and had tea or coffee when we finished. That morning I had made it a point to bathe and change my clothes before meeting her on the porch. "Going to town honey?" she asked.

I didn't want to tell her about meeting Iris. "Going to meet some friends," I answered her.

She asked about my job and then, "Have you seen Iris?" Before I could speak, she continued, "Johnny Flynn, there will be many loves in your life, but there's only one true love...one perfect love for you."

I smiled, got up, and kissed her on the cheek, "I know Granny, I know." I walked to town and over to Country Joe's for a quick hot dog. I made my way over to the mill; I noticed Iris called it our bench. It made me smile. I was nervous. I didn't know what was going on and why she was so angry with me. I didn't like it.

I spotted Iris sitting on the bench in front of the mill. The place where our relationship started and ended. She looked like a woman now, not a girl, and still beautiful. I made my way over to her and stood silently. She had an envelope clutched in her hands. She handed it to me. I recognized it immediately. It was the letter I wrote her from Greenville.

"I just got this," she explained, "Daddy got it in the mail and didn't give it to me.... until I ask him about it last night."

"Did you read it?" I asked.

Shaking her head, "No, I couldn't.... I'm afraid of what it says or what it didn't say..."

I took the letter from the envelope, unfolded it, and slowly read the words that were written two years before...

Iris,

Writing this letter is the hardest thing, besides being away from you, that I have ever done. I don't know when I'll be able to come back to you. I know I will be working every day to find a way for us to have our life together as we planned.

I don't want you to be hurt, alone, to not enjoy each day we must be apart. I'm telling you to always know I'll see you again when it is forever. Until then, I will leave you alone...so you can heal and have some happiness somewhere. This is so hard for me, but I'm trying to think of you. Remember, it is not forever. I think of you each day and am working hard to return to you to stay.

Love you always,

Flynn

Iris dropped her head; tears running down her cheeks, "I'm sorry. I thought you had forgotten about me and moved on with that girl, Joan."

I explained to her how I went to work after school, opened a secret bank account to save money, and planned to come back to make a life for us. "When I didn't hear anything from you...."

She stopped me, "Flynn, I didn't know..."

I continued, "When I got back here, I expected to find you waiting for me. I heard how hurt you were for so long; it broke my heart. Charlie told me about Elijah.... I watched you both...you were happy. I decided I couldn't mess that up. You've been through enough."

Iris looked anguished and confused as she whispered, "Elijah... yes... Elijah."

CHAPTER 46

IRIS

Elijah had been gone for a little over two weeks. The note he left me in the mill window was a short message, with a big meaning, "Save me a seat." It was taped to my mirror at home; now the letter I just found out existed from Flynn was taped right beside it. I looked at them both every day; knowing I had a choice to make.

I hadn't heard from Elijah since he left, except one time. He called Vivian; he told her he was ok. I couldn't help but be a little hurt he called her and not me; it took me back to a hurt I felt while I was with Flynn; his mother always seemed to come before me. I tried not to think about it; with everything else going on, it was just too much.

Tessa having her baby girl had caused tension at home and now I was angry with my Daddy for hiding the letter from Flynn. If he had given it to me, it could have meant my life taking a different direction, but he took my choices away. All these thoughts were flooding my mind as Flynn and I were talking the next day.

He was asking about Elijah, "I don't know what to think or do about all of this?"

I looked at him; his eyes were still just as blue; he was still handsome. He told me how hard it was for him when his mother moved him to Greenville.

He explained, "That's why I sent the letter. Then when I came back; I thought you had moved on; found someone else; Elijah…"

I tried to explain to him how Elijah and I were just friends at first, "It was so hard losing you. He was there to listen and now we are taking the time while he's gone to see how we feel about each other."

Flynn spoke up immediately, "Ok…I get it, but shouldn't we use the time he's gone to see if anything is still between us? Don't I deserve that much?"

He took my hand; it was the first time I had touched him since his mother took him away. It still had the same effect on me. I pulled my hand back, "We can be friends, Ok?"

"Ok friend," he smiled.

Breaking the silence, "I've got to go." Without thinking I gave him a quick hug and turned to walk away. I took a few steps when I remembered the letter, I turned and ran back, "My letter please." He handed it to me.

I reached to take it from him, he pulled me close and whispered, "Are you promised to Elijah?" I shook my head no; he took my face in his hands and kissed me. I didn't resist. I felt the kiss run down my body and weaken my legs. I pulled away out of fear of someone seeing us. "You like me," he smiled.

I turned and walked away. Oh no, I thought, "Now what am I going to do?" I tried to reason with myself all the way home, back and forth between Flynn and Elijah. Is it possible to love two men? Yes, you can; I do, I think; I don't know. What I did know was I couldn't let anyone know what was going on between me and Flynn. They wouldn't understand it, because I didn't understand it.

CHAPTER 47
ELIJAH

I was inducted into the military the same day I left LaGrange. I was known as service number, 34764175, Foster. We were tested, poked with needles, head shaved, and probed every which way you can imagine. The first week there, we ate, slept, and whatever the Drill Sargent told us to do. There was no time for anything else. We were allowed one phone call during the second week; I called Vivian, so she could tell my mama, daddy, and Iris I was ok. It's about all I could say in a two-minute call. I didn't have an address to give to her; all I knew was I was at a base in Atlanta.

I never thought too much about writing home; there was not time. All I was worried about was making it through each day of this new life I had signed up for.

By the end of the week, we were told we would be leaving for a new base located in Florida. We foolishly thought we might get some leave time to go home, or at least be allowed to have visitors. Instead, we were instructed we would be leaving on Sunday; be packed and ready to board the buses at noon. I had no time to write Iris or anyone else.

Sunday arrived, and we loaded our duffle bags onto the bus

and sat in the seats assigned to us. The bus was quiet; none of us knew what kind of training we were going to be doing. We did know the war had gotten worse since December when a military base in Hawaii was bombed.

An hour into the trip, our Sargent announced we had been assigned to an Infantry Division, and our training was marked as TOP SECRET.

He continued, "You are not to discuss, disclose, or discharge any information concerning the training you will be receiving. You're going to learn to perform as a unit; as one; to contain and eliminate pockets of enemy soldiers."

He sat down as another officer stood up to instruct us, "There will be no further discussion on the subject."

Silence fell like a blanket over the bus. There was a lot to think about and my thoughts were all over the place. They were interrupted by a sight I never thought I would see as we entered the state of Florida. The ocean was overwhelming; suddenly I felt like a tiny spec in a big world. I wasn't sure what was going to happen next, and if I would survive it. All I could think of at that moment was Iris.

As we arrived at the gates of our new home, the bus pulled up right in front of a row of buildings they called barracks. Our Sargent stood again as we readied ourselves to get off the bus, "Welcome Privates; over the next month we're going to become best friends." His sideway smile said different.

Inside the wooden buildings, I walked looking at the names on the trunks at the foot of each cot. I found the one which read, "Foster, Elijah" followed by my number. I stopped and slowly looked at the cot with blankets and sheets lying on top; thinking this six-by-eight little area would be my home for the next thirteen weeks.

Following the lead of the others, I took my duffle bag and threw it up onto the shelf behind the cot; thinking I could rest before unpacking it. Suddenly, I heard a familiar voice, "Soldier, that is the only mistake you will be allowed."

We all stood and saluted. He instructed us on how the bed

would be made; how the contents of our duffle bag was to be unpacked and put away in a particular order and how our uniform was to look. "Get it done NOW!" he yelled. We did.

Hoping to have time to rest after all the Sargent' orders were complete, we were instructed to report to the mess hall to eat; afterwards, we had one hour before the lights went out. I lay on my new bed in my new home and pictured Iris' face.

I knew I needed to write but the words to explain what my life was like wouldn't come, and I was afraid she would sense how I was really feeling. I would write tomorrow I thought. Little did I know tomorrow would be the hardest day yet.

The next eight weeks were grueling. Every day was the same, basic training they called it. Reveille at 5; dressed; marching until we were told to go to the mess hall. The rest of the day was hours of exercises and classes learning to use firearms and other weapons; obstacle courses; one after another then repeat for ten to twelve hours a day. It was clear we were being tested...for what we were unsure.

We were given one hour each night before lights out and most of us were asleep before then from pure exhaustion.

They explained to us, the next eight weeks were meant to teach us to take care of ourselves and each other in conditions we could not imagine.

The Drill Sergeants told us, "We're tearing you down to rebuild you all into one unit; you need to be able to stand alone or together. We are preparing you for what you are going to face."

I was homesick; worried about what was to become of me and my unit after basic; and I missed Iris more than I thought I would. That first Sunday after we arrived at our new base, I managed to write to Iris for the first time.

Iris,

We have arrived at our new location. We train every day, from sunrise to sunset. We eat, shower, and sleep. It is so hard. The only thing that keeps me going is the dream of our future together. I'm saving my monthly paychecks for us to use when I get home. I'll try to write on Sundays when I can. It's the only day I get any free time at all.

We aren't allowed to call anyone yet, but as soon as we can I will. I miss you more than I can tell you in words...I'm worried...I long to hear your voice. Please write as often as you can. I hope your family is well. Tell everyone hello.

I know I shouldn't ask, but have you seen Flynn?

All my love,

Elijah

CHAPTER 48

IRIS

Elijah had been gone for three weeks, and I hadn't heard anything from him. Other than the call he had made to his sister. I asked Vivian every day, her response was the same, "No honey, I haven't heard a word. I'm sure we'll hear something soon."

I nodded and smiled; a little worried and a little irritated, thinking, "Surely, he has had time for a short letter." Elijah was on my mind, but so was Flynn. It was hard not to see him every day at the mill. Working together had slowly brought back some of the old feelings I had for him, but I still insisted, "We're just friends; that's all."

He would agree and smile in a way I knew he was thinking something else. I knew crossing that line would only complicate my life and my life didn't need any more confusion than what I was already feeling.

Missing Elijah was hard; I was worried about him, and Flynn was trying hard to break down the walls between us. Leaving the mill on Friday, walking toward home, worrying about Elijah, thinking out loud, "Almost three weeks and hardly a word, Elijah what is going on?"

I was jolted out of my thoughts by a voice calling my name, "Iris...Iris Reed." I turned to see Flynn hurrying toward me, "Iris, Granny wants you to come over today."

I smiled, he knew I had a soft spot for Mrs. Burton, but I was sure he was using her to get me to spend time with him outside the mill, "Really? Are you just trying to trick me into coming to your house?"

He just looked at me, "Iris...come on, I wouldn't do that; I'm telling you the truth. You can call your house, let them know where you are; we have a phone now. Charlie is coming by later to take you home; so, you don't have to worry about it getting dark."

I was irritated he had taken away any excuse I could have, "You planned this, didn't you?"

He smiled, "I hoped, not planned." He was walking beside me now, both hands in their respective pockets, he offered me his arm. I shook my head no and walked toward the house on Jefferson Street.

Granny Burton was happy to see me and confirmed she told Flynn to invite me there. I had missed her and wondered how a woman that sweet had a daughter like Naomi. I accepted her invitation to supper. It was as good as ever, fried fish, fries, hushpuppies, and coleslaw. I ate more than I had since Elijah had left; I was startled when I realized I hadn't thought about him all afternoon.

It was a good visit. Looking over at the clock I told Flynn I needed to get home before it got much later, "Mama and Tessa are expecting me..." I stopped before I said more than I should about Tessa.

I always left that house on Jefferson Street feeling safe and happy; it was one of the few places I felt totally at ease...most of the time. That night felt as though no time had passed at all. Mrs. Burton made me promise to "come by and sit with her for a while" as I hugged her bye.

Charlie was waiting in the driveway in the yellow taxicab he drove part-time on weekends to take me home. Flynn walked me out and opened the taxi door; "Scoot over girl, I'm riding with Charlie tonight."

As I moved to the middle of the seat, "I can get in the back," I replied.

"Don't be silly," he smiled and tucked both hands between his knees, "You're safe."

Charlie knew where we were living, but I wasn't sure Flynn did, "Out on Old Hamilton Road."

As we pulled into the driveway Flynn asked, "Your daddy going to be mad if I walk you to the door?"

"I wouldn't push your luck," I answered. "Bye Charlie, thanks for the ride." He nodded.

Flynn walked a few steps and then held a flashlight so I could see up to the two-story white house where we lived. "Iris," Flynn said quietly, "See you tomorrow in town?"

I nodded, "Thanks for taking me to see your Granny tonight; I had a good time."

"Me too" he answered as he closed the taxi door. I stood on the porch and watched as it disappeared down the long driveway thinking "What am I doing?"

Daddy was sitting on the side porch and walked around to the front door as I opened it to go inside, "Can't believe that boy is back; he doesn't need to come around here" as he spit his tobacco out into the yard. "You heard from Elijah?" he asked.

I shook my head still too angry at him for hiding Flynn's letter from me.

Daddy continued, "Sure he will write when he has the time…."

I interrupted him, "Well, maybe you won't hide his letter when and if it comes." I hurried into the house before he could say anything else.

Into my bedroom, my sisters were asleep. I washed my face, slipped into my nightgown, and quietly got in my bed. I felt confused and unsure of my feelings for the first time since Flynn came back. I thought for a moment about Granny Wilson's words, "The good book says, mornings bring joy." I sure hope so. I drifted off to sleep; not knowing how I felt about anyone or anything and hoping the morning would bring answers.

CHAPTER 49
FLYNN

"**M**an, what are you doing?" Charlie asked as I closed the taxi door.

I looked at him, "Charlie, I still love her. What am I supposed to do? Just walk away and let Foster have her?" Answering my own question, "No way man; not without a fight."

We were silent on the way back to Jefferson Street. As Charlie pulled back in the driveway he said, "Just watch yourself Flynn...ok?"

"I will, I am" placing my hand on his shoulder, "I'm moving slow. See you tomorrow?" He nodded.

The house was quiet and dark; only the light in my bedroom was on; I fell on my bed. Exhausted by the week's work, my thoughts went to my getting back my life with Iris. It was progressing the way I planned. I had to move slowly; Iris was torn. I knew she had feelings for Elijah, but I believed she still had feelings for me too. I fell asleep wondering if she was worth everything I had been through or everything I was going through now.

Saturday morning, I slept late. When I got up, Granny had put me a breakfast plate on the stovetop. Paw Burton had left to go downtown to meet his friends like always. I spent the morning helping Granny; catching up on chores she couldn't do anymore. I took a bath, got my work clothes ready for the next week, and then headed downtown.

I knew Iris used to come to town every Saturday to do her errands, but I wasn't sure if she still did or not. I stopped at Kessler's and grabbed a drink to go, then headed toward the fountain. I noticed Iris sitting on a bench in deep thought. I stood staring at her for a minute, then walked up to her, "Hi there" as I sat down, offering her a drink of my soda.

She took the cup from me. When our hands touched, a shiver ran down my body. She took a drink, "You are complicating my life."

I looked straight into her eyes and spoke, "You don't think you have made mine easy, do you?"

She continued, "I didn't think your mother would ever let you come back here; at least until we were both married to other people."

I defended myself, "My mother doesn't run my life anymore. I'm soon to be seventeen... Are you promised to Elijah?" I waited for her answer a second time.

She shook her head, "But everyone thinks we'll be married, he hasn't asked me.... we talk about being together and traveling..."

"Stop," I interrupted her, "I don't want to hear about you and him." It was silent for what seemed forever as we both sat and stared at the fountain as it shot water into the air. I finally stood up and faced her, "Iris do you love him? Should I move on...try to forget you and find someone else...?"

She spoke up, "I thought you had already; Charlie told me about Joan. How when he visited you..." she stuttered, "And yes I love Elijah; but in a different way than I loved you."

I took her hands in mine our fingers interlocked, "Loved?" I whispered, "I'm in the past?"

She took her hands from mine and sat back down on the bench, "I thought you were until now..." She put her face in her hands, "I don't know...all the old feelings are coming back...and what do I do?"

"I don't know," I answered and sat beside her. There was silence between us again.

The afternoon sun was setting as it shone on the water in the fountain a beautiful rainbow appeared. I took it as a sign to move forward, "Look, Iris, it will be a couple of months before he comes back; can we spend some time together to see what it is between us...or do you just think we are over? It's your call."

I waited for her answer. "And you and Joan," She asked, "What's that?"

I told her the full truth, "Joan and I are and have always been just friends. She wanted more, but she knew my heart was here. Nothing happened or will happen there." I waited for her to answer.

"Yes, we can spend time together," she explained, "As friends... to see if anything else is still there."

Relieved she was willing to give me a chance I said, "Ok. Let's get some coffee...friend." I smiled and held out my hand.

Seated in a back booth at Tasty Café, we ordered coffee and shared a slice of caramel cake and didn't worry about who saw us together. It was like old times.

She looked at her watch, "I have to get home. It's getting late."

We said our goodbyes; we wouldn't see each other until Monday at the mill; the first real test to see if Iris meant what she had said.

She did. She stopped by the office early that morning and ask me to have lunch with her and her friends. I smiled and nodded. We had lunch together every day, but she was careful.

We were never seen together just us, "That would be disrespectful," she declared.

On Friday, she said she was busy that weekend. When I ask her if she wanted to come home with me for supper, she explained, "Me and my sisters are singing at the church revival Sunday. We are practicing...."

What?" I replied, "I didn't know you sang together."

"We don't normally in public, but we always have at home.

Granny Wilson ask us," she explained. She went on to tell me her grandfather had helped to start a church …

"Can I come?" I asked.

"Really, must you?" she smiled, "Charlie knows where it is." I was surprised Charlie had been going to church there; he had never mentioned it.

He picked me up that Sunday. On the ride over he explained how he really enjoyed the small church, and he was right; the service was good; not boring. Iris and her sisters were better than I thought they would be. Sitting in the church pew watching Iris sing alto, I took note that all of the Reed girls were lookers, but Iris stood out; wearing a light blue dress…I was amazed each time I saw her. She took my breath away.

After the service was over, she walked up to me, "Can we talk?"

"Sure," I took her elbow and guided her to Charlie's car… "What's wrong?"

She dropped her head, "I have to tell you something, my feelings for you are getting stronger…"

I smiled at her, "I know you better than you know yourself…. and there is something else…what is it?" She opened her purse and held up a white envelope, "I got a letter from Elijah."

"And?" I said.

"You look nice today," she replied in an effort to change the subject. I didn't let her.

"Iris, what?" I said.

"Flynn, he's having a hard time…I feel guilty …he's struggling; missing me and home, and I'm spending time with you."

By this time, I was angry over her feeling bad about our time together, "You want to stop? Can you stop seeing me…stop the feelings between us? Maybe you should question the feelings you have for him. Maybe you feel guilty that your feelings for him aren't what you thought…"

I knew I had crossed a line…She turned and walked away without a word.

CHAPTER 50
ELIJAH

I got my first letter from Iris in the middle of the next week. I was relieved she wrote to me as soon as she did. After that, I got one about every three days. I looked forward to them; they brought me comfort and news from home; but she never answered the one question I was most interested in, "Was she seeing Flynn?" I didn't have time to worry about it during the day, but at night it was my last thought before I slept.

My days were filled with the training the military said we needed to protect ourselves when we shipped out. The thought shook me to the core; I wanted to be ready. The training was monotonous, but I took it seriously and tried to give it my best each day.

My life was out of my control and the only thing I could depend on was the routine of each day; rise at 5:00, reveille at 5:30; march to the mess hall; breakfast at 6:00, hours of training, exercising; running 3-5 miles; practicing on the shooting range; lunch; more marching; weapons training using guns; grenades, gases. We built shacks; went on maneuvers, ran obstacle courses, learned to drive tanks, and more that I'm not allowed to talk about.

Most days I couldn't imagine what situations I could be in where I would need to know all the stuff they were throwing at us. They were staying true to their promise, tearing us down one day and building us up the next. If not for the letters from home, I'm not sure I could have handled it.

She never talked about us or our future and it made me wonder if she was seeing Flynn. I would soon know the truth. We were given permission to call home that Sunday. Only a five-minute call, but her voice would tell me everything. I needed to know if I still had a girl at home waiting for me. Although I had never asked her, I was planning a future with Iris. I thought she felt the same. Now six weeks and some odd days away from each other seemed to changed things between us, and I was ready to find out just how much.

That Sunday felt different. Everyone was excited to call home. We attended the required breakfast together; and then marched to the base chapel for services. After lunch was the time to shine our shoes and our brass for the weekly inspection, write letters; whatever we needed to do. Finally, we were given an index card with a time to report to the sergeant's office where we would be allowed to make our call and speak privately to our families. My time was 2:30 PM.

It was a beautiful day as I walked over to the Sargent's office, I was nervous; my thoughts were everywhere; what if she didn't answer? Should I split the time between her and Vivian? I saluted the officer as I walked through the office door and sat in a chair to wait for my turn. I took out the piece of paper Iris had carefully written her telephone number on that last night we were together.

My Sargent's voice brought me back to the present, "Foster, you are up...Five minutes after someone answers, understand?" I nodded. We entered the door; he stood by as I dialed the number; waiting to start the timer that sat on the small table with the phone. I was nervous as it began to ring.

I heard Iris' voice accept the charges; the Sargent set the timer and left the room. "Iris," I spoke softly, "It's so good to hear your voice."

CHAPTER 51
FLYNN

I 'm not sure what happened after the church service; I knew Iris had gotten a letter from Elijah. Something about the letter upset her. I tried to talk to her about it, but she wasn't going to talk to me; so, I left. I thought leaving her alone was the best thing to do; I didn't want to push her.

By work time on Monday, I was convinced she was going to break it off with me, after hearing from Elijah. I walked my usual route to the mill that morning the same way I had since I was a kid. I headed up the sidewalk to the entrance; glancing up at the mill window I thought about how it had been such an important place in my life. I stopped in my tracks in awe of Iris sitting there perfectly framed by the window's arches. Just like she had done all those mornings I walked to school...once again all the past memories of us flooded my brain and passed in front of me like they were happening all over again. It overwhelmed me to the point that I backed up and sat down on our mill bench. Watching her, tracing the outline of her profile, fifteen minutes until the whistle blew. I had to clock-in or be late. While I was punching my time-card, Charlie informed me I was assigned to work on several machines in the loom area.

"Why?" I questioned him. I knew he had put me there for a reason. "I need you there today; suck it up and just do the work; ok?" grinning at me all the while. I'm not sure why he always seemed to know things before everybody else, but he did, whether it was good or bad.

I went to our office to collect the tools I would need and headed over to the area I would be working that day. I barely made it in time. The whistle blew minutes after I got to the part of the mill I had avoided for the past four months. I didn't speak to Iris or look over at her machine; the loom I was working on was several feet from hers. She walked up to where I was, "Lunch?"

I stared at her for a moment, "Ok, sure." The whistle blew, and our workday began.

Mondays at the mill were always busy; seemed like everything slowed down or broke over the weekend. I didn't have time to worry or try to figure out why all of a sudden Iris wanted to have lunch with just me.

Frankly, I was getting a little frustrated by the situation between us; I never let any girl dictate what I did and was getting tired of playing her game. I felt like she should just make her mind up between me and Elijah. I decided by lunch she was going to cut me loose, or I was her. I was ready for it either way. I convinced myself I would be ok no matter what.

The lunch break whistle blew; the loom area came to a halt as workers emptied into the lunchroom. I made my way to the bathroom to wash up; opening the door coming out I saw Iris, lunch pail in hand.

"Hungry?" she asked.

I nodded yes as I noticed she was headed in the opposite direction of the lunchroom.

I followed her; no questions asked. I was surprised when she stopped for a moment in front of the mill window; our window, she sat first, "Are you going to sit with me?" Still silent, I walked over and took a seat next to her. Iris opened her pail and laid out two sandwiches, a thermos of soup, and fried pies. She handed me a sandwich. We ate in silence.

Iris always had a way of cooking; even a sandwich made by her was better than most. She was a master at it, "I forgot what a good cook you were."

Iris stopped eating, "You forgot me not my cooking; me; you left me and never looked back. One letter; did you think that was enough?"

I tried to explain what I thought the letter already had, "I wanted you to find some happiness while I was gone; I thought you knew me well enough to know I would find a way back to you. Instead, you went and fell in love with some guy from …"

She shot right back, interrupting me, "Don't talk about someone you don't even know, and don't try to tell me how I feel about anyone or anything."

"Oh, so you're defending him now?" I was hurt.

She stood up, "You don't even know me now; what I went through; what your actions cost me…"

I couldn't let her finish something I knew was not true, "I didn't leave you; I was taken. I was a kid, but I grew up and came back just like I promised." I threw the sandwich I was holding in my hand down into her lunch pail and decided I wouldn't speak in anger. I turned to walk away.

"That's right Flynn, walk away; that's what you do best." Her words cut deep and angered me even more.

I turned and stared into her eyes, "I'm going to say this one more time and never again. I was taken away. I wrote the letter. I wanted to be fair to you because I love you; I wanted you to have some happiness. I didn't think you would fall for anyone; you told me I was the only one you could ever love. You lied to me."

The whistle blew, and the loom area filled up with workers. I went back to my workstation and a note, "Machine 36 down." I picked up my tools and headed over to the area where it was located.

I noticed Iris was back at her work line, and our mess was still in the window. I collected the half-eaten food, the trash, and her lunch pail. I walked over and sat her pail down.

She turned around, "Thanks, can I see you for a minute after our shift ends today?"

"Sure, why not?" I responded sarcastically, "Lunch went so good."

The afternoon went by fast. Machine thirty-six was a mess, and it took me a while to figure out what was wrong and to repair it. I left a couple of times to get the tools I needed and noticed Iris seemed to be in a good mood, laughing, and joking around. She didn't seem upset by anything that had happened between us. I guess she's over it and me.

The shift whistle blew on the dot; 4 o'clock; I didn't see Iris anywhere. Her machine area was clean, and all of her things were gone. I wasn't sure what to make of it. I put away my tools, cleaned up my work desk, and walked out of the mill into a warm sunny afternoon.

As my eyes adjusted to the light, I noticed Iris sitting on our bench, "You love to keep me waiting, don't you?" I didn't take the bait and remained quiet. I sat down beside her and waited for her to speak. She did.

CHAPTER 52

IRIS

I felt a lot of anger at Flynn leaving for two years. The letter my daddy hid from me helped me somewhat to understand the reasons he thought he was doing what was best for me. I still had feelings for him, and I was mad at myself because of it. I felt confused; pulled in two directions; I faced the fact: I was in love with both of them.

The call from Elijah took a while to sink in; I thought he would spend the time on the phone telling me he loved and missed me, and he did in a way. He was concerned to find out if I was seeing Flynn. I told him I had a few times at work.

His response was unexpected, "Iris, right now we have no definite commitment, and we never will until you can tell me Flynn Fisher doesn't mean anything to you. I'll not live in the shadow of another man." His words hurt me; they weren't what I wanted to hear from him during his first phone call. He continued speaking in my silence; "You have eight weeks until I hope I can come home for a while; figure it out; if you need to see him…, do it…I don't like it, but I would rather you do it now than later. I want you to be sure about what and who you want to have a life with. I'll call you when I can. Writing is hard; I'm so tired at the end of the day; but will you please write to me even if you are seeing him?"

I broke my silence, "You know I will. Elijah, I don't know what to say...."

The operator interrupted us, "Your phone call will disconnect in 30 seconds."

Elijah rushed to say, "I love you Iris."

I replied, "I love..." but before I could finish the sentence, the operator ended the call. I was so stunned by our conversation; I played it over and over in my head. What man tells you to see another man?

Then I realized how much love it took Elijah to encourage me to see Flynn to be sure of what I felt. His selflessness made me feel guilty. He should not be worried about me when he was going through so much.

Not knowing what to do, I went to the person who always helped me figure out my problems, my Grandpa Reed.

His advice was put in simple terms, "Iris, you can't ride two horses at one time. You have to choose one that's right for you. If you don't, people are going to be hurt more than they already have; including you."

I knew he was right. I had to choose. The only way I could do it was to see if the feelings I had for Flynn were still there or if they were remnants of puppy love between two kids. At that moment, I wished Flynn hadn't come back. I didn't expect he would. Naomi Fisher said she would never let him. I believed her. Now he's here, and the old feelings are bursting out of me for this man I once loved.

Sitting on that bench that Monday afternoon I told Flynn about Elijah's call. I could see it made him uncomfortable, but he had to know the truth, "I love you both, but it's a very different kind of love. Y'all are very different men." I could tell he didn't like what I was saying, but after Elijah's call, I felt a little empowered. "Flynn, I'm going to give our relationship a chance until Elijah comes home, eight weeks, no more hiding. I have no promises to either of you." I was waiting for him to explode in anger but was pleasantly surprised.

Flynn agreed, "That's fair. I'm ready to figure all of this out."

I nodded and got up from the bench to start home. He stayed seated for a minute, then I felt him beside me...he took my hand, and we walked...no words were spoken between us. Just out of sight from the mill and the workers leaving to go home, he stopped pulled me to him and kissed me. The feeling of his lips on mine, his arm around my waist pulling me to him caused chills to run down the whole of my body. I pulled back from him, "I've had enough surprises for today. Let's sleep on this tonight."

He whispered in my ear, "Ok Iris, you know better."

I don't know how to explain how he made me feel, but I had never felt it with Elijah. I wasn't sure if it was good or bad.

Flynn told me Charlie was waiting to take me home; he didn't want me walking after a long hard day at work. I was impressed by how he always thought of me as we walked back to the mill.

Flynn hugged me, and helped me into the car. I saw him wink at Charlie as he said, "Take care of my girl." I smiled at him as the taxi door closed, and Charlie pulled away from the curb.

CHAPTER 53

ELIJAH

To say joining the service was the best thing I had done would be a lie. I may believe that later in life; but not now. The last five weeks of training were unexplainable unless you have experienced them. The military's goal at that moment in time was to win a war; now a world war. They tore men down to build them into someone who had the know-how to survive the fight. Men who couldn't imagine what they would face when shipped overseas.

They called it basic training. There was nothing basic about it. We were placed in units formed from the results of tests we had taken that first week. We did everything together. We had not a moment alone, until lights out. That part was ok because we were so tired sleep came easy. We had no outside contact those first few weeks, no writing home, no calls, no visitors, and no leaving the base.

I had plenty of time to think and all I thought of was Flynn and Iris. I was ready to tell her to figure out what she wanted. I was tired of it all. I loved her, but I realized sometimes love wasn't enough.

When I called that Sunday afternoon, I was ready. I wanted to tell her what I was going through to make her understand why I seemed so harsh. She wouldn't understand, but after what I had gone through in basic training, I wasn't going back home to fight with anyone, especially Flynn Fisher. I told her straight up to figure it out; to date him; do whatever...but make a choice, me or him.

I do love her; ask her to write to me and "To get rid of the ghost from the past if she wanted to move forward with me." It sounded noble, but it wasn't. Being gone, I wouldn't be there to see them together.

By this time, I was assigned to a replacement division unit, and I knew where I would be going if this war didn't end soon. I couldn't worry about stuff at home if I wanted to survive; it was the first thing we were taught.

Iris had to choose, and I had to set her free so she could.

CHAPTER 54

IRIS

The next eight weeks brought back feelings for Flynn I thought had long passed away for me. We became almost inseparable. At the mill sitting cross-legged in our window sharing lunch, talking, and laughing just like old times.

When we weren't at the mill most of our time was spent at the Burton's house; even occasionally at my house although, Daddy never seemed to like Flynn like he did Elijah.

I'll say right now; you can love two people at the same time, but the love you feel for them isn't the same. I love Flynn, but I love Elijah. The love I felt was different because they were different. One is not better or worse than the other. I cannot explain how it happens, but it does.

I hadn't been writing Elijah as much as I should have; and he hadn't written much to me. It was difficult writing to him while spending time with Flynn. The few letters we wrote were full of nice words; not the way they were at first.

Elijah's letters never mentioned our future; so, I didn't mention it either. He called a few times. His voice told me one thing; he was a changed man ...more serious...a worried voice. We both decided not to talk about our relationship until we were together, face-to-face.

I was about to find out how soon that would be.

CHAPTER 55
FLYNN

After Iris' declaration of "Eight weeks to figure out what we felt for each other," I decided to make them as special as I could. I loved our time working together at the mill, sitting in our window eating lunch, laughing, and planning our time together. I wanted to make each weekend something Iris would remember, even if she chose Elijah.

I planned each one with care. I knew Iris and I knew what "fun" meant to her. We fished, swam in the backwaters, picnics, and finally talked about the future watching the sunset.

Weekend nights we loved going to the movies especially, the balcony sections where we could be alone. Afterward, it was coffee at Tasty's just talking. We loved just being together.

Although Iris wouldn't admit it to me, the attraction was still there. Wherever we were, our hands were touching each other's; and the times we found ourselves alone we couldn't get close enough. The feelings would overtake us, but Iris would always stop things before "We went too far" as she put it. I was frustrated. I wasn't used to a girl not giving me whatever I wanted, but with Iris it was different, I was totally committed to her. I decided to wait as long as I needed to.

I felt like I had a right to date other girls, but I didn't. After all, she had Elijah coming back soon. I was determined to show her I would never cheat on her; I had no desire for anyone but her.

The eight weeks were passing quickly. July arrived with two important things happening, both of which weighed on my mind and heart. I would turn seventeen, and Elijah would be returning; both could change my life. I didn't like the fact another man could change the path I wanted my life to take after my seventeenth birthday.

CHAPTER 56

IRIS

Those eight weeks Flynn and I had together came to be some of the most important times of my life; our love was special. I was sure of it, but it hadn't changed what I had built with Elijah. It was July; Flynn's birthday and our last week together before Elijah's leave should begin.

Elijah and I had been writing, The letters were strained and full of niceties. Neither of us mentioned the future. His letters told me he was worried about shipping overseas. "The war," he said, "was in full force." I tried to reassure him, but I knew little about what was happening or what he was going through. I didn't let him know; I was worried too. Every headline in our local newspaper was about the war; someone losing a husband or son. It scared me.

Both of us signed our letters, "Love." He had been able to call a few times, but his voice sounded different. I tried to catch him up on what was going on at the mill, but it all seemed so unimportant with what he was going through.

What he was facing changed him. He seemed like a stranger. I didn't want to make any serious decisions until he was home; face-to-face we could tell better how we felt. That wouldn't be long, his last postcard arrived the second week of July;

Iris,

Leave will be soon...not sure what day...15 weeks...Now we know?

Elijah

I was shaken by his written words; I didn't realize it had been longer than we had planned, but all I could do was tell him I still didn't know.

How do you choose between two men when you can't imagine your life without either one of them? I decided to face each day as it came, and what was coming next was helping Granny Burton with Flynn's surprise birthday party.

CHAPTER 57
ELIJAH

I didn't tell Iris much of what my training entailed; we were instructed from the first day to "Not talk about what you do; see; or hear." I wouldn't have told her anyway; it would cause her to worry.

The training we were going through taught us what we needed to protect ourselves, survival techniques they called them. Now, they say we are part of a unit; to operate as one, to protect each other and our country.

I was learning every day what that really meant. Unit training was ten times harder than basic training; mentally, physically, and emotionally. Training to fire grenades, becoming a superior marksman on several different types of weapons, and maneuvering tanks the size of houses, I didn't have time to think about things back home. Those thoughts would only sneak into my brain at night when sleep overtook them.

We were informed we would be facing more intense training meant for an infantry division going overseas. Our job was to be ready to replace troops already involved in the war. I was assigned to the armor division; exactly what that meant I didn't know; but was soon to learn at a new military base. We were told we would relocate to a base in Arkansas. We packed the unit's supplies on military trucks that were meeting us there.

I let Iris know I would be getting leave to come home sometime in July. Our thirteen weeks had turned into longer; I was sure Iris hadn't noticed.

Finally, we were told our leave would begin in three days. I would have two weeks at home before reporting to the base in Arkansas. Part of me wished I could skip going home. It would be easier to report directly to my next assignment, but I had to figure out what was going on with Iris, Flynn, and me.

Everyone was ready to go. I chose to ride the bus. It would give me a chance to think about what I was going to do when I arrived home.

CHAPTER 58
IRIS

July arrived and Flynn's birthday was soon. Granny Burton was excited to give him a surprise birthday gathering. We had been planning it for the last two weeks. She did most of the work; I helped by bringing all the groceries she needed. Charlie invited the people from the list Granny and I made. I paid Loretta to pick up his favorite cake from the Box Bakery downtown and drop it off at his house.

His birthday fell on a Thursday; we both worked that day. Granny Burton had told him she was cooking him a birthday supper; and to invite me. I agreed but told him I would need to go home to change clothes.

Charlie knew I was in charge of making Flynn "late" and said, "I'll help you out; drive ya'll out to your house."

The whistle blew, I took my time getting my things together to leave work; Charlie took the long way to my house, using the excuse; "There's road work going on." I took my time changing clothes as they waited for me.

I called Granny Burton to tell her we were on our way, "We're ready honey; Y'all come on." I could tell she was excited.

As I started out the door, mama reminded me of the present

184

she wrapped for me that day, "Thanks, Mama." I picked up the gift for Flynn; Elijah popped into my head. It wasn't long ago I was celebrating his birthday just three blocks over from the Burton's house.

I wondered when he would be home; he didn't give me an exact date just, "The end of the month." No word from him in a week; I pushed it from my head. I just couldn't handle anything but right now.

Out the front door, Flynn looked angry; but he was trying not to show it. He met me at the door, "You look sensational," as he grabbed my hand. Our fingers folded between each other's; we hurried to the car where Charlie was waiting.

As we pulled into the driveway of the Burton's house, it looked like no one was there. Flynn was worried and told Charlie to go in with us in case something was wrong. We walked through the front door. Charlie flipped the light switch and everyone shouted, "Surprise." Flynn's worried look changed to his famous smile.

The party was fun; food, presents, and singing as Flynn ushered in 17 years. We looked at each other as the cake with candles was carried in by Granny Burton. I remembered our plan long ago and wondered if he did.

He blew out the candles and as everyone was clapping, he leaned over and whispered, "I remember." My heart melted into sadness thinking how far away all our plans seemed to be.

Friday was a work day. The party was ending early as people began to say their goodbyes. Flynn looked tired. I suggested Charlie drop me off on his way home. Flynn agreed, but said he needed to talk to me on the front porch for "just a minute."

We walked outside, he immediately began thanking me in a soft sincere voice, "Iris, thank you for tonight; for helping Granny. I know you have a lot on your plate…" As I started to respond, he placed his finger over my lips and pulled me close. He just held me for a long while; like he was afraid it might be the last time. I could feel his trembling, "I just want you to be happy. You deserve so much more." We could hear the telephone ring, as he leaned down and kiss me softly.

185

"Flynn, it's your mother," yelled Granny from the kitchen.

Charlie stuck his head out the cab window, "You ready Iris?"

Flynn opened the front door to answer the phone, I stuck my head inside it "Good night." No reply from inside meant the Burtons had retired for the night. As I started down the steps, I heard Flynn, "When mother?" A call from Naomi Fisher meant she was up to something.

The ride home was quiet, and I was glad. My mind was all over the place. As we pulled into my driveway, I thanked Charlie. He waited until I made it into the house. Everyone was sleeping; even the new baby girl Tessa had just brought home from the hospital. I quickly changed into my nightgown. Lying in my bed, I tried to clear my thoughts; I wondered when Elijah would be home and what Naomi Fisher could be up to. I could do nothing about either. I drifted off into an exhausted sleep.

CHAPTER 59
ELIJAH

My unit's leave started on the afternoon of July 28th. A lot of the guys had already left base, but I decided to catch a bus the next day. I didn't want to get home in the middle of the night. The barracks were quiet; just a few of us remained behind.

Up at four the next morning, we paid a taxi to take us to the bus station. The ride home was long; the sun was setting and darkness was taking over when the bus pulled into town.

It was good to be home again; I grabbed my duffle bag and decided to walk the few blocks over to Vivian's. I took a shortcut down Jefferson Street. I admit I went that route because I wanted to see if Iris was at the Burtons. I intentionally hadn't told her I was coming home that day; it was a plan to see firsthand what was going on between her and Flynn.

Jefferson Street was completely dark, except for the Burton's house. It was lit up inside and outside. People filled the yard. They were having a get-together. Probably family I thought; I saw Iris standing on the front porch with Flynn. I ducked behind some hedges; I didn't want her to know I was home yet. I stood for a second and stared at the two of them…they looked like a couple.

Feeling tired and defeated, I cut through the houses and made my way to Jenkins Street. Vivian wasn't expecting me. I knocked on the front door; the porch light came on as she peeked out it.

She opened the door, she didn't speak. She hugged me and cried, "What are you doing here?"

I smiled, "I live here. No really, I'm on leave before I go to Arkansas... for more training..." I stopped there not telling her what was really happening.....

"Well, at least you aren't being sent overseas" as she hugged me again.

I took my duffle bag and put it in my bedroom. It still looked the same, Vivian said it would. Walking back into the kitchen, "I'm glad to be home, sis."

She had already started making me a sandwich and warming up some cornbread and homemade soup, "I know you're tired, but you need to eat something."

"I'm both," I said as I sat down at the familiar table. For a moment I thought about the last time I sat there with Iris right beside me. Vivian put the sandwich and soup on the table. I ate every bite. "The best thing I've tasted in months." I pushed the empty plate forward on the table, "How's Iris?" Vivian looked troubled, like she didn't want to break bad news.

Allen walked into the kitchen, he shook my hand, "Glad you're home.... she's been seeing Flynn."

Vivian touched my arm, "Elijah, he stayed in town; works at the mill..."

Wanting to stop Vivian from worrying any more than she already did about me, "Sis, it's alright; I know." I told her and Allen the short version of what was going on between Iris and me.

She seemed worried, "What's going to happen between you two...Y'all going to call it quits?"

I shrugged my shoulders, "Doesn't look good...I cut down Jefferson Street tonight; Burton's were having a get-together... there she stood on the front porch with Flynn... guess we'll see."

Vivian explained, "It was Flynn's birthday."

Quietness filled the room, I broke it, "I love her; but I don't want or need someone who is straddling the fence between me and another guy; especially right now."

Quietness again; Vivian started cleaning up the kitchen, "Elijah go to bed; get some rest. You look so tired."

I kissed her cheek and looked over at Allen, "See you in the morning, night brother-in-law."

I closed the door of my bedroom and crashed on the bed without taking off my boots. The last thing I saw as I fell asleep was the image of Iris and Flynn standing on that front porch. Thankfully, the tiredness overtook me, and I slept without dreams or nightmares; the first time since I left home.

I got up early the next morning, bathed, shaved, and got dressed. Out in the kitchen Allen had made coffee. I poured a cup and sat down at the table. Vivian was still getting ready for work. Allen was talking about her quitting soon; he had bought the house from the mill. I nodded as I got up from the table to scramble some eggs and check on the biscuits she already had in the oven.

Vivian and Allen grabbed a biscuit filled with egg I had made for them and headed out the door. Holding the knob to close the door, Vivian stopped, "I hope you just hang around here baby, just rest; think about things before you do anything. I won't mention anything to Iris if I run into her." I nodded.

Sitting there at the table in LaGrange seemed strange. I decided to just stay at the house and think about what my next move should be. By the afternoon, I was restless, not used to just sitting all day. I went for a walk to see what all had changed since I left. I walked downtown; not on the main square but side streets; I didn't want to talk to anyone. I grabbed a copy of the local newspaper, "The Daily News"; everything seemed the same, except for the War Board in the town square. I stood in front of it and started to read the list of the names of soldiers who were overseas fighting. Halfway down the list, I turned and walked away. I wanted to put the war out of my mind.

Without realizing it, I found myself standing in front of the mill just at closing time. I could hear the machines begin to shut off. I knew Iris was there, but so was Flynn. I wasn't ready to face either. I found a bench out of view of the people leaving work; I waited to see if they walked out together. I didn't see them at all.

The sun began to set; I started home, but found myself standing below the mill window. I wondered if she sat in it with Flynn. It was dark inside, except for one light from the window; her window. How could a simple empty window play such an important part of my life? I stood just staring up at it as a wave of shock flooded over me; it wasn't empty at all.

I took a couple of steps closer to be sure I was seeing what I thought I was seeing...I stood there frozen, not sure what to do or react...two figures appeared...their bodies embracing in what looked to be a kiss. The woman's face came into view...Iris...I couldn't see the man's face...but was sure it was Flynn. Question answered I thought.

I turned and walked home and disappeared into my bedroom; not speaking to Vivian or Allen. I needed time to think about all of this; to sort it out; it looked like Iris Reed and I were done.

CHAPTER 60

FLYNN

The night of my party I didn't get much sleep. I didn't get to spend much time alone with Iris. I knew Elijah would be back home, and after that point, I didn't know when, or if I would see her again. Mother always seemed to know how to interfere between Iris and me even when she was miles away. Worse, she was coming for a visit, and Iris wouldn't come to the house when she was there.

The next morning, I was anxious to get to the mill to see Iris; but took the time to thank Granny for all she had done the night before.

She hugged me, "Honey, I'm so glad you enjoyed yourself. Iris did most of the work; she's a good girl."

I winked at her, "I love you" as I ran out the door. Arriving at the mill, I grabbed two cups of coffee and headed toward our window. I hoped Iris was there, and she was, "Good morning beautiful."

"Hey," she smiled. I handed her a cup of coffee, and she gave me a biscuit with bacon.

"Thank you again for last night," I said.

She turned her head a little sideways, and smiled, "Oh it was nothing...What did your mother say?"

I paused and shook my head, "She's coming to visit this weekend." The whistle blew. She jumped up finished her coffee and sarcastically replied, "Well, isn't that great news."

As we reached her machine I asked, "Movie tonight baby?"

She nodded, "See you at lunch?"

I leaned in and whispered in her ear, "You know it."

It was a hard day at work that Friday morning; machines broke down and lines were halted on the opposite end of the mill from where Iris worked. By lunchtime, I was exhausted as I made my way to our window for a break. I had forgotten to bring lunch. Thank goodness Iris thought about me; she made us a sandwich, potato salad, and a slice of cake. We ate in silence; both trying to catch our breath. She knew me well, "You've had a rough time today haven't you? ... I heard the other end of the mill isn't running smoothly, and you were saving the day."

"Just doing my job," I answered.

"You look tired; we can go to the movies another night."

I was shaking my head, "No way!"

Iris sat for a minute and then continued, "I'm getting off early today. We're finished with our run; won't have time to start another one. Why don't I go into town and get us some hot dogs from Country's? We'll have a picnic; right here when you get off."

I smiled relieved, "That would be great; you're so sweet..." I wanted to kiss her right there but was afraid we would get into trouble.

My last repair was made; the mill was closed. No one was there but the security guard at the door. I walked through the dimly lit mill and wondered if maybe Iris had changed her mind. I turned the corner coming out of the bathroom from washing up.

In our mill window sat Iris with supper spread out in the middle. We sat cross-legged in the window facing each other as the sun was setting over the river. We talked, laughed, and ate.

We knew we needed to get out of the mill. The guard was ready to lock up and we were both tired. I helped Iris pack everything back into her bag. We stood silently in front of our window looking at the sun almost fully set now. I pulled her close to me and kissed her. Our bodies fit together like puzzle pieces.

Suddenly, Iris jumped back from me, staring out the window. "Elijah?" She whispered; like she was seeing a ghost. I followed her eyes and sure enough there he stood; Elijah Foster was back.

CHAPTER 61

IRIS

I was stunned to see Elijah standing there. It had been almost four months since he had been home. Flynn and I got our work things together and walked out of the mill door. I wasn't sure if he would be waiting for us or not. He wasn't. I was mad at him at this point. I hadn't heard from him in two weeks; he didn't let me know when he was coming home. I didn't know what to think.

Flynn called me a taxi; saying he didn't want me to walk after a long day. The taxi pulled up, and it was Charlie. Flynn opened the car door; I got in and Flynn turned to start home.

I remembered the plans we made for Saturday; I rolled my window down, "Hey Flynn." He turned around, "You still want to meet in town in the morning?"

He answered, "Around ten, ok?"

I nodded, "In front of the studio; remember to wear your green t-shirt?" He laughed and nodded. I gave him a sitting at a photography studio for his birthday. Most people didn't own cameras, so to have your picture made was a big deal. We were excited, but seeing Elijah changed our moods. I know he was worried about him being back; So was I. The ride home was quiet. My thoughts were focused on what the coming weeks would be like with Flynn and Elijah both in the same city.

I knew Daddy wouldn't want either of them coming to the house. He hadn't been the same since Tessa's baby arrived. She wasn't married, and it wasn't acceptable for an unmarried girl to raise a baby. She went back to work at the mill, so mama was left to care for baby, Jeanine.

Daddy thought the answer to this never happening again was to be even stricter than he already was. He didn't want any of us girls to have anything to do with any boys, "They're only after one thing," he would say. My thoughts were scrambled everywhere.

The house was quiet as I opened the front door and made my way to our bedroom. My sisters were all there. I knew Tessa felt bad about Daddy being so hard on all of us, but I didn't blame her.

"Where's the baby?" I asked.

"Asleep, finally," she smiled. Loretta and Ester were listening to the radio I bought for our room.

"Guess who's back home?" Loretta said looking up from her movie magazine.

I shrugged my shoulders, "Why don't you tell me."

Loretta always knew everything that was happening every-where. Ester turned the radio up a little, she knew Daddy was listening more now than ever.

Loretta sat on the side of my bed, "Elijah is home."

I whispered back mocking her, "I know."

"Seriously, Iris what are you going to do?" Ester asked.

"I'll be glad to take Flynn off of your hands," Loretta offered with a smile, "He's so handsome." She always had a crush on Flynn, and I was pretty sure she was half serious.

"I'm not going to do anything tonight," as I got up from my bed. "I'm going to iron my clothes for my studio pictures tomor-row." I pressed my overalls and yellow shirt. The room got quiet again and I noticed my sisters were all asleep.

I slipped into the bathroom for a long soak in the tub hoping it would help me gain a sense of what I needed to do. The more I thought about it the more confused I was. I slipped quietly back into the bedroom. Lying in my bed, I drifted off to sleep still asking myself, how a woman is supposed to choose between two men she loves?

CHAPTER 62

FLYNN

I was glad to be home after work on Friday. My supper with Iris was romantic, but I was shaken by seeing Elijah standing below watching us through the mill window. I knew exactly how that felt and couldn't help but be a little sad about it. I just wanted to take a bath, eat a piece of my chocolate birthday cake, and go to sleep. I did just that.

Saturday morning, I woke up to the ringing of the telephone and Granny's voice, "Ok Naomi ...I will tell him...No, he is not awake. He worked late yesterday. He was bone tired...went straight to bed. Yes, Naomi, I'll tell him." Only my mother would call someone this early on their day off, I thought as I slipped into the kitchen.

She hung up just as I sat down at the table, "I'll call her back later today. Granny, I want to thank you again for my party. I know it was a lot of work." I poured myself a cup of fresh coffee and grabbed a hot biscuit as she took a pan from the oven.

Paw Burton came in and sat at the table with me, "I heard Elijah Foster is home on leave."

I nodded, "Yes Sir." I listened as he gave me advice on how to manage the situation "You are in," secretly I was thinking I needed to get dressed so I could meet Iris at the studio downtown.

Wearing jeans and a green t-shirt, I walked to the photography studio. During my walk, I thought about what I should do now that Elijah was home. Iris and I had rekindle our relationship and I didn't want to mess it up. Seeing her in the distance waiting outside the studio door, I realized why she asked me to wear the clothes I had on. She was dressed exactly the same as the first night I saw her...outside of the movie theater...overalls and a yellow shirt...she remembered what we both were wearing after all this time; that had to mean something.

She smiled, "No matter what happens, when we see these pictures we'll always remember the night we first saw each other." Without a word, she took my hand, the bell on the door rang as we went inside the studio to have our pictures made separately; only married couples had portraits taken together. I waited outside the studio door while she gave them the address to mail the pictures when they were developed. I was nervous. I knew we had a talk coming, and I didn't know what or where it would lead us.

The bell on the door rang; she came outside. We walked together silently along the sidewalk in town, passing stores without stopping.

We ended up in front of Tasty's Café, "You want to get lunch?" I asked as I opened the door for her. Seated we held hands across the table until our burgers were ready. As we ate, I was first to bring it up, "Have you seen him yet?"

Her voice was low, nervous, unlike her, "No, I'm not sure what to say to him." Silence again.

We finished eating, "I tell you what, Iris, let's just spend this day together; just us; not talk about him."

She looked relieved; outside in the warm of the afternoon, we walked toward the other side of town; down Broad Street to the mill. It seemed like we always made our way there when we needed to be together. We sat on our bench below our window. I couldn't help but ask her what she was going to do about Elijah.

She stared straight ahead, "I don't want to hurt him."

"What about me, do you want to hurt me?" I asked her. I was angry; I wanted her to say she chose me; but she didn't. I got up from the bench and began to walk toward the mill.

"Flynn," she cried, "What am I supposed to do?" I kept walking; I was mad at myself for getting in the middle of this.

She caught up with me and grabbed my arm, "Listen, I do love you, but I love him too…just different…"

I didn't want to hear anything she had to say; I circled her waist and pulled her close to me; we kissed. I leaned back on the mill door, "Iris, please…" I stopped knowing what I was about to say wasn't right. We couldn't go any further without the chance of getting into trouble.

I was frustrated, and I knew girls before, but Iris wasn't that way. I wanted to wait until we were married, but I didn't know if that would ever happen. It felt so hopeless, "Iris, I want to do it the right way with you…but I don't know how long I can wait… you need to make your decision."

She nodded, "I know, but please for right now just hold me tight."

I pulled her inside the mill corridor and in the warmth of the July night we became closer than we ever had…I stopped before it went too far, "Iris…you aren't that kind of girl." She looked shaken. We straightened our clothes, and I walked her back to town to get her horse.

I helped her up onto the saddle, "See you tomorrow, church?"

She nodded, "Giddy up." Moses began a soft trot. She looked back to see me standing there watching as she rode off into the sunset. "Damn," I shook my head; "just like in a movie, and I'm the one who loses the girl."

CHAPTER 63
ELIJAH

The image of Iris and Flynn in the mill window was stuck in my mind Friday night. I was sure it was over between us. Vivian and Allen went out for supper leaving me with my thoughts. I made a pot of coffee and cut a slice of apple pie. I remembered the promises we made to each other at that very table before I left for boot camp. Those promises were gone; not broken only by Iris, but by me. The military changed me and honestly I wasn't sure I even knew myself much less Iris.

I hadn't written or called her as much as I could have. I couldn't blame her for doing exactly what I told her to do, but I didn't like seeing it. My mind was settled. I needed to see Iris; talk to her but not tonight or tomorrow. I needed time to think about what to say. I washed my cup and saucer and lay down across my bed. The sleepless night before gave way to a good night's sleep.

Waking up that Saturday morning, I was still confused and hurt about seeing Flynn and Iris the day before. I heard voices in the kitchen. Mama and Daddy were sitting at the table with Vivian and Allen eating breakfast. Their arrival pushed the thoughts of Iris from my head. I decided spending the day with my family was the best thing I could do. Being with them almost took away my worry over what was going to happen between Iris, me, and Flynn…almost.

CHAPTER 64
IRIS

Daddy and Mama were glad I was home; worried I was later than usual. The first thing they asked was if I had seen Elijah.

I boldly declared, "No, I spent the day with Flynn." I was tired of sneaking around and thought out loud, "I'm old enough to make my own decisions; especially about who I am going to eventually marry; Flynn, Elijah, or maybe someone else."

Daddy wasn't happy with my declaration, but he didn't say anything. Mother sat a plate on the table; She hugged me, "Iris be careful…you don't want to end up like your sister…" she whispered. I ate a few bites, cleaned up the mess, and went to my bedroom.

Ester and Loretta were staying at Granny Wilson's that night to help her cook Sunday dinner. Tessa was on the bed with baby Jeanine….it reminded me of the afternoon with Flynn and how close we came to going too far. I loved Tessa, but I didn't want to be in her place with a baby and no husband.

I changed and told Tessa, "I'm going to take a bath."

"You ok?" she asked with genuine concern. I shrugged my shoulders as I closed the bathroom door. Laying back in the bathtub, radio playing, I thought about the decision I needed to make. I didn't know how to choose between these two men. I went over and over the things I liked about both of them. It didn't help. I finally dried off and changed into my nightgown.

As I lay on my bed, Jeanine asleep; I ask Tessa, "What would you do?"

She thought for a minute, "Wait; see who stands the test...It's only a matter of time before Elijah goes back to the base. Flynn will probably be drafted...give it time."

I nodded, I could see her point, and time was all I had. I fell asleep remembering the feelings Flynn and I shared; I had never felt that way about Elijah. My mind was made up...I chose time. I didn't need to decide right away, Tessa was right; time was on my side, or so I thought.

CHAPTER 65
FLYNN

I couldn't believe I stopped things with Iris. I had never been one to stop physical closeness with a girl. It confirmed my feelings for her. I love this girl, and even if she chooses someone else, I would always love her.

When I got home on Saturday, Mother had arrived with news...a notice that I needed to register for the draft. I thought I did before I left Greenville, apparently, I had to wait until I turned seventeen. My mother wanted me to take the bus back with her the next day, Sunday, to register on Monday. I told her I was going to church. I could take care of registering in LaGrange. She wasn't happy but decided to go back alone the next afternoon. I went to bed satisfied with my day; looking forward to seeing Iris on Sunday.

The next morning, I dressed for church. I heard Charlie blowing the taxi horn. He was picking me up to go to the little church where Iris went. Mother was livid that I was going to the same church as the Reeds. I didn't give her time to say much. I grabbed my thermos of coffee and biscuit and was out the front door, "Bye Mother, see you soon."

I filled Charlie in on everything; he was surprised Iris hadn't seen Elijah, "Man that should tell you how she feels about you. She and Elijah were close before he left."

I shook my head, "I don't know; I'm tired of all of it. She has to decide soon, or I will walk." We pulled up in the church parking lot, got out of the car, and made our way inside the church.

Charlie and I sat down on a middle pew. I was looking around for Iris but didn't see her. The choir began to sing... *"Jesus Loves..."* Iris came in and walked down the aisle of the church. My eyes followed her as she passed by us without speaking. She sat down beside her sister, Ester. Ester leaned over and whispered in Iris' ear. She turned and looked back at me and Charlie and smiled. I felt better after she acknowledged we were there.

The preacher stepped up to make announcements; I heard the back doors of the church open. Elijah Foster walked in with Vivian and Allen. They sat down directly across the aisle from us. I could see Elijah looking around, I'm sure to see if Iris was there. He and I had never met. It was awkward seeing the other man. I had respect for him; I had to; he was serving our country.

The preacher did have a message...but...my thoughts were on how to handle things after the service. I knew what I had to do. It was the only thing I could do. We sang, *"Just As I..."* and church was over.

I shook the preacher's hand at the backdoor and started toward Elijah; I could tell Charlie was worried as he followed behind me. Iris started up the aisle; Elijah had left without speaking to her. We were all outside. Elijah was walking toward their truck,

"Elijah," I called his name to get his attention. He turned around and we were eye to eye. I felt the whole congregation standing around us and whispering; I'm sure they thought a fight was about to begin, I held out my hand to shake Elijah's, "Hey man, thought we should at least meet each other. No hard feelings. I'll respect your time with Iris if you'll respect mine."

Elijah shook my hand, "I agree; I will. Thanks." I nodded, and we parted ways. I felt good I handled it like a man and not a young, hot-headed kid.

Charlie patted my back and chuckled, "Flynn you have finally grown up."

Iris walked up and hugged me, "Thank you, I'm going to spend the day with my family. I'll see you tomorrow." I nodded and kissed her on the cheek. I knew Charlie was wondering why I didn't tell Iris I wouldn't be at work the next day.

"I'll be there." I explained to him, "I'm going to the draft office first thing; get this stuff straightened out, and then I'll be at work."

Charlie dropped me off at the house and decided to head home, "To rest up for work."

I nodded, "Me too...after I eat some dinner." Keeping her word, mother left for Greenville without protesting my choices. I hoped it was a sign she realized I was making my own decisions. I did what I told Charlie I was going to do; ate, helped Granny clean up the kitchen; got clothes ready for work the next week, and laid down on my bed to rest. Thinking I should have told Iris I would be coming into work late the next day, I decided to call her.

I didn't call her often; I knew Mr. Reed didn't like boys calling on the telephone, but Iris paid the bill each month. I thought I had a good reason to disturb their Sunday afternoon.

The female voice answering the telephone wasn't Iris, "Hello, Reed house." I nervously asked to speak to her. Loretta on the other end replied, "She's not here." I said thank you and hung up the phone. My imagination got the best of me. I figured she was with Elijah; I soon found out I was right.

CHAPTER 66
ELIJAH

Flynn Fisher approaching me at church Sunday morning caught me off guard. I was glad he did. We agreed to respect each other's time with Iris. I hadn't talked to her; truthfully, I was angered at the entire situation. I didn't want the first time we talked in person to be in a place surrounded by people. I hated my time at home was going to be filled with stuff I thought we had settled before I left. My mind was too overwhelmed with what I was facing after my leave to worry about Iris and the drama of it all.

Surprised when Iris called me that afternoon wanting to see me; I suggested we get together that afternoon. I wasn't sure what we had to talk about, her choice was clear. With hesitation, I told her I would pick her up around two o'clock.

Iris ran out the door as my truck pulled up in front of the Reed's house. She looked pretty as always; her hair had been cut a little shorter; her dark blue dress with flowers reflected the blue in her eyes. My heart began to beat faster as she opened the door and climbed into the truck. It was strange being with her after so much time had passed.

"You look older, wiser," she remarked. "Can I hug you?" she

asked. I leaned over and gave her a quick hug. I drove back down the long driveway in awkward silence. We didn't talk for a while.

As we drove by the local dairy I asked her, "You want a milkshake?" She nodded yes. We both ordered vanilla with whip cream. I smiled thinking about how much we had in common; even milkshakes. Sitting at the curbside waiting for our order, she asked me if I had gotten to see my family.

"Yes, I have. Mom and Dad came up on Saturday." I explained to her, "I got home late Thursday on the bus."

She looked surprised, "Why didn't you call? I would have met you."

I stared at her, wondering if I should tell her the truth. I decided to let her know everything, "I walked to Vivian's; down Jefferson Street by the Burton's. I saw you on the porch with Flynn."

She seemed shocked by what I was saying. "You planned it? You were checking up on me?" she asked.

I answered in a half-angry voice, "Yes, I wanted to see how involved you had become with him," I explained. "I wanted to know where I stood. I guess I found out after I saw you at the mill."

She stopped me before I could say anything else, "What do you know; tell me because I don't know what to do. I still feel the same about you." The waitress brought our order, and we both sat sipping on our shakes.

I was confused, "Tell me how you love two men? We are different as two men could be." Iris offered no answers to my question. I continued, "I have ten days before I report to my next base; I don't want to spend my time worrying about this. I have other stuff on my mind." I cranked the truck, and we rode uptown to the fountain. I looked her directly in her pretty blue eyes "Iris, I'm about to give up on us; are you ok with that?"

In an angry voice, she responded, "I understand the pressure you are under, but it's not easy for me either." We sat silent for a while and then she declared, "I'll tell Flynn I need to spend some time with you while you are home. I'll see him at work, but you come first." silence; then she took my hand, "Tell me what it has been like."

I thought for a minute. What could I tell the beautiful girl who couldn't take the truth about what my life had become? How it has changed me, and how I might not see her for a very long time. "It's ok; hard; but I try to remember why I'm doing it. It started as a way to make our lives easier; but now seeing what is really happening, I'm doing it because they are trying to take our way of life." I stopped for a minute; I could see the look of worry on her face; like it was her fault, "Iris, you aren't the reason I joined; don't stay with me or choose me because of guilt.."

She didn't speak for a while; we started back to her house when she finally said, "How about we have supper together tomorrow night, to catch up, just you and me?" I nodded as we turned into her driveway. I stopped the truck and went around to open the door for her.

She jumped out, "See you tomorrow night?"

I replied, "Yes, I'll pick you up?"

She thought for a minute, "Around 4:30 for an early supper?" I wondered why she wanted to eat at that time, but I agreed, and she ran inside the house. I felt strange; Maybe I didn't know this girl at all. A feeling of sadness spread over my entire body; it was a feeling I was getting a lot when it came to Iris Reed.

CHAPTER 67
IRIS

Seeing Elijah Sunday afternoon was strange; he was a different person; more than thirteen weeks had passed, but neither of us knew if we belonged together or not. Time away from each other had changed us for different reasons; his life in the military; my life with Flynn. I knew I loved him. I wasn't sure what kind of love it was…that was what I hoped to begin to find out at supper the next night.

Telling Flynn about seeing him wasn't going to be easy, but being honest with each of them was the best thing to do. I decided I would tell Flynn at the mill in the morning before our shift began.

I got to work at my usual time and brought a biscuit for me and Flynn. I sat in the mill window waiting for him and the cup of coffee he always brought to me. I was surprisingly calm about telling him I was having supper with Elijah that night. I felt sure he would understand. I waited until it was time for work, but Flynn didn't show up. I was a little worried; he never missed work. By the time the whistle to begin work blew, I looked around for Charlie; he wasn't there either. There was nothing I could do but start work as the looms began to run.

By lunch, Charlie had shown up at the mill; I learned Flynn went to the local draft board to register. I knew he had to do it; I wasn't upset because he went, but I was upset he didn't take the time to let me know. I knew I had no right to be mad; I was going out with another man that night.

Flynn showed up to work after lunch. I saw him standing in the office talking to one of our foremen. Flynn did most of the talking; the foreman walked over to him and patted him on the shoulder. Now I was worried. What was going on? Was he in some sort of trouble?

Flynn came out of the office and walked over to me, "Hey, everything is fine; I'll explain after work. Meet me outside?" I nodded yes.

CHAPTER 68

FLYNN

I know Iris was mad I hadn't told her what was going on that day, but I did try to call her again the night before. Loretta answered, "She isn't home. She had a date with Elijah. She's a popular girl these days…" Loretta giggled, "I'm available, will I do?" I politely declined her offer and hung up. I was a little mad or maybe hurt; though I knew I shouldn't be surprised.

When I finally got to work that morning, Charlie left. He had gotten the same draft notice I did. I wasn't sure what was happening with him, but the news I got at the draft board that day wasn't what I had hoped. I stayed to myself the rest of the day at the mill trying to get caught up and thinking about what I was going to say to Iris. The afternoon went by fast; and before I knew it, I was sitting beside Iris on our bench outside of the mill.

I had noticed Vivian watching us many times, and that day I felt like a thousand eyes and ears had joined her. Usually, I didn't care, but now I knew she was reporting back to Elijah everything she knew, heard, or saw. I didn't like it.

My mood wasn't good as Iris and I sat together. When she let me in on what she did the night before and what her plans were that afternoon, I felt like I was going to explode. I have a hard time hiding my feelings, "I guess it's up to you how you spend your time, but don't expect me to stay here and watch you and him. I can't." I felt like the news I got at the draft board office was something I couldn't share with her. She got up from the bench and walked away. For once, I didn't follow.

She turned around. I could tell when she was mad; fire came from her eyes and the words she spoke were harsh, "You knew this was coming. I told you I still have feelings for him, and I need to find out what they are. I hope you'll be around so I can see you too."

Her words angered me, "Have your cake and eat it too; I'm not sure I can stand it; for God's sake make up your mind. I think you enjoy all of this, two men scrambling for you; well not me."

She didn't speak as she turned to walk away. Stubborn as I was, I got up from the bench and walked in the opposite direction. Her footsteps faded as we moved further from each other.

Iris and I were as far apart from each other as we had ever been and honestly, at that point in time, I felt relieved. I was tired of all the back and forth.

Once again, Iris Reed and I were going to be separated by distance. This time it wasn't my mother; it was the draft board's and Iris Reed's fault.

CHAPTER 69
ELIJAH

I didn't feel like I thought I would seeing Iris alone for the first time. She looked and acted the same, it was me who had changed. My training and time away from LaGrange had turned a 19-year-old boy into a man; it made me look at the future differently. I felt the same for Iris, but I was tired of the back and forth from Flynn to me. It wasn't fair to any one of us.

After our talk at the dairy bar on Sunday, I was angry at her. That afternoon, Vivian filled me in on how Iris was eating lunch with Flynn every day, that part didn't bother me. I knew she was going to see him. We agreed to it. The thing that made me stop and think was where they sat when they were together, the mill window. She never sat with me there. She told me it didn't mean anything to her anymore, now I knew different. Despite everything, I felt more relaxed than I had in months, and as I fell asleep that night, I decided I wasn't going to let Iris spoil it.

The next day I worked around the house until it was time to pick up Iris. I did want to see her, but the excitement I used to feel before was gone. It was replaced with a determination to tell her I was through waiting. She had to choose before I left again. I wouldn't give her the green light to see Flynn or anyone else. I didn't know what her decision would be, but at that point I didn't think Iris Reed was ready for a commitment.

Driving up the driveway to the Reed's house, I hoped Iris would come out to meet me. I spent the day practicing what I was going to say to her, and I wasn't ready to see her entire family.

Normally I would have pulled around the back of the house not to block the driveway. That afternoon I stopped the truck at the end of the front sidewalk as a sign to her I wasn't coming inside. It was 4:30; just as we had planned. I waited. Iris came out of the door looking much like she did after a day at work. I was surprised she hadn't changed clothes; don't get me wrong she was always pretty, but normally she would have taken the time to change before our date. It bothered me, but I decided not to mention it as she climbed inside the truck. I was so deep in my thoughts, I forgot to get out and open the door for her. As she was climbing inside I said, "Sorry, I was daydreaming."

"It's ok," she said, "I just got home, didn't have time to change. Is it ok if we just grab a burger somewhere?"

I nodded, wondering why she was late getting home from work. I asked, "Over time at the mill?"

She was silent for a moment, "No, I was talking to Flynn, telling him I was seeing you tonight."

I stared straight ahead as we drove to town, "How about the Main Street Café?"

She nodded, "Sure, anything you want.."

We rode in the awkward silence that seem to follow us since I had been home. I thought about how quickly things can change in someone's life. It was only a few months ago I felt I knew this town and this girl inside and out; now they both seemed like strangers to me.

I pulled up in front of the cafeteria and parked. Before I could get around to the other side Iris was closing the truck door. I placed my hand on the small of her back to guide her inside the restaurant to a corner booth. Making small talk I asked her about her sister, "How is Tessa and the new baby?"

Iris' voice whispered, "The baby is so cute. Tessa is adjusting; trying to work."

I wondered out loud, "What about the father?"

Iris explained to me, "No one knows who he is but Tessa, Mama, and Daddy."

I nodded, "So he's not going to be in her and the baby's life?"

"No, I don't think so," she continued, "I think he knows about the baby, but he can't be in her life. I'm not sure why."

The waitress appeared at our table, and we both ordered a burger with fries and a shake. I smiled as she told the waitress; "Cheese, tomato, and lettuce…everything else on the side."

For a moment, the old feelings surged; "You want to tell me how you are feeling about all of this?"

She took a deep breath, "I can tell you I'm happy to be here with you; I missed you…I guess I'll always love you and Flynn. I just need to decide which kind of love is best for me."

I didn't speak for a minute; choosing my words carefully, "You know this isn't fair to me, you, or even him? I have a lot going on…I can't tell you where I will eventually be sent, but I need to have things in order, sooner than later."

Iris seemed truly concerned about what I had just said, "Can you tell me anything about what you have been going through?"

There would be no way she could understand what I had experienced; I spoke in general terms, "Very hard days; someone always telling you what to do next; exercises; hours and hours. All of it getting us ready for the next step…"

She reached over and placed her hands over my folded hands, "Are you ok?"

I nodded, hoping she wouldn't question me further, "How about you? You saw Flynn every day at the mill?"

She nodded, "It was hard when you first left…. I felt like someone had died…. not being able to talk to you …Flynn stayed away from me…I was alone."

The waitress set our plates on the table; I watched as Iris built her burger just the way she liked it; took the first bite…. then a fry…a drink from the shake. I smiled watching it play out in my brain; I wondered if Flynn knew her that well. Our eyes met; we busted out in laughter; it was the first time the old us peeked its head out from underneath the change that time had brought to us.

We left the café and began to walk down the sidewalk. The streetlights on each corner lit the way as we walked and talked about how the next weeks of my leave would look; I told her, "If you're going to keep seeing Flynn; I can't sit around and watch it."

She tried to explain, "I plan to spend most of my time alone, with my family and friends. I think being by myself will give me time to make up my mind and both of you time to make up your minds. I know things are different, but I still feel the same about you. That's what I'm sure of right now."

I could feel myself getting a little mad, "How can you say that to me when you just told me you were seeing Flynn?" I shook my head, "This is all crazy......" I stopped talking; trying not to make things worse, "You ready?"

She reached out to take my hand as she tried to change my mood, "Let's go sit on our bench at the fountain, ok?"

I shook my head, "Don't think so, those people are gone.... maybe they'll be back...I don't know...I was so sure of us before I left...but now...I don't know what I feel."

She looked surprised, and I knew Iris well enough to realize she was angry at my words. She said in a prideful voice, "Well, just take me home...I guess."

We rode back to her house in silence; it hadn't gone the way I had hoped. I tried to make small talk on the way back to Mountville, but Iris wasn't interested and ignored my questions with a stare out the window.

I hadn't seen this side of her before, "Iris, listen to me," I said as I turned into her driveway, "I still love you, but I need to protect myself as much as possible, because I don't know what you are going to do...do you understand?"

The truck came to a stop. She leaned over and put her arms around me. We held each other tight...close... she placed her lips softly on mine...and I couldn't help myself. I kissed her to make up for all the times I had missed while I was gone.

She pulled away, "Daddy will kill us." She opened the truck door and started up the steps of the porch. I called her name and she turned back to look at me, "Guess I was wrong," I said. She looked at me with confused eyes. I responded. "Thirteen weeks... and we still don't know. Maybe not knowing is the answer."

CHAPTER 70

IRIS

The rest of that week was quiet. I didn't talk to Elijah or Flynn until that Friday, and I was still as confused as ever. A part of me just wanted to run away from both of them; I wondered if the fact that I couldn't choose meant neither of these men was the one for me; maybe my future husband was still out there.

I came home from my date with Elijah tired and decided I would go to sleep. I slipped into my nightgown and into bed. Tessa and baby Jeanine were both sleeping. Loretta was spending the night with Granny Wilson, and Ester was focused on the latest magazine about movie stars.

Remembering what Grandpa always told me, "Things always look brighter in the morning." As I tried to fall asleep, I hoped Grandpa was right. I laid in bed wondering what Elijah meant when he said, "Maybe me not knowing was the answer," and what Flynn was up to. All was quiet in the Reed house as I finally drifted off to sleep.

Saturday arrived and I felt more optimistic. I smiled thinking my grandpa was right. I had the entire day to myself, no plans with Flynn, no plans with Elijah.

I got up early to help Mama cook breakfast for the family. We all gathered at the big round table built by Grandpa and enjoyed the meal and the time together. It felt like the old days.

After I finished, I got up to help Mama clear the table. She stopped me letting Ester know it was her turn since she didn't help with the cooking, "Iris, you go ahead to town. Your Paw Wilson is coming by to get my list for the grocery store, and you can ride with him if you want to."

Paw and Loretta were coming in the front door as Mama finished her sentence, "Anita, you got any coffee?" That meant he was going to visit for a while.

I decided to walk on to town; it would give me some quiet time to think. I hugged Mama, "I'll be back soon; I need to wash my hair; you want anything?" She shooed me away with her hand, motioning me out the door. I walked to town, thinking it was only about one week before Elijah's leave was ending; I thought about his ultimatum. I knew he was serious, but I didn't like the pressure he was putting on me.

Flynn on the other hand just walked away; something he was good at doing. I pushed the thoughts of both of them out of my head and went about town getting my shopping done; the bank, McClellan's Five and Dime, and Hollywood Clothing. I slipped into a back booth at Tasty's for a quick lunch, a chicken salad sandwich, and coffee. I ate quickly; I wanted to go by Box Bakery and take home some treats for everyone; coffee to go and out the door. I took the shortcut down by the bus station. I wish I hadn't.

Flynn was placing a suitcase in the luggage compartment on the back of the bus.... I crossed the street to the next block as he was stepping on board. The doors closed. I ran up to the bus intending to ask him where he was going. I reached the door and had my fist ready to knock.

"Iris, Iris," I heard a voice calling my name; I turned; it was Elijah. He looked upset.

I turned and ran to meet him, "Elijah, what's wrong?" Before he could speak, the bus started its engine and begin to pull away from the curb.

I looked up to see Flynn opening the bus window, "You just made your choice." He said as he closed the window, and the bus drove off. My heart was about to explode.

CHAPTER 71

FLYNN

For me, it was as plain as the nose on my face that Saturday morning at the bus station. Iris made her choice. She saw me leaving town, and for a minute she was coming to ask where I was going. As she reached the bus, I heard Elijah call her name, and she turned and ran to him. What else was I to think? I had a lot happening those few days before I left to go to Greenville; a notice from the draft board and dealing with Elijah being back in town; to me her actions were a clear choice. She chose him over me.

When I told Charlie I needed to be off on Monday to go downtown, he told me he got a notice too. We planned it so we both could go there on Monday without leaving the mill uncovered in case a line broke down. I would go the first thing that morning; then he could go that afternoon. Charlie promised to meet Iris with her coffee and tell her what was up. He didn't get a chance to do either; the major line at the mill shut down from mechanical problems that morning.

By the time I got to work after lunchtime, he left in a hurry. I had to finish the repairs on the line and clean up all the tools. I was busy, but still made a point to go by and see Iris. I was surprised to find her upset. She hadn't seen Charlie, I whispered I would meet her after work to explain where I had been. She wasn't happy when I commented, "Work had to come first."

By the end of the day, the news from the draft board that morning and the news she had spent the afternoon before with Elijah had dominated my thoughts as I worked. I was ready to push her for an answer to this crazy triangle going on when I sat down on the mill bench. To add fuel to the fire, Vivian was hanging around outside watching us; seemed like everyone wanted to know what Iris was going to do. I could tell she was aggravated; and so was I; not a good combination. "I tried to call you last night," I said, "Thought you were staying home all day."

"I didn't tell you that," she insisted, "but I only went for a short ride with him; not gone more than an hour. I'm seeing him this afternoon; I told you when he came home, I was going to spend time with him."

I accused her of playing a game. Her hot temper flared. I didn't feel like I could explain the reason I would be leaving on Saturday. The rest of the week we only saw each other at work; we spoke but didn't talk. She insisted she needed time away from both of us. I gave it to her.

Maybe by the time I got back, she would listen to me, instead of the gossip at the mill. The gossip like Charlie wasn't working that morning or I had been drafted. Both were untrue; Charlie was at the mill and I had to register for the draft. The notice informed me I had to register after my 17th birthday. When I went to the draft board in LaGrange, they told me I needed to register where my official address was, which was still Greenville.

My mother brought me the letter the weekend she came for my birthday. When I tried to explain to Iris I would be leaving for just a couple of days, she continually cut me off saying, "Please, just give me some time." I didn't push it; I could be just as stubborn as she was. She wanted time so I gave it to her. I figured by the time I returned from Greenville she would be ready to talk.

I tried to call her the morning before I went to the bus station, but she wasn't home. I left a message, but I knew she wouldn't get it. When I heard Iris calling my name at the bus door, I thought I was going to have the chance to let her know where I was headed, and to reassure her I wouldn't be gone but a couple of days. When I let the bus window down to call her name, I saw Iris running away from me to meet Elijah. What was I supposed to think? It was clear to me; She made her choice.

The bus ride seemed longer than usual; I was anxious to get there and try to forget everything going on in LaGrange for a couple of days. I called Iris as soon as I got to Granny Fisher's house; I wanted to tell her what was going on with me and to give her a chance to tell me why she ran to Elijah. I left another message, "Loretta, please have her call me at SC-555 collect."

She promised she would, "I will sweet thing, I promise."

CHAPTER 72
ELIJAH

The only thing predictable about Iris Reed was that come hell or high water she would be in town on Saturday. I knew that. I thought a lot after our time together the day before, and I had some things I needed to make clear to her. I decided to drive downtown that morning to try to find her. I knew her Saturday routine. It was just after noon, so I knew she would most likely be at Hollywood Clothing or Tasty's Café. I drove by Hollywood; not there; by Tasty's; not there. I thought I missed her and started toward home, then I saw Iris knocking on the door of a bus. In my head, I thought she was leaving town. I parked, opened the truck door, and ran toward her.

I called her name, and she turned and ran to me, "What? What?" She asked what was wrong. "Are you leaving town?" I questioned her.

She shook her head, "No, I was trying to talk to someone on the bus." She explained what had happened. I didn't see Flynn get on the bus or hear anyone say anything out a bus window, but Iris did. I could tell she was upset.

What I wanted to say to her would need to wait. I apologized, "Sorry, I swear I thought you were trying to get on the bus."

She smiled, "I would never leave town without telling you; unlike some people." I knew she was talking about him. She turned and watched as the bus pulled away from the curb and disappeared out of sight.

I took her by the elbow; "Where are you headed?"

"I was going home," she answered.

"I'll drive you?" I asked her. She nodded. She gathered her packages from the bench and as we walked toward my truck, I told her the news I had received the day before from my unit commander. I would be traveling to Arkansas in two days. I explained to her how anxious I felt about being further away from home; not just the situation with her; but my family; things were changing; including me and my life.

She slid over beside me in the truck and placed her arm on the seat behind my shoulders. She hugged me lightly, "It'll be alright; how long will you be there?"

I shook my head, "They don't tell you how long you will be anywhere. The orders will tell me, I should be getting a special delivery letter today to give me more information."

She thought for a minute, "The post office is still open; go by and see if it's there. At least you'll know."

I just looked at her and wondered how she always seemed to know what I needed as I turned on Vernon Street toward the post office. I hopped out of the truck; "I'll be right back; thanks."

She smiled, "Hurry before they close."

Inside the post office, I saw the clerk; one of Flynn's friends. He reached over and picked up an envelope, "We were just going to deliver this?"

I nodded, "Thanks, figured I would just pick it up; a little curious about where I will be living next."

Placing the delivery notice out for me to sign, "I get it, good luck; I hope it's still stateside." I reached out my hand to shake his and walked out of the post office with an eight-by-eleven manila envelope that held my future.

CHAPTER 73

IRIS

It was the perfect storm and I walked right into it. I thought Flynn was leaving town. Elijah thought I was leaving town, and all of us made life-changing decisions without knowing the reality of what had happened. I was instantly angry at Flynn. It brought back all the feelings I felt when his mother forced him to leave. My anger at him would later cause me to make a decision I might not have made otherwise.

The bus drove off; nothing I could do about Flynn; Elijah, however, was standing in front of me upset. I needed to find out what was going on with him. He began to tell me he was leaving; he didn't know when or if he would be back...I could hear him still talking but all I could hear was the words, "I'm leaving in two days."

Flynn was already gone; I didn't know if he would ever be back, and now Elijah was leaving, too. I felt lost...as Elijah took me by the elbow and said he would take me home.

Inside the truck, he explained he was expecting mail that would tell him more about his military orders. I convinced him to go by the post office to see if he could pick it up. He walked out of the post office door with a yellow manila envelope with "CONFI-

DENTIAL: Private Elijah Foster" written on the outside. He looked worried as he slid back into the truck seat. We sat silent for what seemed like forever; then he spoke, "Iris, I'm a little scared."

"Just put the envelope down, and let's get out of here" I smiled at him. I couldn't understand what he was going through, but I felt the worry and pain he was feeling.

We stopped at Whatley's Grocery, I hopped out and went inside and bought us a drink, crackers, a chunk of hoop cheese, and an apple. We drove out of town to the river and found a place under an oak tree near the water. Elijah got out a blanket from the truck and spread it on the ground.

We sat for a long time talking about what he wanted to do after the war ended. It was the first time he had mentioned the war; he told me he knew he would be going overseas.

As I peeled and sliced the apple and cheese; he opened the caps on our drinks, "I can't even think of how you must be feeling," as I handed him a slice of each on a cracker. Silence draped over us; neither knowing what to say as we drank our sodas and ate our crackers.

I got up; went to the truck and got the envelope, "You want to open it, or should I?" He pointed to me. I opened it slowly and read the top line, "Arkansas, Replacement Unit Training." He nodded and took the papers from my hands and read "REPORT: August 12, 10:00 A.M. City Bus Station; LaGrange."

"What does all of this mean? What is the training?" I asked.

He took my hand and folded his around mine, "It means my unit is preparing to go overseas to replace soldiers who have been killed or wounded in battle. It means I won't be home for a while. It means I'll be without you, my family, and everything I love." He looked over at me, "I love you Iris,"

It was the first time he had said the words, and my heart filled with emotion for this man who had been so patient, so kind, "I love you too." He took me in his arms and kissed me with every emotion he was feeling. I kissed him back. Our bodies slowly melted into one body and one soul as the sunset over the river. It happened. Elijah and I crossed the line; I was instantly scared. I thought of Flynn; I thought of Tessa.

Elijah looked as scared as I was, "Iris…" he began.

I stopped him, "Please, don't say anything…just take me home." We dressed. I waited in the truck as he folded the blanket. During the drive to my house, no words were spoken between us. I hopped out of the truck and ran inside.

Luckily, it was quiet; Mama and Daddy had already gone to bed. I went straight to my bedroom, grabbed my nightgown, and closed the bathroom door without speaking to Tessa, Ester, or Loretta. Standing in front of the mirror as I undressed, the thought of how hurt Flynn would be if he found out made the guilt of what I had done worse. I turned the radio on and climbed into a hot bath hoping it would wash away what had happened between me and Elijah.

CHAPTER 74

FLYNN

I was tired when I finally got to Granny Fisher's house. I hugged Granny extra hard.

Mother fixed me something to eat while she explained, "Granny is getting older and losing Grandpa Fisher had broken her spirit. She misses him." Mama told me she and Daddy had something to tell me, "He'll be home soon."

I whispered not to upset Granny, "Is something wrong?"

Mama answered, "Just wait."

"Where are Jacob, Jack, and Bobbie?" I asked her.

Mama explained they were with Daddy, "Watching him play baseball; you heard of that new game everybody is playing?" she asked.

I nodded I had; the mill in LaGrange had a team. Just then they all four came busting through the door. It had been a while since I had seen them, but Bobbie's fire-red hair was still the first thing I noticed.

Granny Fisher insisted all three of them take a bath. She reminded the boys, "Let your sister go first; it's nearly her bedtime." With a promise of a snack, the three of them raced to the bathroom.

"Ok, what's going on; I know I have to go to the draft board on Monday, but what else is wrong?" I asked.

Daddy poured a cup of coffee and sat down, "We need your help son." He explained, "Granny needs to rest; three young kids are hard for her. Your Uncle George and Aunt Rachel bought the house next door, and they'll be close to watch after her."

I could tell Granny was relieved and sad at the same time. She had grown closer to all of us, but her health wasn't the best. I understood what Daddy was saying, but I wondered where my family would live after the move.

Daddy got up from the table, "Stay here Naomi, come with me son." I followed him to the driveway. Two trucks were parked there, "We're moving back to LaGrange; it's better for Mama."

I shook my head, "Ok, you need me to help you pack up your truck and drive back to LaGrange?"

"Yes," he continued, "and pack up yours too." He walked over to the newer green truck beside his, "Drive it back to LaGrange."

I was so surprised I couldn't speak. I walked over to Daddy and hugged him, "Yes sir…thanks, Daddy."

"You deserve it son," he hugged me back. Inside the house, I told them all I was going to bed; I picked up the phone to call Iris one more time. I stopped myself knowing it was too late to call the Reed's house and besides, I left her messages, and she didn't call me back. I thought out loud, "I guess she did make her decision."

In bed that night, I went over what had happened at the bus station. I decided it was most likely over with Iris. I was hurt and mad and vowed to myself to never let her know she had broken my heart.

Sunday morning arrived and though I usually went to church, I decided to start packing up everything Mother had marked to move. I would go to the draft board first thing the next day; take care of the problem there, and we would leave on Tuesday to go back to LaGrange.

I thought about calling Iris all that day, but I had left her several messages. She didn't call me back. I was angry and determined she should make the first move.

Daddy and I worked all morning loading his truck; we packed the pieces of furniture they were taking; household stuff; and some of the kid's toys. As we were covering the truck, Joan walked over to the yard.

She immediately hugged me, "So good to see you Flynn." I smiled and hugged her back. She seemed like a breath of fresh air; no drama; no choosing me or another guy; I knew where she was concerned, I was always her first choice. We caught up for a few minutes and decided to get together that night for supper. I watched her cross the street back to her house and wished I felt about her the same way she felt about me.

When mother came home from church she told me, "We are going over to George's new house next door for Sunday dinner. You come on over."

I finished loading the truck and made my way next door. They were seated at the table eating when I got there. I wasn't hungry, but in my family that didn't matter, you still sat at the table.

My mind was all over the place; I wanted to be alone to think. I excused myself and went back to Granny's house. It was quiet, and as I lay on the bed; I fell asleep.

Jacob woke me up, "Flynn." He shook me until I was awake, "Brother, some girl is on the phone."

I jumped up thinking it was Iris; my heart beating as I picked up the receiver, "Hello."

Joan was on the other end of the line, "We still on for tonight?"

I told her I was tired and wondered if we could meet tomorrow after I went to the draft board.

Always agreeable Joan said, "Sure, I understand, you just call me when you get home." I agreed.

My staying home that night and waiting for Iris to call didn't change anything. She apparently had made her decision. By bedtime, I decided I could live my life as a single man and felt I owed Iris nothing.

CHAPTER 75
ELIJAH

I ris wasn't my first, but I knew after that afternoon at the river, I was hers. I had a lot of feelings about it; I was happy, but sad that it happened before she decided who she wanted to be with. Mostly, I was worried about how she felt afterward.

We didn't speak on the way home; the next day at church she wouldn't even look at me. The guilt of what happened consumed me, but I didn't know what I could say to make it right with her. I decided that she needed to come to me to talk; she didn't have long; I was leaving on Tuesday for Arkansas. I would be gone for at least a month.

I thought about what a woman must go through after her first time with a man and decided I needed a plan to show her how serious I felt about us. I knew what I had to do.

CHAPTER 76

IRIS

I didn't sleep much Saturday night. I kept thinking about what Elijah and I had done. Asking myself how I allowed it to get so out of hand. I knew what could happen when two people went too far; Tessa was a constant reminder of it.

I thought about Flynn and how mad and hurt he would be when he found out; especially after we had stopped ourselves from the very same thing just a few days ago.

Yes, I would tell him; it was the right thing to do; but I had no idea how or when; No, I'm not going to tell him; it has nothing to do with him; after he left like he did. At that point in time, I didn't know if he would even be back or not. I was so confused. I reach the conclusion; I would decide what to tell him when and if I ever saw him face to face. Once again Flynn Fisher had disappeared from my life or so I thought.

After Sunday dinner, I decided to call Elijah. We definitely needed to talk.

I went to the phone and saw a note on the table; "Iris," Flynn called; "Call him at this number."

I could tell it was written by Loretta, I went straight to our bedroom, note in hand. "Loretta, why didn't you tell me Flynn called?"

She replied, "You weren't home." Loretta seemed unphased by my being upset, "You were out with another man…and I had a date; so, I left the note. You didn't see it?" She smiled in the usual Loretta style to aggravate me. I wanted to slap her, but instead, I turned and walked out of the room, picked up the phone, and called the number Flynn left.

"Hello." It was Naomi Fisher's voice on the other line; I wouldn't talk to her. I hung up the receiver and called Elijah.

He answered. "Elijah?" I asked.

"Yes Iris, it's me," he said softly.

"Can we talk?" I asked him.

"I'll pick you up in 30 minutes…if that is ok?" he replied.

"Ok," I quickly answered and hung up the phone. I felt embarrassed just talking to him. I washed my face and went to the kitchen to tell Mama I would be back soon. She could always tell when something was bothering one of us, "Iris, you feel ok; is it your time of the month?"

I smiled thinking I wish it were, "I'm fine; no not yet…I'll be back soon…Elijah is leaving for Arkansas on Tuesday. We got some talking to do."

Daddy smiled, "Proud of that boy; serving his country."

I grabbed my purse and walked out to the porch thinking, "If daddy only knew; he would hurt *that boy*."

Elijah pulled up. I ran down the steps and got inside the truck. He smiled, "You ok?"

I thought it was a strange thing to say to a girl afterward, "I'm worried; Elijah what if I am pregnant?"

He didn't speak for a minute, "Look, I would marry you tomorrow; even if it hadn't happened."

I smiled and took his hand, "Thanks, that means a lot to me; I don't want any man to marry me because they have to; I wanted to wait until I was married; now…"

He interrupted me, "Now, nothing…no one knows what happened but me and you, and no one will…got it? No matter if you decide to marry Flynn or someone else." He pulled into the Dairy Bar and ordered two vanilla shakes.

He knew me so well, "I'll know in three weeks if I am pregnant or not…"

He stopped me there, "Iris, I got my orders from Arkansas. I'll be back here around September 9th; with plans to marry you either way." He took out a small black box. He opened it. It held an engagement ring with three small diamonds, "You be wearing this when I get back if you want to marry me? No one knows I bought it; No one…. not even Vivian…this is between you and me. I've had it since Laurel; hoping I could one day give it to you."

I was so touched, but I couldn't make him any promises; he insisted I take the ring as he slipped the box into my dress pocket. I thought what a good person he was, but I wished it hadn't happened. Our shakes came. We decided to drink them on the way back to my house.

I could tell he was worried about me; I tried to reassure him, "I'll be ok; I'm not going to worry until I have to."

He patted the seat beside him; I slid over until our bodies were touching. He put one arm around my shoulders; "We're in this together. Do you want me to tell Vivian before I leave? She will help you if you need it."

I shook my head no, "Please don't tell anyone, Ok?" He nodded. I told him I was just going to take a bath and go to bed.

"I'll call you after you get home tomorrow." He explained, "I have a lot to do; I'll be leaving Tuesday afternoon at two."

I told him I would try to get off in time to be there. Silence filled the truck as we turned into my driveway. He got out and opened the door; "Remember Iris, I love you; you are the only girl I've ever said that to." I went inside feeling a little better knowing he would stand by me no matter what.

CHAPTER 77
FLYNN

After Joan call, I decided laying around doing nothing would be the worst thing I could do. I still hadn't heard anything from Iris, and I was tired of thinking about a girl who obviously was thinking only of herself.

Me and Joan had a good time together, just friends. We ate at Pete's Hotdogs and caught up on what had been going on with each other. I was glad to hear she found someone and was happy. She definitely had moved on from our relationship, and I was secretly jealous because my relationship with Iris seemed to be over.

When I got back home everyone was asleep but mother. She was hanging up the phone after talking to Grandpa Burton.

Mother told me, "He is getting ready to retire from the mill; that means they will move from the house on Jefferson Street." She looked worried, but Grandpa had told her he would talk to her about it more when we got back to LaGrange on Tuesday.

I assured her it would all work out, and we both needed a good night's sleep. Leaving the kitchen, she commented someone called and hung up the phone when she answered, "I think it was Iris."

I was too tired to worry about it. I just wanted to sleep, and I did without one thought of Iris, Elijah, or anyone else.

The next morning, I was up and at the Draft Board when it opened; it was a pretty easy process to register. I filled out the front and back of a little 4x6 card, and I was done.

The officer there talked to me about joining; "If you enlist you get to choose the branch you want to serve; if you're drafted; you go where they put you." He told me, "think about it." He gave me a folder with all the information; he informed me I could enlist there or in LaGrange.

He reminded me I had to be eighteen or get my parents to sign. I took the folder with the papers and brochures about each branch of the military and put them inside my jacket pocket. There was no way my parents would sign for me to join now.

Back at Granny Fisher's, we loaded the back of my new truck, had supper, and said our goodbyes to Uncle George and Aunt Rachel next door. We would leave early the next morning around 9:00; I could tell Granny was sad, but she knew it was best for her and my mother not to live in the same house; two strongminded women together with three small kids was too much for both of them.

Lying in bed that night, I pulled out the brochures I got at the draft board and read about each branch. I learned when I turned 18 I would most likely be drafted, especially if the war hadn't ended. If I had to go, I wanted to pick where I would serve myself. I decided that night I wanted to join; the only way I would wait would be to marry Iris. I was pretty sure that wasn't going to happen. I convinced myself going into the military would be the best way to start my life over without her.

The next morning, we ate breakfast and loaded everyone in a truck. Me driving with Jack and Jacob; Daddy driving with Mother and Bobbie. We were on the road by 9:30 for the three-hour trip to LaGrange. Pulling out of the driveway, I saw Joan standing in her front yard, waving bye. I rolled down the window and yelled, "Bye Girl…take care…call if you can."

Jacob nudged me in the side, "She likes you; boyfriend or no boyfriend."

I winked at him, "You think so…" We both laughed.

The drive back to LaGrange was kind of fun. The whole family together; listening to the radio, stopping at a rest stop for a picnic mother had made. It went by quickly and by 1:45 I was pulling into LaGrange's city limits; down Highway 29; turning on Church Street by the bus station. My thoughts flashed back to the picture of Iris running to Elijah the day I left.

I heard Jack calling, "Flynn…Flynn…" I followed his pointed finger and what I saw chilled me to the bone. Iris hugging Elijah. I pulled my truck over, and Jack, Jacob, and me watched Iris kiss him on the cheek and walk him to the door. Elijah dressed in his uniform disappeared stepping onto a bus. Iris stood waving until it was out of sight. She turned and walked down Bull Street. I hadn't heard from her for five days. The small thread of hope I had for a future with Iris disappeared.

CHAPTER 78
ELIJAH

I wasn't thinking much about the military on my ride to Arkansas. I didn't like leaving Iris when she was so worried. I wanted to marry her the first time I saw her at the house on Troup Street. I bought the engagement ring soon after without telling anyone afraid they would think I was crazy. I was worried she thought she would have to marry me, but I didn't care. I knew I could make her happy.

I had no idea what the new base in Arkansas held for my unit now that the war had ramped up. The 15-hour bus ride gave me plenty of time to think about all of it. For the first time, I felt like my life was out of my hands. The military and Iris Reed were in full control of what my future would be.

We arrived at the camp after dark; all military units seemed to be the same, except for the barracks. The difference here was the roofs of each building were made of canvas, and whatever weather was outside was somewhat inside too. We unloaded our duffel bags, found our bunks, and slept in complete exhaustion.

Over the next four weeks, our days were filled with much the same as they had been. Still, it was hard. I knew the key was to lay low, follow the rules, and try not to make mistakes that would land me or my unit on extra duty or worse.

After the first two weeks, we were informed we would be trained in an additional duty. I was assigned to the armor division. That meant I would become an expert in everything tanks. I have to admit I was kind of excited about learning to operate a vehicle that large. From that point on, I spent my days learning to drive over the rough, wooded terrain at the camp, learning the mechanics, and concentrating on how and when to use the escape hatch. When I wasn't training on the tank; I was training with weapons and survival techniques. It was pretty clear they were getting us ready to go overseas, and it was weighing on my mind.

Unlike the bases we were stationed at before, we did have some free time. While a lot of the guys went to dances organized by the camp, I stayed at the barracks to write to Iris or call her when allowed. She was on my mind; always wondering... is she wearing my ring?

The few times I called her, I made it a point to never questioned her about how she felt. I left it to her to tell me what she felt comfortable talking about, besides, I didn't want her to think I cared if she was expecting or not. I wanted to marry her either way. I was pretty sure she would have told me if she wasn't. I could do the math; I had been gone three weeks; it had been about four weeks since we had...well, anyway I figured she hadn't started her cycle or she would have said something. I wanted her to know I felt bad she was going through all of this without me. My letters were clear; she was my girl; my family; either way. I wanted her to marry me for no other reason other than she loved me.

CHAPTER 79
IRIS

Loving Elijah was never a question for me. I loved him, but I loved Flynn, too. The question for me was more about which one I could see myself living without. The fact that Elijah and I had gone "all the way" had nothing to do with the decision I needed to make. I knew this all had to stop. I had to as Grandpa would say, "quit straddling the fence, jump one way or the other."

I heard Flynn was back in town, but I hadn't seen him. Once again, he didn't come to see me. I felt like I was reliving the same thing with him over and over. I knew he was mad about what happened at the bus station, but he didn't tell me he was leaving. Would I ever be able to depend on him?

It was hard for me to let Flynn go. He was my first love. He had a part of my heart no one else could ever have. If Mrs. Fisher hadn't interfered, he and I would still be together. I would have never dated Elijah.

Elijah on the other hand always seemed to be there when I needed him. The love I felt for them was very different but very real. My heart had found a place to hold the love for each of them.

Letting one of them go would mean my heart would never be filled; always half empty.

I knew the day at the backwater changed everything. I hadn't started my cycle. I looked at Tessa with new eyes and was feeling some of what I imagined she had gone through. I was struggling to make a decision about Elijah; I didn't want him to marry me because he felt obligated.

I knew I needed to tell Flynn what happened. It wasn't fair to anyone not to tell him, but he had to come to me. He's the one who left.

Flynn was back at work that Wednesday. I heard he was steering clear from the end of the mill where I worked. Rumors about him and Charlie were all over the mill. I knew for sure Charlie had been drafted. I heard the same thing about Flynn. It was hard to believe he wouldn't have told me something that important, but when he was mad, he was very stubborn.

Unfortunately, I was the same way. I knew sooner or later we would run into each other at the mill. It was later. Charlie turned in his notice to leave for basic training that Friday. It was his last day at the mill; a going-away party was happening that afternoon. I thought there would be no way Flynn would miss it, but he did.

Charlie said, "He's hurt, Iris. He told me you made your choice, and it wasn't him."

I smiled and decided not to bore Charlie with any details, "I'll miss you, Charlie. Keep in touch, I'll be there to see you off on Friday." I hugged him.

As he hugged me back, he whispered, "Iris, these two men will probably be fighting overseas before long; they don't need a broken heart to weigh them down. Get it done, one way or another."

I smiled nodding my head in agreement. It sounded so easy, but my heart was torn between the two men I love.

Charlie left on Friday; the bus station was crowded. I saw Flynn immediately. Surprisingly, his family was with him. Jack saw me and darted to me from the other side of the bus station. I hugged him.

Flynn made his way over to us. "Jack, Mother said to get back over there with her," Flynn said staring at me the entire time. He took Jack by the arm and turned to walk away.

I spoke without thinking, "Can I talk to you…tomorrow?"

He nodded, "I have to work. I'll let you in the door at 11:00?"

I nodded and he disappeared into the crowd of cheering people waving goodbye to another busload of our young men leaving home to fight a war that seemed to never end.

CHAPTER 80
FLYNN

So much had happened since we move back to LaGrange; Pa Burton retired from the mill. With money saved over the years, they bought a little house on DeGroat Street and were packing up to move out of the mill-owned house on Jefferson Street.

My mama and daddy bought five acres, on the outskirts of town near the backwaters. My daddy said, "It was time they settled down in a place of their own." We had already started clearing a place to build a small house for them to live in while they built a bigger one.

I was trying to convince them to let me join the military. I decided being on a ship would be best for me. I wanted to see the world, and serve my country, but mostly get as far away from Iris Reed as I possibly could. I was convinced she was playing with my heart, and I couldn't take it any longer. The only problem was I was still crazy about her.

Saying goodbye to Charlie was hard; he was my best buddy. I hoped to see him again after his basic training, but wasn't sure when that would be. The fact was none of us knew what was going to happen.

Since the war, working at the mill changed. Mills in general had a shortage of men to work in them. With more women working and fewer machines running, I was able to keep up with the loom maintenance and the repairs needed by working on Saturdays. It gave me extra money to help my family get settled.

When Iris asked if she could talk to me on Saturday, I wasn't sure I was ready to have a conversation with her. I had avoided her since coming back from Greenville. I told her to come to the mill, secretly I hoped she wouldn't show up. I was afraid of what I would say; I was still hurt and angry; not a good combination for me.

I waited by the locked door of the mill to let her inside. I saw her sitting on the bench she had always called ours. I whistled to get her attention, "Iris, are you coming inside?"

She got up and walked slowly over to the door; I closed it behind her.

"It's strange in here without the looms running," she said as she walked in the direction of the mill window and sat down.

I stood, "No need to drag this out; say what you need to say." She didn't look well, "Are you sick?"

She replied, "Just nerves, I guess." She dropped her head, avoiding looking into my eyes.

I spoke next, "Look, I know you're here to tell me it's over. I already know it."

Still, she wouldn't look me in the face; she stared out the window and talked about how she would sit and watch me walk by it in the mornings on my way to school, "Seems like an eternity ago. I'm not sure what happened to those people…" she paused for a minute. I didn't know how to talk to her; what she was thinking.

She continued "I thought your mother made you go back to Greenville; I didn't think you were coming back."

I saw no need in trying to explain that I had left her a message, or I tried to call; she knew it. "I don't think we have anything to say to each other," I turned to walk away, "I saw you choose between me and him at the bus station."

She stood up and called my name. I turned around; she was perfectly framed by the arch of the window, "I'm going to marry him; I'm sorry; I have to...I mean I want to" she changed her words.

"You have to?" I asked... "You are preg..." before I could finish my sentence, she grabbed her pocketbook; ran past me and out the mill door. It was really over; she had slept with him. I could never forgive her. In my head, I was mad as hell, but in my heart, I was a broken man.

CHAPTER 81

ELIJAH

I wrote to Iris on the first day of September to tell her I would be taking a bus home on the ninth for three days. Three days didn't seem like a long time, but those days would determine my future. I wasn't sure what Iris was thinking or if she was seeing Flynn; but I didn't think so; her last letter was short and to the point.

Dear Elijah,

Hope you are doing good. I'm not feeling so hot; thinking I will feel better in about eight months. HA! HA! Will be glad when you come home.

Love, Iris

I didn't know if she had been to the doctor or was basing everything on her cycle. I tried to push it to the back of my mind and concentrate on the survival training I was going through. At this point, we were all pretty sure we would be shipped out within the next year if the war didn't end.

The only good thing about being so busy was the time went by fast and before I knew it, I was on a bus on my way back to LaGrange. I thought about the letter Iris had written making a joke about eight months. Even though I desperately wanted a family, I hoped she wasn't pregnant. I wanted her to marry me because she wanted to, not because she felt like she had to.

I arrived late in the day on Saturday and went straight home. As usual, Vivian was glad to see me, but she also looked concerned, "What's going on with Iris; she isn't well. Do you know what's wrong?"

I sat for a moment, "I do, but I have to talk to her before I tell you the whole story. I'm beat. Can we talk in the morning?"

She hugged me, "Of course, but Iris isn't sick, is she?"

I shook my head, "I don't think so."

I slept that night from pure exhaustion. The next morning, I woke up before sunrise, I got dressed and was drinking a cup of coffee when the phone rang.

I hurried to pick it up; "Hello."

The voice on the other line spoke softly, "Elijah?"

"Iris?" I answered, "Is that you?"

"Yes, are you coming to church today?" She spoke in a worried voice.

"Yes, I am. You want me to pick you up?" I asked her.

"Yes soon?" she replied.

"I'll be there in 20 minutes," I assured her as I grabbed my keys and coffee.

As I drove up the driveway, I could see Iris standing on the front porch. I smiled and thought, as beautiful as ever. She hopped into the truck, bible in hand, and hugged me for a long time, "I'm so glad you're here," as she held out her left hand with my engagement ring on it.

I had to ask, "You're pregnant? I don't want you to marry me; just because of...."

I stopped when I saw the look on her face, "That's not the reason; I might be going to have a baby, I don't know, but I need you. I want to be with you for good."

My heart jumped out of my chest. I pulled over on the side of the road, "Give me the ring, please." She looked confused as she carefully removed it from her finger. I thought she would cry.

Out of the truck, I walked around to her side. I opened her

door and down on one knee, "Iris, I have loved you since the first day I saw you under that big oak tree on Troup Street. Will you marry me tomorrow?"

She began to cry, "Yes, of course I will."

I carefully placed the ring on her finger, "Promise you will never take it off?" She nodded.

We walked into church that day together. At the end of the service, we announced to everyone there we were getting married the next day. I walked right up to Mr. Reed, "Sir, may I have your daughter's hand in marriage? I know it is quick, but I most likely will be shipping out overseas soon. I want to make sure she is taken care of forever. I love her sir."

To my surprise, Mr. Reed said I could marry her with his blessings.

Iris and I spent the afternoon together at the kitchen table at Vivian's planning the small ceremony and our future. Afterward, we sat on our bench in front of the fountain spurting out red, white, and blue waters. It was a perfect day...

CHAPTER 82
IRIS

I felt some sense of relief. I was happy, but inside I felt a deep sadness of loss for the part of my heart that belonged to Flynn. I was sure he heard about us getting married; news like that traveled quickly around LaGrange. It was the one thing I didn't like about our little town.

After Elijah drove me home Sunday night, I had a lot to do. I had bought a new dress, hoping we would get married while he was home. It was light pink; his favorite color on me. I thought about a white dress, but decided against it, not because of the reason you may think. In my heart, I thought white was meant for pure love and that love had belonged to Flynn.

Nanny Wilson was making me a bouquet and Mama and Vivian talked after church and were going to prepare a meal for everyone after we were married. Daddy, who was sharecropping for the sheriff, called and asked if he would arrange a time with the local Justice of the Peace for us on Monday. Everyone insisted Elijah and I couldn't see each other until then.

I took a long bath and talked with Mama about what Elijah and I decided that afternoon. We both saved money, and were going to open a bank account together. I would stay at home for a while if it was ok, until we could find the right place for us. I would move in there and get the house ready for when he came back home. Mama sounded relieved I wasn't going to move to the town where he would be stationed.

I told her we thought he would be going overseas soon and he wanted me close to family.

She hugged me, "Iris, being married is hard, but I think Elijah will be a good husband." She said goodnight satisfied that her oldest was ready to be married.

The next morning, the phone rang. Thinking it was Elijah, I ran to answer it, "Hello?"

"I wanted to wish you congratulations," it was Flynn's voice.

A chill ran up my back, "Thank you…Flynn, I want…" The receiver went dead.

He had hung up. I sat down on the nearest chair at the table and cried for what was lost between two young people truly in love.

I thought about me and Elijah and our life together. If anyone asked me that day, I could honestly tell them I loved Elijah, but I still loved Flynn too, and suspected I always would.

The marriage ceremony didn't last long. It was hard to believe ten minutes were supposed to change who you were, your name and all. Elijah looked handsome, wearing his uniform. I wore the pink lace dress; he said, "You look beautiful." Not many people were there, his family, my family, and a few close friends.

Afterwards, we all gathered at Vivian's house. Elijah was anxious to spend time with everyone thinking he may not see them again for a while. It was a happy time. Elijah looked over the moon proud of his new wife.

After an hour or so, he announced to everyone, "My bride and I are leaving now for our one night together…in peace, I hope." Everyone laughed. His good-byes to some were for the last time; he was leaving to go back to camp on the 2:00 bus the next day.

We ran to his truck, rice filling the air, mama handing me a picnic basket, and an overnight case. We pulled off, cans rattling behind us. We looked at each other and smiled.

The ride over to Ridley Avenue to The Colonial Hotel was silent. I lay my head over on Elijah's shoulder and drifted off to sleep. I felt the truck come to a stop. Elijah scooped me up in his arms and carried me over the threshold of the honeymoon suite. He laid me softly over on the bed and went back downstairs to park the truck and bring in our things. He looked exhausted as he sat everything down and lay beside me on the bed, both of us fully dressed fell asleep in each other's arms.

CHAPTER 83

FLYNN

After the news of Iris and Elijah's wedding, I couldn't stay in LaGrange. Back at the Jefferson Street house, they looked as if they saw ghost when I walked into the room. I was so broken I couldn't speak. I lay the folder with the paper from the draft board, permitting me to join the military open on the kitchen table.

Mama shooed the children out of the room, but they all knew; even Bobbie, "It's ok brother." She declared her love for me as Mama took her to the other room.

I spoke first, "Daddy, I can't stay here; please just sign this. I'm going to Macon to enlist, before I leave I'll come back to help you build the homestead."

Daddy was almost as disappointed as me, he loved Iris and always thought we were right for each other. Grandpa sat silent at the end of the table; Granny was making coffee.

Silence draped the kitchen; waiting to see what Daddy would do. He picked up the pen and signed the paper. I just couldn't hold my hurt inside any longer and broke down in his arms, "Thank you Daddy."

I calmed myself and drank a cup of coffee. Grandpa told us Mr. Clyborne agreed to let the family stay there as long as needed. I was relieved Mama and Daddy had a place until they could get something built on their new property.

Grandpa said, "Flynn don't you worry about the mill; I'll call them in the morning to let them know you'll be on military leave." I nodded.

I packed a bag for the trip the next day making sure I had all the paperwork I needed to enlist as soon as I got there. I couldn't sleep. Thoughts of Elijah and Iris sharing the same bed was too much. I was up and down all night.

Mama was too, "Flynn, you know I'm against you joining the military; but I understand. I told you she was trouble honey." I know the words were meant to help me, but they only made things worse.

The next morning, I was up and ready to leave by 7:00. Daddy wanted me to take the bus; it would be safer, but I insisted the truck was better. It would be cheaper, and that meant more money to help them. I loaded up my bags, grabbed the thermos of coffee Granny had poured, the lunch pail she had prepared and was on the road. I was relieved everyone else was still asleep. I hated goodbyes.

I drove slowly through town; it was still quiet; too early for the hustle and bustle a Tuesday morning usually held. I traveled down Main Street to Ridley Street to hit Hwy 29 to Macon. Passing the Colonial Hotel, I noticed Elijah's truck parked with cans tied to the back bumper and "Just Married" on the back window.

I pulled over next to the curb; opened my door and was sick. I closed my eyes and pulled myself together, "She is nothing special, man…forget her." I repeated those words I cannot tell you how many times on the two-hour drive to Macon. I wondered why I couldn't make myself believe them.

I arrived at the recruiting office, walked in, and lay the signed parent permission paper in front of the officer. He smiled and pulled out the necessary paperwork for me to sign-up. It took only twelve minutes for me to give the next four years of my life to the military.

I was told to report the next day for the induction process. Mother wouldn't be happy, but I was. Strangely enough, I felt like I paid Iris back for everything she had done to me. I would be as far away from her as I could be. Surely, I could forget her then.

CHAPTER 84
ELIJAH

I woke up early Tuesday morning; it took me a minute to remember where I was; next to me Iris was sleeping soundly; I remembered I was a married man. I smiled; I liked the sound of it. We didn't consummate our marriage, still I felt closer to her than I had ever felt to anyone in my life.

I reached over quietly to get my watch from the nightstand. I checked the time; 5:30 AM. I noticed Iris and I were both still fully dressed. I chuckled; that will be something to tell our children as I thought of the little one growing inside of her. I made my way to the bathroom, showered, and dressed. I called for room service to be delivered at 9:00. I ordered all of her favorites; I knew she had not eaten much the day before.

I opened the door to go get us a cup of coffee. A tray with a pot left by room service was there; with a note that read, "To the happy couple, love Vivian and Allen." I tucked the note in my pocket as I sat the tray on the small table beside the window. I poured myself a cup. Looking at Iris sleeping soundly, I thought of the years to come, and how happy we would be together.

Iris was awake by seven; I was glad, I was getting in my head way too much and she always brought me back to reality; "Good morning wife."

"Good morning, what time is it?" she asked.

"It's 7:30; breakfast will be here at 9:00. Are you hungry?" I went over to the bed and sat beside her. I could see she wasn't feeling well, "Are you ok? Morning sickness?"

She smiled, "I hope so."

I nodded, "You want to wash up so you can eat something? We'll have a couple of hours together before I have to be at the bus station."

I stood up and held out my hand to help her up from the bed; I held her close as she leaned her body against mine, "You keep that up, and we aren't going to have time for breakfast."

I smiled at her; she excused herself to go to the bathroom.

As she turned to walk away, I noticed the back of her clothes were soaked with blood. Dread filled my heart. I didn't say anything to Iris; I thought it might embarrass her.

CHAPTER 85
IRIS

Waking up something didn't feel right; I thought it was morning sickness. I headed to the bathroom to shower and change into my new gown for breakfast. I noticed the red stains of blood; I didn't know what to think...I thought I was having a miscarriage and called out to Elijah, "Please come in here."

Inside the bathroom; he just held me, "I know. I saw it...You think you need to go to the hospital?"

I shook my head, "No, a shower, clean clothes, and to eat breakfast with you is what I need. I feel ok, right now"

He nodded, "Ok, but I'm sitting here until you get out of the shower." I hugged him, "How do you put up with me?"

He smiled, "Easy, you're my girl." I showered and rushed him out just as someone was knocking on the door. I dressed in the new nightgown I bought for my wedding night; I noticed a tinge of blood. Alone in the bathroom; I was worried; and wondered, "Is this what a miscarriage feels like?"

I decided I would go to the doctor after Elijah left. This morning I was going to try making it as special as I could for us. Out of the bathroom; he had ordered all my favorites; I sat at the round table, and we had our first breakfast together as husband and wife. I explained "I don't think we will be able," trying to apologize for the lack of physical…

He stopped me, "Iris, I know…we'll be together when we figure out what is going on with you. That's what I'm worried about."

We finished breakfast and lay together on the bed; making plans for me to come to Arkansas for a real honeymoon. Hopefully, we would have time before he was shipped overseas.

CHAPTER 86
FLYNN

The trip to enlist and back to LaGrange was tiring; I had to tell my family I would be catching a bus back to Macon the next day for my induction. I didn't know when I would be coming home again. My time in the service would begin immediately. I was a little scared. I was just a seventeen-year-old kid with a broken heart.

We arrived back into town just in time to see a bus with a sign on it that said "Arkansas" pull out of the bus station. Iris was standing there with his family as it left. I turned in the opposite direction down Broad Street and over to the house on Jefferson.

Inside, Mother was busy packing; Daddy was out at the new homestead working to build a small one-room house for them to move into. I hated to tell him I wouldn't be around to help him finish it. I decided to wait until supper when I would only need to say it one time.

I went directly to the bathroom, took a shower, and began packing what few personal items I was instructed to take with me the next day. They didn't fill the small duffel bag I had pulled from underneath my bed.

Walking outside I joined in a game of horseshoes with Jacob and Jack.

Bobbie was on the tire swing and ran to me as soon as she saw me, "Can I play brother?"

"Sure-thing sis," I said winking at the boys. A lump formed in my throat as I thought about not seeing them every day.

Sitting at the supper table, it was time for me to tell them all my news, "I did get to sign up today." Everyone stopped eating and looked at me, "I'll be leaving tomorrow, back to Macon. Then I'm not sure where, but I'll call you or write to you as soon as I can."

Daddy didn't seem surprised, "What time tomorrow do you leave?"

Mother was surprisingly calm, "Son, I can't believe you are leaving because of Iris."

My daddy interrupted, "Naomi, be quiet; that's over; we don't need to talk about it. He was going to get drafted anyway."

Paw Burton was glad I joined to serve our country; Granny Burton just hugged me, "Everybody eat now; let's enjoy our time together."

We had a good night; I talked to Daddy about the family's move, "I'll send as much money as I can home; maybe you could hire someone to help."

He told me not to worry about home, "We're ok; you worry about you."

I was touched by Daddy's show of concern. It was unusual for him to show emotion; caused by being married to my mother who could be critical.

The next morning, I got up, showered, dressed, and went to the kitchen. I told Mother the night before not to make a big deal out of me leaving. She promised it would just be family seeing me off the next day. She made me a care package; letter paper, envelopes with stamps, my favorite peanut butter fudge, and a box of change to call home.

I knew this was hard for her. She did what she had thought was best for me. I was finished blaming her for everything wrong in my life. I was on my own now, and I was going to grow up in ways I never dreamed.

I decided to go by the mill before I met the family at the bus station. I wanted to tell my supervisor to please give my last paychecks to daddy. While I was there, I took a piece of paper and scribbled a note to Iris, and left it in a secret place inside the mill window.

It was noon. I was ready. I arrived to catch the bus and found my mother and daddy, my brothers and sister. I hugged all of them and told them I would call or write as soon as I could. Mother kept saying to send the address where she could write. I nodded. I kept looking around for Iris. I didn't see her. I thought about calling her; then I remembered she was not Iris Reed; she was Iris Foster. I felt sick and just wanted to get as far from her as I could. I was relieved she didn't show up.

The bus was loading; I was instructed to put my bag in the back and the recruitment officer announced, "Final warning to report." I opened the double doors that led to the bus to see Iris standing there. I looked around for Elijah; he was nowhere in sight. I was confused and hurt; surely, she knew she was the last person I wanted to see. I started past her as if I didn't see her standing there and noticed Mr. Reed standing off to the side. My family saw what was happening and made their way to the door.

I heard Iris's voice, "Flynn?"

I turned and faced her, "Why would you show up here; today of all times?"

She stepped toward me, "I just wanted to tell you goodbye; let you know I do care about what happens to you."

I nodded as I struggled with what I should say to her, "Thanks, I guess."

She stepped towards me to hug me; I stepped back just as her daddy stormed up screaming, "She's a married woman, don't touch her."

My parents started towards us and stopped as I held my hand up for them not to come any closer. I walked over to Mother and Daddy; hugged them, my two brothers, and Bobbie. I rushed onto the bus to my assigned seat in the back near a window. My eyes surveyed the crowd; I didn't see Iris.

The bus pulled away from the curb and started down Bull Street; people lined the sidewalk waving goodbye. As the bus turned onto Main Street, Iris was standing on the corner; her eyes shielded from the sunshine by her hand. She saw me; I saw her. The bus stopped at the red light. I was clutching the seat so I would not jump off the bus to ask her what the hell she was trying to do to me. She stepped toward the bus. My window was down; I could hear her voice, "It wasn't because I don't love you."

I spoke with the cruel truth, "You think that helps?" I pulled the window up and turned away from her.

CHAPTER 87

ELIJAH

Iris kept telling me how sorry she was our wedding night was "not what it should be." I kept assuring her I understood. I insisted she go to the hospital or doctor as soon as she could. We shared some special time. I knew from that day forward I would always come first with her, but I also knew a part of her still loved Flynn. You don't just turn those feelings off and on like a faucet.

I explained I wouldn't get to come home for a while, but maybe she could come to Arkansas; she agreed. The morning passed quickly; it was time for me to be at the bus station. Iris dressed; I called Vivian and asked if they would come to the station to drive Iris home after I left. I explained, "She doesn't need to be driving; she is feeling sick."

I packed up our things and loaded the truck. Iris asked the desk clerk to take a picture of us. We walked out of the hotel hand in hand...happy.

We got to the bus station just in time; I gave her the keys to my truck, "You get it when you feel better; I don't want you walking everywhere." She hugged me; I kissed her softly and whispered, "You're my girl, Mrs. Foster."

She smiled and told me not to worry, "I'll let you know what the doctor says; I'm ok. You take care of yourself."

I stepped onto the bus and just that quick, once again I was leaving my family; my wife; with no idea when I would see them again.

CHAPTER 88

IRIS

I felt like I had cheated Elijah out of a honeymoon; we didn't have but one night together and I had been sick. I wondered if it was caused by stress or nerves. I felt fine. The bleeding had all but stopped by the time we left the hotel; just a little spotting, but I had terrible pain in my stomach. I hoped it was nothing; I didn't want to lose the baby. We walked hand in hand inside the bus station; I had grown to hate the sight of buses; it seemed they were always taking someone I loved away from me.

Elijah's bus wasn't ready; we made our way inside the station to find a seat; Vivian and Allen were there. Elijah was talking to them as I excused myself to go to the restroom. I checked to see if I was spotting; it had gotten worse. I was getting worried, but I couldn't tell Elijah. He had enough on his mind; no need to give him one more thing to worry about. I washed my face and came out of the bathroom.

The bus was getting ready to load; I found Elijah putting his duffle bag in the luggage compartment. He came over to me; he was anxious and didn't want to leave. He was reminding me of all the things I needed to do; the account at the bank; add his name;

find a place to live for me and the baby, "Iris, please go get checked out; make sure you are ok. If anything happened to you or our baby…"

The bus driver called, "last call."

We walked over to the bus door and at that moment I didn't care who saw us, I kissed him like a wife kisses her husband when she doesn't know how long it'll be before she will be able to kiss him again. We hugged, and he disappeared onto the bus. I followed him as he found a seat and lowered the window, "I'll call you as soon as I can."

"I'll be waiting," I shouted as the bus pulled away from the curb and disappeared.

Vivian was standing waiting for me over at the Military Bulletin Board, staring up at the list of the recruits leaving, "Did you know this?" She pointed to Flynn's name listed under new recruits leaving for service the next day.

I shook my head, "No why would I?" I was shocked and hurt; he hadn't told me. I had no right to feel either.

I told Vivian I was all right to drive home on my own; she asked if I was sure. "I'm going straight home to rest," I promised her, "Let me drop you off first." I knew that would give me the perfect opportunity to drive by Flynn's house. I dropped Vivian off and rode slowly back up to Jefferson Street past the Burton's house. I didn't see anyone.

At home, I dodged questions about my wedding night. I took a bath and decided to call to report off work the next day. I needed to do two things; find out if I lost the baby and go to the bus station to see Flynn off. I wanted him to know I still cared for him and would be praying for his safe return. I told myself it was ok, but sure Elijah wouldn't approve. I was so tired; I hoped a good night's sleep would make me feel better the next day; the bleeding would be stopped, and the pain gone. The next morning I did feel better, but the bleeding was still there; I washed and dressed quickly; I called the mill, grabbed a cup of coffee, and headed to Dr. Hammond's office.

I spoke to the nurse first. I told her I was about five weeks pregnant and was bleeding with cramping. She took me back to the examination room; I put on the gown she gave me and sat on the chair. The doctor came in afterwards. He asked me the usual questions doctors ask; how long; how many; I answered. He examined me and asked the nurse to take blood and get a sample when I used the restroom. She did both, and I waited.

The doctor delivered the results of the test. I was shocked by the news; a little sad; a little afraid; but a lot happy. I left the doctor's office feeling much better about my life; happy to be married and couldn't wait until Elijah called.

Flynn's bus wasn't leaving until two; I had time to do some errands. The bank first; deposited the money Elijah gave me and added his name; grabbed a quick lunch and coffee to go.

I walked over to the bus station. I was worried how Flynn may react to me being there but, I felt I owed it to him to tell him bye and help him to understand.

I saw him as he came out the door; no one was with him. He walked right by me as if I wasn't there. I called his name, and walked over to him, "I wanted to tell you goodbye; you didn't tell me..." He didn't speak. I moved toward him; He stepped back away from me at the sight of his family coming out the door. Before he could say anything, my daddy appeared hollering like a crazy man. I looked at Daddy and shook my head. I walked away.

A few blocks down the street, I waited for the bus to pass; praying the light turned red; praying he was sitting on the right side of the bus...praying I could say something to make him feel better.

I saw the bus coming; the streets were lined with people waving; the light was green....it turned red. I walked over to the bus. The window was open; Flynn looked straight ahead, not looking at me. I stepped under the window; "It wasn't because I don't love you; We weren't good together."

Flynn sarcastically replied, "You think that helps?" He turned his back to me. The bus rolled forward and disappeared out of town and Flynn disappeared from my life.

I walked back to the truck thinking about Flynn; about Elijah, and what the doctor told me. I headed home to wait for Elijah to call. I was worried what he would do when he found out... and for just a moment I wondered if I had gone to the doctor earlier; would he still have asked me to marry him; and would I have said yes?

CHAPTER 89
FLYNN

I was glad to see Iris before I left; though it did hurt my heart and make me a little angry. I didn't know if she would find the note I left her; I didn't want to leave things unsaid between us. Yes, I was heartbroken, and I thought with an ocean between us surely I could forget her.

When we arrived at the induction center in Macon, they immediately shaved our hair into what they called a "buzz cut." I know it's only hair, but it was a rude awakening of what to expect in the coming weeks. We were given uniforms to wear. They didn't care what our size was; some were too big; some too short; didn't matter, "just put them on." It was mentally hard. We were all tired, but we didn't dare complain. They instructed us to "pack up our civilian clothes in a box; put our address on it." to be mailed back home.

Finally, they took us to a local hotel. After our induction's "last meal," we were given a room. I made a note in my head as I drifted off; "I hadn't thought of Iris all day." Despite how hard the day was, I had made the right decision joining the service.

I called home collect the next morning to let them know we

271

were leaving for Pensacola Beach for basic training. Mother talked like I had been gone for years, but it made me feel good; someone missed me.

We were given seabags as we enter the barracks with a list of what would be inside them; in the correct order, folded and arranged in a specific way. I didn't know what basic training meant. I soon found out it was the same routine every day; marching, physical training, instrument operations, and training to use weapons on a battleship. Going over them all in the correct order and in a specific way; day after day until eight weeks were completed.

I hardly remembered how to do anything else but spend hours and hours working on the skills they told me would save my life one day; "You need to be prepared for what you are going to see and do."

I was exhausted, and had no time to call home or write. The only good thing that came out of it all was I had no time to think of Iris.

When the two months were done, we were sent to an aircraft training center. They would determine what level of job you would be expected to perform on a military ship based on tests we took. Though each of us learned a specialty; we would be expected to know how to do all the jobs on the ship we were stationed on.

We wouldn't know where that would be until our orders came. We had been together as a unit for three months and assumed we would move on together.

We learned to never assume anything when we were each handed a yellow manila envelope. Our orders were clear; our unit wouldn't return together. We each would move on to a different location. I would be stationed in Boston, Massachusetts. It was the last time we would be together and the last time I would see many of the men I had grown so close to.

I would have a two-day layover in LaGrange to spend with my family if I went home; it was a big if. Did I want to put myself in the place where all the memories I had tried to forget were? Could

I go home and not run into Iris? Trying to get over the past three years of loving someone is hard, but I needed to see my family, and they needed to see me.

CHAPTER 90
ELIJAH

I got to the base in Arkansas with my mind filled with hope and worry. I decided it would be best if I spoke with my Sargent. I told him about my change in status and ask his permission to call home that night; explaining about Iris being sick and the circumstances around it.

He was concerned, "Foster, you need to get your head in the game; your survival and your unit's survival will depend on your mental state. Call your wife; I'll notify personnel of your marital status to upgrade your pay."

"Yes sir, thank you sir," I saluted and returned to my unit.

The day went by quickly and after going to the mess hall to eat that evening; the Sargent sent for me and ushered me into a small office with a phone on the desk, "Report to my office after your call."

I saluted, "Yes Sir!" He closed the door as he left the room; I sat for a moment staring at the phone trying to get my thoughts together. I was excited to hear Iris's voice and hear what she found out at the doctor's office. It had only been two days, but it seemed forever since I had seen her; touched her. I dialed the telephone.

Iris picked up immediately. I wasn't prepared for what she was about to tell me.

She immediately began talking to me about Flynn leaving for the service; and how her daddy showed up and "showed his tail." I was confused about why she was telling me about Flynn and not our baby.

Suddenly her voice changed, "Sorry, my family just left for church; the house is empty now so we can talk." She continued, "How are you…"

I interrupted, "Iris I'm fine. Did you see the doctor?"

Her voice changed, "Yes, I did. I'm afraid to tell you what he said."

I was losing my patience; I only had a certain amount of time, "Tell me…Please, I have been so worried." What she told me crushed my world, and I couldn't help but wonder if I had made a mistake in marrying her so quickly.

My Sargent stepped to the door, "Foster, two minutes."

Iris hesitated and then ask, "Elijah, do you want to end our marriage?"

I paused for a minute, "It feels like I have lost a part of me. I don't know what to think; how could you not know what was happening?"

Silence…finally she replied, "I don't know; I can't explain it."

My time was almost up, "I need a while; you do too…"

She interrupted me, "We're married; I do love you. I want it to work, but you have to decide what you want."

I replied a little mad at her, "I have to think about it; I'm confused right now; I don't want to say anything I'll regret."

Her voice cracked, "Ok, we'll talk in a week or…two?"

I said goodbye, reported to my superior's office and explained. He was understanding, but vocal in making his point, "Foster, get your head in the right space; figure it out; settle it. Your life or someone else's could depend on it. Do you understand what I'm telling you?"

I saluted, "Yes sir…am I excused now?" He nodded.

The barracks were quiet. Lights out came just after I arrived. Laying on my cot, my brain was going in circles. I loved Iris, but wondered if she married me to get even with Flynn.

CHAPTER 91
IRIS

My call from Elijah went like I thought it would. I hoped he would reassure me he loved me. I was asking myself the same questions, he was. My monthly cycle was never late. When it was, and Elijah and I had been together I naturally thought, I was pregnant ...Dr. Hammond examined me and saw the results of the blood test; he gently told me I had never been pregnant.

Telling Elijah the truth was the hardest thing I had ever done. I realized he might think I tricked him into marrying me. I hoped after he had time to think about it, he realized I would never lie about something so precious.

Looking forward to going to work the next day as a married woman, I slept better than I had in weeks. There were lots of congratulations at the mill. Everyone shared their opinion; some declared, "You chose the right one," and some who "couldn't believe I gave up Flynn Fisher."

I just smiled and worked; glad to be back; thinking of Elijah. The humming of the machines always seemed to calm me and help me think, but this day was different. All I heard was noise, I felt anxious and worried...what was going to happen to us?

Questioning our choices... would we have married if we had known the truth? By lunchtime, my thoughts were all over the place. I needed to think, and the only place I could think was in the mill window.

My lunch pail in hand, I made my way to my window seat and crawled up inside; sitting sideways I could see the trees turning colors outside. Eating my sandwich; I turned my thermos up to take a drink. I noticed a piece of paper stuck between the two cracks in the rocks that circled above me. I pulled it out slowly not to tear it; intrigued I opened it and silently read the words...

Iris,

Please remember me as we travel this life separately; I will always remember you.

Flynn

I reread it wondering when he wrote it. I sat back and carefully folded the note and tucked it inside my pocket. I felt at peace.

Back to work on my line, the machines were humming again; Flynn had soothed my soul; I felt at ease. The note was his way of saying he accepted my decision. I realized he was right our journey was over. I would remember him often; see him seldom; but knew my journey for now was with Elijah if he wanted me.

Over the coming weeks, wondering and waiting to hear from Elijah; I would take out Flynn's note and read it, and whisper to the universe we shared, "I remember Flynn." It didn't have anything to do with still loving him. It was a recognition of what he and I had; what Elijah and I were working toward.

A couple of weeks passed. I wrote him a letter and ask Elijah if I could come to see him in Little Rock when he had leave. Two more weeks passed; still no word. I was getting worried. Had he left the States? Was he in a place where he couldn't contact me?

Normally, I didn't discuss my problems with anyone; but at the mill the second week and still no call, no letter, I asked Vivian on our way out of the mill if she had heard from him.

She nodded, "You haven't talked to him?"

I shook my head, "No, we had a little..." I stopped there remembering the vow we made to each other on our wedding night not to involve family in our private life. I shook my head, "I'm sure I will."

Vivian smiled, "He's fine; homesick."

I nodded, "I know; I just miss him."

At home that night, I wrote him another letter. I told him I was sorry; I asked him to please understand I truly thought the situation was different. I ended my letter with these words:

I won't write again; it is up to you; if I don't hear from you by October 13. I'll end our marriage. I hope you are safe. I only wish you happiness.

Love, Your Wife, Iris.

Then I waited.

Finally, on October 1, when I got home from work, a letter was laying on my bed postmarked from Arkansas. I decided not to read it. I was nervous about what it would say and how I would react.

I tucked it under my pillow and went to the bathroom to soak in the tub before helping Mama with supper. By the time I made it into the kitchen, everyone had gathered there. Assuming I had read the letter, Mama asked me how Elijah was. I told her he was good; setting the plates on the table; I thought about not reading the letter I tucked inside the dress I had put on after my bath; my stomach was turning as everyone was asking about it. I slipped into the bathroom, sat on the side of the tub; opened it slowly, and cried.

CHAPTER 92
ELIJAH

It took me some time to get over losing a baby I never had. It did make me wonder if Iris thought she was expecting or if she just wanted to get married to spite Flynn.

My days were filled with training that kept my mind focused away from Iris and our problems. We were constantly reminded, "What you're learning could determine if you live or die." We were aware our next orders would tell us we were shipping out overseas. It was taking a mental toll on all of us. My mind was occupied with the thought of leaving the country with my life with Iris so unsure.

Nighttime was different. Laying in my cot, I thought of everything Iris and I had been through the last two months. Once the shock and grieving for what I thought my life would be was over, I remembered I loved her and had planned to marry her early on. The truth was Iris knew she didn't need to trick me into marrying her.

I decided that night to write; lights out had already been called. I took out my flashlight, a sheet of paper, and I wrote,

Three-day pass October 22-26; please plan to come to Little Rock
I love you, still. Elijah.

I mailed it the next day.

Things settled down into a routine over the next weeks. Training was easier to handle without the worry of losing Iris. We were in a better place and ready to spend some time together.

CHAPTER 93
FLYNN

Plans were made for a graduation service before my unit was split apart and we each were sent to our next assignment. We were hoping our families could be there for the service; but quickly learned in the military things could change overnight. The war escalated. There would be no graduation ceremony.

Our last week of training intensified. The drill sergeant got harder. The physical and emotional training was intense, hours and hours every day; making sure we achieved the ability to operate the machinery on a warship.

I was glad to be busy and focused on something besides going home. I was more nervous about going to the place I grew up; than leaving to go to another country on a warship.

CHAPTER 94
IRIS

I planned the reunion with Elijah with care. I was more nervous about this visit than I was for my honeymoon. I had gotten my train ticket; roundtrip, booked a room at the Marion Hotel, and bought new gowns for our time together. I saved every cent I could to take with me.

He was concerned about where we would live after he got out of the service. I decided to take our bank statements to show him we would be able to buy a house soon. All we wanted was a little house in LaGrange.

Thursday morning, Tessa drove me to the train depot. On the way she was telling me about a guy she had met named Ernie. I could tell she liked him, "Tessa, go slow...we'll talk when I get back." She looked happier than I had seen her in a while. I winked at her as I got out of the truck.

She winked back "I will, I promise. Have a good time."

I closed the truck door and walked into the station. I was happy to be on the train; luggage stored; and seated. I took out my purse to make sure I had the paperwork I needed and settled back in my window seat. Taking in all the new places we were going through I was amazed at the beauty of the countryside and cities.

The trip was over sooner than I thought, and I was getting off in downtown Little Rock. I checked into the Marion Hotel. I went to the room I had rented for the next three nights. I unpacked and hung my clothes in the closet and placed my toiletries on the vanity facing the window in the room. I bathed and put on the pink dress and heels that I wore when Elijah and I had married.

I waited in a small coffee shop in the lobby of the hotel. It would only be a few minutes until I would see my husband for the first time since we were married.

CHAPTER 95
ELIJAH

I waited for the Little Rock-bound bus leaving at 4:15 that Thursday; a bus I had been waiting on for two months. I wondered if I would recognize her; this girl I married. I was nervous; would I feel the same about Iris.

Thirty minutes later I was walking into the Marion Hotel. The bus let me off right in front of it; I walked up to the double doors; the doorman opened them. Standing there was my wife, Iris Foster.

All my questions were answered, and all my doubts disappeared. I fell in love all over again; just like I did the first time I saw her. I walked to her and put my arms around her, and she put hers around me. We stood in the lobby of the Marion Hotel and held each other for a long moment; people clapped and cheered like they knew us and what we had gone through.

We took the elevator up to the room, the honeymoon suite. We ordered room service for dinner and pretended it was our wedding night all over again; only this time we were able to be together with no worries. Iris was fine, not sick, not pregnant. She was beautiful. The night was beautiful. Just like I had dreamed of for three years.

CHAPTER 96
IRIS

When I saw Elijah come through those doors of the hotel in his uniform, I fell more in love with him. I knew I had made the right decision; all the confusion and doubts we had about each other had disappeared. Our first night together was perfect; like a fairytale. I fit perfectly in his arms as our bodies molded together into one.

We slept soundly and didn't wake until almost noon. We decided we would stay in that morning and have room service bring our breakfast. We wanted to sit and talk about our future; I was proud to show him our bank statement and pictures of houses I had cut out of the newspaper.

He was more interested in us being together; we stayed in bed until the knock on the door forced him up to let them deliver our order. I got up behind him and ran into the bathroom. Teasingly I fussed, "See what you caused; the bellboy is going to see me without my clothes."

Elijah smiled, "Best he will ever see!"

Inside the bathroom, I dressed and washed my face. I looked at myself in the mirror closely to see if I could notice any change. I smiled at myself as I brushed my hair. Opening the door, I could see Elijah waiting at the table; I hugged him as I sat down. I felt content.

CHAPTER 97
ELIJAH AND IRIS

The next three days were perfect. We agreed it was exactly what we needed. We spent a good bit of it in room 313; we knew we were facing a long period of time away from each other. We were together in ways only two people who truly love each other could be.

A guy in my unit told me about a restaurant, Lassiter Inn, that served fried fish. It was Iris's favorite. We changed clothes for dinner together. Watching her get dressed I was still amazed by her beauty. I slipped behind her and encircled her waist with my arms. "I can't believe you're all mine...I'm the luckiest guy in the world."

She turned around and put her arms around my neck, "Yes, you are," she smiled, "And your wife is starving."

I laughed, "Always!" We walked hand in hand down two blocks to the restaurant. After we ordered our dinner, I thought it was the perfect time to have a serious talk. I began slowly. I considered not telling her at all, but I wanted her to be ready, "Iris, it's real; if this war doesn't end soon, I'll be sent to fight, and I don't know if I'll be able to see you before I leave."

She began to shake her head, "No, no..."

I took her hand, "Baby, it's alright. I want you to stay at your parent's house. You will be safe there, have people around you."

She nodded, "I don't want to be by myself. I'll miss you so much after this weekend."

I leaned over the table and kissed her quickly, "You've done a good job at saving for our future. When I get back, we'll buy a house wherever you want."

She shook her head, "Can we not talk about it anymore?"

Our waitress brought our food at just the right time. After we ate, we decided to have dessert later; and explored Little Rock as the sunset. Iris spotted a little bakery. She loved to look at how everything was decorated and would talk to the bakers about how to make things. She picked out two special treats for us to have later in our suite: a slice of pecan pie and a slice of chocolate cake. I teased her all the way back to the hotel, but secretly I loved the way she got excited about baking.

I took a quick shower and put on one of the gowns I had bought for this weekend. As I walked out of the bathroom, I heard Elijah ordering room service; coffee and milk. I smiled as I realized just how well he knew me.

He hung up the phone, walked over to me, "You take my breath away every time I see you."

I responded with a kiss, and once again we melted into each other. Our time together was unexplainable; something that cannot be put into words. I truly fell in love with him every day and night.

We had our desserts in bed, "I could get used to this," I teased.

He teased back, "I could get used to you." It was a perfect day and night; we fell asleep curled up together. Waking up the next morning, we talked about how to spend our last day. We decided just us together. We had a quick breakfast in the hotel's café and went back up to the room.

Iris curled back up in bed and wanted me to join her. I felt relaxed; no stress; no weapons, no tanks; no marching. We watched television; talked about our future together; how many kids we wanted. She laughed when I said I wanted all girls.

"You are crazy," I said laughing. I fell asleep happier than I had been in a long time. Still, Flynn crossed my mind…I hoped he was ok.

All too soon it came to an end. It was time for us to leave each other. Elijah wanted me to get on the train before he caught his bus back to the base, "I'm always the one who has to leave first; this time I want to see you off; make sure you're on the train and safe."

We checked out of the hotel. She wanted to go back to the bakery we had gone to the night before to get something to have on the train. I knew she had a love of anything sweet. We sat at a small round table near the window while the lady packed up the cookies and crème horn she had picked out. I pulled out a small box and placed it on the table.

I smiled and thought about how sweet he was to me. He told me not to open it until I got back home. I promised.

I couldn't believe Iris and I were going to be separated because of this war. Knowing that made it more difficult to let her go; I made sure she was on the train back to LaGrange, and her luggage was in the compartment above her. I paid the purser for her lunch and gave him extra to bring her coffee and soda. I kissed her one last time. I held her to me and devoured her smell; how her skin felt, and the pattern of her breathing hoping they would sustain me until I was with her again.

I looked out the window of the train, and for the first time, I felt the emptiness Elijah must have felt as he left the people and places he loved. The thought of Flynn popped into my head; how lonely he must have felt to have no one there for him as he left; yes his parents, but not me. I felt guilty as I waved and blew Elijah kisses. I didn't want him to feel that way, but I didn't want Flynn to feel that way either.

CHAPTER 98
ELIJAH

I took the next bus back to the post; the barracks were empty. Most of the guys had leave and those who didn't have time to go home were over at the canteen. I unpacked my things, went to the laundry room, did my wash, and got my uniform ready for the next day's inspection.

I had just laid down on my bed to write Iris a letter when the other guys started to arrive back. They were acting different; I knew something was up. I sat up on the side of my cot and whispered to the guy next to me, "What's going on? Another maneuver?"

He whispered, "We got general orders; we're going overseas; they haven't told us where or exactly when we will leave; but we know it will be soon. We may get leave around Christmas; but even if we do, we have to be back here before Christmas Day to begin 'intensive training' to join the troops overseas."

I was heartbroken I wouldn't be home for my first Christmas with Iris. I decided to write Vivian so the family could make their plans for the holiday. I asked her not to tell Iris. I didn't know when I would tell her. I wanted it to be a phone call, not a letter.

The barracks were somber; we knew changes were coming, but we didn't know what the changes were.

Christmas was five weeks away. Four weeks until I saw Iris; Christmas or not; didn't matter to me. I needed to see Iris.

CHAPTER 99
FLYNN

I'm not going to lie I was nervous about living on a ship, but felt confident I was prepared more for that than returning to LaGrange. I convinced myself I was over Iris. I knew I would love her forever. She was my first love; the only girl I dated for years. Maybe that was all it was meant to be. I had remained true to her; and she betrayed me. I decided to be with whoever I wanted.

The base in Pensacola organized "social gatherings" at the cantina once a month. I met a few girls at them; we slipped off and did what boys and girls do. They wrote to me after we were together wanting to see me again, but I built a thick wall around my heart. I swore I would never let a female hurt me that way again.

After we learned we were shipping out, we packed our seabags, said our good-byes, and headed to the train station. It was strange saying goodbye to the guys in the unit. We had become each other's support.

The train took me to LaGrange for a two-day visit; then on to Boston. I tried not to think about what was to come in either place.

I saw Daddy standing outside the train depot as the train pulled to a halt. He was smiling, but under the smile was a face filled with worry. Focused on what had been going on with me; I hadn't even considered what he had on him. We hugged; got my seabag and jumped in my truck.

I drove as he told me how to get to Granny and Paw Burton's new house. Daddy made small talk; ask me how boot camp had been; talked about how Mother may go to Greenville while he is working on the new place. Finally, he mentioned Iris had been driving by the Jefferson Street house a lot before they moved.

I shook my head, "She's married; she needs to act like it; stay away from me and my family…Daddy, don't have anything to say to her."

He paused and then declared, "I like Iris…always have…with you or not."

I nodded, "I know Daddy…just don't tell me about her or what she does." He agreed as we pulled into the driveway of my grandparents' new home. It was nice, and I was proud of them; to be retired and in a good place.

Our time together flew by as we ate supper and caught up on family news. Jacob wanted to join the military; Mother said because I had.

I looked over at him, "Don't rush it, little brother," as I pushed back from the table. We were staying there while I was home and Mother showed me where I was sleeping.

"I'm beat; I'm going to turn in," I said goodnight to everyone and told Daddy I would help him the next day. I crawled under the covers and passed out from sheer exhaustion.

CHAPTER 100
IRIS

After I returned from Arkansas, my daily routine fell back into place. The mill had changed; the majority of workers were women; the men were off fighting in the war or getting ready to. Working with mostly women had its advantages; we all brought food for big luncheons. We talked about men, fashion, makeup, and love. The downside was women loved to talk. If you wanted to know what was going on in Troup County all you had to do was listen to the mill gossip.

The big news that week was Flynn was home on leave. My heart dropped as I heard his name; and how some of the girls were going to town that night with the hope of running into him. I knew I had no right to feel jealous, but I did still love Flynn. It had nothing to do with my loving Elijah. I knew I had to pretend I didn't care, so I did.

After work, I went to town to pick up some things from Big Store Grocery and couldn't help driving down Jefferson Street. The Burton's had moved, and the house was empty, but still, I like to drive by to remember all the good times I had there.

I turned left in front of Clyborne's Mansion; across the bridge, I saw a truck in the yard of the Burton's house. I drove by slowly and stopped right in front thinking about all the times I sat on the porch drinking tea. I missed Mrs. Burton and hoped I would see her in town sometime.

Suddenly, the front door of the house opened and Flynn stepped out. He stood just looking at me for a minute, "Iris, what are you doing here?" He walked down the front porch steps over to the truck and sarcastically remarked, "Mrs. Foster, good to see you; nice truck."

I could not speak; the words in my heart were stuck there.

Flynn continued, "What? Nothing to say about how you betrayed me. I heard you were with child." Silence filled the stare between us. "I hope you will be happy." He turned to walk off.

I called to him, "Flynn!"

He turned to face me.

Rubbing the small gold heart necklace from the little box Elijah gave me in Arkansas between two fingers, "I'm not...going to have a baby...I just want you to know marrying him had nothing to do with not loving you."

Flynn's words were angry, "Do you think that helps? Go away Iris, and don't come around me...I can't think about you anymore...we're done. You made sure of it." He turned and disappeared into the house.

CHAPTER 101
FLYNN

Daddy and I went over to the house on Jefferson Street to sweep it up and get a few last things they had left there. We had almost finished with the last load when I noticed a truck parked by the curb. I didn't recognize it and walked out to see if it was the new mill workers getting ready to move there. I was surprised it was Iris. Daddy was right about her coming by the house. I walked out to try to talk to her, but I should have let more time pass. I wanted to hurt her as much as she hurt me. My words were angry, but I meant them all. She looked different; no longer a girl; a woman. Still as beautiful to me as ever, I was mad at myself for still having feelings of any kind for her. She was a married woman; off limits to me. I could never cross that line. I told her to stay away from me, but secretly I still hoped for the impossible.

Daddy and I finished at the Jefferson Street house and worked a couple of hours on the homestead he had started on the new land. He had done a lot of work. Jacob had helped a little, but he was back in Greenville finishing the school year. The homestead had just three rooms; a kitchen and bedroom and a side room for the kids to sleep. He only had a little work before they could move in, and we finished most of it. That took a lot off of my mind. I wanted to leave them in good shape.

Back at Granny's house, I decided to take a shower before supper. I packed the clean clothes Mother and Granny had washed that day in my seabag. I decided to spend as much time as I could with the family, not knowing for sure when I might see them again. It was a good time; playing canasta, eating snacks, and a good night's sleep led to my goodbyes at the bus station the next morning. I looked around as I boarded the bus; halfway thinking maybe Iris would be standing in the shadows somewhere to say good-bye. She wasn't.

CHAPTER 102
ELIJAH

We still hadn't heard anything about getting leave or when we would be shipping out overseas. Things had been tough; we woke up at midnight; freezing cold outside; to go on a 25-mile hike. They were preparing us; all too soon we would understand why.

It was two weeks before Christmas. We knew we wouldn't be given much notice if and when we were able to get leave. Iris was understanding. She told me we would celebrate whenever I got home, and I knew she meant it.

I relived the three days we spent together in Little Rock each night as I fell asleep. The thought of my life with her was the only thing getting me through the uncertainty the war caused.

CHAPTER 103
IRIS

Three weeks had passed since I saw Flynn at the house on Jefferson Street; about a month since I saw Elijah. Two weeks before Christmas, the city was decorated with the colors red and green; the fountain spewed water the same.

All the signs of Christmas were there, but there was a sadness that filled the holiday season that year. Just about every family had at least one member missing; fighting in the war, missing in action, or waiting to be sent to fight. Families hoped and prayed their loved ones would be coming home for the holidays, but it didn't happen. The war raged on with no end in sight.

Elijah was unsure if he would get leave at Christmas time, but if he did, it might not be long enough for him to come home. I was waiting and worrying about him. Secretly I was doing the same about Flynn. I knew I was married now; I wanted to be with Elijah; but you don't just stop the feelings you have for other people. The heart doesn't work that way or at least mine didn't.

The mill was going to close the week of Christmas, a usual move for the company. The day before the scheduled closing, I heard a familiar voice call my name, "Iris Reed?" I turned to see Charlie standing there, home on leave.

I smiled and hugged him, "Iris Foster."

He seemed surprised, "What? Not Fisher? Flynn didn't mention that."

I asked him if he had stayed in touch with Flynn. He said they had exchanged a few letters, but Flynn hadn't told him I had gotten married. I wasn't surprised.

We talked for a few minutes, and he told me some important news that would eventually affect us all. He was advised before he left his military base; they were going to "ramp up the fighting by sending more troops overseas in December." He explained, "They want to win this war and bring it to an end."

At home after work Elijah called with the news, "He would be home that Sunday, but he would leave on Wednesday." That meant he wouldn't be home on Christmas Day; the following Saturday. Still, I was so excited to see him again. I only had two days to get ready for his arrival. I finished my shopping for the family; we weren't planning to exchange many gifts. Now, I could concentrate on Elijah's visit.

After supper that Friday evening I went to tell Vivian about the news. She was so excited about her brother being home, "It will be our Christmas Day; Hey, why don't y'all stay here with us?"

I thought about it for a minute. I had planned to get a hotel; I knew we wouldn't have any privacy at my house. I agreed with Vivian, "It would be good for us to be there." I knew his family was anxious to see him too. Vivian and I made plans. I told her if Elijah called, "Don't tell him we are staying here." I was excited to surprise him!

CHAPTER 104

FLYNN

I arrived in Boston the same day I left LaGrange; I was surprised at how large the ship was compared to how small our private quarters were. I soon understood why. Every inch of the destroyer was used to defend the air and waters of our country. We were given a tour of the ship the day we arrived, but it took me a while to learn where everything was.

It had been two weeks since I began my life as a sailor and I had adjusted pretty well to living on ship in such close quarters. We were still docked and preparing for the ship's next tour of duty even though we weren't sure when or where that would be happening. There were some advantages about being docked. We were able to get our "sea legs" and lessen the chance of getting sick when we were seabound. Sea sickness was the one thing I didn't want. So far, I had been lucky.

Three weeks after I arrived, we found out we would be shipping out on Christmas Day; "destination not specified". We did know we would be joining the war effort overseas. The good news was we were given a four-day leave beginning on the Monday before Christmas. I would leave to go home on Sunday by bus.

I was glad to spend time with my family before I shipped out, but I wasn't excited about going back to LaGrange. I planned to be under the radar during the visit; I didn't want to see any Reeds or Fosters. It sounds immature, but I was still getting over a broken heart and all the one-night stands with other girls weren't helping.

CHAPTER 105
ELIJAH

I settled on the bus that Sunday; ready to be home for the short visit I had before Christmas. I heard troops in all branches were to be back on their assigned bases by Christmas Day. That told us the rumors we heard were true; the military was ready to end the war. It meant my unit would be shipping out soon.

I wasn't afraid of fighting; my fear was much deeper; something I couldn't control. I was afraid of missing Iris to the point I wouldn't be able to think. How do you control your love for someone?

After so many trips, I felt at home on buses and trains. This trip was going to be a long one. I would have an hour's layover in Atlanta to transfer to the bus that went to LaGrange. I made sure the presents I had bought for Iris were with me; in case my duffel bag didn't make it. My thoughts were all over the place, but as I fell asleep on the train ride, my anticipation of being with Iris made everything worth it.

CHAPTER 106
IRIS

I told Mama Elijah and I would be staying at Vivian's while he was home. She seemed disappointed, "I hope y'all come for supper one night?"

I promised her we would if he had time, "I just want him to do what he wants while he's here. His family is coming up one day, but we will try to come by." I promised her I would be back home for Christmas Day.

Tessa and Ester understood why we were staying at Vivian's; Loretta didn't seem concerned, but she didn't miss the chance to let me know she heard Flynn was coming home for Christmas, too.

"Maybe I'll run into him. Now that you are off the market..." She stopped without finishing her sentence, flipped her hair, and walked out of the room.

That night I wrapped the gifts I had bought for Elijah, a new shirt and pants to wear while he was home, some cologne, and a picture of me, signed "Love, Iris Foster."

I packed my overnight case and made sure I took my best nightgowns and outfits to wear for him. The next morning, I put everything in the truck.

Mama made him a special cake; his favorite; chocolate. I hugged her, "We'll be by to visit, if we can. I'll call you."

I stopped at the gas station to fill up his truck and the grocery store to buy some things I knew he liked to eat. All errands finished; I headed over to Troup Street.

Vivian was already cooking when I got to her house. Her phone was ringing, "Iris, can you get that?" she asked. I grabbed the phone as I set the grocery bags on the counter.

It was Elijah, "Hey baby, where are you?" He explained he was in Atlanta during a layover waiting to catch a bus to LaGrange.

"I can't wait to see you" he whispered into the phone.

"I know, me too" I whispered back. I heard the announcement in the background, "Last call for bus 316 to LaGrange, Georgia... All Aboard."

He hurriedly said, "I'll be there..." With that, the phone went dead.

I brought my luggage from the truck and put them into Elijah's bedroom. It was strange being there without him, yet comforting to know he would be there soon.

A night together was what we needed. I couldn't wait.

CHAPTER 107
FLYNN

Sunday came. My seabag and myself were settled on the bus back to LaGrange. It was going to be a long trip; I opened my book, a western, a new one, just released. The trip was easy; the scenes along the way were beautiful to see during the sunrise of the early morning.

I had breakfast at the bus station in Charleston, and we continued to Atlanta where I would make a transfer to a bus going to LaGrange. I was glad the seat beside me had been empty, now I noticed a purse in it; soon a pretty young girl sat down beside me. I smiled and went back to my book; almost finished, and proud of myself for resisting my practice to read the last page first.

The girl beside me, busy reading a book of her own, leaned over and softly asked, "Want me to tell you how it ends?"

Confused I responded, "You don't know; girls don't read westerns...do they?"

She shrugged her shoulders and focused again on her book, clearly a love story. I smiled at her pointing to the cover of the book she was holding, "See?"

She laughed, "I tell you what, I'm going to write down the

ending of your book on a piece of paper…when you finish the last page…read it to see what you think?"

We both laughed. She stuck out her hand, "Hi Sailor…. I'm Cathy."

I took her hand, "Flynn." I took the paper she handed me and placed it between the pages of my book, then stuck all of it in my duffel bag.

Cathy and I talked about books, politics, and life. She asked me where I was headed, and before I knew it I spilled my whole life story to my new friend. She took my hand and said all the right things that were supposed to help someone heal a broken heart.

Time passed quickly and soon we were arriving in Atlanta; stepping off the bus going our separate ways, Cathy hugged me, "Flynn, I know we'll see each other again," she whispered.

I hugged her back, "I hope so." I grabbed my seabag and ran to the waiting bus for my last trip home for a long time.

CHAPTER 108
ELIJAH

I was on the bus out of Atlanta to LaGrange when the driver announced we were waiting for a few passengers running late. Trying to be patient; watching as one by one people passed by my bus window. I was surprised, I saw Flynn hugging a woman I didn't recognize, "It didn't take him long to get over Iris." I was shocked to see him with someone new, but secretly glad he had moved on to other conquests.

I had heard he was a "lady's man"; I guess it was true. I silently scolded myself for caring what Flynn Fisher did when I realized he had just thrown his seabag in the luggage compartment and boarded the bus.

He sat down on a seat at the front; I was glad he didn't see me. I still felt threatened by the idea of Flynn being in the same city as Iris; and glad I was going to be in LaGrange while he was there.

CHAPTER 109
IRIS

Everything was ready for Elijah; Vivian and I decorated the Christmas tree; wrapped presents; and cooked cakes and pies all afternoon.

I showered and put on the new dress I had bought and headed to the bus station to pick him up. He would be tired and hungry; you can't get decent food on a bus trip. I just wanted to get him home.

The bus station was crowded. I immediately spotted Mr. Fisher standing over by the door where buses pulled up to let passengers off. I didn't know if I should speak to him; I didn't have to decide; he was walking toward me, "Hello Ike, good to see you."

I smiled when he called me Ike. I never understood why he chose that nickname for me, but I liked it.

I smiled and hugged him, "So good to see you. Who are you here to pick up?" He told me Flynn coming home. We talked about him being on a ship and how he would be leaving to go overseas on Christmas Day.

As I was about to tell him I was waiting for Elijah, the bus pulled up to the curb; and the door opened. The first person off the bus was Flynn. I couldn't help but notice how handsome he looked in his sailor uniform. Mr. Fisher stepped forward to meet him; I stepped back. They hugged; I could see he was truly glad to see his daddy. Mr. Fisher walked over to get his seabag.

Flynn and I didn't know what to say to each other; he spoke first in his usual sarcastic voice, "I know you're not here to meet me. Are you waiting on your husband?" Before I could answer, I heard Elijah's voice.

He walked up to us at the same time Mr. Fisher returned, "You ready to go home son?"

Flynn turned to leave; shook Elijah's hand, "Hope y'all have a good Christmas."

I tried not to show my emotions, "I hope you all do too." Two things were still truly clear to me that night, I loved the man I was married to, but I still loved the one I lost. I felt happy and sad at the same time. Merry Christmas to me.

CHAPTER 110

FLYNN

I was glad to be in the truck away from the bus station; it seemed I had spent more time on buses than anywhere else. I was tired, and I could tell Daddy was too. The ride was quiet; then he asked me a question I had thought about a lot in the past weeks, "Are you over Iris?"

The only answer I had was the one I gave him that night, "Do I have a choice? She is married; done deal. I don't mess with married women."

We pulled into the driveway of Granny and Grandpa's house. Daddy placed his hand on my shoulder, "You never get over your first love; you just learn to move on."

I nodded, "Yes sir;" I paused for a minute not letting my mind go where it had started, "The house looks quiet; the kids in bed?"

Daddy answered chuckling, "Let's hope they all are." Inside he put my seabag in the small room off the back of the house they had fixed up into a bedroom for me. I was thankful for some needed privacy; not to be sharing a place with my two brothers and sister.

Daddy said goodnight and went straight to bed. It was late and everyone else was asleep. I read the short note from my mother,

"Johnny Flynn, sandwich in icebox; cookies on the counter; see you in the morning, Love Mother." I grabbed a couple of cookies and a glass of milk and headed to my little room to finish the end of my book.

I thought of Cathy and smiled as I finished the last ten pages; I read the last page twice and closed it. Cathy's note fell out. I remembered what she had said, "Some girls do read westerns," On the blank sheet, she had written the last page of the book almost word for word; then, "This girl loves westerns; Cathy Baker, 555-3167, Boston, MA. Call if you're ever in town."

CHAPTER III

ELIJAH

Let me be clear, I didn't like seeing Iris standing there with Flynn. I immediately thought the worst after seeing him with the girl at the bus station. I learned to wait before saying anything to Iris about him; she was still defensive about my judging her feelings toward him. I held my tongue as I approached the two of them in the bus station.

Iris immediately stepped over by my side; Flynn and Mr. Fisher didn't wait around too long. I was surprised when Flynn held out his hand to shake mine. I felt like he was letting me know he had moved on. I decided to keep quiet and not ask what was said between them.

I was ready to get to Vivian's and just get some rest. I was looking forward to spending some time with my family. The house was fully decorated, and the smell of Christmas filled the air as we walked in the door. It was late, but Vivian and Allen were still up and sitting at the table in their robes.

I dropped my duffle bag and hugged them, "Boy I'm glad to be home." We visited for a minute and agreed we all needed sleep.

Iris had already excused herself to get ready for bed, and I was ready to join her. We snuggled together and fell asleep in pure exhaustion. It was the best sleep I had since our time in Little Rock. All I needed was to be near Iris. The thoughts of fighting in the war left; all was right with the world. I didn't think about anything but holding my girl.

CHAPTER 112
IRIS AND ELIJAH

We had a perfect time celebrating our first Christmas together as a married couple. Vivian was mindful of the time we wanted to spend just the two of us. For us, it was our Christmas Day.

We ate a big breakfast, opened presents, and Elijah's parents surprised him with a visit. It was a nice day, though shadowed by the looming sadness my husband wouldn't be back home for a long time. All I wanted to do was be near him.

There was a Christmas parade in town going on that night. Iris was excited to go to the singing around the fountain. She insisted we all would love it.

Vivian and Allen decided to stay home, "Y'all go on now, we'll stay here and clean up. You need time together just you two."

I decided not to change clothes, but Iris insisted she needed to. I knew her well and she was giving me some time with just them. I was glad. I had some things I wanted to tell them about my orders. I knew Iris was going to need some support.

Vivian and I were sitting at the table, "Sis, I know the time is getting closer for me to go overseas to fight. I'm ok with that; I can

316

take care of myself as long as I don't need to worry about Iris. She is more fragile than she acts. Will you kind of watch over her?"

She assured me she had been, and she and Allen had already talked about it, "We will take care of whatever we need to; You take care of yourself." She got up from the table and hugged me, "Right now enjoy yourself with your new wife...It will work out hon."

The bedroom door opened, and Iris walked into the kitchen in a red dress, "Baby you look beautiful." She grabbed my hand and playfully pulled me out the door. In the truck waiting for it to heat up, we started kissing and before we knew it we had started something we had to finish.

CHAPTER 113

IRIS

In that truck the night of the parade, we came together with all the passion, love, and worry of two people who didn't know how long it would be until they were together again. Afterward, we put ourselves back together, clothes back in place. I whispered in his ear "It's going to be funny if we have to tell our kid one day, they got their start in a truck." We laughed as I snuggled up under his arm. He cranked the truck and headed to town.

The parade had started when we got there; I loved downtown during the holidays. The store fronts all lit up in different colors, the tree in the square sparkled from the moon's light, and the fountain's water in red and green seem to announce the celebration of our Savior's birth.

We parked across the street from Tasty's Café and walked over to the curb to watch the parade with Santa in his sleigh throwing candy to the waiting hands of children surrounding him. Their excitement was catching and for a moment I forgot Elijah would be leaving soon.

Elijah smiled and pulled me closer to him as if he knew why sadness swept over me. He took something from his coat pocket,

"Santa told me to give you this." He handed me a bag of Nut Goodies.

CHAPTER 114

ELIJAH

We went home after the parade; we didn't talk about anything. We just enjoyed being with each other. We hoped a baby would happen during that visit. We felt like we had lost one even though we hadn't.

On my last day, we visited the Reeds; everyone was there. It was good to see them all, especially Robert. We remained close and talked often as we could. He was good friends with Flynn too and though he tried to stay out of it, I knew he felt right in the middle.

We had a good visit; Tessa announced she was getting married to a man named Ernie. Iris was happy for her, but no one else seemed to be, "She deserves some happiness," Iris declared as we climbed back into the truck.

We decided to go by Tasty's Café, "to get a hamburger and fries for supper?" She slid over to my side of the truck as I stepped out; I smiled and put my hands around her waist to help her down. She wrapped her arms around my neck, and we kissed. Kiddingly I asked her "Iris Foster, what will people say?"

CHAPTER 115

IRIS

I looked around as Elijah put me down. My stomach went into my throat. Of all the people to run into, Flynn was coming out of the café, and he wasn't alone. I never met her, but I was sure the girl with him was Joan, from Greenville. I felt a pang of jealousy, but I also felt glad he had someone. I waved at them; I just couldn't speak. He gave me a nod; just one; his way of acknowledging my wave.

Elijah and I walked toward the café door; Flynn held it open for us. We sat at our usual corner table near the window; I watched as Flynn placed his hand on the small of the girl's back as they climbed into a truck.

I knew it bothered Elijah for me to watch them. He wasted no time asking me about my feelings, "Does it bother you to see him...especially with a girl?"

I told him the truth, "No...it's strange...not speaking to him...but I'm glad he has someone."

He took my hand across the table and smiled, "I'm glad I have you." I felt a warmth go through me; he was so sweet.

"Let's get ours to go...eat it in bed," I smiled.

"Good idea" ...he answered.

We slipped into the quiet dark house with our dinner and made our way to the bedroom. I turned down the covers; Elijah laid out his uniform for his bus ride back to the base. We both slipped into our pajamas and had our hamburger and fries picnic.

We talked about when he might get leave again, "Iris this might be the last time I'm home for a while."

"Well, I replied, maybe we should take advantage of this time." I pulled him down under the covers with me. It was the best part of being married.

CHAPTER 116
FLYNN

I was glad Joan came down for a couple of days to see me. The morning after I arrived, she was sitting at the breakfast table like she belonged there; happy she accepted my mother's invitation.

Joan loved me, and I loved her, but she knew my feelings for her were like a friend. We always had good times together. This visit was no different.

She helped me find a tree and decorate it. We shopped for gifts for my brothers and sister; a doll for Bobbie; a BB gun for Jack and a pocketknife for Jacob. Joan wrapped each one and place them under the tree.

It was her idea for us to go to the Christmas Parade in town; She knew how much I loved that time of the year. I explained to her, "I don't want to run into Iris and Elijah again." It was too hard.

Joan announced, "We can watch from Tasty's Café; come on… it will cheer you up." We drove downtown; Christmas lights lit the way; Joan was right; I was feeling better.

We chose a back booth at Tasty's and decided to order a burger and shake.

We were one block over from the main parade route, but we could still see the float as they travelled down Broad Street over to Bull Street. Santa's sleigh arrived signaling the end of the parade.

Joan and I started out of the restaurant ready to ride through town to see more decorations. As we left Tasty's, the first thing I see is Iris kissing Elijah. I couldn't get away from her. She was everywhere I went. Joan saw the look on my face and suggested we go on back to Granny's house. I went straight to my room closed the door and tried to sleep Iris from my mind.

Standing beside the bus she would take home, I tried to reassure Joan I would be ok. She just hugged me. I remember the last thing she said to me as she turned from the step to board the bus, "Maybe an ocean will be enough for your heart to forget Iris; but I doubt it."

I looked at her for a moment and replied, "I hope so."

She stepped back and placed her arms around my neck; she whispered in my ear, "Iris is a lucky girl and doesn't even know it. Flynn Fisher loves her."

CHAPTER 117
ELIJAH

My Christmas was coming to an end; duffle bag packed, I said my goodbyes at Vivian's. Iris was taking me to the station to catch the bus back to Arkansas. I dreaded leaving her but was ready to get back to camp. I wanted to get my tour overseas finished and get back home to her for good.

We had the routine down and went about checking in and loading my bags. We were not alone; the place was a green sea of uniforms; other couples in the same boat as us. It got harder to say goodbye every time I left her, but I knew I had to.

She handed me a bag and a thermos of coffee, "I made you lunch for your ride back; it will be better than anything you can buy."

I smiled and kissed her quickly, "You go back inside; it's too cold out here."

I watched as she stood by the glass door as the bus pulled out of the station. She placed her open hand on the glass window; I placed mine on the bus window. It was our way of saying I love you when one of us left.

Just as I settled back into my seat, I noticed Flynn Fisher at the station with the same girl from the night before. I watched as he hugged her. She boarded the bus in front of mine, and he turned to walk back through the door. The same door Iris was headed for as my bus pulled away from the curb. I knew Iris loved me, but the thought of Iris and Flynn in the same town still unnerved me.

CHAPTER 118

IRIS

I turned to walk out of the bus station and ran into Flynn; We actually bumped into each other. My first instinct was to laugh. He didn't respond as he pushed by me and kept walking. I couldn't help myself, "Flynn, wait..."

He turned around, "Wait for what? You didn't wait now, did you?"

His sarcasm was hurtful, but I tried to ignore it, "I wanted to explain...I thought you were over..."

He stood looking at me; hurt and confused, "I'm not going to stand in a bus station full of people and talk about this..." he turned and walked out into the parking lot. I watched as he got into his truck.

For a moment I wanted to run after him, but I was a married woman. I love my husband, but I still cared for Flynn. The realization of loving two men filled my head, and it broke my heart that I had hurt one of them.

Back at Vivian's, I decided to pack my things and go back home. I didn't want to sleep in Elijah's bed without him. I already missed him and strangely enough, running into Flynn made it worse. I just wanted to go home for Christmas.

I thanked Vivian and Allen. They sent a care package to my house with the cookies, cakes, and candy we had made.

I blew the horn of the truck as I pulled up in front of the house; Robert ran out to help me take my luggage inside; I grabbed the box of goodies and placed them on the long kitchen table. Mama made a pot of coffee. I told them about Elijah's news as they devoured the cookies.

Daddy spoke first, "Damn war..." That summed up exactly the way I felt.

I excused myself and decided to unpack and go to bed, "Tree looks pretty mama."

She smiled, "See you in the morning."

I took the special gowns I bought for Elijah and hung them in the back of my closet; no need to wear them here. As I hung each one, I remembered the nights we spent together. Under the last gown was a small, gift-wrapped box with a note attached, "Do not open until Christmas morning." I slipped back into the living room and placed it under our Christmas tree.

Lying in bed, Tessa talked about getting married to Ernie, "Iris you like being married?"

I turned over to face her, "I guess so, I'm not sure I've been married long enough to know."

I reached out to take her hand, "You love him?" She nodded.

I smiled, "Then it will be alright."

CHAPTER 119

FLYNN

I was glad to be home; glad Joan had left; and glad I didn't waste my time talking to Iris at the bus station. I was over being hurt by her, now I was just mad. I didn't want to hear her explain anything to me. I wanted the image of her face that appeared every time I closed my eyes to go away. I had two more days before I was to report back to the ship; I hoped to lay low and spend time with my family.

The next morning, I slipped out of the house while everyone was still sleeping and drove downtown to meet Clyde and Charlie at Tasty's for breakfast; it was good to see them. We exchanged addresses and promised to keep up with each other.

Charlie finally brought up the subject, "Have you seen her since you've been home?"

I nodded, "I can't seem to escape her; she is everywhere I go. I guess her husband went back yesterday. I saw her at the bus station while I was putting Joan on one."

Clyde spoke up, "You'll find someone, Flynn; just have some fun for now."

I nodded as we stood up to pay our check and Iris walked in the door. I turned to Charlie, "See what I mean?" I laughed.

Iris ran over to Charlie and hugged him, "It's so good to see you; how long are you home?" They continued idle chatter as I excused myself.

I paid my check and started out the door when I heard her call my name, "Flynn, can I talk to you for a minute?"

I walked over to where they were, as the guys left Charlie said, "Flynn keep in touch man."

I nodded and turned to Iris, "Why? I'm not sure what we have to talk about. Why don't you just leave me alone?"

She didn't answer and insisted it wouldn't take long as she sat down in a booth.

I hesitated for a moment thinking about the gossip it might create for her, "You sure you want to talk here...you know it'll be all over this town."

She shrugged her shoulders. Against my better judgment I sat down across from her. I looked her straight in the blue eyes that had captured my soul and spoke one word, "Talk."

CHAPTER 120
IRIS

I knew word would get around about Flynn and I having coffee together. I thought it was important he knew what happened and that I still cared about him, "I just want us to be ok when we are around each other. You know I will always care about you." I explain to him, "I thought I was going to have a baby..." he stopped me,

"Iris, I don't want to know the details about you two; you're married; doesn't matter how it happened or why it happened; I know you care about me, but I cannot be your friend. It's just too hard."

I tried to explain, "My feelings for you haven't changed..." those words seemed to only make him angry. He stood up to leave without speaking. I reached for his hand.

He snatched it away, "Iris, just leave me the hell alone; it's hard enough; don't rub it in my face." With that, he walked out the door. I thought it would be the last time I spoke to Flynn Fisher for a long time.

CHAPTER 121
ELIJAH

The bus ride back to camp was long. I was glad to be back. It was the first step in getting what I had signed up for finished and starting my life with Iris.

I thought she might be expecting after my visit home at Christmas, but she told me she wasn't. We talked about it while I was home on leave, and agreed we were ready to start our family.

After talking with Vivian, I wasn't sure what was going on with Iris. I was troubled; not a good way to be when I needed my full concentration to complete the training I was faced with every day.

The program to deploy overseas begun immediately. It meant long days filled with what they referred to as "endurance training." It seemed to never end.

By the first of the year, we were notified we would be leaving to continue deployment prep from a military base in Alabama; closer to home.

We hoped to get leave before we shipped out, but that wasn't in the military's plans; it was just the opposite.

At the new base we were told, "We wouldn't be allowed to leave or to have visitors. Their excuse was "We are getting you used to being away from home." We were only to be "focused on our upcoming mission."

Iris and my relationship was strained by letters I received after my trip home at Christmas. Vivian wrote to me saying Iris was with Flynn at Tasty's. She was told by several people, and she said they wouldn't have told her if it wasn't true.

When I asked Iris about it, her attitude hadn't been forthcoming. She had never been someone who felt the need to explain herself. We had agreed we wouldn't talk about it until we were face-to-face, but it was looking like that might not happen for a long time. It was putting a strain on both of us.

On top of that, morale at the base was low. A few times we would report to reveille with guys missing; AWOL they called it, Away Without Leave. After a few weeks, they were back with the unit and all seemed to be forgiven; however, a few times the guys just disappeared with no explanation. I thought at the time it was something not worth the risk, but I was missing Iris and needed to see her.

CHAPTER 122
IRIS

After the conversation at Tasty's Café, I was sure I wouldn't see Flynn again during his visit at Christmas. I was wrong. The supervisor at the mill called me that afternoon and asked if I would be interested in coming to work the next day. The mill was running one line during Christmas to help with the war effort. I told them I would; it was the least I could do. Mama was all for it; she told me she could handle the baking and cooking for our Christmas dinner along with help from Granny, Ester, Tessa, and Loretta.

I arrived early the next morning at the mill; it was quiet as I walked back to where I was scheduled to work. It was in my old area near the mill window; a flood of memories filled my head. As I turned the corner; I thought I was seeing things. Flynn was sitting in the window staring at the sunrise. In shock, I quietly turned to walk away.

He spoke, "What are you doing here; are you following me?"

"No, I still work here...... working for the war effort today," I said.

He stood up. We were again face-to-face, "You're a married woman; I won't say what I think of that. My coming here was a mistake; I was remembering the young girl I fell in love with three years ago, but she no longer exists. She has turned into someone I no longer recognize."

Tears streamed down my cheek, "I'm still the same person; I'm sorry I hurt you. I can't change it."

Flynn walked closer, "I've never heard you say you love him." He waited for an answer from me.

"I owe you nothing and your cruelty only makes it worse. I told you I would always care for you, but you are making it hard for me."

Flynn stepped closer; our bodies were only inches away from each other as we stared into each other's eyes. It was broken by the lights turning on, and people filling the work area.

"Go away, Flynn; You have Joan, and I do love my husband." The words I spoke were true but spoken in cruel anger to hurt him the way it hurt me to have him think so little of me.

CHAPTER 123

FLYNN

I walked out of the mill that day with a new resolve to get over Iris; I felt like the girl I knew was truly gone. Out of everything Iris had said, what surprised me the most was her remark about Joan; it was almost laughable. There was nothing between Joan and me except friendship, that was it. I had told her as much a thousand times. Now it didn't matter.

I went to the mill that morning to collect a paycheck they were holding for me. I wanted to cash it and give the money to Daddy to help with building the new house. I went home after going to the bank; the house was quiet as I slipped into my room and fell asleep on the bed. I woke up to Mother calling me to eat supper. It was my last night there; they cooked all my favorites. Mother had collected all my presents together for me to take back to the ship, my idea. I wanted to have some kind of Christmas.

I asked Daddy if he would help me with packing my seabag; we walked to my room. I handed him the envelope from the bank; "Merry Christmas …this is for the house…to help you get started with it."

He opened the envelope, "Son, take some of this with you… you may need it."

I shook my head, "No, I'm ok. I get paid every month; I've put back some."

He hugged me, "Thank you, son...I promise to use it wisely. I will send you pictures if I get that camera I want from Santa." We both laughed.

Back in the kitchen, I said my goodbyes to Jacob, Jack, and Bobbie; I told them to be sure to check under the tree for a present from me on Christmas Day. I hugged the rest of the family and told Daddy I would see him the next morning. He was driving me to the train station in Hogansville.

I laid down and replayed my conversations with Iris; I wondered if she was having regrets. She said she loved him. The words hurt my heart. As I fell asleep, I prayed for the war to end. I prayed God would let me come back home safe. I prayed for my family... and for Iris.

Daddy and I were up and ready to leave for the train station by 8:00 AM; Mother made me a thermos of coffee and biscuits for breakfast to carry with me. While I was saying goodbye to her, Daddy was loading my stuff in the back of my pickup truck.

As he came back into the kitchen, "Son, Iris is outside...You want me to tell her to leave?"

Mother was raving, "Well, the nerve...she is a married woman."

"Mother calm down, we're just friends; believe me I have no feelings for her," I lied. Daddy pulled Mother back into the kitchen as I went out the front door to see what Iris could possibly need to say to me.

She was sitting in her truck, Elijah's truck, I refused to get inside. She jumped out, "Flynn...I heard you were leaving this morning. I just didn't want things to be bad between us. Yes, I love Elijah. Yes, I'm married, but I will always love you; you were my first love."

I didn't know what to say. I nodded, "Ok, I appreciate the words; but they don't mean a lot to me right now. I don't want any bad feelings about anybody. You married who you wanted...I'm fine, but I'm not your friend."

Iris dropped her head, "Can I hug you?"

Daddy came out the door, "Flynn, we need to leave; you don't want to miss your train."

I noticed the sadness on her face, but still couldn't help saying what I needed to say, "Go home Iris. We were over when you married Elijah; not friends, not anything."

She looked defeated as she climbed into the truck and backed out of the driveway. She stuck her head out the window, "Flynn, be careful."

I didn't answer her; there were no good answers to any of it.

Goodbyes at the train station were quick; and before I knew it my last trip to LaGrange for a long time was done. I made a promise to myself to never speak to Iris again. It would be a hard promise to keep.

CHAPTER 124

ELIJAH

I wrote to Vivian about Iris, "Was she spending time with Flynn after I left?"

Vivian not wanting to spread gossip, answered back, "She has been seen a couple of times with Flynn; she was talking to him at the mill…and other places."

She insisted it was between me and Iris.

She wrote with certainty, "If she was with Flynn, I'll bet she has a good reason. I know she loves you, Elijah."

I wanted to trust Iris, but being so far away from her made me doubt everything.

After the news my unit received that day from my Sargent, I had more important things to think about; I needed to talk to Iris. He told us we would get to call home on Saturday. I thought about it all week.

The phone was ringing, I planned what I would say to Iris when she answered. I heard her voice and everything changed.

Before I could say anything, she asked, "Are you ok?" I told her I was. She immediately said, "I know you have something important to tell me, but I wanted you to know about me seeing Flynn before you hear the gossip going around." She explained what had happened between them and why she tried "to make things right." She just wanted everyone to be ok.

"I trust you baby. Don't worry about gossip; I'm not. I need to tell you something important."

Her words were quiet, "Ok, what is it?"

I explained, "We are going to a base in Alabama to finish training… we're shipping overseas in six to nine months. They're telling us we need to be prepared mentally and going home is not advised; that means no leave."

She told me she understood and asked "If I come to where you are, will I be able to see you?"

"I don't know, but I hope so. I have to go, I will write." My phone time was ended. We were cut off before we could say we loved each other. I didn't like it; those words gave me strength.

CHAPTER 125

IRIS

I got a letter a few days after my call with Elijah. He was leaving for the base in Alabama the next day. I looked it up on the map; it was near Dothan, about two hundred miles away. I was worried how I could get there, and if I could see him if I did.

Three months passed, and all I could do was work, wait, and worry. It was hard to say everything in letters. Some things needed to be said in person.

I found the words to let him know I wasn't pregnant. We both hoped I would be before he went overseas. It was part of our plan. He wanted to come back to a "home, wife, and a baby."

His next letter said, "It's not your fault; don't blame yourself." Somehow, I felt like it was. Now he was closer to home, but out of reach; the military was prohibiting any visits before his unit was to ship out. My only prayer was that the war would be over before the fall.

Flynn was on my mind. I heard he shipped out on Christmas Day. I didn't know where he went. Was I wrong to worry about him; pray for his safe return? Maybe, but I wanted him to have a happy life. It was difficult to love and care about two men. People didn't understand it, but I felt different types of love for the two of them, always had and though I made my loyalty well known; no one knew my heart was split in two pieces.

CHAPTER 126

FLYNN

I shipped out on Christmas Day, December 1943. I was officially engaged in the war that was ravaging the entire world. The fighting had picked up; word of what our orders were floated around the crew gossip chain. The gossip soon became reality.

We were assigned to patrol the Eastern Coast of the Caribbean Sea and eventually headed to Casablanca controlled by France. It had been less than six months since the invasion by sea, and our orders were to protect our homeland's interests there and Casablanca's neutrality in the war.

By mid-1944, we were reassigned to return to a base in Rhode Island to serve as a plane guard for the movement of troops deploying to fight and aircraft carriers. We maintained the ship and the weapons in ready condition to protect them from enemy attack.

Life on the ship was hard; busy enough that Iris didn't crossed my mind too often during the day. At night just before I went to sleep, I would see her face and the hurt she felt the last time I saw her. The anger was gone. I had to move on, and I was trying.

When we were in port, no matter what country we were in,

there were always girls who were willing to spend time with a sailor. I was determined not to get involved with any of them. It was better to move from one to the other. The strange thing was no matter how many girls I was with; I never felt the way I had just talking to Iris. I know what people would say, love was the difference. I laughed at the thought. I had become cynical about love; I no longer believed in it.

CHAPTER 127
ELIJAH

We were in Alabama for about three months of training when we received new orders. We were leaving for a departure station in New Jersey by October to begin our move to Germany. Morale among the unit sunk to a new low; we were advise, "No leave would be approved." We were given weekly call time every Sunday afternoon, but calls were different from being able to hug your family.

Iris managed to get down to Dothan, but she wasn't allowed on base. I only saw her for about five minutes through a fence. They tried to keep us busy during our downtime, which wasn't too often. They showed movies, had dinners, and let us play cards at the cantina, but it didn't keep any of us from wanting to go home or at least have visitors.

The grueling training day after day made our homesickness worsen. It was the reason some guys in the unit were choosing to slip out of the barracks, off of the base, and go home on their own. I didn't agree with it, but I understood why they did it. The military had instigated strict rules about being AWOL because of the number of men who were making that choice. I wasn't sure what their punishment was, but they never returned to our unit.

My calls home to Iris were hard; hearing her voice made me miss her more. She tried to encourage me by telling me what was going on at home. She never mentioned Flynn; the Fishers or Burtons. I was glad.

We spent our time talking about our future; We agreed the best thing for her to do was stay at home with her parents and save money. I acted like I was doing good, for the most part, I guess I was. The training was hard work, but I didn't mind it.

The days passed quickly, so they were bearable. It was the quietness of the nights that let the thoughts of home slip into my head and caused me to fall into a dark abyss of sadness.

CHAPTER 128
IRIS

I tried to see Elijah, but they wouldn't allow any visitors. The separation between us caused both of us anxiety. To cope, I had sunk into a routine of working, coming home, helping Tessa with Jeanine, writing a letter to Elijah, and sleeping; then doing it all over again. I worried about him, and Mama worried about me.

One afternoon after work mama was telling me about all the news she heard in town, "I ran into Mr. Burton; You know Naomi isn't living with them now."

I remarked they were probably back in Greenville.

"No," Mama said shaking her head, "They're living in a shed, while they are building a house out on Old Turner Road."

I nodded, "I'm surprised Mrs. Fisher would live in a shed."

Mama continued, "You should visit Mrs. Burton; be good for you to start getting out of the house some. Get your mind off the war and worrying about Elijah."

I nodded, "I'll think about it; not sure she would want me to, though. They weren't happy with how things ended with Flynn."

"That's water under the bridge; at least that's what Mr. Burton said," Mama smiled.

I liked Mr. Burton and always had a special bond with Granny Burton. The next day after work, I drove by the Dairy Bar and picked up milkshakes, and went by the Burton's new house on DeGroat Street. They seemed happy to see me and touched that I remembered how much they loved a "treat." After that day, I visited them when I could. I looked forward to it. We didn't talk about Elijah or Flynn.

Elijah's phone calls home were coming less as spring was ending. His letters were filled with information about what his days were like. How lonely his nights were. He always ended his letters with talk about our future; his love and desire to get "this thing" behind him and come home to me; buy a house; and have children.

By May, his letters begin to change. He was homesick and began to tell me about other soldiers slipping off the base and going home. I didn't understand what he was saying, "Don't they get in trouble?" I asked him. I remembered a girl at the mill talking about her brother slipping out of the barracks one night and showing up at home. When he was caught, he had gotten into big trouble.

He never answered.

"Elijah, don't do it. I will always be here. It's not worth it. Elijah, promise me." The operator came on the line, and we were disconnected before he could answer.

CHAPTER 129
ELIJAH

I wanted to see Iris. How could I go home for just a few days? There didn't seem to be an answer; except one…go AWOL. I began working on a plan.

Just in time, we were given orders we would be leaving for New Jersey for our final training. We were going to fight this war on the front lines.

With that news, we were advised our families were permitted to visit the upcoming weekend…. to tell us good-bye. Finally, I could see, touch, and talk to my Iris. At once, some of the stress was gone and we had something real to look forward to. My plans to leave without permission disappeared, at least for a while.

CHAPTER 130
FLYNN

Life on the ship was hard during the cold winter months of 1944 into 1945. We had been designated as "a warship; a plane guard." Our job was to rescue, assist and protect aircraft and their crew while on their way to their destination. If the aircraft took a hit from the enemy, we rescued them from the water and fire.

I got first-hand experience with top-secret protection during our first assignment. Our ship traveled back to Casablanca to protect the waters from the enemy, both on land and at sea. It lasted for 14 days.

After the mission was completed, we got a three-day leave. I was nursing a broken heart unable to forget Iris. I admit I used the girls I met for the reason men do, but it didn't help; the sadness I felt remained.

My last night of leave, I met a woman from France. In Casablanca to escape the war-torn conditions of her home country.

She told me, "I see the pain of a broken heart. She said, "Just remember on the other side of the pain happiness waits."

Her words gave me hope somewhere in my future the pain would give way to happiness.

After we shipped out she wrote to me and I answered. I wasn't sure what would become of it, or if there was any possibility of something between us. I was willing to find out. She was the first girl since Iris I even considered seeing more than once. I didn't know if I would ever be in Casablanca or France again, but her letters to me made me forget Iris for a while.

My military duties took us to many countries. During those assignments, I saw amazing places. In each of them I tried to forget Iris with different women. Not one of them stopped the images of Iris in my head as I fell asleep each night; I wondered if I would ever stop being haunted by a woman I couldn't have.

CHAPTER 131
IRIS

I was looking forward to visiting Elijah in Alabama; I wasn't sure how long my visit would be or if he would be allowed to leave the base. I packed and was ready to leave the coming Friday. All I had to do was buy my bus ticket.

I drove downtown, parking close to the bulletin board the city had placed in the square. It listed the names of the men fighting in the war under their branch of service. They identified the wounded with a yellow star; missing in action with a blue star, and the ones who were killed with a red cross. I knew Elijah was ok; he was still in the country. I didn't know about Flynn. I needed to know; I still cared about him.

I approached the board; my eyes followed the names. Flynn's name had no stars and no cross. I let the breath I was holding out. I ran across the street to the bus station and got my ticket. I felt happy. I was going to see Elijah, and Flynn was ok. I loved my husband, but something always told me my connection with Flynn hadn't ended and never would.

My bus left early Friday just as the sun began to rise. The ride to Dothan was long; most of the passengers were headed to the same military installation and finally, we arrived. The soldiers were all there. I scanned the crowd of men all dressed alike; there he was waving; he rushed towards me.

We embraced and just held each other; no words, some tears. Finally, I felt whole again. Elijah made me feel like everything was right in the world, but we both knew it wasn't. Sadness overcame me thinking this might be the last chance we see each other for a long time.

CHAPTER 132
ELIJAH

I stood in front of the bus as the door opened wondering if Iris was on it. We hadn't had a chance to talk to each other since I told her she could visit. Iris being in my arms was the only thing I wanted and needed to face the months of not being able to see her. When I saw her stepping off the bus, I felt ok for the first time since we had last seen each other. As I embraced Iris I whispered, "I'm so glad you made it."

She whispered back, "Me too." We walked slowly with the other families over to the base cantina; lunch was ready for us. There were round tables set for us to eat the fried fish they had cooked for lunch. I picked a table in the corner; only two chairs. I needed to tell Iris some things, and I knew she wouldn't be happy with the news.

She asked me, "When will you be able to go to the hotel?"

Explaining to her I had no choice in the decision, "I can't leave the base, but you can come again tomorrow; we're on lockdown because two soldiers went AWOL."

My prediction was right; Iris fumed, "They are punishing the rest of y'all because of what they did? That's not fair!"

I ask her to calm down, "Iris, nothing about this is fair." She could see I was getting upset.

Her voice changed, and she spoke softly, "It's ok; I need some rest anyway. The bus ride was tiring." After we ate, she whispered, "Can we go outside and walk?"

I nodded as I stood up, "Yes, let's do." Outside we sat on a bench; no words and enjoyed being together. I wondered if she had heard from him and finally asked, "You heard anything from Flynn?" It always seemed to come back to him.

CHAPTER 133
FLYNN

My first letter from home finally caught up with me, and it was filled with Iris's name: what she was doing, where Elijah was...things I didn't want to hear. I wrote home to ask them not to write to me about her. I wanted to hear about the new house, how they were, and pictures. It took a while, but finally, there was no mention of Iris in their letters.

Mother sent me letters often filled with stories of how Jacob, Jack, and Bobbie were doing along with pictures of the little homestead they were living in while they worked on the house. I looked forward to the news of what was happening back home as the ship took us to places I knew I would never see again.

I thought of the young girl from France. I hoped I would see her again, but when we crossed over the equator into countries far removed from her; any chance of seeing her again disappeared. I did what we all did, look for love...if only for one night.

I tried everything to forget Iris, yet panic filled me when I couldn't picture her face when I closed my eyes. I opened the bible I kept beside my bunk; turned to the place where I kept the picture of Iris I taped back together. I would study her face until once again it was burned into my memory. I began to hate myself for not being able to forget her.

CHAPTER 134
IRIS

The weekend hadn't started like I thought it would, and now Elijah was asking me about Flynn, "No, I haven't. Why would I?" I told him about the military board, and how I saw Flynn had shipped overseas.

He nodded, "I'll be joining him soon, except I'll be on the ground fighting."

I changed the subject, "Will you be able to call me at the hotel later?"

He said he would try, but he stressed, "We haven't been told what the rules are for tomorrow. They are telling us day by day."

The bus to take us to the hotel began to load. Elijah took my hand. We walked slowly over toward the line of women and children waiting to board the bus. Elijah kissed me bye. I stepped on the first step; turned and ran back to him. We held each other for a moment.

Seated on the bus, I watched as the soldiers marched away in perfect unison. He didn't call that night, but we were given a piece of paper outlining the next day; at the top in bold letter: BUS LOADING AT 10:00 AM. The night seemed to last forever; all I could think about was getting back to Elijah.

The next morning breakfast was at the hotel restaurant where we all compared notes on what we knew. Some of the wives were saying our husbands wouldn't be allowed to leave the base; for fear they wouldn't return. We were all upset; but knew any misbehavior on our part would only hurt the ones we love.

We arrived back at the camp at around 10:30; Elijah was waiting and grabbed my hand as we walked to the cantina. I noticed the couples were pairing up, and the families were going another way. They gave the married men a free day to spend alone time with their wives, but not private time.

Elijah told me right away, "This will be the last time we will be together until I get back..." He stopped talking and took my hand, "About three weeks, June 3, for New Jersey to get ready to ship out...not sure where we will be." He explained there would be no visitors during the preparations on the top-secret base. We could write and maybe call. He was upset; I could tell he was shaken.

I tried to reassure him, and told him to focus on right now, "Let's make some memories to get us through it."

We did have a special day; I told him about a little house I had found, "I think we should get it. I'll have everything ready by the time you get home." We hugged, we kissed, but we couldn't do the one thing I knew he wanted the most.

I left to go home that night thinking it would be the last time I saw Elijah until the war was over.

CHAPTER 135
ELIJAH

Iris was gone; too short of a visit. I tossed and turned... no sleep. I couldn't understand how they had the right to deny men time with their wives or families. They did it under the premise of it being the best thing for us. I decided they didn't know what was good for me; the thought of not being able to be with my wife before I shipped out was too much. I decided to go home no matter what the cost, but I had to wait for the right time. I didn't tell anyone my plan, not even Iris.

The right time arrived the next week. We had liberty and could go off base for eight hours; I slipped away from the others, bought a bus ticket, and was in LaGrange around ten that night. I hid in the darkness as I walked out of town to the Reed's house. I knocked softly on Iris' bedroom window. Tessa looked out and saw me, and I heard her tell Iris, "It's Elijah!"

I heard the springs of a bed squeak as Iris came to the window, "Elijah, you didn't? You go back right now...." I pulled her through the window and kissed her.

Iris whispered, "Climb in..."

Looking at Tessa she continued, "Tess, don't tell anyone he's here until morning?" The room was quiet as Iris and I melted once again into one person and fell asleep. Finally, I could breathe.

CHAPTER 136
IRIS

I got up early and slipped out of bed covering Elijah; he looked tired. I went into the kitchen where Mama and Daddy were sitting at the table having their usual first cup of coffee and explained to them what was going on, "He's shipping out and he needed to come home before he did... he's going back."

Daddy wasn't mad at him but worried the sheriff would find out he was there and fire him from his sharecropping job, "I understand, but think it would be safer at his folk's house...this will be the first place they come."

I called the mill and reported out sick, packed my clothes, and took the truck to fill it up with gas. Mama cooked breakfast and afterward, Elijah and I were on our way out of town. I was happy to be with him, but I was worried about how the military would punish him.

Arriving at his parent's place, we saw a black car in the driveway. It had an emblem that said something about the government. With his brother, Jake, sitting on the front porch with his daddy, we knew why it was there. Elijah and I looked at each other, "Now what?" I asked him.

He told me to stay in the truck. He jumped out and walked up to the porch. They all three stood and talked. I wasn't sure what was happening, but I hope Elijah would go back with him. I was worried; I didn't want him to be in trouble.

CHAPTER 137

ELIJAH

I knew Jake had been sent there to pick me up; he was assigned to a Military Police Unit. He explained to me if I went back before seven days passed, I wouldn't be thrown in the brig and punished too severely.

I told him, "Give me five days to spend with my wife before I ship out, then I'll go back with you."

He made a couple of calls, and an agreement was made. I had five days with the love of my life to carry me through the war and back home.

Those five days couldn't have been more perfect; we spent every minute together. The family let us be alone when we wanted to and were there when I needed to spend time with them. I enjoyed seeing my mama and daddy but being with Iris was all I wanted.

We held each other each night as we fell asleep and woke up to hours of loving each other. Then it was over. I kept my promise and went back to face the consequences of five days in heaven with my wife. It was worth every minute; no matter what it cost.

CHAPTER 138

IRIS

I watched as Elijah drove off with Jake to report back to "the nearest base."

He told me not to worry if Elijah couldn't call for a while, "I'll keep you informed about what's going on. Girl, I have never seen a man who loves a woman like he does you."

I nodded, "I love him too. Please help him if you can."

They were gone and after a good cry with my in-laws, I headed back home. I walked in the house a few hours later; and went straight to bed. Tessa asked me how I was; I told her what had happened and then remembered her husband was in the service too, "How's Earnie?"

She shrugged, "I haven't heard from him in a week."

I hugged her, "I'm sorry." We were both quiet in our own heads until we fell asleep.

Elijah had been gone for a little more than a month; I hadn't heard from him; but Jake called me a couple of times to let me know he was ok, "not behind bars; but waiting on orders." I was so worried about what was happening to him, it was beginning to make me physically sick. Two weeks later, still no word from Elijah, and I was feeling worse each day.

Mama called Dr. Hammond's office, "You be there right after work. You hear me?" I nodded as I went out the door. I was sick most of the day; my stomach was churning; the smell of food made it worse. I worried so much I had made myself sick.

After the doctor examine me, he smiled, "Iris you're expecting...about five weeks...the baby will come in February," he explained. He gave me a list of what I could and couldn't do; what to eat and not to eat. Neither was a problem; I didn't feel like doing anything and everything I ate made me sick. I was excited to tell Elijah... if he ever got to call me.

I wanted to tell him, not write a letter, but I wasn't sure if I would get the chance.

CHAPTER 139
ELIJAH

Jake took me to turn myself in as agreed; I was there for over a month and wasn't allowed to contact anyone. I was held at a base in Georgia waiting for a decision from my superiors about the consequences of going home.

Finally, it came. I would be transferred to a division out of Texas. The thought was it would be harder for me to get home if I decided to go AWOL again.

I didn't know anything about the unit I was being sent to, but assumed it would be much like the one I left. I was leaving to join them in three days. Hopefully, they would accept me.

Finally, they let me call Iris...what she told me made everything we had gone through and everything I was facing worth it.

Iris said, "Elijah, you're going to be a daddy!"

I was so excited and didn't want my news to ruin it, but time was important. I didn't know when or if I would see or talk to Iris again before I left the country.

She brought it up first, "When are you going back to your group?"

I chuckled silently about her calling us a group, "I need to tell you about that...I'm being sent to Texas..."

She asked, "Can I come there to tell you goodbye?"

It was one of the things I loved most about her, she always thought of me first, "I'm not sure, but do you think it would be good for you to travel...I want you to take care of yourself and the baby...I'm going to be ok."

Silence on the line...she spoke... "I think it will be...but I'm not sure I can get off at the mill."

We talked about it and decided it would be best if she didn't come, "You stay there; I want you to start looking for a place for us and our baby girl."

She laughed, "Girl?"

I explained to her, "I have always dreamed of having a daughter; I know it's a girl." The base operator broke in and gave us a two-minute warning. We said our goodbyes, promising to write, and then her sweet voice was gone.

Two days later, I was in Brownsville, Texas, fully accepted into the division with the news I would be processing to the front lines of the war in two weeks. I was ok with it; the sooner I left, the sooner I could get back home...hopefully for the birth of my first child.

CHAPTER 140
FLYNN

After our orders to protect troops and aircraft in Casablanca was completed, we were sent to Rhode Island. The military decided it was a perfect place for a shipyard base right before the war had started. I worked hard and did my job when I was on duty. Life on the ship was trying; protecting aircraft carriers and the operations took us all over the globe.

After ten days at sea, we docked and were given liberty to leave the ship. It was the perfect opportunity to help me forget Iris; women were available and willing to fill my time. I was doing what young men do when they were trying to forget another woman.

I decided with how things ended with Iris; I would never let my feelings get that involved with anyone again; and I didn't. I did what most sailors were doing, trying to survive; the love of a woman helped; even if it was only for one night. I knew I had no one at home waiting for me and it broke my heart.

I'm not proud of how I chose to spend my personal life. I was looking for a way to harden my heart against love. Using women and wine, I had hoped Iris would become a faint memory; I was wrong. All my shenanigans did nothing but hurt me in the long run.

CHAPTER 141
IRIS

After Elijah's orders were issued, they sent him to Brownsville, Texas; he promised to call when he could, but I got a letter first. He never wrote too many details about what he was doing or where he was going, but this letter was more vague than usual. The last time I heard from him his unit was getting ready to go by ship to England.

His main concern was always me and the baby. I assured him we were fine, but the truth was I was suffering from morning sickness that lasted all day. Still in my first three months I prayed it would get better, I spent my days working and looking for a house for Elijah, me, and our new baby. Hoping he would be home before the baby came, there was no way to know when either would happen.

Each day after work, I would ride to the city's military information board; it had changed...one by one names were added to the Killed in Action, Missing in Action, or Prisoner of War. I prayed for every man and woman whose names appeared there, but I prayed extra hard for Elijah and Flynn.

Yes, I still loved Flynn or maybe I should say I love the Flynn I knew long ago. I prayed he was safe, and he would find someone who he loved and who loved him back. I had no right to feel any other way. My life was changed forever; I was going to be a mother in seven months.

CHAPTER 142
ELIJAH

During mobilization, there was little time to write to anyone. We were equipped with barrack bags containing essentials for the trip. Shortly after, we were put on high alert; that meant we would be leaving in 12 hours. It was physically and mentally tiring.

Instructed to remove our patches from the sleeves of our uniform; to keep anyone from knowing who we were or what country we represented. Numbers were written on our helmets in the order we would be lined up for the long march down the docks.

The trip took two weeks on an aircraft carrier. We were on edge. The military was concerned about how our troops would get along with the troops there. They didn't particularly like us and some considered us as beneath them.

We arrived in England in July worn from the long journey. Our orders to join the ground forces were put on hold until we knew where our assignment would be. It would be the last time we would know any of the comforts of home.

We were prepared as a unit to fight, but the realization of what we would be facing hadn't hit us. We were trained to think only about what was in front of us. It was the only way to survive what we would be facing.

I wrote to Iris every day; careful not to tell her anything to worry her. We were given liberty a few times and were able to visit local shops in the small village where we were waiting for orders. I wanted Iris to know I was thinking about her and our life together. I saw a beautiful silverware set; bought it; sent it to Iris; unsure it would even make it to her.

My unit was anxious...wondering where our orders would dispatch us to fight concerned us all. We were in a strange country and the only family we had was each other. Orders in, the wait was done; we were going to Northern France. We were nervous, but ready to do our job so we could go home.

It was August; six months before my first child would be born.

CHAPTER 143
FLYNN

The war ramped up and every ship, including ours, was used for transporting replacement ground troops. The trips were somber; these men knew what they were facing and we did too. We were on heightened alert; knowing the possibility of a strike from the enemy could come at any time; wanting to stop our men and our supplies from landing.

While our involvement in the war seemed like an easy way out, it wasn't. Boats that weren't part of the military carried supplies vital to the survival of the troops who were in foreign lands. Our assignment was to protect the supply boats from the frequent attacks from enemy submarines. We were on watch from our ship twenty-four-seven, rescuing and preventing attacks; our lives were on the line more times than I care to remember.

About every two weeks we would dock in a port for our ship to be refueled. Allowed to go landside, those were the times you looked for some way to convince yourself life was normal and all wasn't lost in the mist of the war.

For a lot of the men, it was found in the arms of a woman. For me it was my way of trying to hurt Iris like she hurt me. My life turned into a not-so-healthy cycle of doing my job on board the ship and trying to forget Iris when I was given liberty. I blamed my downward spiral on the war and her. I would one day realize my battle wasn't the only battle being fought.

CHAPTER 144
IRIS

My pregnancy was going well; I was into my fifth month and had gotten used to Elijah not being home. I enjoyed working at the mill, and decided to continue as long as the doctor allowed me to work.

I felt better there; a sense of calm flowed over my soul sitting in the window; my window. It was still my place where I would make decisions, face regrets, and dream of my future with Elijah.

I was excited about becoming a new mother and was experiencing all the worries that come along with it. I decided to stay at my parent's house until the baby came and then look for a place for us. It should be about the same time Elijah would be getting back from overseas.

Finally, we could begin our lives together. I didn't hear from him often. The mail was slow to get to us, but he sent me a silverware set from overseas.

He said, "It will be a reminder when the war was over to never take life for granted." I placed it in the cedar chest my Nanny Wilson gave me; filling it with the things I would need when we got our house.

I tried to keep up with the war; by listening to the radio

speeches given by the President. I stopped going to the military bulletin board every day after work. I would only allow myself to look on Saturdays when I was doing errands. Each time, holding my breath as I walked up to the board to see if any names of men had been moved to MIA, KIA, or POW; when I didn't see Elijah's or Flynn's name, my breath returned. The knot in the pit of my stomach disappeared for a while, and I was able to enjoy lunch at Tasty's Café.

It was always busy on Saturdays and with Fall in the air, more people seemed to be out. There was a renewed hope the war would soon be over because of a news report on the radio of the successes our forces were having. I didn't really understand the war; all I knew was if it ended, Elijah would be back home safe and sound.

Sitting at the counter at Tasty's, I heard a familiar voice call me a familiar name; only one person used, "Hello Ike." Mr. Fisher sat down on the stool beside me, "I see you are eating for two; how are you Ike?"

I leaned over and hugged him, "I'm ok, how are you…the rest of the family?"

He nodded, "We are good…trying to get that damn house built…still going back and forth from here to Greenville." We talked on as we ate our lunch; neither of us mentioning Flynn's name. I knew it wouldn't be the right thing for me to ask about him; but eventually, I couldn't help myself.

As we each paid our bill and walked out into the cool air of the fall I spoke up, "Mr. Fisher, how's Flynn?"

He told me where Flynn was stationed and the ship he was on; what their job in the war was. I could tell he was proud of him but worried like everyone else. I told him I was happy Flynn was doing ok.

He hugged me and said, "Ike, you'll always be special to me."

It was a good day.

CHAPTER 145

ELIJAH

Our unit received orders to move inland with the hopes of securing the ports located there. It was necessary we controlled them to allow our troops and supplies to land safely. By the time we arrived, the enemy was being attacked by sea, air, and on land. Our forces successfully cleared the beaches of land mines buried there. We successfully overtook the beaches and surrounding lands; with the mines cleared, our landing on the beach from the sea was successful with little resistance.

We were given orders to advance inland toward the enemy borders. The move was slow and what we encountered during our invasion was horrific to see; the concentration camps and the mass murders of the people there. We rendered help for them when we could.

Our movements were successful as we surrounded the enemy. Their desolation allowed us to move quickly. We reached our goal. We had penetrated the enemy's border; now surrounded by our troops.

It was the last of September and the battles continued, all I could think was, "We made it this far." Every day I survive, I was one day closer to going home. When I was scared or discouraged, I took the picture of Iris out of my front pocket thinking to myself my baby would be coming soon. Maybe, I would be there by then.

CHAPTER 146

IRIS

My days drifted into a routine of working and being exhausted at the end of the day. I knew it was time to take a leave from work and start preparing for the baby who would be arriving soon. I was no different from most of the families in LaGrange waiting for this war to be over.

News was slow to come across the radio; letters were even slower. There were weeks when no letters came then two or three would show up; I looked at the date and read them in reverse; thinking if the last letter had no bad news; then I knew he was alive. I still made the trip every Saturday to the city bulletin board; still holding my breath; still relieved that Elijah's name hadn't been moved; still feeling guilty when other names were moved to one of the dreaded columns.

I didn't understand the war. Why Elijah was fighting; not really. He never complained or wrote about what he was doing or seeing. He talked about his dreams of coming home and our lives together.

I read everything I could about the war; not understanding all, but enough to know he and others were in danger all the time. I knew when he came home it would take a long time for him to return to a normal life. I could never understand the things he went through or the things he saw.

Still, his thoughts were about us. He made sure his pay was coming to me. He would say, "Buy everything we need for the baby and yourself." I wondered how he could worry about us when he was facing such danger. I felt so helpless. All I could do was end each day writing to him; telling him every detail; trying to give him the feeling that we were still connected, but the truth was I felt lonely and afraid all the time. I couldn't let anyone see me that way, so I hid inside myself and concentrated on having my baby.

CHAPTER 147
ELIJAH

After the invasion and the movement into enemy territory, the rumors began the war was about to end; but there had been no surrenders on either side. We were on the move trying to penetrate further into the western borders of enemy territories. All the time trying to help the people there devastated by what was happening.

Winter had arrived. The sub-zero temperatures and the deep snow on the ground were something we hadn't experienced. We heard enemy troops used all their supplies and many starved or froze to death. I don't think any of us thought it could go on much longer. With orders to move deeper into the enemy's country; we were about to find out they had one more try in them.

Our new assignment was to protect the thin line we held there against the enemy. The first few days it was quiet; some of us had managed to write letters and get them mailed during the redeployment.

On the night of December 15th, I wrote a letter to Iris; I told her the war was coming to an end; I would be home soon...hopefully for the birth of our baby. I told her I loved her. I knew she may or may not get it, but it did me good to write it. I fell asleep thinking about my life with Iris after this hell was over.

I woke up the next day to the news that the enemy had begun to attack; breaking through the lines we were holding with hundreds of tanks and troops. They came through the forest and began their advance against the line we held. It looked as if they were going to have some success in defeating us, but we fought in small groups in the cold weather; and began to make some headway in stopping the enemy seize.

Along with the help of troops from other countries, we were able to increase the size of our hold. We attacked from the South as another division attacked from the North. Finally, the enemy began to stand back. We didn't retreat, all of our training kicked in and our division along with others continued to make advances taking away all the gains they thought they had made. Everyone was quietly celebrating what they considered a win against the enemy. I didn't think anybody had won, but I was alive.

CHAPTER 148
IRIS

Christmas had come and gone; it was January and although the city of LaGrange decorated and held a huge parade to honor the men fighting; Christmas wasn't the same that year. The entire city was covered with a blanket of sadness.

I hadn't seen many people since I took maternity leave from the mill. I missed my friends and the peace that covered me when I sat in my window; mostly I missed Elijah.

The winter months arrived and my visits to and from Vivian were few and far between. We called each other to see if either had heard from Elijah, but that was it. I stopped going to town much; just once a month when I had to go to the bank or the doctor. By the end of January, I was ready to have the baby. The bed was bought, put together, and the clothes were ready.

There were days Flynn slipped into my mind; I wondered where he was; was he ok? There wasn't any way to find out except for the bulletin board. Seeing all those names made me have an empty feeling, I just stopped going.

At my usual appointment at the beginning of February, Dr. Hammond told me I was ready to deliver at any time. I was happy and waiting. I decided to drive into town afterward and have a hot dog at Country Joe's. Inside seated at the table, I noticed Mrs. Fisher and Bobbie seated at the counter. Luckily, school had just let out. Loretta saw my truck and came to get a ride home.

We ate our hot dogs and started out the door; Mrs. Fisher saw us, "Iris Reed...oh that's right...Mrs. Foster.... you're really showing, aren't you?" in her usual condescending voice.

I nodded and hurried out the door. Naomi Fisher hadn't changed a bit.

CHAPTER 149

ELIJAH

After the victory of our last invasion, we were given a short break. We hoped they would tell us we were going stateside. No orders arrived; I finally got my letters from home. I looked at the dates and opened the latest one dated February 20.

When I opened it a small picture of Iris holding a new baby fell out; on the back was written, "Beverly Jo Foster." Tears rolled down my cheeks as I read the letter from Iris. I wasn't sure if the tears were happy or sad as her words told me about the baby; the delivery;

"She is healthy, weighed almost eight pounds. I will send more pictures when I can. We love you and are waiting for you to come home. Iris."

I tucked the picture of Iris holding our daughter in my front pocket. I couldn't believe I was a Daddy. This war needed to end, so, I could go home to hold both of them.

The next day our division received orders; to meet another unit at the river for what was planned as a surprise attack, but the enemy forces knew we were coming. We were prepared for a fight.

Our job was to encircle a territory that housed a major industrial area. We met little resistance as we completed our task.

We continued capturing city after city but were surprised to see a major bridge still standing. As we tried crossing it to take control of the city on the other side, enemy forces attempted to blow it up.

The fighting was fierce; they released the dams and reservoirs in an attempt to stop us. They were attacking on all sides, and we were retaliating.

Gunfire came at us from the bridge ledge. Men from my unit were dropping to the ground as bullets were flying past. The smoke from the weapons thickened; I looked around to check the placement of our troops. I couldn't see them. I panicked as blackness suddenly overcame me...I felt excruciating pain...then I was back home...LaGrange.

I saw Iris sitting in the mill window holding my baby girl...I sat beside her knowing my dreams had been fulfilled...I felt complete as I passed through them; leaving part of my soul with my girls; I knew we three would always be part of each other... Then everything went black...then everything was beautiful...the pain was gone...only happiness, beauty, and a light, a peaceful light...I had to follow it. It was God's perfect plan...and it is beautiful.

CHAPTER 150
IRIS

I hadn't heard from Elijah since I had the baby, but the news reports were hopeful the war was about to end. I fell into being a mother quickly and was surprised by my love for this chubby little girl. I had a tough delivery. It took a couple of weeks to get better, but there were plenty of people to help me.

Vivian visited often after the baby, and I learned Elijah's parents were staying with her for a while. I could tell they would be good grandparents. I started looking for a house for Elijah, me, and Beverly.

March passed and still no letter from Elijah. Everyone said not to worry, it was hard for mail to get through. I felt darkness overcome me, but I tried not to think about it and to concentrate on when he would come home to us.

It was a day like any other; early afternoon; mama, Tessa, and I were getting ready to start supper. A car driving up the drive caught our eye; it was a military car with an emblem on the side we recognized. Two men got out of the car and walked up the sidewalk: one was a chaplain.

We met them at the front door. Tessa and I glanced at each other wondering which one of us they were looking for.

Then he spoke, "We are here to see Iris Foster?"

My knees weakened below me as Tessa caught me, I replied, "Yes?" The chaplain handed me a telegram. I opened it slowly and handed it to Mama.

She read the message and shook her head at me, "Honey…she paused…Elijah was killed." Tessa caught me as I felt myself crumbling to the floor.

I don't remember much after that…I remember the chaplain prayed; they said "It could take a while for him to be returned home" … "that his things would be shipped to me." I turned and walked out of the room into my bedroom, picked up the baby, and rocked her the rest of the day.

Elijah was gone; not coming home, I dressed and fed the baby and put her down to sleep. I lay on my bed and cried until the next morning. Everyone left me alone that night, and I was glad. I couldn't face this. I was sure I would die too.

CHAPTER 151
FLYNN

We received a telegram that spring, it was over, the war was over. We were given orders to assist in transferring any remaining troops home. We were sent abroad and immediately completed our mission. After returning to the ship, we were informed we would be returning stateside.

On the trip back, I became ill and began running a high fever. I reported to the ship's infirmary and found I wasn't the only one who had contracted an illness. After many questions and exams, we learned we contracted a newly discovered disease they thought was transmitted through physical relationships. We were admitted to a local hospital when we arrived stateside. I was there for three weeks getting treatment; I slowly began to feel better.

I had a lot of time to think about how I had been living my life since losing Iris. I realized how wrong I had been; my acts went far beyond sowing my wild oats. I decided during that time I had to be done with the pity party I had been wallowing in.

I planned to stay up East and build a new life with or without a woman in it. I thought about Iris; I figured she was waiting for Elijah to come home now that the war was over. It still hurt me to think about her with someone else, but if she was happy, I figured I should be too.

When the hospital released me I was transferred to Virginia. I learned when I arrived the military was releasing men based on the point system. I would begin processing out immediately and would be officially classified as a private citizen.

While in the hospital, I decided to make a life in Boston and applied for a job working at the railroad. I broke the news to my family; they were disappointed I wouldn't be coming home to live in LaGrange. They knew why I was staying away. They respected my wishes and never mentioned Iris. I didn't ask. The less I knew about her life, the better off I felt I was.

CHAPTER 152
IRIS

The weeks and months after the news of Elijah being killed in the war were the hardest that I had known. He and I talked about what kind of life we wanted before he left, and I struggled to get the things done that were important to him. I was receiving a widow's pension from the military, but the need to keep busy and the peace my window brought me led me right back to the mill. I was happier there.

Beverly was growing; mama kept her for me while I worked. She was loved by the Fosters, and she reminded me of her daddy in many ways. Elijah's remains still hadn't been brought home, but I bought a place at the cemetery for him to be honored. Nothing to do but wait and try to heal the hurt that broke my heart.

The months passed, and the days slowly became bearable; I still thought of Elijah every day, instead of crying I smiled remembering the love between us. I lived isolated as the year passed and Elijah's body finally arrived home. He was buried with honors in the city cemetery. He was a hero. Everything I could do for him in this lifetime was done. I knew he would always be in my heart. My love for him remained and gave me strength. With that thought, it was time to try to rejoin the world.

The first time I went back to town after Elijah's service, I noticed the military bulletin board was taken down. I was glad to see things going back to the way they were before the war.

I hadn't heard any news about Flynn. He hadn't returned to town. I thought about him off and on; I still cared about him but didn't dare ask questions. I had no ideas of having a life with him; that was surely over, there was no me and him.

CHAPTER 153

FLYNN

I settled in Boston and was working at a railroad as a tower watcher, with hopes of becoming a conductor. I was living in a boarding house saving money until I could buy my own place.

I didn't need a car. I was living in a city where I was able to walk everywhere I needed to. I made friends at a local pub, and a couple of days a week, I would go there for lunch. It was there I heard a familiar voice ask, "You still think girls don't read Westerns?" It was Cathy. I couldn't believe it.

We started seeing each other; I was trying to convince myself I loved her, but every time I closed my eyes to kiss her, Iris' face appeared. I hadn't thought about Iris much in the last months of the war. I had accepted she was living in LaGrange; happily married.

Suddenly without warning, she seemed to be everywhere. I smelled her perfume; I saw her favorite flowers and those damn nut goodies were in every store. The constant nightmares were the worst. I was haunted by visions of Iris sitting in the mill window crying. It left me with a strange feeling.

I was haunted by another man's wife. I refused to be the man who wanted a married woman. I made up my mind I wouldn't give up my life for a memory of something I lost. It was hard. Some days I fell into a depression over what could have been, but I was determined to move ahead; to build a life, a family of my own.

I continued to date Cathy. It was comfortable. I knew she loved me, and I really liked her. I decided to ask her to marry me. I was ready to settle down.

Early one morning my landlady called me from the stairway, "Flynn, phone call."

CHAPTER 154

IRIS

The mill had once again become my refuge; I found my way back to the mill window. It still seemed to hold a magic for me. I sat in it, thought of Elijah, and released the tears I held back at home. I missed him and what would have been, but I knew he would want me to move forward to make a life for me and Beverly.

Ernie returned from the war and he and Tessa married and were expecting a baby. I realized it was time I created a life for me and Beverly outside my parents' house. I bought a duplex house for us. Tessa and Ernie were moving to the other side with their new baby. Mama took over the raising of Jeanine; she insisted she stay with her. Tessa didn't agree but decided it would be too hard on Jeanine to rip her from the life she already knew.

Things fell into place. I wasn't looking for love. I found it twice and lost it twice. I had the same love for the same two men and had accepted I wouldn't be with either. I had lost them both, but I was ok with my life the way it was. I had more love in my life than most people would ever have.

Charlie came back to work at the mill when he got out of the service; he said he was sorry about Elijah, "He was a good guy." He paused for a minute… "You heard from Flynn?"

I told him I hadn't, and I didn't expect to. He nodded and smiled. It was the only time Charlie and I mentioned Flynn. I thought we both realized he was out of our lives for good.

CHAPTER 155
FLYNN

I answered the phone that morning expecting to hear someone was sick, and they needed me to come home.

"Hello?" as I picked up the receiver. It was Daddy. I was relieved. I didn't want to deal with my mother so early. My weekly calls home were full of her asking a thousand questions; especially after I had told her about Cathy. "Daddy, what's wrong; you sick? Mother?" I asked.

He stopped me mid-sentence, "Your mother says you are about to ask a girl up there to marry you?" he said.

"Yes sir, I am," I told him about Cathy. Daddy listened and then he spoke slowly, "Your mother didn't want you to know this; but you need to know everything before you make a serious decision like getting married."

"What's going on? What are you talking about?" I asked trying to understand what he was saying.

"Flynn, Iris's husband was killed during the war. She is raising her baby alone; back working at the mill. I told your mother you were going to find out. She's hoping you would already be married to someone else by then. I think the right woman for you is here."

I understood now why the memories, nightmares, smells, and images of Iris came back to haunt me. I knew what I had to do.

I immediately found Cathy and explained everything to her, "I don't mean to hurt you..." I told her upfront about Iris; how she was my first love; that I always thought we would be together one day. I didn't know how or where, but now I had to try.

Cathy was hurt. I saw it in her eyes. She didn't speak. She simply turned and walked away. I never saw her or talked to her after that day.

Without any thought, I quit my job; packed up what fit in a few bags and took a train as far south as I could; then rode a bus to LaGrange. My daddy was there to drive me to the house on DeGroat Street to stay with my grandparents. My mother was at the homestead west of town. Daddy hadn't told her he called me, "You find Iris before your mother finds out what is going on." I hugged him.

Being back in the little bedroom off of my grandparents' house felt strange; I couldn't sleep. I dressed and drank coffee with Grandpa Burton until just before sunrise. As soon as I knew the mill was opened, I made my way there to find her.

I found Charlie instead. It was a happy reunion, like old times. I told him why I was there.

He replied, "I know. I'm the one who called your Daddy and told him what was going on with Iris; it's time you two get this thing figured out. Flynn, don't mess around about it; this girl has been hurt a lot."

I nodded; thinking he had no idea how hurt I had been; no need to tell him now. "Where is she?"

"Where do you think?" he pointed in the direction of the mill window.

Walking through the quiet of the mill brought back memories, good and bad, that were rushing through my head. For a moment I panicked. I stopped and turned around to walk away from it all. Was I ready for a life with her after being her second choice? Could I live with knowing that and a new baby? How would I feel about being a father to Elijah's child? The questions rushed through my head. I stood still for a moment, knowing if I walked away; I would never come back.

The answer to all my questions was yes because I knew my life would never be complete without her in it. I turned back and started toward the mill window; not sure what my reaction would be when I saw her after so much time had passed.

The morning sun shone through the window. She was there like always; sitting drinking her coffee; eating her biscuit staring out it. She looked older; like a woman who had been hurt, but still beautiful.

I stood hidden by a loom and just stared at her. This person who had brought me such happiness and sadness, could I have a life with her after everything that had happened?

CHAPTER 156

IRIS

It was early in the morning; the rising sun was framed by the arch of the mill window.

I thought of Elijah; then Flynn; and how I had lost them both. Saddened by it all, my life was so different from what I had planned. I missed Elijah; I had been haunted by his death; the military didn't give me many details, about how he was killed; just killed in action. He died on the battlefield. It worried me he was alone.

The Chaplain who had visited after the telegram arrived said he had died quickly. He returned a few things he had with him when he had passed away; dog tags, and a wallet.

The Chaplin said, "They wanted you to know, this picture was in his front pocket when he died."

It was the picture of me holding Beverly; the one I had sent right after she was born. I held on to that picture every night; somehow it helped me sleep.

Nightmares haunted me for weeks. Mama took over the care of the baby while I wasn't able to function. Like always Elijah made everything ok, just like he always did. People tell me it was a dream, but I know it was real...He came to me the night of his funeral service; no words were spoken, yet I understood he was ok, it was ok; he would always be with me and Beverly.

From that night forward, I was able to slowly begin to build a new life. I started back at the mill; things were getting better. Sitting in the mill window in that morning watching the sun come up, I felt Elijah with me; he was beside me as I sat in the window. I knew everything was going to be ok; Beverly and I were going to be ok.

Over the next few days after seeing Elijah, I was startled when the image of him began to fade into black and Flynn's was there. I had thought of Flynn over the weeks. I hoped he was ok, but knew things between us were over. Charlie told me he was about to get married. I wanted to be happy for him; I had no right to feel anything else. I knew I had never stopped loving him, but it was buried deep in my heart by the sadness of losing Elijah. I wasn't sure I could ever feel again.

Suddenly, I felt someone standing behind me watching, I turned and was speechless. I was so glad to see he was ok. The sheer happiness of seeing Flynn Fisher filled my heart. The love for him I had stored away came flooding back.

I told Elijah before we married, he had as much of my heart as I was able to give. I always felt a part of it had died when Flynn and I were separated. Elijah understood, and he knew it had nothing to do with my love for him.

We both were soaking in the feeling of seeing each other for the first time in years. He had matured; the young boy I fell in love with was gone; a man stood in front of me. For a moment, I felt Elijah with me as if he were telling me, it was ok. Silence filled the mill as neither Flynn nor I knew what to say.

I struggled with the words as I asked, "What are you doing here?"

CHAPTER 157

FLYNN

I didn't answer her right away; I took time to survey this woman who haunted me all these years. I felt the same way I did the first time I saw her outside the theater. She still looked beautiful, but with a strength I didn't know a woman could have.

I stepped forward. I took her hand in mine and pulled her up close to me. I whispered in her ear, "I came home to marry you." She fell into my arms. I pulled her closer and we kissed each other. She went over to the window; then patted the place beside her where I always sat.

I walked over and sat down. I felt the years that separated us disappear. Just like that, all the bad feelings between us were gone. We talked about our lives, the past, and the future.

She showed me the pictures of her baby, a girl. We realized we were still connected by the love between us. We talked about how our families had pulled us apart. We decided we wouldn't ever let anyone come between us again.

Iris spoke softly, "I understand if you want to move slowly; just be friends first."

I smiled as I remember all the things that had happened to us sitting in that mill window. There was no better place to start our lives together. I pulled out a small velvet black box... "We've waited long enough."

We were married two days later with the mill window outlining our shadows as the sunset over LaGrange.

As we finished our vows, She leaned over and whispered in my ear, "He's here. Elijah is here."

I smiled and replied, "As it should be."

CHAPTER 158
IRIS

Looking up at the mill window 54 years later, I knew I had to correct the decision Flynn and I had made sitting there the year after we were married. It was in the mill window I told him I was expecting our first son. He was so excited.

Flynn fell in love with Beverly instantly and wanted to protect her from the whispering gossip of our small town during that time. We decided we wouldn't tell anyone who didn't already know Beverly wasn't his daughter. He truly felt she was. I wasn't sure it was the right decision, but I did agree our children no matter how many we ended up having together wouldn't understand it.

We didn't plan to hide or change our marriage date, or the existence of Elijah in our past. When the five children were young our anniversary wasn't mentioned, as they got older and began to ask, we changed the year we were married to 1944; to include Beverly as our child.

Sitting on the new bench outside the now boarded-up mill window, I knew it was time for everyone to know the truth. We had told Beverly, but our other children had no idea of our lives before them.

When Flynn passed away the wrong date was chiseled into his headstone; it haunted me each night. We lived with a lie our entire marriage; a lie which all but erased the part Elijah had played in our lives. A lie that took away the special bond Flynn had always shared with Beverly. I knew what I needed to do. I got up from the bench and took one last look at the mill window, smiled, and walked back to my car.

Driving back through LaGrange past the old building that was once the Colonial Hotel; the place where Tasty's Café stood; the fountain, the bus station, theater, and Country Joe's the memories of time flashed before me. I realized how important each place had been in my life. This town was truly my heart's home.

I made my way to the city's cemetery. Out of my car, I walked through the sea of headstones toward Elijah's. I stood facing it. I smiled remembering him and our time together.

The love was still there as strong as ever, and I knew it was the right thing to do. He deserved for the world to know who his daughter was.

I felt Elijah's love with me through this journey and it filled me now as I leaned down and ran my finger over his name etched into the granite. Tears filled my eyes as my finger traced over the words engraved below his name, "We Knew." A chill ran down my spine, as Elijah's love filled me now.

I spoke to him "I have always loved you. I still do; See you soon." I turned to walk to my car. My heart was filled with love knowing Elijah heard me and understood. The tears were replaced with a smile as I remembered our short time together.

During the drive back to the small cemetery where Flynn was, I thought about the decision we made years before; it seemed such a small thing, but no matter how little a secret seems it still has a consequence. I worried how my children would react to knowing I had been married before…I walked into the house and picked up the phone to call the funeral home to have the headstone replaced.

Now when I stand in front of Flynn's grave, I feel a sense of peace. Inside the heart, he had insisted be carved on his headstone, was our truth, January 11, 1947. The love was still there; stronger than ever.

We three had come full circle; one woman who loves two men and two men who love her. I'm sure they are together and waiting for me. I pray every night I will be with them soon.

ABOUT THE AUTHOR

A retired teacher holding a Doctorate in Education from Liberty University, Janelle Freeman Garner resides in Georgia with her husband. She has carried a love of writing from a young age and is proud to present her first novel, *The Mill Window*, dedicated to her parents.